The Dead and the Dying

By Lin Anderson

Driftnet
Torch
Deadly Code
Dark Flight
Easy Kill
Final Cut
The Reborn
Picture Her Dead
Paths of the Dead
The Special Dead
None but the Dead
Follow the Dead
Sins of the Dead
Time for the Dead
The Innocent Dead
The Killing Tide
The Wild Coast
Whispers of the Dead
The Dead and the Dying

STANDALONE NOVELS
The Party House

NOVELLA
Blood Red Roses

The Dead and the Dying

LIN ANDERSON

MACMILLAN

First published 2025 by Macmillan
an imprint of Pan Macmillan
The Smithson, 6 Briset Street, London EC1M 5NR
EU representative: Macmillan Publishers Ireland Ltd, 1st Floor,
The Liffey Trust Centre, 117–126 Sheriff Street Upper,
Dublin 1 D01 YC43
Associated companies throughout the world

ISBN 978-1-0350-2925-9

1 3 5 7 9 8 6 4 2

A CIP catalogue record for this book is available from the British Library.

Map artwork by Hemesh Alles

Typeset in Meridien by Six Red Marbles UK, Thetford, Norfolk
Printed and bound in the UK using 100% Renewable Electricity by CPI Group (UK) Ltd

Visit **www.panmacmillan.com** to read more about
all our books and to buy them.

For all at the Orkney Library and Archive

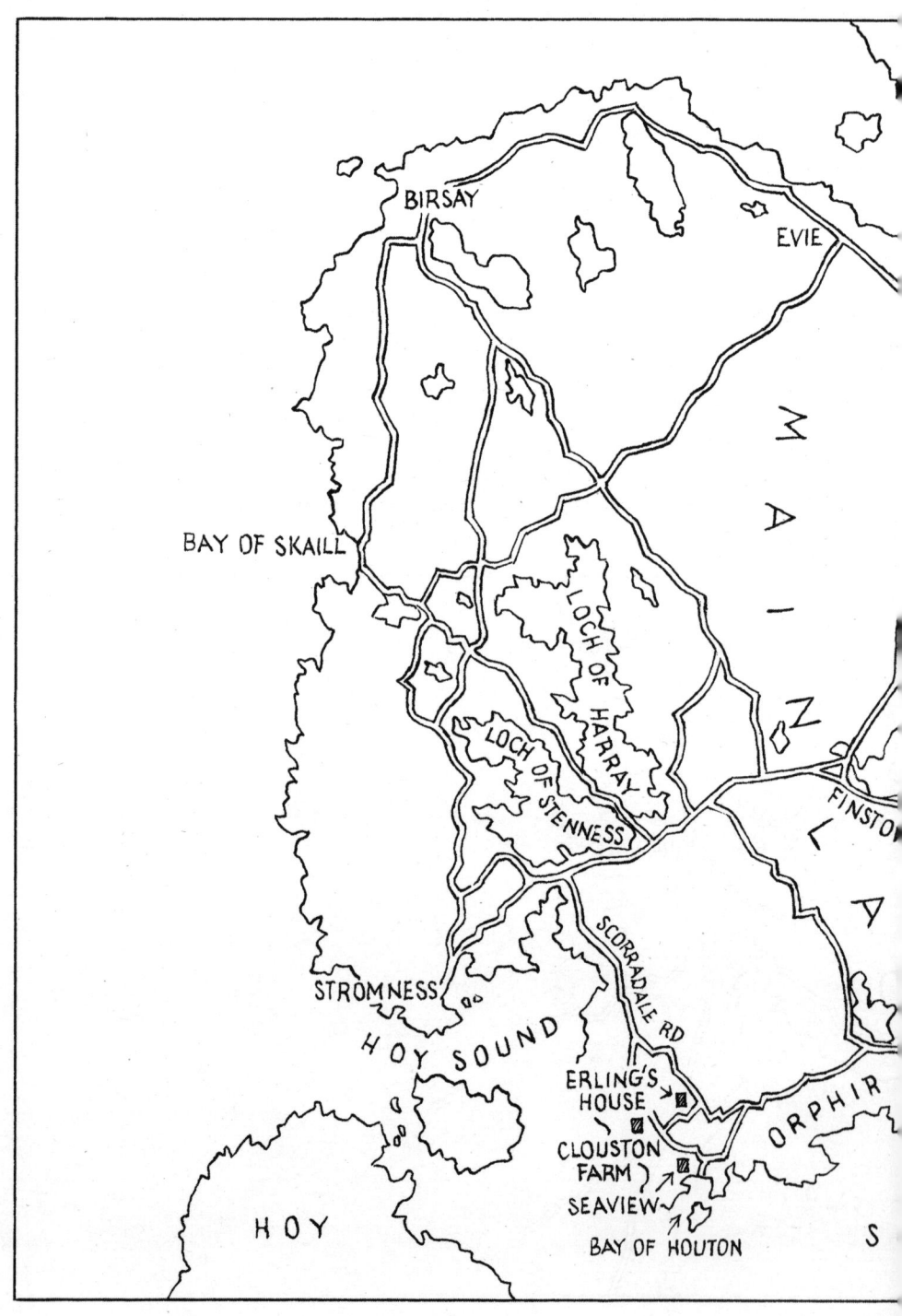

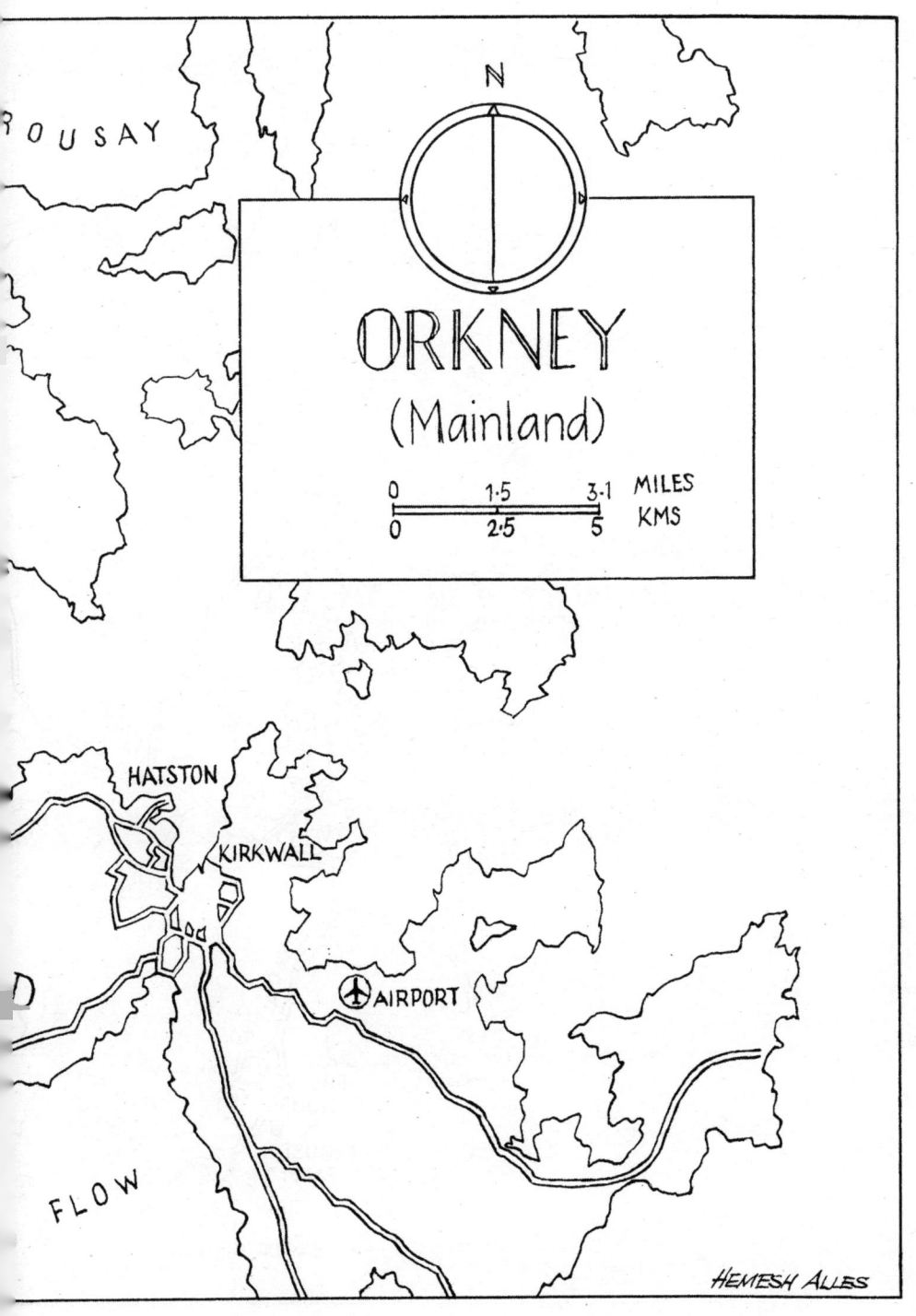

The moment he stepped off the train in the busy station, he felt his heart rise.

It would be different here, he decided.

Exciting. New. He could even be himself. He smiled at such a thought.

He took his time walking along the platform, the other passengers passing him by, eager to leave the station or perhaps meet someone.

There would be no one waiting for him beyond the barrier, but he was used to that. To being alone. He liked it better that way.

So once he emerged from the station, what to do then? Where to go?

Find a hostel? Or just wait and see what life in the big city might offer him?

He'd been standing there thinking for barely five minutes, when a man addressed him.

'You look hungry,' the man said with a smile. 'Fancy a Big Mac?'

He contemplated what exactly a Big Mac might entail and decided he'd be safe enough at a McDonald's. Plus he was hungry after the long train journey.

Nodding his acceptance, he followed the man out of the station.

1

Orkney

The moon was full in a starlit sky as the pod of pilot whales swam steadily up the western flank of Hoy.

Why the pod should suddenly change course and come so close to the Orkney mainland shore could only be surmised.

Some would say that the noise emitted by the cruise ship *Hercules*, bound for a morning berth in Kirkwall, might have been the cause. Others would suggest that their favourite prey of squid had drawn them into the shallows.

At this moment, however, the pod was within view of the said *Hercules*, much to the excitement of those who had remained on deck after photographing the dark red pillar that was the Old Man of Hoy lit up in a mix of moon- and starlight.

Such a wonder was now eclipsed as one by one the passengers spotted the sleek bodies of the pilot whales coming alongside. This would be what they would remember, possibly even more than the Neolithic wonders they would visit when the sun rose in a few hours' time.

Past the entrance to Scapa Flow and Stromness, both the

ship and the pod were now skirting the cliffs of Yesnaby, although the pod, moving at near twice the speed of the cruise ship, would soon be lost to view.

But not yet, it seemed.

A cry went up from the crowd as the pod appeared to suddenly change course, turning eastward towards the great Bay of Skaill, soon to disappear between its twin rocky headlands, where the southern one, being home to the famous Hole o' Rowe, was seen to spout a whale-like fountain of water as though in welcome.

2

Orkney

Seated at the table in the original flagstone-floored kitchen of the famous Ivy House on Albert Street, Kirkwall, Rhona glanced around at her fellow guests.

To her right sat Magnus Pirie, Professor of Criminal Psychology at Strathclyde University. Orcadian by birth, he had the appearance of a Viking warrior, further enhanced by his recent decision to grow a beard.

On her left was Detective Inspector Erling Flett, also a local, and as tall as Magnus. They'd gone to school together back in the day and usually met up when Magnus came back to his home in Houton Bay during university holidays.

Across from her at the table sat their host and current owner of the Ivy House, Professor of Archaeology Colin Nelson of the University of the Highlands and Islands, who was listening intently to the two men's conversation, which had moved into the rich Orcadian accent.

Sitting here in the warm light and scent of a peat fire, the room lit solely by the antique silver candelabra in the centre of the old oak table, Rhona could imagine being back in the original building of 1650. Especially since they'd been given a tour of the upper floors, lovingly furnished with antique items from Orkney's seafaring history.

Rhona had often wondered what lay behind the oft-photographed yellow-painted windows and ivy-covered walls of the house on Albert Street.

Now I know, she thought with a smile.

At this moment the conversation shifted from the popularity of the Ivy House with visitors to the impending start of the tourist season.

'So,' Magnus was saying, 'March sees the beginning of the cruise liners docking in Kirkwall. I think the first one to arrive is called *Hercules*, which I believe holds three thousand passengers.'

'I saw one easily that size in Stavanger in Norway,' Rhona said, remembering. She'd been over there for a forensic conference, staying in the beautiful old town. 'It was berthed in the old harbour and towered like a colossus above the original wooden buildings,' she added.

'Well, the ones that come here berth out at Hatston, so they're not so obvious, although we know when one's in by the influx of tourists all intent on visiting the better-known Neolithic sights,' Colin said. 'Skara Brae, Maeshowe, the Ring of Brodgar . . .'

'Your first time here in Orkney was because of the body we found at Brodgar, if I remember correctly?' Erling said.

'It was midsummer,' Rhona recalled, 'but still so windy we couldn't erect a forensic tent. Plus you had a major problem with the tour buses from the cruise ships not being able to gain access to the standing stones.'

'A midsummer nightmare,' Erling said, turning to Colin,

whose main work consisted of the study of all archaeological sites of interest on Orkney mainland and its islands.

'Where are you working at present?' Rhona asked.

'We're out of season now, but we'll be back in June on Rousay,' Colin said. 'At Skaill Farm on the southwest coastline, where we've uncovered the remains of a Norse hall.'

'So Viking?' Rhona said.

'Most definitely.'

'Any problems with interested onlookers?' she asked, thinking about her own forensic work in the field, which usually involved a buried or hidden body.

Colin, reading her meaning, replied. 'It's different in our line of work. Any remains we're likely to dig up won't involve a police investigation. Also, I like the public showing an interest in what we find,' he admitted. 'After all, archaeology is about the study of ordinary folk and how they lived here on Orkney, throughout all the ages and weathers.'

Even as he said this, the wind, having picked up, reminded them of its presence via the spluttering fire and a smattering of rain against the window.

'It's maybe time we headed for Orphir?' Magnus suggested, glancing at his watch. 'You have your flight back to Glasgow in the morning,' he reminded Rhona.

Rising, Rhona thanked Colin for his wonderful cooking and the chance to see the inside of the famous Ivy House.

'The number of times I've walked past here and tried to peer in the window,' she admitted.

'Next time, please just knock at the door,' he told her as he said his goodbyes.

Erling, who lived minutes away from Magnus, had insisted on being the designated driver this evening, for which Rhona and Magnus had both been grateful.

'You missed out on that delicious wine Colin served with his casserole,' Magnus said as he buckled up in the car.

'I was on call tonight anyway,' Erling told him. 'So I'm just grateful I got through the meal without interruption.'

The rain had come to nothing, and the sky was now clear with a full moon, although as they drove along the coast road towards Orphir, the power of the wind and the retreating tide was obvious in the froth and surge of the surface of Scapa Flow, with the dark hills of Hoy a smudge on the horizon.

Looking out from her seat in the back, Rhona thought of her upstairs room at Seaview, Magnus's home, with a view similar to this one, the waters of the Flow lapping at its stone foundations. Built below the high-water mark by fishermen in the last century, it had its own little harbour where Magnus kept his boat.

Erling's mobile rang just as they reached the road leading down to Houton Bay. Hands-free, he answered.

The voice that spoke was almost drowned out by the howl of the wind, so whoever it was, they were definitely outside. All Rhona could decipher from the swift Orcadian interchange was the word 'Skaill', which she assumed meant Skaill Bay on the western coast.

Ringing off, Erling explained. 'A pod of pilot whales are in difficulty in Skaill Bay with some already beached.'

At that moment Magnus's mobile sounded an incoming message. 'That'll be my call-out too. I'm a rescue volunteer when at home,' he explained.

'I'd like to come with you, if I won't be in the way,' Rhona said, both intrigued and worried about what she was likely to see.

'Okay,' Erling said. 'We'll head straight there.'

Rhona and Magnus remained silent as the radio messages streamed in, indicating how swiftly word of the beaching had gone out and been responded to.

In the short silences in between, Magnus explained what to expect to Rhona.

'Our initial response is to give first aid to the animals until a vet makes a judgement as to whether they're healthy enough to attempt to refloat them. Be prepared to discover that many of them are likely already dead,' he added. 'It was sheer luck that someone was out and about in these conditions at this time of night to spot them.'

'Does this type of beaching happen often?' she asked.

'Not normally. We get plenty of individual animals washing up, harbour seals, single whales, dolphins et cetera. The same rules apply. SMASS, the Scottish Marine Animal Stranding Scheme, investigates all deaths of stranded cetaceans on our shores. Bit like what you and the forensic services do for humans,' he added.

As they approached the great western Bay of Skaill, they found the long stretch of sand, famous for its nearby Neolithic settlement of Skara Brae, lit up by a line of mostly 4x4 headlights.

Exiting the car, Rhona stood atop a grassy dune to look down on the scene below.

Beneath the moonlit sky, the sea was wild with shoulder-high white water, illuminated by the eyes of the beams. The shiny sleek bodies of the ocean creatures, which should by rights be dancing through those waves, were instead strung out unmoving along the beach.

At Erling's voice, she turned.

'We need to get kitted up before we go down there. The dead and the dying are full of bacteria. But hey, you know that already,' he said, his words echoing her own thoughts on the scene below.

Protective gear and various tools were being distributed from the back of a police van. Once kitted up and equipped, she and Magnus headed for the shore.

As they picked their way down the slope of giant rounded boulders, flung there over centuries of high seas like tonight, Magnus told Rhona what was expected of them.

'The routine is to keep any live ones wet, being careful not to get water in their blowholes,' he explained. 'Get them upright and stable, dig trenches under their fins and cover them with damp sheets to protect their delicate skins from the light when it appears.'

Amid the whales now, Rhona watched as the tasks Magnus had described were being carried out by at least six folk who'd brought sheets and towels, buckets and spades to channel ocean water through the sand.

'They go for the youngest whales first because of their size and the possibility of moving them. An adult pilot whale grows to about six metres and weighs up to 2.3 tonnes,' he added, 'so most are beyond saving. It's exhausting work going backwards and forwards to the sea with buckets of water to pour over the live ones, with the tide slipping ever further away.'

Magnus suddenly halted and pointed.

As Rhona's gaze followed his finger, her heart found its way into her throat.

The dead newborn lay at the centre of a protective circle of adult whales, none of which showed signs of life.

'I suspect this is what brought them ashore,' Magnus said, his voice full of emotion. 'If the birthing mother was showing signs of distress, the matriarch of the pod would—'

'Instruct the pod to stay with it,' Rhona finished for him. 'So when one strands, they all do.'

Erling came towards them. 'Three survivors so far,' he said grimly.

'And high tide?' Rhona asked.

'Not nearly soon enough,' Erling told her.

3

Orkney

It was almost dawn when the helicopter arrived carrying the director of SMASS, Dr Donald Main from the department of Veterinary Epidemiology at Glasgow University.

Rhona immediately recognized his figure as he stepped from the chopper.

'You know him?' Magnus said, noting her expression.

'We've encountered one another socially on campus,' Rhona told him.

'He's here to do the post-mortems and decide what should be done with the carcasses.'

'You've met before, then?' Rhona said.

'We have,' Magnus said. 'This isn't the first time he's been here to examine a stranding.'

There was a mutual recognition on both their faces when the SMASS director spotted Rhona.

'What brings you to these parts, Dr MacLeod?' he said in surprise.

When Rhona explained that she was visiting Magnus, but

had also been here before in her forensic capacity, he asked if she wanted to watch him at work.

'If I may,' she said.

'Okay, stay for as long as you have the stomach for it – although I guess a strong stomach is your forte?' he said.

Rhona nodded at that. 'Although I usually deal with one body at a time,' she said sombrely.

'They aren't humans, but they have much in common with our own species with regard to their sociability and intelligence. And their care for one another. *All for one and one for all*. Which, sadly, is probably the reason they came ashore.'

He led her back to the baby calf. 'I suspect the birth of this one is maybe the cause of the stranding. That or perhaps some noise out there on the water.'

'That was what Magnus thought too,' she said.

'Skara Brae's too near to do anything here. The visitor centre is open all year round, so the tourists will start arriving soon. Plus, once the word goes out about the stranding, we'll be a focus of interest in general. So we'll need to remove the dead whales from the beach to perform the necropsies. DI Flett has spoken with a local farmer who has offered us a place to use for that, and the means to take them there.'

He knelt down beside the calf. 'As for this little fella, DI Flett indicated that he's happy for us to deal with him here, then bury him nearby.'

Even as he said this, the crack of a gunshot confirmed what Rhona had been expecting. One of the remaining three from the pod, which the volunteers had worked so hard to keep alive, had finally been put out of its misery.

*

Rhona watched the small digger work on the hole in the dunes that would be the final resting place for the newborn whale. She'd decided not to head back to Kirkwall with Erling so as to catch the earlier flight back to Glasgow, but to stay here for the forensic examination of the calf and its subsequent burial.

It was mid-morning now, and further along the bay she spotted the arrival of a bus at the visitor centre, no doubt carrying a contingent of tourists, possibly from the cruise ship *Hercules*. Mercifully, the beach had been cleared of the carcasses, although from where she stood, the pungent smell of death still hung in the air.

In the bright daylight it was difficult to imagine the fear, hope and despair of the previous night. Briefly relieved by the two young whales they'd succeeded in towing back out to sea alive.

But for now, the post-mortem over, the burial of the new-born still had to be completed.

As Donald had said, pilot whales weren't human, and yet their instincts in many ways were. Laying the youngest one to rest here, where some of its family had died, seemed fitting, although still immensely sad.

Rhona could only hope that the study of both its body and those of the others would provide Dr Main and his team with insight into what had brought the pod ashore in the first place.

The small digger that had brought the calf's body from the beach to the dunes was now in the process of digging its grave, with herself, Magnus and Donald in attendance.

Once the upper layer of marram grass had been removed, the silver sand beneath had made for easy digging until this moment when a loud grating noise suggested the shovel had met a much harder object.

As the driver reversed back from the hole, it was clear to see what the shovel had encountered.

The large flagstone slab lay at a slight angle as though shifted by the digger's shovel.

Flagstones were in common use in Orkney both in past and present times, bountiful as they were on all the foreshores. The main streets of both Kirkwall and Stromness were constructed with large flagstones, and in the older houses like Seaview and the Ivy House, flagstones provided the coverings on the ground floors.

Flagstones had also been used in the past for field delineations. Was this what they were exposing? Rhona wondered. The remnants of the edge of a pasture that had eventually been buried in sand, driven in on high seas or winds?

Or something much older and more interesting than that?

'It might be the capstone of a burial cist,' she said, noting the now fully exposed rectangular outline with upright stones beneath.

Anyone who'd heard of Skara Brae, or been here to visit it, knew the story of the ferocious storm that had exposed the abandoned stone Neolithic village buried in sand further along the bay. So finding something buried beneath a nearby sand dune wasn't really a surprise.

'I think you should call Colin,' Rhona told Magnus. 'Tell him about this.'

Donald agreed. 'And I'll go and organize the calf's carcass to be buried with the rest of the pod.'

Magnus, stepping away to make the call, was swiftly back. 'Colin will be here directly. He sounded very excited at the find. Unfortunately, I have an online meeting so will have to get back to Seaview. Are you okay to hang on here?' he checked with Rhona. 'You've already missed one flight?'

'I'd like to see what's in the cist before I head back to Glasgow,' she told him. 'Colin can drop me at yours when we're finished.'

Watching the digger trundle off with the calf, Rhona registered that the tide was almost fully in now, any evidence of their frenzied attempts at preserving life being currently washed away.

Although not from memory, she thought. Neither from her memory nor, she suspected, the memories of all those who had worked so hard last night.

4

Orkney

The cist lay open, the lid having been lifted and placed to one side with the aid of the digger.

The skeleton, now fully exposed, lay on its right side, knees bent, a burial form Rhona had seen before in forensic archaeological images.

In those first moments as the lid had been lifted free of the cist, Rhona had thought she'd caught a whiff of something that gave her cause for concern.

'Did you smell that too?' Colin said, seeing her expression.

The remains appeared to be fully skeletonized, but the brief scent of decomposition when exposed to the air, plus what looked like faint body-staining in the grave, indicated that the remains might not be as old as they'd initially assumed.

'A burial in sand,' Rhona said, 'particularly at this latitude where it definitely isn't warm, would take some time to skeletonize. But . . .' She halted there.

Colin nodded, seemingly aware of what she was thinking. 'The burial *definitely* looks similar to others we've found here in Orkney, including the cist. But I've never encountered that particular scent before, no matter how slight, on opening either a prehistoric or Viking grave.' He regarded her, his expression serious. 'You're thinking we might have a more recent burial than that?'

'We may have, despite initial appearances,' Rhona admitted. 'When Erling checks in with us, we'll voice that thought, but until then we progress as normal. If we find anything about the skeleton that identifies it as a more recent death, then it'll become my responsibility. Plus we'll have a police investigation on our hands.'

They both knew that it was almost impossible to tell a fifty-year-old bone from a two-thousand-year-old one without using carbon dating, unless there was something distinctive about the skeleton, such as a titanium plate in a healed fracture, or dental work that definitely wasn't available to the Neolithic residents of Orkney. Nor the Picts or the Vikings.

'When my assistant, Chrissy, and I exhume a body,' Rhona remarked as they set to work with small brushes and shovels to remove and bag the sand from around the remains, 'we hope the killer might leave some evidence of themselves behind. Most obvious being handcuffs made from cable ties, which Peter Tobin and many other murderers have done. It also helps the time frame if there's clothing present. Or if I'm really lucky, I might find a coin, a phone or a SIM card.'

'Whereas in a Viking grave I'd be more likely to find the deceased's sword, knife and spear,' Colin offered. 'Although you can often also find evidence of everyday life in there. Needles, combs, beads, jewellery et cetera.'

Rhona sat back on her haunches. 'None of which clues, modern or ancient, seem to be present here,' she finished.

Erling appeared at that moment, coming within earshot just as Rhona made her announcement.

'You think it's not Viking?' he immediately said.

Registering his worried expression, Colin took pity on him. 'It's buried in a stone cist not far from other Viking burials we've unearthed here,' he offered.

Erling switched his gaze to Rhona. 'What do you think, Dr MacLeod?'

At Rhona's explanation regarding the fleeting smell when they'd opened the casket, Erling said, 'And Viking graves don't smell when you open them up?'

'Every grave we exhume has a scent,' Colin told him. 'Just not like this one.'

Erling seemed to be contemplating this worrying thought when his radio crackled into life. Before walking away to answer the call, he said, 'I sincerely hope it is a Viking grave. Once you decide for sure, let me know.'

Photographing the skeleton in situ, Rhona had surmised, from the size and shape of the skull and pelvis, that they were likely dealing with a male. Although both its sex and age would be better decided when measured and examined in detail, and DNA from the bone would establish the biological sex for certainty. Along with both hair and eye colour.

Now, as they carefully removed, itemized and bagged the remains, bone by bone, to be reconstructed later, they found no obvious breakages or injuries that might point them to how the occupant had met their end.

Handing the skull to Colin, Rhona said, 'The teeth look

healthy. No obvious modern dental work done. What were Viking teeth like?'

'It varies with diet. But they were unlikely to have as complete a set as this specimen.' He gave her a wide smile to illustrate the point.

Having processed the skeleton, Rhona began to bag the film of sand that lay on the bottom of the cist, stopping when she caught a glint of what might be metal jammed between the base and one of the side walls.

'What is it?' Colin said as she directed the beam of her forensic torch on the object.

'Can you hand me the tweezers?' she said. 'I'll try to ease it out, whatever it is.'

The object seemed reluctant to abandon the space between the stones, but eventually she managed to extract it, laying it flat on the sand for Colin to see.

'It's a torc bracelet,' he said in an excited voice.

'So it's Viking?' Rhona asked, thinking it had the appearance of a longship with its curled ends.

'It looks like it,' he said, his eyes alight.

Rhona watched as he weighed the heavy object in his gloved hands, studying it intently.

'Old or not so old?' she said.

'In 2022, a team of Swedish archaeologists unearthed a trove of torc necklaces similar to this, north of Stockholm, which dated back an estimated thousand years to the Viking era. Despite their age,' he stressed, 'when cleaned, the pieces looked brand new.'

'This piece doesn't appear to need any cleaning,' Rhona offered. 'Apart from some sand caught in the swirls.'

'Exactly,' Colin said with a nod.

*

They'd taken Erling at his word and phoned him with news of their find. His return had been swift, and he now stood with them at the site of the excavation, studying the torc bracelet safely in its evidence bag.

'You're saying if this was from the Viking era, it wouldn't be this clean?' When Colin nodded, Erling double-checked. 'So, if it is more recent than that, the remains may be too?' He looked to Rhona for confirmation of this.

Rhona affirmed his suspicions. 'My initial examination suggests the remains are those of a young male who's lain here for maybe twenty years. However, I'll need to take both the remains and the torc to Glasgow for a full forensic examination and evaluation. I've already spoken to Dr Main from SMASS and he confirms he'll be finished with the necropsies on the whales today and I can share his return helicopter tomorrow morning. Until then, you'll need to store both the skeletal remains and the torc at the station.'

Erling gestured to the bracelet. 'Viking jewellery like this is popular with tourists. Some are made here in Orkney. Is there a craftsman's mark on it?'

Rhona handed Erling a magnifying glass. 'There is a mark,' she said. 'On the back of one of the swirls.'

Erling checked where she'd indicated. 'Might be initials. E or maybe B M? Right, send me through the photographs and I'll await news on the forensic examination of the remains and the bracelet.'

The tone of his voice indicated his concerns, which were, Rhona thought, broadly in line with her own. A Viking burial would have been both a normal and a welcome find. A more recently buried body would mean Erling had a murder investigation on his hands.

'You'll text me when you plan to leave in the morning and I'll bring the evidence to the airport?' he said.

Rhona assured him that she would.

Colin drove back to Kirkwall via Orphir, dropping her off at Seaview.

'You'll be in touch?' he checked as she got out of the car.

'I'll let you know the outcome as soon as we do,' she promised. 'On the body and the torc bracelet.'

'Good. I'll keep my fingers crossed the body's too old for a formal investigation even if it's not Viking. For Erling's sake at least,' he added. 'Remember what I said, though, about the Ivy House. Any time you're passing, just knock at the door. No need to peer in the window any more.'

When the car headed up the hill to the main road, Rhona stood for a moment looking out over Scapa Flow, noting that the wild frothing of the previous night had been replaced by a calm swell that was softly breaking against the foundations of the solidly stone-built house.

At that moment Magnus, having likely heard her arrival, emerged to greet her. Reading her expression, he said, 'Something wrong?'

'Possibly,' she admitted, without elaborating.

Ushering her inside, he asked if she wanted a drink or a shower first. 'There's food ready. You must be hungry. And tired,' he added. 'I managed a short nap after my class.'

Up to that point she hadn't realized just how hungry she was. And tired. The night had passed swiftly with their efforts in trying to save the stranded whales, the time that followed consumed by the discovery of the cist and its contents.

'A shower first,' she declared, 'then the food and drink.'

Upstairs and in her usual room, she stripped off and

headed for the shower, deciding not to linger too long under the warm water because of the smell of something delicious that had accompanied her upstairs.

The ring of her mobile ended her shower even more swiftly than she'd planned. A glance at the screen confirmed who it was. Although impossible scientifically, Chrissy McInsh's calls seemed to have a particular tone and insistence all their own. Much like her forensic assistant's voice.

'Hi, Chrissy, I was just about to call you,' she fibbed.

'I heard you dug up a Viking?' Chrissy said, her tone one of glee.

'Where did you hear that?' Rhona said, with a hint of sarcasm in her voice, aware as she was of her forensic assistant's network of informers, which, it appeared, extended beyond the Central Belt.

'Well, is it true?' Chrissy demanded.

'Not exactly,' Rhona told her. 'It was in a stone cist, buried in the sand dunes at Skaill Bay, but the age of the skeleton is in question.'

'Why?' Chrissy sounded suspicious.

Rhona explained about the torc bracelet.

'Jeez,' she hissed. 'That is weird.' There was a brief pause as she fully assimilated this information. 'I take it you'll be bringing back the bones? And the bracelet?'

'I will,' Rhona told her. 'I'll be back tomorrow morning with both.'

Ten minutes later she was seated by the fire with a glass of Highland Park whisky and a starter of fish delicacies prepared by Magnus.

Unlike Chrissy, Magnus hadn't deluged her with questions, but rather waited until she was ready to tell him what had happened after he'd departed Skaill Bay.

When she'd consumed possibly more than her fair share of the casserole, Rhona had explained the day's proceedings and was now watching as Magnus mulled her story over.

'So,' he eventually said, 'you suspect you may be dealing with a much more recent burial, because of this torc bracelet? Do you have a photograph of it?'

Rhona brought up the ones she'd taken on her mobile.

'Erling says it may have been made here on Orkney,' she told Magnus as he studied them.

'It looks pretty heavy,' he said.

'It is,' Rhona confirmed, remembering the weight of it in her hand. 'And made to look like the real thing, according to Colin.'

'Fashioning jewellery like this on Orkney has become popular for the tourists.' He paused there. 'Could it be a later addition to the cist?'

'I don't think it could have got there by accident,' Rhona said. 'The digger removed three feet of sand before we hit the cist. Plus the lid was pretty firmly in place.'

'The dunes shift all the time,' Magnus said. 'Depending on the winter storms. Maybe someone discovered the cist earlier and added the bracelet?'

'Someone found what might be a burial cist, then didn't report it, but decided to add a modern Viking bracelet to it instead?' Rhona wasn't convinced by such a scenario.

'We used to do some crazy things here as teenagers,' Magnus said. 'If Erling and I had discovered a cist buried in the sand, who knows what we would have done? Especially if we were high at the time.'

Rhona couldn't envisage the now Professor of Criminal Psychology or the island's Detective Inspector getting high, no matter how hard she tried.

Reading her expression, Magnus laughed. 'We were pretty crazy back in the day. We're lucky to be alive after some of our escapades. Wild coasts and seas were our playground. Not to mention Neolithic monuments and tombs. It wasn't only the Vikings who wrote rude things inside Maeshowe,' he told her with an apologetic smile.

Rhona was playing out some of these scenarios in her head, just as Magnus was obviously doing.

Eventually he said, 'Any idea as to the sex of the remains?'

Working with the bones, marking each one off on the chart as they'd retrieved them, noting the signs that inferred biological sex and age, she suspected a full lab study would conclude that the victim was a young post-pubescent male. She told Magnus so.

'How long's he been there, do you think?' Magnus said.

'He was buried naked, so no clothing to help identify the time zone, apart from the bracelet. Plus there was faint staining and a slight scent on opening the cist.' She halted there for a moment, considering her thoughts up to now. 'Skeletonization when buried in sand takes time, especially in cool Orkney temperatures, so twenty years or more.'

'Twenty years ago I was a teenager about to head for university.' Magnus checked her expression. 'You're wondering if I remember anyone going missing around that time?'

When she nodded, he said, 'No one comes to mind, although as a teenager I was pretty caught up in my own affairs. Also, there was a lot of coming and going in Orkney. Oil workers on Flotta. And folk from down south who were trying to escape to what they imagined would be a better life. Then leaving when it wasn't. Or they couldn't cope with the weather.'

They'd moved back to the sitting room where Magnus replenished the fire and topped up her whisky glass.

'So when do you head back?' he asked.

'Tomorrow morning,' she told him. 'Donald said he would text me in advance of the helicopter's arrival. Erling will meet us at the airport with the evidence.'

'How long before we know if it is a murder investigation?'

'I believe Erling already thinks it is,' Rhona replied.

5

Orkney

Erling lowered the driver's window, hoping the fresh air would keep him awake. The adrenaline surge of the previous twelve hours would wear off soon, but there were still things to do before he could head home for a sleep.

Rory was away on a diving job, so no need to keep him informed as to when he would get home. The downside, of course, was that he'd have to cook for himself. Something he was well able to do, although what he conjured up never reached the culinary heights of Rory's endeavours in the kitchen.

Thinking about food had made his stomach rumble as he realized just how many hours had passed since the Ivy House meal. There would be coffee at the police station. Maybe even biscuits if he was lucky. Enough to stave off the hunger until there was time to eat properly.

Caught at roadworks in Finstown, he called ahead to warn DS Green he was finally on his way back and would be with her shortly.

'Can you get the team together?' he said. 'There's been a development at the excavation site.'

A short silence followed as though she was waiting for him to say what the development might be. When nothing was forthcoming, she assured him they'd be ready and rang off.

This wasn't a subject to broach en route, he thought, even at a particularly long red light. In fact Erling was still trying to assimilate the outcome of the excavation himself. Rhona had been cautious in her analysis of what she and Colin had unearthed, but whatever way they looked at it, the discovery of a torc bracelet, which had definitely not been forged in Viking times, together with a healthy skeleton had presented them with a mystery.

And, if Rhona was right about the condition of the remains, they were possibly looking at the death and burial of a young Orkney male around twenty years ago. Or maybe a visitor or itinerant worker.

Picturing himself two decades ago in Orphir, he was reminded that he'd been more likely to be breaking the law, rather than upholding it. Plus, if anyone had told him back then that he would become a police officer and be serving in Orkney, he would have thought them drunk or mad.

Yet, despite his misspent youth, he'd still managed to go to university to study mathematics. And the boy who'd entered university, he reminded himself, wasn't the one who'd emerged four years later.

His arrival with the set of bones and the torc bracelet was bound to cause some consternation, he thought as he drew up outside the station. His colleagues were used to the unearthing of Neolithic burial mounds. However, the discovery of a stone cist at Skaill Bay that might contain a more recent body wasn't something they would be expecting. Or wishing for.

He found PC Ivan Tulloch on the front desk and ordered him out to the vehicle to help retrieve the boxed evidence and place it in storage.

Once that was done and the evidence room door locked, PC Tulloch ventured to ask if Dr MacLeod's forensic assistant, Chrissy McInsh, had been at the excavation site with her.

'No,' Erling told him. 'Dr MacLeod was here on a short break. Not work.'

Noting his constable's disappointed expression, Erling suddenly remembered that PC Tulloch had developed a bit of a crush on the young and feisty forensic assistant the last time she was in Orkney, but decided not to mention that.

He found the rest of the team assembled as requested in the upstairs meeting room, including his second-in-command, Detective Sergeant Jo Green, recently relocated from Inverness.

Transferring the photographs taken at the scene onto the overhead screen, Erling explained what had happened at Skaill Bay.

'As you all know by now, the hard work of the volunteers did result in two of the beached whales being saved. Dr Main of SMASS transferred the other remains to a nearby site for the necropsies, but decided to bury the body of a newly born calf among the dunes.

'That's when the digger struck something that turned out to be the capstone of a burial cist,' he continued. 'After which local archaeologist Professor Nelson was summoned and he and Dr MacLeod set about opening it up.'

An image of the partially open cist was now on the screen.

'Dr MacLeod thought she caught a faint scent of decomposition when the lid was initially lifted,' he told them. 'Professor Nelson noted it too.'

There was a murmur at this from the team.

'However,' Erling went on, 'they were still working under the assumption that they were likely dealing with a Viking burial.'

He switched photographs. Now the screen held the image taken when the capstone had been removed.

'As you can see, the body is lying in the typical fashion of many of the burials already unearthed here in Orkney. There were, however, no weapons or any other articles that Professor Nelson has commonly found before.'

He continued. 'The skeleton, which Dr MacLeod suspects will prove to be that of a young male, gave no indication of how he might have died.'

He paused there, remembering his own reaction to the news he was about to tell the expectant faces before him.

'It was when they'd removed the bones and were inspecting and collecting the sand on the base that Dr MacLeod found this Viking-type bracelet.'

The photograph of the torc now on the screen, he awaited their reaction.

It was DS Green who spoke first. 'I've been on archaeological digs here as a student, sir. That bracelet is fashioned like a Viking torc, but its condition suggests it's not that old.'

'That was Professor Nelson's opinion too,' Erling said, pleased by her knowledge.

'So they think it may be a more recent burial?' she added.

'That is a possibility, yes.'

As Erling said this, murmurs went up from the group.

He spoke firmly to silence them. 'So while we await the

outcome of the forensic examination of the remains, we'll try to trace this bracelet, which doesn't appear to be mass produced.'

Enlarging the image on screen, he pointed to the two possible letters engraved on one of the spiral ends.

'Any thoughts on the markings?' he asked, keen to see if the team's reading of them matched his own.

'E and M?' Ivan offered to murmured agreement.

'Right, let's start checking out if bracelets like these are or have been made here on the mainland or anywhere on the islands. But let's keep this low key, in case the torc becomes a vital piece of evidence in a murder enquiry. Plus we start looking into any young males reported missing here in Orkney, say initially in the past twenty years.'

He motioned DS Green to join him in his office.

'They really think it's recent?' she said, her voice full of concern.

'Dr MacLeod's an expert in buried and hidden bodies, so we need to take her concerns seriously. I think we start investigating it as a suspicious death and hope the bones turn out to be older than a century.' Erling tried to stifle a yawn.

'You haven't slept yet?' his sergeant checked, looking sympathetic.

'Not yet, no,' Erling admitted. 'Nor eaten. Although we were treated to a three-course meal at the Ivy House last night before all this began.'

'Coffee and a biscuit?' she offered. 'Maybe even a chocolate one if PC Tulloch hasn't been in the tin.'

'Great,' Erling said. 'Has anything else happened in the interim that I should know about?'

'Nothing major. The reports are already on the system,'

she told him. 'When does the evidence from the cist go south?'

'First thing tomorrow by helicopter with Dr MacLeod and Dr Main.'

'I could take it to the airport for you?' she offered.

'I was going to ask you anyway.' He paused, taking time to study her. 'How are you settling in?'

'Okay.' She gave a wide smile. 'I know Orkney quite well, having visited a lot and worked on digs here.'

'And the flat?' he said.

'Small. I couldn't swing a cat if I had one. But it's handy. Not that far from the Ivy House, in fact. Always fancied a look in there,' she added wistfully.

'You'll have to wait your turn, Detective Sergeant,' he told her with a smile.

Ten minutes later, his brain back in action after a mug of tea and a chocolate biscuit delivered by PC Tulloch, Erling began writing up the events at Skaill Bay.

The report on the pilot whales and the subsequent man-agement of this was standard. Although, in this case, he was glad there had been two survivors, which was rarely the outcome of such beachings, either here on Orkney or on the Western Islands of Scotland.

Moving on now to the decision to bury the calf in the dunes and the resultant discovery of the capstone, he went through the photographs again, recalling when he'd been back to look at the open grave, recording what Dr MacLeod had said about the scent. Plus the fact that Professor Nelson had also noted it, and had declared that he had never encountered such a smell when opening a Viking grave before.

It seemed Magnus had already left by the time this had happened, which was a pity. If Magnus had registered the smell, it would have left no doubt as to its existence – however fleeting. His friend since childhood had hyperosmia, and experienced smells more strongly than other people. It had tortured him when younger, but he'd managed to control it the older he became.

Erling, along with others, had tormented Magnus about it, especially during adolescence, exposing him to dead carcasses found on the beaches or in fields just to see his reaction, which was often instant vomiting.

As for anyone smoking dope, Magnus could catch that scent a mile away.

That wasn't all he could pick up from you, Erling's memory reminded him. Back before he would admit to being gay, he'd had a crush on Magnus. One day when they were alone together, Magnus, like the professor he eventually became, explained that he could smell the pheromones that he, Erling, was giving off in his presence.

So Magnus would have confirmed Dr MacLeod's suspicions. As had Prof Nelson, and he knew what a Viking burial smelt like. And all of this before the discovery of the bracelet.

He indicated in his report that the evidence was being transported with Dr MacLeod to Glasgow tomorrow morning and, while awaiting her results, he had made the decision to investigate the origins of the torc bracelet and also to check on any young males reported missing in Orkney initially in the last twenty years.

That task now complete, Erling allowed himself to return to the two thoughts that had been niggling at him ever since his most recent visit to Skaill Bay.

If a young male *had* gone missing around twenty years ago here on mainland Orkney, wouldn't he remember such a thing happening? Orkney wasn't a big place and its population was a fair bit smaller then than it was now.

It had seemed to him back then that you couldn't do anything without someone knowing about it. Struggling with his own sexuality, and a desire to escape to somewhere he could be himself, it had seemed impossible to go unnoticed. Anywhere, at any time.

So, if a young man had gone missing, would he not remember that? He resolved to ask Magnus if he recalled that happening. Seeing as they'd spent most of their time together.

Then the other thing that was annoying him.

Looking again at the enlarged image of the torc bracelet fashioned to look like a Viking longship, he had the feeling he had seen one like it before.

A shop window on the main street perhaps?

There were lots of jewellery shops in Kirkwall now. Most were high-end, since the cruise ships had started docking nearby at Hatston and disgorging their passengers who were keen to buy fashionable and good quality mementoes of Orkney.

Or somewhere else?

He closed his eyes and tried to picture where it had been and when, aware that it must have made an impression at the time.

It took a while but eventually it came to him.

It had been on a male wrist. A wrist and hand that he'd been sexually attracted to.

And there it was.

Rory had been wearing one just like it the night they'd first met.

6

Glasgow

The helicopter ride south to Glasgow was uneventful and for the most part undisturbed.

After enquiring briefly about her excavation work on the cist and receiving a guarded reply, Dr Main left Rhona to concentrate on her own thoughts. Which were, as usual, full of her dislike of flying and her continuing belief that, despite the physics of flight being proven, she still remained unconvinced.

Had Chrissy been here, of course, there would have been constant 'oohing' and 'aahing' as they crossed the Pentland Firth and made their way south. Chrissy had no qualms about the emptiness beneath them or how long they were required to be up in the air.

Rhona was still contemplating this when Glasgow thankfully reappeared.

Transferring the evidence into the forensic van, Rhona, her feet now safely on terra firma, gave her forensic assistant, who had come outside to meet her, a big smile.

'Have you eaten today yet?' Chrissy enquired.

'Nope,' Rhona told her.

'I knew you wouldn't eat before the chopper ride. Even if Magnus offered to cook something delicious for you.'

Poor Magnus, ever the excellent host, had definitely tried, but to no avail.

Customarily, it was Chrissy who provided breakfast at the lab, which she picked up on her way to work. It consisted of a traditional filled roll with egg, tattie scone, bacon or sliced sausage, or a mixture of your choice.

There had been a period when she'd tried a move to instant porridge in various flavours, but thankfully it hadn't lasted too long. Rhona wasn't averse to home-cooked porridge, especially when it was served with fresh cream, something Sean was good at. However, that was kept for a non-working day.

'The rolls are in the oven,' Chrissy declared when they reached the lab. 'Coffee's on too. I'll check in the evidence. You help yourself to breakfast.'

Sitting by the window now, coffee and roll in hand, Rhona looked out over Kelvingrove Park. Glasgow University, which housed her forensic lab, had to her mind the most enviable location in the city.

Perched on a hill, its gothic towers rising high into the sky, it had a bird's-eye view of another architectural masterpiece, Kelvingrove Museum and Art Gallery, which itself was surrounded by the park. Straddling the River Kelvin on its way to join the River Clyde, Kelvingrove Park consisted of eighty-five acres of grassland and trees, providing an urban haven for wildlife and, of course, its West End citizens, of which she was one.

Her own flat was in Park Circus, which sat atop a neighbouring hill. She'd purchased the flat when the Circus was less salubrious than it was now, but it too had an enviable view over the park.

Although, like any open space within a big city, Kelvingrove had had its own share of police incidents. Even when walking through it to work, she still acknowledged the locations where she'd had to attend a crime scene. However, none of this affected her fondness for the place in all seasons.

Now March and officially spring, the park was already taking on a vibrant green hue.

'So,' Chrissy pronounced as she took a seat alongside her, 'you can't go anywhere without being called on to look at a dead body?'

'It would likely never have been found if the pilot whales hadn't come ashore,' Rhona told her. 'We were coming back from dinner when the call came in on Erling's phone about the beaching.' She paused for a moment, an image of the scene springing up before her eyes.

'I saw it on the news,' Chrissy said. 'All those folk trying to save them.'

Rhona explained that the matriarch had likely led her pod into calmer waters because of a difficult birth. 'Then they got caught in the swell.' She fell silent, before adding, 'The volunteers did manage to save two of the young males.'

'What about the mother and her calf?' Chrissy said, looking upset.

'Sadly not,' she said, aware that Chrissy, herself the mother of a young child, wee Michael, would be particularly stung by this. 'Donald decided we should bury the calf in the dunes rather than take it away with the others. It seemed kinder, somehow. He brought in the digger and . . . that's when the shovel hit the capstone.'

She brought the photographs up on her phone. 'I'll

download these after we've talked, but take a look at what we found inside.'

She watched as Chrissy went through the images, studying each one intently.

'The skeleton was complete?' she said.

When Rhona indicated it had been, Chrissy asked about injuries.

'None obvious,' Rhona confirmed.

'The teeth look in good nick,' Chrissy commented. 'What are Viking teeth usually like?'

'Depends on the diet, but unlikely to be as good as these, according to Prof Nelson.'

Chrissy sat back, looking pensive. Rhona could almost hear her assistant's brain in action. Chrissy had worked with her on numerous buried remains. Rhona was sorry she hadn't been at Skaill Bay to view these in situ.

Rhona now brought up a photograph of the torc. 'This was the only thing in the coffin apart from the skeleton and sand.'

Chrissy gave a little whistle. 'A Viking torc bracelet. That's a bit of a find . . . if it was old,' she added with a quick glance at Rhona.

'Prof Nelson said pretty much the same thing. He's dug up numerous pieces of Viking jewellery and they can and do look like this *after* they've been cleaned up.'

'I take it DI Flett thinks he has a more recent victim?' Chrissy said.

'He's working on that assumption, while waiting to see what the post-mortem comes up with,' Rhona told her.

The remains had been taken directly from the police helicopter to the morgue where a full examination would take place involving Dr Sissons, a forensic team and an osteologist, whose expertise in bones would likely confirm what theories she and Colin had discussed at the gravesite.

'Any idea when they'll do the PM?' Chrissy said.

'Tomorrow or the day after and I think you should come along this time.'

'Great,' Chrissy said enthusiastically. 'It's not often I get to work on a skeleton, Viking or otherwise. Can I take a proper look at the photographs?'

'I'll send them to your laptop. Come and tell me your thoughts when you've had time to study them.'

Rhona hadn't voiced her own thoughts on the age and sex of the remains and Chrissy hadn't asked. But she knew as she watched Chrissy settle in front of her laptop that she'd be looking for all the visible signs that could lead her to give her judgement on both characteristics.

There were many differences between male and female skeletons. The most certain indicators were found in the pelvis and the skull. In females, the pelvis was flatter and more rounded, proportionally larger to allow a baby's head to pass through. Females usually had narrower ribcages, smaller teeth, less angular mandibles. Their brow ridges were less pronounced, their chins less square. The small bump at the back of the skull less pronounced.

'Well,' Chrissy said, approaching with her laptop. 'The heads of the long bones are just fused to the shaft.' She pointed at the screen image for emphasis. 'See the line? Plus look where the two hip bones join onto the pelvis. I'd say our victim's likely under twenty years old.' She looked to Rhona for confirmation.

'My conclusions too,' Rhona admitted. 'It's difficult to be more precise than that. And the sex?'

'I'd say male, but DNA from the bones to confirm.'

'Agreed.'

'That doesn't mean he was living as a male, of course,' Chrissy said.

Rhona nodded. 'True, but in the first instance it looks like a young missing male we're seeking.'

'How long do you think he's been there?'

'Buried in sand in a temperate climate like Orkney, I'd say twenty years or so,' Rhona suggested. 'There was a faint scent of decomposition when we pulled back the lid. Plus some staining.'

Chrissy absorbed all of this before saying, 'Why bury him naked?'

'I've been thinking about that,' Rhona admitted. 'Perhaps the killer, fearing his victim might at some point be unearthed, didn't want to help us with the time frame. Or the death and naked burial were ritualistic in some way.'

'And the bracelet?' Chrissy asked.

'I'm not certain the bracelet was meant to be in there,' Rhona told her. 'It was jammed between the wall and the base.'

She enlarged the torc image sufficiently to expose the letters on one end.

'It doesn't look mass produced. More like handcrafted,' Chrissy said.

'Erling's going to check out the Orkney jewellers first. See if they recognize their work and the inscription.'

'We might get more than just the initials from it,' Chrissy said, with a hint of excitement.

'I thought you should get started on the bracelet,' Rhona said. 'I'm keen to know about the sand caught in the end swirls.'

Chrissy gave her a look. 'You're thinking about that case on Sanday?' she said, reading Rhona's thoughts.

The wider public tended to think that sand was pretty much the same whichever beach it came from. But sand, like soil, was unique to its location. When a small digger, like the one used in Skaill Bay, had been used to break up a former school playground on the island of Sanday, it had unearthed a human skull, bringing Rhona and Chrissy north to exhume the grave. There had been no thought of Vikings in that particular case, the era of the death being identified via the remains of the clothing. But in the end it was a sample of sand that had eventually led them to the killer.

'Right,' Chrissy said. 'I'll get back to my torc examination. We could go for a drink later and catch up on other things?'

Rhona nodded her agreement and went back to writing up her report on the excavation.

Hours later and despite a detailed and thorough study of the photos she'd taken, Rhona had to admit that the skeleton had provided not one clue as to how the victim may have died. No broken hyoid bone to indicate strangulation. No evidence of head trauma, or possible bullet or knife wounds. No fractures, small or large.

Which might suggest the victim had died by ingesting something. Or perhaps suffocation before or after he'd been put in the stone cist? Although, from her study of the photos she'd taken of the inside of the stone coffin, it was clear that all surfaces were devoid of scratch marks, which pointed to him being already unconscious or dead when entombed.

How strange, she thought, *that this young man might never have been discovered had the pod not turned into Skaill Bay to try to save a birthing mother and her calf.*

Eventually Chrissy reappeared with a self-satisfied look on her face, which led Rhona to believe that her assistant had had some success with her work on the bracelet.

'How'd it go?' she asked.

'Good,' Chrissy said. 'I retrieved some sand particles from the twirls. Did you find any evidence that his hands had been tied at any point?'

'No, but we still have bags of sand to sieve yet,' Rhona told her. 'Why?'

'I extracted a fragment of plastic from the initials on the torc, which might have come from electrical tape.'

Rhona nodded her pleasure at this. 'Good start.'

'Now, I want to head for the jazz club while you tell me all about Orkney,' Chrissy said with a grin. '*Before* the beaching and the body,' she added.

'You mean, all about Magnus, and maybe PC Ivan Tull-och?' Rhona suggested with a smile.

Chrissy raised an eyebrow. 'Could be,' she admitted.

Rhona heard herself laugh for the first time since she'd stood on that headland looking down on the carnage below. It was striking, she thought, and not for the first time, how the death of innocent creatures could affect people so powerfully.

'What are you thinking?' Chrissy demanded as they went to don their coats.

'Just the way folk sometimes seem to care more about the suffering of animals than humans,' she said honestly.

Chrissy appeared to be considering this as they made their way through the main gates and headed down the hill towards Ashton Lane, before suddenly saying, 'I got a dog from the rehoming centre. His name's Rocket.'

Whatever Rhona had expected to hear, it hadn't been this. 'When?' she managed to say.

'When you were away in Orkney,' Chrissy told her. 'A cat would have been easier, but then if I let it out it might get run over. I wouldn't like that. So I got a dog.'

There were so many questions associated with this, Rhona didn't know where to begin. Luckily, she didn't have to say anything before Chrissy continued.

'He keeps Mum company when I'm at work and wee Michael's at nursery. I drop him off at hers and pick him up when I go home.'

Rhona wondered if perhaps Rocket was more her mum's dog than Chrissy's, but then thought about how often she farmed out her cat, Tom. Either to a neighbour or more recently to Sean.

As though reading her mind, Chrissy said, 'Have you spoken to Sean since you got back?'

She hadn't, Rhona told her.

Sean Maguire, her erstwhile male companion in what could only be described as an on/off relationship, played saxophone at the jazz club, and was a co-owner of the establishment where they were now heading.

What she didn't tell Chrissy was that she hadn't spoken to Sean since she'd left for her mini break in Orkney. Not even to check up on her cat.

'I need to find a man like Sean,' Chrissy said wistfully. 'Who's handsome, sexy and a good cook. And who'll happily take care of Rocket when I'm away on a job.'

'Your mum does all of those things except the handsome sexy male part,' Rhona said with a laugh. 'Maybe just concentrate on that.'

'You're right.' Chrissy looked thoughtful. 'Perhaps Rocket

will turn out to be the female equivalent of a babe magnet. I think I need to start taking him to the park in my spare time.'

'You've got spare time?' Rhona said as she reached the stairs to the jazz club.

That question went unanswered as they entered the room that served as the auditorium, incorporating a dais with a piano where the various musicians played, plus the long bar, where they usually congregated after work.

'Not sure whether McNab'll be here,' Chrissy told her. 'He's been on a course the last couple of days with the guy from IT, Ollie.'

Since Detective Sergeant Michael McNab didn't like computers on principle, that sounded odd to Rhona. 'Was Janice with him?' she checked.

'No. But she tells me that McNab wasn't enamoured of the said course,' Chrissy informed her.

'And did your spies tell you what the course was about?' Rhona tried.

'They did,' Chrissy said with a broad smile as the drinks she'd ordered appeared.

Chrissy's revelations, as Rhona well knew, were carefully timed for maximum effect. And eventually the words were spoken after Chrissy had sampled her wine.

'I believe the course was about using Artificial Intelligence in police work,' she said.

Rhona almost choked on her own drink. 'You are joking,' she eventually managed.

'Nope. Next big thing – but, of course, we already knew that, didn't we?'

Chrissy was right. Developments in digital technology had been at the forefront of forensic science in all its forms. AI was here and could and would eventually be utilized too. But knowing McNab as she did, she knew he wouldn't be of the same persuasion, which was probably why his superior officer, DI Bill Wilson, had sent him there.

Rhona found herself glancing over at the door, hoping to see McNab's tall, auburn-haired figure enter, so that she might hear his take on all of this.

Chrissy, catching her glance, said, 'Think I'll give him a call. Tell him you're here. That should bring him in double-quick time,' she added mischievously.

Rhona didn't respond to this, merely told Chrissy that she was going to check if Sean was about.

Sean usually played in the latter part of the evening, and could well still be at his flat. *Or perhaps at mine*, she thought. Arriving outside the office door, she suspected by the silence that it was empty, but checked anyway.

The office looked as it always did. Untidy, with a selection of clothes lying about, and a pillow and blanket on the couch, signalling the likelihood that Sean had slept there the previous night.

It was at this point she heard the sound of the shower.

So he is here, she thought. Before she could call out, her mobile rang with Sean's name on the screen. Puzzled as to who might be using his shower, she answered.

'Are you back?' Sean's Irish voice asked.

'I am. In fact I'm in your office at the club, where someone, who I thought was you, is having a shower.'

A short silence was followed by a laugh. 'Right, that'll be my cousin Connor. He arrived late last night and I told him he could sleep on the couch in the office.'

Rhona tried to recall if she'd met Connor when in Dublin the previous Christmas, but Sean's extended family had seemed to reach biblical proportions at that time, so she couldn't be sure.

As though reading her mind, Sean said, 'You haven't met Connor yet.'

Even as he said this, the bathroom door opened and a naked Connor emerged, rubbing his dark hair with a towel.

'Jesus, Mary and Joseph,' he said when he spotted Rhona and quickly moved the towel to cover his embarrassment.

As Rhona confirmed that she was neither Jesus, Mary nor Joseph but Rhona MacLeod, a friend of Sean's, the office door was flung open and Chrissy entered.

It wasn't often that her forensic assistant was at a loss for words, but the sight of a naked and handsome Irishman was one such occasion. As the two exchanged glances, Rhona did the introductions.

'Connor meet Chrissy. Chrissy meet Connor, a cousin of Sean's from Dublin,' she added.

Smothering her laughter at their expressions, Rhona chose that moment to step into the corridor and explain to Sean what had just happened.

'Excellent,' he said. 'I've been promising Chrissy to introduce her to one of the better male members of my family.'

'Well, you've done that. In more ways than one,' Rhona told him with a laugh.

'So are you coming home soon?' Sean said.

'You're at my flat?' Rhona checked.

'I am in the kitchen preparing a meal for you,' he told her.

'Then I'll be there shortly,' she promised, before shouting to Chrissy that she was heading home.

7

Orkney

It was already dark as Magnus watched the lights of a car wind down the road towards Houton Pier. As it drew closer, he registered it as Erling's vehicle and knew he would be heading for Seaview – and him.

He'd known Erling would visit him from the moment Rhona had described what they'd found buried in the dunes at Skaill Bay. If, as she suspected, the body had only lain there for twenty years, then Erling would be dealing with a murder investigation.

Opening the front door, Magnus went through to the sitting room and added some peat to the fire. He wondered if Erling had eaten or slept properly since all of this had begun. He wondered if Rory was about, then instinctively decided he couldn't be, because then Erling would have likely headed straight home.

In the minutes before he heard Erling's footsteps in the hall, Magnus poured himself a whisky and drank some down. Dutch courage, he thought.

When you bury your past, avoid friends with shovels.

Where had he heard that quote? And, more importantly, why had it appeared in his brain right at this moment?

As Erling entered, Magnus did his best to look both pleased to see his friend plus concerned by his obvious exhaustion.

'You look terrible,' he added for effect. 'Are you hungry too?'

A light seemed to flicker in his eyes, before Erling nodded. 'Starving,' he admitted.

'There's food if you want to eat here with me, unless Rory . . .'

'Rory's away on a job. I was planning on a ready meal,' Erling admitted. 'Then bed.'

'Well, I have a meal ready. Lasagne okay?' Magnus said.

'Lasagne would be great.'

Was he imagining it, Magnus thought, or was Erling's swift acceptance of food a way to cover the real reason he'd come?

Ladling out a plate of still-warm lasagne, he added a couple of pieces of garlic bread and, bringing it through, handed it to Erling. 'You want anything to drink with that?' he said.

'I still have to drive home.'

'Less than five minutes away,' Magnus said. 'And not even on the main road.'

'A lot can happen in five minutes,' Erling said with a small laugh.

They fell silent then as Erling set about demolishing the food. Magnus finished his whisky and poured himself another, turning his back to Erling while he did so. He was beginning to question whether he'd been right about the visit. Whether it had anything to do with the Skaill Bay discovery after all.

But even as he thought this, he knew that Erling was here for that reason. He just wasn't ready to talk about it yet.

'Coffee?' Magnus offered as Erling finished clearing his plate.

'Please, then I'll get out of your hair and head for my bed.'

In the kitchen, Magnus poured the coffee, leaving it black just as Erling liked. The action reminded him of when they were teenagers and had tried using coffee to appear less drunk when they got home. He considered pouring a mug for himself, then decided against it. He didn't want to smother his Dutch courage in case he might yet need it.

Re-entering the sitting room, he found Erling standing at the window looking out into the blackness of the night. Accepting the coffee Magnus handed him, he said, 'Remember when the ghost ship *Orlova* was towed into Scapa Flow? It blocked your view of Hoy.'

'Only part of the time,' Magnus told him. 'As it turned on the tide.' He felt himself relax, thinking they weren't going to broach the difficult subject after all.

Erling looked at him. 'I just heard from my dad via Dougie that Ava's coming home on a visit,' he said.

'That's good,' Magnus offered, while wondering why she should come now.

Ava Clouston had gone to school with them. She'd left Orkney to become an investigative journalist, working in many of the world's hotspots until both her parents had died in a car crash. Dougie, her wee brother, had been seventeen at the time, so she'd come home for a while to be with him.

Her visit had coincided with the arrival of the *Orlova*, a deserted Russian cargo ship that had been washed against the cliffs at Yesnaby. The *Orlova* had held many secrets, which she'd reported on, endangering her life in doing so.

47

Could her visit now have anything to do with the body discovered buried in Skaill Bay? It would make an interesting story, no doubt about that, and the true crime podcast she'd begun after her report on the *Orlova* was proving very popular. Magnus often listened to it himself.

Ava could scent a story and one here in Orkney would be ideal, giving her the chance to spend time with her brother.

Erling was observing his reaction to this news.

'She'll no doubt be interested in the discovery at Skaill Bay,' Magnus said. 'Maybe feature it in her true crime podcast.'

'Which will put even more eyes on it.' Erling didn't sound happy about that.

'If it proves to be a murder investigation, she will be restricted in what she can say,' Magnus reminded him.

There was a brief silence before Erling responded to that. 'Ava published information during the *Orlova* case that compromised both the investigation and those involved.'

He was right, Magnus thought – Ava Clouston was dogged and determined. But what exactly did Erling fear she would reveal? He waited, hoping Erling might explain.

'Dr MacLeod thinks the body's been there around twenty years,' he said. 'She also thinks it will prove to be a young male, possibly late teens.'

Magnus gave a small nod. 'I know.' He wondered what would come next.

'So around our age?' Erling said. 'That last summer before we left Orkney for university?'

Magnus stayed silent, yet acutely aware of what Erling's next question would be.

Erling held his gaze. 'Do *you* remember anyone going

missing that summer or even that year? Anyone around our age?'

'No one we knew went missing,' Magnus told him. 'But someone we knew left the island.' He willed Erling to remember who he was referring to, without having to say his name.

After Rhona had left, he'd gone online himself, looking for anyone who'd been reported missing from Orkney back then. Someone who might fit the description Rhona had given of the victim. It was when he'd looked back through the photographs of their senior year at high school that he'd suddenly remembered.

'Who?' Erling said cautiously.

'Ben Bradley.' Magnus watched Erling's reaction to the name. When the light didn't immediately dawn, Magnus added, 'His family came to live in that red corrugated-roof cottage near the Ring of Brodgar.'

Erling considered this for a moment before throwing Magnus an agonized look. 'Jesus. I remember him now. The family came from somewhere down south. They kept pigs for a while, but had no idea what they were doing. When the piglets died they buried them in the slurry.'

Magnus nodded. 'Ben took the brunt of that story at school. That and other things,' he added.

'He trailed around after us.' Erling shook his head at the memory. 'And we were pretty mean to him.'

'We were,' Magnus agreed. All the instances of their behaviour had arrived at the forefront of his memory now, with one in particular.

'That night at Skaill Bay when he turned up at our midsummer bonfire . . .' Erling was echoing Magnus's own thoughts.

'Exactly,' Magnus said.

'I was totally pissed and high when we spotted him spying on us.' The look he threw Magnus told its own story.

'You didn't hurt him,' Magnus said. 'Not physically, anyway.'

'But I might have.' Erling looked shocked by what he could now remember.

'But you didn't. He walked away unharmed.' They both fell silent, as though trying to fully recall what had happened that night.

The whole thing had been a horrible mess. Erling hadn't yet come out as gay, even to himself, although Magnus had already known the truth. Instead Erling had made a play for Ava and they'd gone into the dunes together. Magnus suspected Bradley had a thing for Ava, or maybe Erling, and that's why he'd gone to spy on them.

Magnus had been sitting by the fire, pretty drunk himself, talking to Shona Bain, who was so high she was considering going swimming in six-foot-high waves. He'd stopped her by coming on to her in a big way.

What he'd admitted to Rhona about their behaviour as teenagers had been true.

'It can't be him,' Erling was saying. 'Didn't he leave the island with his family before winter?'

Magnus nodded. 'It can't be Bradley.'

'But it might have been,' Erling said. 'If you hadn't helped Ava stop me from attacking him.'

Magnus didn't deny that and neither, he thought, would Ava.

'I'll head home now,' Erling said, still looking grim. 'Thanks for the meal. I really appreciated it – and the talk,' he added.

Minutes later, Magnus watched the lights of Erling's car as it wound upwards to eventually cross the main road and head home to his stone cottage on the hill.

The difficult topic of Ben Bradley had been broached and discussed. Surely now it could be forgotten?

Even as he thought this, Magnus knew that when Ava arrived it might well present itself again. Plus there were others on the beach that night. Not just the four of them. He struggled to recall who exactly. It was so long ago, and they were all out of their heads one way or another.

It didn't matter anyway because Ben Bradley had left the island at the end of that summer with his family, he told himself.

But even if he did leave, that didn't mean that he hadn't come back.

8

Orkney

Erling emerged from his vehicle to stand for a moment in front of the Grammar School. This was the last place he'd wanted to be this morning, especially after his talk with Magnus the previous evening. In truth, he'd forgotten this visit was in the diary and he'd had to be reminded of it by DS Green. Thanks to her, he was on time.

Sleep had evaded him the previous night, despite his exhaustion. Arriving home, he'd gone straight to bed, but though his body craved rest, his brain had immediately gone into overdrive, replaying the scenes from the past he'd discussed with Magnus, then merging them with the scenes of the dead and the dying at Skaill Bay.

He'd finally given up and risen from his bed to swallow a large dram before he set about looking through Rory's things, trying to locate the Viking bracelet he'd felt sure he'd seen on his lover's wrist that first night in Stromness.

Despite his thorough search, which he strove not to feel guilty about, he did not locate the said bracelet, which made him question if he'd ever seen it on Rory's wrist in the first place.

A second attempt at sleep had worked after a fashion, although his tumultuous dreams – or nightmares – found him buried alive in a stone cist, screaming to Magnus to let him out.

Hence why returning to his old school hadn't featured on his wish list for today.

Bracing himself, he headed for the entrance. He was here at the head teacher's request to talk to senior pupils about careers with Police Scotland. Basically to outline his own path from being a former pupil of Kirkwall Grammar School to becoming a Detective Inspector here in Orkney.

It sounded straightforward, but as he knew, the result would depend not on him, but on the sea of faces that awaited him. Too well did he remember a similar visit when he'd been in the sixth form. He'd been hung-over that day, in a belligerent mood, and he hadn't contributed to the discussion except to annoy his teacher so much that he'd been told in no uncertain terms to leave the room.

Perhaps he should tell them about that, Erling thought.

Always remember, it's not about you. It's about your audience, Magnus had once informed him with regard to public speaking. *Get them to laugh with you and they'll be on your side.*

Since his audience often consisted of reprobates, Erling hadn't made use of Magnus's advice. But today he would, he decided.

Making his arrival known at reception, he didn't have long to wait for the head teacher, Ms Claire Brown, to appear. Already known to one another, she gave him a big smile and thanked him for coming.

'My pleasure,' Erling told her, 'although I can't stay long.'

'The burial at Skaill Bay?' she ventured with a sympathetic smile.

'That and other things,' he told her, wondering just how much news about that had already made its way around the local population.

'Of course,' she said. 'We won't take up too much of your time. As discussed, if you could tell them how you went from being here as a pupil to where you are now. And maybe take a few questions at the end?'

Erling nodded. Now he was here, he found himself up for the task in hand. It was strange, he thought, that even at his age, just walking into the school assembly hall brought trepidation plus a rush of memories, most of which he would prefer to forget. Currently occupied by around two hundred pupils, the hall was in fact equipped to hold the entire secondary school population of around nine hundred.

As Ms Brown entered, the place fell silent. Erling took this to be a good sign, although there were some murmurs when he appeared behind her. The introduction was brief, after which she encouraged those present to listen carefully to what Detective Inspector Flett had to say and to have suitable questions ready for him when he finished.

As she took her leave, a ripple of sound moved through his audience and all eyes turned towards him. Many of them he already knew by sight, simply by living among them. A few he'd met because they'd got into trouble in some way, but none of them, as far as he was aware, had seriously broken the law. Not yet anyway.

Magnus had suggested he tell them a little about his time here as a senior pupil, warts and all. Including the fact that the last thing he'd ever imagined was that he would become a Detective Inspector in Police Scotland, and be back here in Orkney, talking to them.

His admission caught their attention, even the group of boys together at the back, where he and Magnus had chosen to sit in their day. When he was rewarded by laughter, he was glad he'd followed Magnus's advice.

Expanding a little on this, he explained that his favourite subject had been maths, basically because he found it easy, so he didn't have to work at it, unlike English. Or read books.

The groan at the word 'maths' was countered by an even bigger groan at 'English', particularly among the boys.

'I wanted off the island as soon as possible, so I chose to do maths at university. Thought I could always become a teacher. The thing about teaching maths is, it doesn't change, and the answers are at the back of the book,' he said. 'So, I thought, no hard work required there. Except it's not only maths you're dealing with in a classroom. It's people. People like you.'

There was more laughter at this point.

'Maths is beautiful and logical. It can describe the physical world, but it can't describe people and how or why they think the way they do. There is no formula, no certainty about that. And definitely no answers at the back of the book. Policing, on the other hand, involves striving to keep people safe, and to do that I have to try to understand their motives and their fears. So I didn't become a maths teacher but a police officer, which eventually led me back here as Detective Inspector.'

His little speech over, he watched the hands go up. The first and nearest was a girl who asked about female police officers and sexism in the police. He told her his second-in-command, DS Green, was female and, in his opinion, would go far in the force. He also pointed out that Police Scotland was currently headed up by a woman.

'That doesn't mean they don't face discrimination at work, just as in other walks of life,' he added. 'But it's something Police Scotland is working hard to eradicate.'

'What about gays?' a male voice from the back demanded, without raising his hand.

When a babble of voices followed the question, Erling stood in silence until they died down before responding.

'Sexual orientation is not a barrier to joining the police force,' he heard himself say, aware that there would probably be some in the audience who knew about his own living arrangements.

'And trans?' the second girl with her hand up asked.

'The same opportunities are open to trans people,' he told her. 'And there have been and are trans officers in the force.'

A brief silence followed this until another male hand was raised.

'The body you found at Skaill Bay, I heard it's not Viking but a boy about our age buried in a stone cist twenty years ago. Is that true?'

It was the question he'd probably dreaded the most, and here it was.

Erling drew breath before speaking.

'We did unearth a burial cist at Skaill Bay, the contents of which have been transferred to Glasgow for a full forensic examination. That's all I can say about what is a current police investigation.'

The rumble of noise that followed this was only brought

to an end by the reappearance of Ms Brown who, with a raised hand, demanded silence.

A relieved Erling thanked them for listening and for their questions, even if he wasn't at liberty to answer the last one, then waited as Ms Brown gave them licence to leave and head for their next class.

'How'd it go?' she asked him as the pupils trooped out.

'Fine. There were a few questions on women, gays and trans in the police force,' he told her.

'I'm not surprised,' she said. 'Young folk are all about equality and inclusion. Much more than we were at their age.'

Erling wondered what age she was, and figured probably near his own.

'The last question was the tricky one,' he told her as she walked him to the exit. 'That one was about the burial find at Skaill Bay.'

'The place is agog with it,' she said with a sympathetic look. 'The word in the school is that you have a more recent murder on your hands. A young man. Possibly not a lot older than them. Hence their interest.'

Erling didn't deny or confirm this. They were at the exit now and it was obvious from the glowering sky and the wet entrance that the rain had arrived in earnest.

'I was a pupil here twenty years ago myself,' she said. 'And I've been racking my brain to see if I could remember anyone who'd gone missing around that time.'

Erling gave her a more studied look. 'I didn't know that,' he said.

She smiled. 'I, like you, left vowing never to return.'

'But you did,' he said.

'Orkney has a drawstring that pulls you back. My maiden

name was Renton. Claire Renton. You were a couple of years ahead of me in school. You and Magnus Pirie.'

'I'm sorry,' Erling admitted. 'I don't remember you.'

'You were in the sixth form and didn't pay the least attention to fourth years. Although we were all very interested in you . . . and Magnus,' she added with a smile. 'We also desperately wanted to be invited to one of your beach parties.'

Erling found himself at a loss for words at this, so swiftly changed the subject. 'We'll need to take a look through the school records,' he said. 'Going back twenty years or so.'

'Of course,' she said. 'You can access them online. I'll send you through the details and password, or you can send an officer here to do that.'

'We'll do it online,' Erling said, keen as he was to establish exactly when Ben Bradley had left the school and hopefully the island.

On the way to his vehicle, he spotted a plane circling the nearby Kirkwall airport, and wondered whether Ava might be on it. If not that one, then she would be on another. And likely soon.

9

Glasgow

Appearing at the lab a good fifteen minutes after Rhona, which was definitely not the norm, an inscrutable Chrissy immediately set about dispensing their usual filled rolls along with the coffee Rhona had made.

'Well?' Rhona eventually said when breakfast had been swiftly consumed and Chrissy hadn't yet broken her silence to reveal the reason for her late arrival.

'It was all Rocket's fault,' she eventually offered.

'So nothing to do with Connor Maguire?' Rhona said, already disappointed by her explanation.

'Perhaps a little,' Chrissy admitted with a cheeky smile.

As she now looked poised to tell her tale, Rhona checked her watch, suddenly remembering. 'Sorry, I'll have to wait until later to hear the full story. Prof Nelson wants a video call in five minutes to discuss the Skaill Bay excavation. It seems he's found something interesting.'

Chrissy's expression moved from disappointment to curiosity. 'I wonder what it is.'

'Well, I'm about to find out,' Rhona told her.

Moving into her office, she settled behind her laptop to await the call, which soon followed.

'I'm at the dig, so I'm using my mobile,' Colin said. 'Apologies if I lose the signal.' He continued. 'As discussed before you left for Glasgow, a colleague and I investigated the immediate area around the cist. And I can report that we found artefacts in the sand that appear Viking in origin and age.' He paused for a moment to let Rhona digest this fact.

'So you think the area is a burial site?' Rhona checked.

'Yes. And since we unearthed the various items, including a knife and pieces of jewellery, we've expanded our search and have now found bones. Human bones.'

This wasn't a great surprise to either of them, she thought. Building a stone cist in the dunes above Skaill Bay would have been a big undertaking, which would have attracted attention. It seemed therefore logical that it had been discovered rather than created. If the killer knew of its existence already, or perhaps simply found it by accident . . .

'And you think these bones may belong to the original occupant of the cist?' Rhona asked.

'I think it's a strong possibility, and what we've found so far points to the probability of it being a female Viking burial.'

Rhona remained silent for a moment, as the full implication of his findings sank in.

'Have you spoken to Erling about this?' she said.

'I've sent Erling the photos of what we've discovered so far and he's coming over to the dig as soon as he can to see for himself,' Colin told her. 'I'm about to send you the same images.'

Rhona was browsing these when Erling called a little

later. 'You've seen the latest photos from Skaill Bay?' she checked.

'I have them in front of me now,' he told her. 'So we think the perpetrator emptied the cist and put his victim in it?'

She confirmed this, before asking, 'Have you had any leads yet on the possible identity of our victim?'

'None,' Erling said. 'But the word is definitely out there. I was at Kirkwall Grammar first thing this morning talking to seniors about my route from being a wild Orkney teenager to a DI in Police Scotland and all they really wanted to talk about was the young male, possibly around their age, who was murdered twenty years ago and buried in a stone cist at Skaill Bay.'

'Wow,' Rhona said. 'They knew that amount of detail?'

'News travels fast in Orkney,' he said. 'Also, according to Magnus, Ava Clouston's due back for a visit soon.'

Rhona had met and worked with the investigative reporter during the *Orlova* case and liked her.

'You think she's got wind of the story too?' she said, sensing Erling's disquiet.

'It's a case that would suit her true crime podcast.' Erling didn't sound too happy about that.

Ava Clouston was known for her tenacity, as evidenced by her work on the *Orlova*. 'That could be good news,' Rhona offered.

'Alternatively, armchair detectives could follow her up here, creating problems for the investigation,' he said, an edge to his voice.

When he ended the call, Rhona got suited up, thinking as she did so that something had spooked Erling and she wasn't convinced it was the discovery of the remains of the original likely Viking occupier of the cist.

Instead, it seemed to be Ava's imminent arrival in Orkney and his memory of her behaviour during the *Orlova* case. She decided she would give Magnus a call later and see if he could enlighten her as to what the problem might be.

Bringing up her photos of the original excavation, she began to study them in preparation for tomorrow's post-mortem. At Skaill Bay she and Colin had collected and recorded the victim's bones. At the PM the bones would be dusted clean with a soft toothbrush and laid out to form the skeleton.

A forensic osteologist would examine each bone along with Dr Sissons, the resident forensic pathologist. Her own findings, she suspected, would be confirmed, but it would be good to hear their interpretation of the evidence.

As to what the victim may have looked like alive, she'd already formed an image in her own mind. Around five feet ten inches in height, he'd been of slim build, his wrist easily fitting into the torc bracelet found in the cist with him.

As for his face . . .

A skull was made up of twenty-two bones, fourteen facial and eight cranial. Complex in structure, the small variations occurring during growth and development, together with soft tissue variations, could and did create the myriad different faces encountered every day.

The face Rhona had fashioned for him was that of a young male with his adult jawline not yet fully formed. DNA taken from teeth and bone, as well as confirming the sex, would also reveal his hair and eye colour.

A 3D scan of the skull would give shape to his features and an AI program could present them with a 3D image, which a 3D printer would then model.

As for now, she would hold her own picture of the victim in her mind, a young man who she'd already named Erik.

'Who are you, Erik?' she said. 'And what terrible thing happened to bring you here to my lab?'

'Is that you conversing with the dead again?' Chrissy called from the doorway. 'When you're finished your wee chat with Erik, d'you fancy sharing my lunch? Mum gave me a double helping this morning.'

'You definitely don't need a man to cook for you,' Rhona said, accepting the offer with alacrity. Until that moment she hadn't registered that she was hungry, intent as she'd been in completing her report on Erik.

'Looks like tuna salad, and definitely enough for two,' Chrissy informed her as she opened the container. 'Plus for dessert you get to hear about my evening with Connor.'

'Sounds perfect,' Rhona said.

'But first I want to hear what Prof Nelson had to say.'

Rhona gave details of their conversation as Chrissy dished up.

'That explains a lot,' Chrissy said, handing Rhona a heaped plate and a fork. 'And I look forward to seeing what they found in the sand. And what *I* might glean from it.'

Chrissy's enthusiasm knew no bounds in the areas of her job she loved.

'So tell me about your encounter with the naked Connor,' Rhona said in between mouthfuls of salad.

'Well, he was mightily embarrassed. Or he pretended to be,' Chrissy laughed. 'Stood there gawping until I suggested he get dressed and meet me in the bar.'

Chrissy was nothing if not forthright in whatever circumstances she found herself.

'By the time I got to the bar, you'd already left,' Chrissy

said. 'But, by what I overheard of your phone conversation, *you* also had a date with an Irishman.'

Rhona had, and a particularly pleasant one as she recalled, but she wasn't going to talk about it, because she wasn't as forthright in such matters as Chrissy. When she managed a nod and a smile, Chrissy gave her a knowing grin in return.

'Sean did say he'd been promising to introduce you to one of the better male members of the Maguire family,' Rhona offered. 'And apparently Connor is that man.'

'Well, we had a drink together and we got on great. I called Mum and she told me to have a nice time and that she would keep both wee Michael and Rocket overnight for me, if I was going to be late.'

'And?' Rhona encouraged her.

'We went for a curry along the lane at Ashoka and things were going really well, when Mum phoned to say that Rocket had jumped the back fence and run away. She was distraught, but couldn't leave wee Michael to go looking for him.' Chrissy threw her a wry look. 'Which took me some time, I can tell you. Hence my late arrival this morning.'

'And Connor?' Rhona said.

'I abandoned him in the restaurant and ran off like a rocket,' Chrissy said wryly. 'God knows what he thought that was all about.'

'Connor's staying at the club,' Rhona said. 'So you – or *we* – could head there again tonight, and you can explain. And maybe this time DS McNab *will* show his face.'

'Oh, he did come last night after I called him,' Chrissy told her. 'But I was too busy with Connor to listen to his AI story, and worse than that, *you'd* already left.' Chrissy pulled a face. 'Anyway, it's your turn to call him,' she added firmly.

10

Orkney

When Colin's call had come in earlier, Erling had been staring at his mobile, wondering again why Rory hadn't called back, despite his attempts to contact him the previous night.

The screen had lit up and he'd grabbed at it eagerly, only to discover not Rory's name but Prof Nelson's instead. Knowing it was unlikely to be good news, he'd momentarily hesitated before answering.

Their usual greetings exchanged, Erling had waited to hear the reason for the call, already suspecting that it would be connected with Skaill Bay. It was.

Colin had swiftly related the tale of having discovered more bones in the vicinity of the cist, which had set Erling's mind racing. Did this mean there was more than one victim of their killer?

When Colin had expanded on this by suggesting the bones were more likely to be Viking this time, Erling had at first been relieved, then puzzled when Colin asked him to come take a look. He didn't normally attend the excavation of either Viking or Neolithic bones, especially considering how many such sites there were on his home patch.

Perhaps sensing this, Colin had explained further, saying he was sending images through, but wanted Erling to come and see for himself, because the bones might belong to the original occupier of the cist. Which made it likely that it was the killer who'd discarded them, in order to use the cist for his victim.

Clear then about the significance of the find, Erling had promised to be over as soon as possible. After which he'd called Dr MacLeod, with the images already open on his screen. Their conversation was like a rerun of the one he'd just had with Colin. Although he'd eventually veered off into a moan about Ava's imminent arrival, plus the surprising knowledge of the sixth-formers regarding the body dug up at Skaill Bay.

En route to the locus once again, he now tried to direct his thoughts away from Ava Clouston and what she might remember of the past, and concentrate on what this latest development might mean for the investigation.

When he'd first heard Colin say the word *bones*, he'd had the immediate and horrible thought that they might belong to a second victim. The naked body in the cist was such a stylized modus operandi that he could hardly believe it was a one-off. So discovering the link as more likely to have been caused by the perpetrator discarding a set of ancient bones in order to bury a more recent corpse had been a relief.

And if the killer had handled the bones and artefacts without care as to what forensic evidence of himself he left behind . . .

Now passing Maeshowe, shortly followed by the Ring of

Brodgar, he was forcibly struck by how the distant past and the present coexisted side by side in Orkney. As a youth he'd paid little attention to any of these monuments or their significance.

He hadn't known that the Ring of Brodgar was older than Stonehenge. He wasn't aware that a group of Vikings had once spent a winter holed up in Maeshowe. Nor did he know that some of the graffiti inside the Neolithic mound were sexual slurs against Viking women.

It had been Magnus who'd eventually enlightened him about that, even etching a message of his own on the inner wall in support of the women.

At the Loch of Skaill he slowed down on the narrow, twisting road that bordered its choppy waters, remembering how often he'd come close to taking his first car into the loch on their way to the Bay O' Skaill. As a teenager he'd never thought about the possibility of death. The only thing he'd truly worried about was his sexuality.

Seeing a car approach, he now drew aside to allow it to pass, acknowledging the driver's wave of thanks before carrying on.

Arriving at the bay, he noted that the waters were calmer than the fateful night of the beaching, when all of this had been set in motion. Had the decision not been made to bury the calf in the dunes, then no hole would have been dug, and no remains discovered.

For a moment he wished that had been the case. Then just as swiftly he regretted such a thought, because no doubt there was someone out there desperate for news of the young man who'd been buried here in the dunes. And that was his job, no matter how difficult it might be.

Leaving the vehicle in the small car park near the toilet

block, he headed for the roped-off area. On approach he spotted Colin, then someone with him, who he realized was female once he got close enough to see.

Colin climbed out of the hole to say hello, then gave him a quick introduction to his fellow archaeologist, who greeted Erling in an American accent.

'This is Dr Deborah Gillam, who's on sabbatical from Princeton University and was keen to help me here,' Colin explained. 'If you come over to the van I'll show you what we've retrieved so far.'

Stepping into the van with Colin, he noted a selection of bones together with a chart partially filled in. Laid out alongside were the retrieved Viking items Colin had described on the phone.

'As you saw from the photographs I sent you, these items were scattered on the western side of the cist. We've found nothing as yet on the eastern side. I think he just picked things out at random and threw them into the sand. However, as well as the bones et cetera, we also found this.'

The said item was already bagged, the contents visible through the clear plastic.

Lifting the bag, Erling took a closer look. His eyes lit up. 'It's a cable tie,' he said. 'Likely used to restrain his victim.'

Had he just thrown it into the sand, never thinking it would be found? Or had he dropped it by accident, perhaps in the dark or poor light, and couldn't find it again?

Whatever the reason, it was there.

'We unearthed it shortly after I spoke to Dr MacLeod this morning,' Colin told him. 'I'll leave it up to you to tell her the good news,' he added.

Erling didn't need to voice how happy he thought she'd be. By Colin's expression, he already knew.

Colin continued. 'The weather's predicted to be poor for the next couple of days, so we won't be able to do any further digging, but you can take what we have as of now and send it on to Dr MacLeod.'

Erling's mood on the way back to Kirkwall was decidedly more upbeat. Hopefully the cable tie would provide evidence of the person who'd used it. And that was a start on the road to discovering the killer.

DS Green called on his return journey. Hands-free, he answered.

'Sergeant?'

'You have a visitor in reception,' she told him. 'A young lady. She says she was at your school event earlier and needs to speak to you.'

Erling wondered what it was about, hoping it would prove to be about a career in the police force.

'I'll be there in twenty minutes or so,' he told his sergeant. 'Depending on the temporary traffic lights at Finstown.'

11

Orkney

Erling recognized the girl who now stood in front of him as the one who'd posed the question about misogyny in the police force. Slim with a cascade of blonde hair, she was no longer wearing school uniform, but jeans and a hoody, plus a pair of very sturdy boots with thick soles that added an extra inch to her already tall frame.

PC Tulloch, showing her into Erling's office, gave her name as Ingrid Donaldson.

Erling suggested that she should take a seat, then waited until she was settled before saying, 'I understand you wanted to talk to me. Something about my visit to the school earlier.'

'It's actually about the body you found at Skaill Bay.' Her voice was firm, though he noted the hands clasped in her lap were trembling a little. 'I didn't want to say anything this morning.' She hesitated. 'But I know of someone who disappeared from Orkney eighteen years ago.'

'We're concentrating initially on a twenty-year interval,' Erling assured her. 'Would you like to tell me who this person was?'

She swallowed, as though the words she sought to say were causing some difficulty. Erling waited, aware that patience was the best way to deal with her obvious trepidation.

'I think it might be my father,' she eventually said.

'Your father?' Erling heard himself repeat this, even as he mentally did the arithmetic. The girl was a sixth-former, which put her at about seventeen or maybe eighteen years old.

As though reading his thoughts, she said, 'My mum was six weeks pregnant when my real dad disappeared.'

His immediate reaction to this was to think she wanted the police to find the man who'd abandoned her pregnant mother, and that the discovery of the body offered her a way of doing this.

'Was your father reported as missing at the time?' he asked gently.

'No. But my mum told me that he didn't leave us through choice.'

Her answer seemed to reinforce his reading of the situation, but her expression was so open and honest, he was determined to be kind.

'Could you tell me your father's name?' he said.

'Yes,' she answered firmly. 'It's Ben Bradley.'

'Ben Bradley,' he heard himself repeat, struggling to assimilate this fact and what it might mean. 'And your mother's name?' he added, wondering if this could get any worse and suspecting it was about to.

'Shona Bain, but she left Orkney for Glasgow after my dad disappeared and there she married my stepfather, David Donaldson.'

Shona's name was a bolt to both his brain and his chest. Shona, who had been on the beach that night with Magnus when he'd tried to attack Ben for spying on his disastrous attempts at sex with Ava in the dunes.

Gathering himself, he said, 'Shona Bain was in the sixth form at the same time as me. Ben too,' he added as though he'd just registered that fact.

'I know. I saw you in Mum's sixth-form photograph,' she told him firmly.

He remembered the day it had been taken. He'd been in the back row with Magnus, looking like thunder because he had a crashing hangover.

And now came the question he'd wanted to ask as soon as she'd mentioned Ben's name.

'I thought Ben and his family left Orkney the autumn after we quit school,' he said.

'He did, but he missed Mum so he came back to see her,' she told him.

Ben and Shona? Could that be true? He remembered Shona, but only vaguely. She hadn't been one of the inner circle. Had she and Ben really had some sort of connection? Enough for Ben to return to Orkney to visit her? And father her child? The girl, he realized, was painting a totally different picture of Ben from the one Magnus and he had discussed the previous evening. And what about that night in Skaill Bay? As he recalled it, Shona had been interested in Magnus back then. They hadn't even invited Ben along. And had no intention of doing that . . . ever.

'I don't remember Ben coming back to Orkney,' he said.

She shrugged. 'When you talked to us this morning, you said you'd left for university and rarely returned. In fact you never imagined coming back to Orkney. Ever.'

He had said that. Stressed it even. He decided to change tack.

'Does your mum know you're here?' he asked pointedly.

'She knows you found a body at Skaill Bay, but she doesn't know I've come here about it.' She hesitated. 'My stepdad died last year of cancer. That's why we came back to Orkney.'

Erling remained silent for a moment, wondering whether Shona's story of Ben being her daughter's father was true. Or whether she'd just made it up. There was one way to find that out, of course, and that would be from Shona herself.

'First thing to do is speak to your mum about this,' he said. 'There may be something she hasn't told you. If she agrees with what you're doing, then she needs to come here in person and give us a full account of Ben's disappearance.'

'I don't want my mother to know I'm doing this,' she said. 'And I don't need her permission anyway.'

'That's true,' Erling said. 'But you weren't born when your dad disappeared. And' – he hesitated – 'if your mum hasn't told you for sure that Ben is your father . . .' He tailed off.

She regarded him for a moment, anger sparking in her eyes. 'She says I've inherited my father's hair colour. Did the corpse have blond hair?'

'I'm not at liberty to give out details in an ongoing investigation,' Erling said, even though he had as yet no idea what colour hair the victim had. Although he did recall Ben as having his hair shorn like a GI, which he took a lot of stick about.

Having made her point, she rose and, thanking him for his help, made for the door. When it shut behind her, Erling eased himself back in his seat and considered what had just happened.

Jo found him there minutes later, so deep in thought that

he failed to note her entrance until she roused him with a 'Sir?'

He looked up. 'Yes, Sergeant?'

'What happened with the girl? PC Tulloch said she was here about the body in the cist.'

So Ingrid had told Officer Tulloch the reason for her visit, Erling thought. Tulloch was from the island of Sanday originally and a fair bit younger than himself, so Erling doubted that he knew anything about Ben Bradley or his family.

Neither, of course, would DS Green. A thought that comforted him a little.

Erling set about describing his meeting with Ingrid Donaldson in detail. Even the fact that he remembered her mother, Shona Bain, from school and the man Ingrid said had been her birth father, Ben Bradley.

'They were together back then?' she said.

'Not that I remember,' he replied honestly.

'Will she speak to her mother about this?' Jo asked.

'I don't think so,' he admitted. 'I'll go and see Shona myself. Explain what's happened and try to get the full story about her and Bradley. And, of course, his supposed disappearance. You can start looking into where the Bradleys went after Orkney.'

'If the body does prove to be that of Ben Bradley, and you knew him back then . . .' Jo halted there, not needing to explain that his position in leading the investigation would be compromised.

Erling acknowledged this with a nod. He would be the one answering the questions if that happened. Not asking them.

All the more reason to find out what he could now, he decided.

12

Orkney

PC Tulloch had informed him that Shona and her daughter lived just off Kirkwall High Street in a block of council-owned flats. Shona also worked in the library part-time, so they might have her mobile number if he wanted to call her.

How he knew this, Erling had no idea and didn't ask.

Instead, he'd called the library before setting out from the police station and requested Shona Donaldson's contact details, which they'd happily given, while also telling him that Shona was usually in with them Mondays and Thursdays, so he'd likely get her at home now.

His advance call to Shona regarding his visit had been nothing short of awkward for both of them. She'd immediately panicked, thinking that something had happened to her daughter. After reassuring her and saying that he was calling about something else, he'd had to reveal that it was with regard to Ben Bradley.

A pregnant silence had followed this before she'd eventually said, 'What about Ben?' in a cautious voice.

'I don't want to talk over the phone,' he'd told her. 'May I call in on you now?'

And here he was, staring at the name 'Donaldson' on the buzzer, his finger hovering above it. On the short walk over, he'd tried to decide the best way to approach the subject of her daughter's visit to the station. But by the time he'd reached the block of flats, he was none the wiser on that front.

The buzzer pressed, he heard the door release and, pushing it open, made his way up the stairs. He realized as he reached her landing that he was having difficulty recalling what Shona had looked like as a teenager. She'd been in a couple of his classes, but he'd never paid her much attention. She was part of the summer beach party crowd, and he'd thought she liked Magnus, but she wasn't the only girl who did. Had she been mean to Ben, like they had? That he couldn't remember.

But I'm about to find out, he thought.

She was waiting at the open door and, with an awkward 'Hello', urged him inside, swiftly shutting the door behind him.

'Come into the kitchen,' she said. 'I've put the kettle on. You'll have a coffee or a tea?'

He agreed to a black coffee and watched as she prepared it, suddenly recognizing in her movements – the way she pushed her brown hair back and the small smile when she handed him his coffee – the young girl he did remember.

'I didn't know you were back in Orkney,' he said.

'We're not back long. Just this last year,' she told him. 'I didn't expect to find you here and as a detective inspector no less,' she said with a wry smile. 'I couldn't believe it, to be honest. But you look the same, just a bit older.'

'A couple of decades older and hopefully wiser,' Erling said.

'So what is this about Ben?' she said quizzically.

'Have you any idea where he is?' Erling said.

'Nope. None.' She stared at him. 'Why would you think I should?'

Erling decided to go straight for it. 'Because your daughter came into the station today and said that the body we found at Skaill Bay might be him.'

'What?' she gasped in astonishment.

'She claimed Ben was her father and that he'd disappeared when you were six weeks pregnant.'

Shona, who'd been standing by the sink, now slid to a seat at the table as though her legs would no longer hold her up.

'She said you told her that he would never have deserted you.'

'My God.' Shona covered her face with her hands.

'So that's not true?' Erling said.

She was silent for a moment. 'I told her that story when she asked about her father. I said I went to senior school with Ben and he was kind to me. His family left Orkney but he came back to see me once, then I never heard from him again. I thought something bad must have happened to him, but I never found out what.'

She'd been gazing into the middle distance as she said all this. Now she turned to look at him, her expression troubled. 'I don't know where he went after he left me that night. He wasn't living at home any more. He didn't get on with his stepfather, who was a homophobic bastard.'

Erling's surprise at her story of Ben, his kindness to her, and the relationship, or lack of one, that he'd had with his father, must have shown on his face, because Shona said, 'You didn't know him at all, did you?'

'No, I didn't,' he admitted.

He allowed the silence between them to settle for a moment, before saying, 'Ingrid asked if the victim had blond hair like hers.'

Something resembling pain crossed Shona's face before she answered. 'And what did you tell her?'

'That we don't give out information on current investigations,' he told her. 'Although the victim's hair and eye colour haven't been established as yet.'

He wanted to ask her who Ingrid's father was if it wasn't Ben, but knew that was too much of an intrusion.

She gave him a small resigned smile. 'My daughter won't give up on this, you know. Whatever you or I say.'

Erling had a feeling she was right.

'Ingrid says Dougie's sister, Ava, is coming back for a visit,' Shona said as she led him to the door. 'It's like a class reunion,' she added. 'I suspect she'll be as interested as Ingrid in the body you found in the dunes at Skaill Bay.'

And with that, she showed him out.

13

Orkney

As the Loganair flight circled, getting ready to land, Ava gazed out at the familiar landscape, her heart rising. The fields weren't yet the lush green of spring, and the kye were still in their winter byres, but her homeland looked good. *It always does*, she thought. Regardless of the season or the weather.

The wind caught them a little on landing, which was par for the course, then the twin-engine aircraft was down and trundling towards the small airport building. Once it had come to a halt, around half the passengers made moves to exit, the remainder continuing on to Lerwick.

In the front seat, Ava was first out and heading down the narrow steps onto the tarmac, where a stiff sea breeze buffeted her as far as the entrance. Inside, she passed those in line to board for Shetland on the second half of the flight that served the northern isles.

Waiting for her case to appear on the little carousel, she looked round, hoping her young brother had got her text and would be there to meet her. Spotting his entrance, she noted there was a young woman with him.

Dougie's smile when he saw her was so welcoming, Ava felt her throat catch. Not that long ago they had been at odds with one another. But thankfully no longer.

The girl was hanging back, allowing them space to meet. Ava hadn't expected a hug from her teenage brother, but she got one nonetheless, before he took charge of her suitcase, then beckoned the waiting girl over.

'Ingrid, meet my big sister, Ava, the intrepid investigative reporter. Ava, meet Ingrid, who was in the year below me at Kirkwall Grammar.'

When he grinned, Ava knew that he was happy to have left school and taken over the family farm. She'd tried to encourage him to go to agricultural college first and let their neighbour Tommy Flett, Erling's father, basically run the place for a while, but Dougie had been adamant. He knew everything he needed to know about running a farm already, he'd told her. Plus Tommy would be helping him. So she'd agreed and even felt relaxed enough about his decision that she'd gone back to London, returning for short stays in between jobs.

'Hi, Ingrid,' she said. 'I don't think we've met before?'

The girl's face lit up. 'No, but I listen to your true crime podcast. It's great. And I know all about what you did on the *Orlova* case here on Orkney,' she added in an admiring tone.

'Then I must get to know *you* a bit better,' Ava said as they made their way out to the car park.

When Dougie smiled at this, she decided maybe Ingrid was his girlfriend, despite the fact he hadn't mentioned her during any of their phone calls.

Dougie had always been a man of few words and deep

thoughts, she reminded herself. And he wasn't her baby brother any more, she thought, with a glance at the big solid hands now gripping the steering wheel of the 4x4, but a grown man and a farmer in his own right.

The general chat as they drove home alongside Scapa Flow was about the weather and the state of the still-confined cattle, which would be set free from their winter hibernation in the byre come the first of May. At this point Ava made a mental note to be back for their release, remembering the wonder of the occasion as the kye virtually danced their way into the fields.

'There's a casserole in the oven for lunch,' Dougie said as he led them into the warmth of the farmhouse kitchen.

'It smells delicious,' Ava told him, greeting Finn, Dougie's collie dog, who'd leapt from his bed next to the Aga as soon as she'd appeared.

The subject of the beaching and subsequent body dug up in the dunes at Skaill Bay was brought up by Dougie after they'd cleared their plates and he'd made a pot of coffee, mainly for Ava.

'Is that why you're here?' he said. 'Apart from checking up on your wee brother,' he added with a grin.

Before Ava had a chance to respond, Ingrid said eagerly, 'I was hoping you would feature it in your podcast,' before she swiftly added, 'I think I know who the body might be.'

Ava was silent for a moment, trying to work out her response to this. In all of her successful investigations, there had been many people who'd felt they'd known the answer before she did.

Dougie broke the silence. 'Ingrid thinks it's someone you went to school with. His name was Ben Bradley.'

'Ben Bradley?' Ava repeated, searching for the name in her memory.

'He was my dad,' Ingrid told her. 'My mum's Shona Bain,' she added.

And there it was. The image of brown-haired Shona Bain, who'd been, if not in their little gang, certainly part of their wider circle.

And Ben? As though her brain had gone on searching her memories of twenty years ago, she suddenly remembered the awkward boy who'd followed them round, desperate to be included, but who never was.

Ingrid believed that boy was her father?

The discomfort of that thought must have shown on her face, because Ingrid suddenly said, 'You did know him?'

Ava nodded, rather than answer.

'I have your sixth-form photo,' Ingrid said. 'You're in it with my mum and dad.'

'And Erling and Magnus,' Dougie added, his gaze focused on her.

'I do remember Ben,' Ava said. 'He came to our school during sixth form, from somewhere down south. His family didn't stay in Orkney very long, though. They left at the end of the school year, I seem to remember.'

'Ben came back to see my mum,' Ingrid said. 'That's when he disappeared. Mum said he would *never* have left us,' she added with conviction. 'And that something bad must have happened to him.' The expression on her face matched her words.

Ava didn't immediately reply, because she wasn't sure how to.

News of the excavation in the dunes after the pod of whales had come ashore had indeed prompted her visit.

She hadn't told Dougie this beforehand, but suspected he'd already guessed. Hence the reason he'd brought Ingrid with him to the airport.

'I am interested in the discovery of the body at Skaill Bay,' Ava admitted. 'I'm also sure that Detective Inspector Flett will be doing everything he can to identify the remains.'

'I went to see him at the police station and told him about my dad,' Ingrid said, her tone one of anger. 'That he'd disappeared before I was born. That the body might be him. He didn't believe me. He said my mum may not have told me the truth about my father.'

God, Ava thought, this was getting more awkward by the minute. Unsure how to respond to the girl's distress, she decided to ask the most obvious question.

'Why do you think it might be your dad?'

'I just heard that they found a Viking torc bracelet in the cist. And it wasn't old. My dad is wearing one like that in the school photo. You can just see it below his shirt cuff.'

At this surprising and concerning information, Ava immediately said, 'You told Erling, I mean DI Flett, about this?'

Ingrid shook her head vehemently. 'I only heard about the bracelet after I spoke to him.'

'So the discovery of this bracelet isn't official?' Ava said, wondering how many more stories involving the body, either true or fabricated, were doing the rounds on the island.

'That doesn't mean it isn't true,' Ingrid came back with. 'The other things folk are saying about it – like the sex and age of the victim, plus how long he's been in the ground – the police didn't announce that formally either, but the word's out there,' she added defiantly.

Keeping pertinent information out of the public domain

was always a problem for the police, Ava thought, but in a small, highly connected community like Orkney it was well-nigh impossible.

Dougie came in at this point. 'Erling would tell you the truth about what they've found, wouldn't he?'

'I'm not a police officer, so no, he couldn't and wouldn't,' Ava said. 'Although once the remains have been forensically examined and the approximate age and sex of the victim established, together with the length of time the body has been in the dunes, all that would be released to the public to help identify the remains.'

'And the bracelet?' Dougie said.

'The discovery of the bracelet, if there was one, would I think be kept quiet, initially that is.'

'Why?' Ingrid demanded.

'So that the killer didn't know it had been left behind.' She checked their reaction to this, then added, 'It's likely the killer is watching and listening to the proceedings just like you and me. If the torc bracelet might provide a link to them . . .' She tailed off.

'So you think we shouldn't tell Erling about it being in the school photo?' Dougie said.

'On the contrary. I think you should. Or *I* should,' she added, aware that she really needed to talk to Erling about all of this, plus other stuff associated with Ben Bradley.

At this point, Ingrid fetched the small backpack she'd had at the airport and extracted a brown envelope. From it she produced the sixth-form photograph and slid it across the kitchen table to Ava.

Ava found herself both fascinated and repelled at the thought of looking at her younger self, but she studied it anyway.

She spotted Magnus and Erling first. Both taller than the others, they were standing in the middle of the back row. Magnus was looking straight at the camera. Erling was looking elsewhere. No doubt on purpose. He'd been in a foul mood that day, she recalled. Likely hung-over from more than just booze. Magnus had probably consumed the same amount, but it had always left less of a mark on him.

She scanned the other faces, looking for her own, in order to delay her search for Ben.

And there she was, hair pulled back into a ponytail, her expression serious. She recalled how she'd felt that day, a mix of relief that her school life would soon be at an end and trepidation at departing Orkney for university in the big city.

Feeling both Ingrid's and Dougie's eyes upon her, she checked for Ben, who she located at the end of a row, standing a little apart as though he wasn't really one of them. Which he never had been, she thought. His expression seemed haunted and wary, as though he was hanging about with a pack of wolves, who might eat him up at any moment.

God, they'd made his short time in the sixth form a misery. Trying not to recall exactly how they'd done that, she focused on his left wrist.

And there it was. Or at least a glimpse of what looked like a metal bracelet.

'See,' Ingrid said. 'I told you he was wearing it.'

Ava wanted to say that it wasn't completely clear what he wore on his wrist, and that they had no idea what the bracelet in the cist looked like, or even if it existed at all. But something stopped her.

'May I take this and show it to DI Flett?' she said instead.

'Yes.' Ingrid's voice held a hint of triumph. 'Maybe he'll listen to you.'

14

Glasgow

Pelting rain accompanied them to the mortuary. Steadily persistent, it never left them apart from their short period of time underground, when they drove through the Clyde Tunnel from Partick to Govan.

Emerging on the other side, the rain was waiting to take its revenge, causing Rhona to flip the windscreen wipers to their highest speed, which didn't improve the view.

Beside her, Chrissy looked gloomily out. Such an expression was unusual if not unheard of with regard to her forensic assistant. In fact Rhona couldn't remember when she'd last seen it.

'Okay,' she said finally. 'What's up? I thought you wanted to go to the PM?'

'I did. I do.' Chrissy attempted a smile. 'I was just wondering . . .' She tailed off.

'Why Connor wasn't at the jazz club last night?'. Rhona tried.

As arranged, they'd gone to the club after work to find

no sign of Connor staying there any more and no Sean to explain the change in circumstances.

'Sean wasn't there either and I have no idea where he is,' Rhona said. She remembered Sean mentioning that Connor was yet another Maguire musician. 'If asked, I'd say they're probably away playing together somewhere,' she added.

'Sean doesn't tell you when he's playing elsewhere?' Chrissy said in surprise.

'I don't always tell him when I go away for work. He knows it's my job and we don't live together anyway,' Rhona said pointedly.

'What instrument does Connor play?' Chrissy said, brightening a little.

'Guitar, I think. And maybe piano.'

Seemingly perked up by this information, Chrissy said, 'Maybe he'll play for me sometime like Sean does for you.'

'Maybe,' Rhona said, joining the queue to enter the large car park that served the Queen Elizabeth University Hospital, known affectionately by Glaswegians as the Death Star, because of its architectural design rather than the quality of its care.

'We're going to be late,' Chrissy said ominously as the windscreen wipers continued to fight the deluge. 'Dr Sissons won't be happy about that.'

Dr Sissons, the forensic pathologist, wasn't known for levity at the best of times and lateness was a bugbear of his, especially when it featured DS Michael McNab, which was often. Rhona had yet to be chastised for it, but today might well be that day, she thought.

The PM had been scheduled for ten a.m. which had given them time for a quick breakfast, but they'd then been delayed by a call from Erling regarding the cable tie Colin had unearthed among the discarded Viking bones, all of which would arrive with her shortly.

This news had caused Chrissy much excitement, which had subsequently evaporated during their rain-soaked journey across town.

'Here we go,' Chrissy said as the queue finally began to creep into the car park. 'Grab the first space you see,' she ordered.

Even at this early hour there was little chance of a parking space that would avoid the need for a dash through the pelting rain to the mortuary entrance.

So a sprint it will have to be, Rhona thought, as she duly parked the vehicle in the first available space and jumped out.

Chrissy's shriek of laughter as they zigzagged their way through the mass of cars indicated that her forensic assistant was back to normal.

Shaking themselves down in the vestibule, Chrissy announced that they should have donned forensic suits before exiting the vehicle, since she couldn't put one on now without removing her sodden clothes first.

Hence it was that when they entered the examination room, they had only their underwear on inside their suits, their outer clothes now draped over the radiator in the changing room to dry.

Fortunately, no one was aware of this apart from themselves.

'Ah, Dr MacLeod. So glad you could join us,' Sissons said, without looking up from the fully assembled skeleton.

However, a quick glance to his left found the smiling eyes

of the osteologist, who Rhona immediately recognized as Dr Ruth Styles.

'Rhona,' she said. 'Delighted you made it through the biblical downpour. And Chrissy. Glad you could join us too. We started early so most of what you're interested in we've already completed.'

She gestured at the skeleton. 'I've read your transcript of the excavation and your conclusions as to the possible age and sex of the victim. We'll confirm with DNA, of course, but both Dr Sissons and I agree that the bones belong to a post-pubescent male. Late teens, early twenties,' Ruth said.

'Rhona named him Erik, with a k,' Chrissy told her.

'Erik it is, then. Much better than Skaill Bay man,' Ruth said. 'I've taken a 3D scan of the skull so I'll send you an image of what I believe he looked like in life shortly. Although from the number of skulls I've studied, I already have my own mental picture of Erik,' she added. 'As I think you probably have too.'

'How long do you think he's been buried there?' Rhona asked the other key question.

'Given your details of the sandy grave and the photographs, I think your twenty years is a reasonable estimate.'

'Any thoughts on how he may have died?' Rhona tried.

'Neither Dr Sissons nor I have found anything on the skeleton to suggest a violent injury of any kind. Although there is an indication of a long-healed fracture to the left wrist. Most likely from when he was a child.'

She showed Rhona the faint markings that indicated this.

'There can't have been that many young males who disappeared in Orkney twenty years ago,' Ruth said. 'If he was a local child, the hospital would have a record of the wrist fracture.'

It wasn't much, but it was something to go on, along with the facial reconstruction.

'I should say we were kept late because of a call from DI Flett from Kirkwall. They've discovered a second set of bones in the vicinity of the first,' Rhona said. 'Which will be sent on here for you to examine.'

'Another victim?' Ruth said in a shocked tone.

Rhona reassured her. 'According to Professor Nelson, they're most likely from the original occupant of the stone cist in which we found Erik,' she explained. 'They were scattered in the sand nearby, together with some Viking jewellery.'

'I'm relieved to hear that,' Ruth said.

They discussed this briefly before Rhona and Chrissy made their exit.

'Well,' Chrissy said. 'Nothing that we didn't think already. Apart from the wrist fracture.' She eyed her still-steaming clothes. 'We could go back in the suits?' she suggested. 'I don't fancy putting on wet clothes.'

Rhona was inclined to agree. 'We can change into dry things at the lab.'

The call to her mobile came as they reached the vehicle. It was McNab's name on the screen.

'You at the mortuary for the Orkney PM?'

'Just about to leave from there,' Rhona said. 'Why?'

'Anything you can tell me about the victim?'

'Male, late teens to twenties, five ten, slim build. Manner of death unknown. Why the interest?' she said.

'The boss briefed me on your Orkney find. He wants us to help with trying to identify your victim.'

The pause that followed suggested McNab's disquiet at this.

'I assumed Glasgow would be involved seeing as you have the manpower,' she said.

'And the AI technology,' he added in that sardonic tone she knew so well.

So that was the problem, Rhona thought. 'I take it this involves the recent course Chrissy told me about?' she said, trying to keep her amusement out of her voice.

'It does,' he confirmed. 'Not sure Ollie is impressed at being replaced by an AI program, especially one he was actually involved in developing.' The laugh that followed signified that neither was McNab.

'They've done a 3D scan of his skull,' Rhona said. 'The results of which should be available shortly.'

She couldn't make out the mumbled reply that followed this information.

'Does that mean you'll be on the case?' she checked.

'The Glasgow end of it,' he said firmly.

It was clear from McNab's tone that he had no desire to revisit Orkney any time soon. It wasn't personal. He just didn't like what he called 'the countryside'. The last time he'd been sent 'into the wilderness' had been for a murder on the island of Sanday, Orkney's second most northerly isle. He hadn't taken to either the location or the locals back then. And they hadn't taken to him.

'Did you catch that?' Rhona asked Chrissy when she ended the call.

'McNab's voice was even louder than the rain on the car roof,' Chrissy told her before falling silent for a moment. 'I was thinking about what Dr Ruth said about the likelihood of the victim being from Orkney.'

'If our victim does turn out to be a local,' Rhona said, 'it could prove awkward for Erling.'

Chrissy considered this. 'Especially if he knew him personally.'

'Twenty years ago, Erling was much the same age as our victim,' Rhona added, wondering if that had been the cause of his obvious discomfort the last time they'd talked.

15

Orkney

Ava had slept badly, her dreams replaying dark memories she'd rather forget.

In them she'd been seventeen again, awkward and undecided, both loving Orkney yet desperate to get away as soon as possible.

She'd felt the same about Erling Flett. Both fancying him and disliking him at the same time, and suspecting he felt much the same way.

All of that had, of course, been resolved in the interim for both of them, but there was still a small part of her that wished it had turned out otherwise.

The night he'd attacked Ben Bradley for spying on them in the dunes had been the moment of realization for her, and she suspected for Erling, that he was definitely gay. That's why he'd flown at Ben with such ferocity.

If she'd been honest with herself back then, she'd suspected already. Even tried to convince herself Erling might be bisexual, which meant he could fancy her too.

The evening, she recalled, had been warm with little

wind, as though Orkney lay at the epicentre of a storm. Earlier in the day, a brisk onshore breeze had whipped up the waters of the bay so that they still broke white and frothing against the beach.

Her flashes of uncomfortable memories found the four of them sitting close to the fire. Erling, his arm about her shoulders as though finally claiming her for his own. Her pleasure at that. Magnus and Shona Bain opposite. Shona wanting to swim and Magnus sensibly persuading her otherwise.

Erling whispering in her ear, pulling her up and walking her towards the dunes. Their stumbling over the big rounded stones, then sinking into the sand as he drew her up behind the marram grass.

She'd already decided she would say yes, knowing he would ask first, for beneath the angry and confused adolescent, she now realized, was the honourable man he would eventually become.

What happened next now replayed with a vengeance. Despite his determined moves, she'd known by his expression that he was both frightened and repulsed by what he was trying to do. And his body felt the same. The more he tried, the worse it became.

It was then that she'd screamed, realizing that both her humiliation and his were being viewed, and by the boy who so wanted to be part of their world that he'd followed them here.

Ingrid's visit yesterday had been the catalyst for both the nightmares about that night and also her concerns about the proposed podcast.

The discovery of a body at Skaill Bay had appealed to her investigative mind. And when it turned out not to be the usual Viking burial, but a possible more recent death with murderous overtones, she'd decided that it was definitely something she wanted to delve into further.

Until, that is, Ingrid had thrown up the possibility of the body being that of Ben Bradley, who Ingrid seemed to think was her father. If Ava was right about Ben's sexuality, then she didn't think that part of Ingrid's story, or maybe her mother's story, was likely true. But that didn't make the rest of her story false.

Now seated at the kitchen table with a very strong cup of coffee, the school photograph laid out in front of her, she considered how she might broach the subject of the possible torc bracelet on Ben Bradley's wrist with Erling. Along with its implication.

If the body did turn out to be Ben's, then she suspected everyone in that school photograph would be drawn into the investigation, in particular those who'd persecuted Ben in all the cruel ways only high school pupils could dream up.

Everyone in that photograph knew about the beach parties at Skaill Bay. Who held them and what went on there. Some of them had been part of it, others rejected, among them Ben.

But Ben had left alive that night. He hadn't been harmed, except by cruel words, she reminded herself. And they'd all thought he and his family had departed Orkney shortly after.

But what if he did come back to Orkney, like Shona had told her daughter?

Before she could wrestle with those thoughts any further, she brought up Erling's number on her mobile. He, she and Magnus had been friends twenty years ago, and more recently when they'd been reunited by the death of her parents and her work on the *Orlova* investigation. It was time all three of them talked about this, and she would begin with Erling.

It was funny, she thought, how the outer person changes with age, and yet the way the voice says your name stays the same. And so it was with Erling. He'd taken only moments to answer and, as soon as he did, she could again picture the teenager of two decades ago with his wild hair and tall, wiry build.

'Can we meet?' she said. 'I need to talk to you about Skaill Bay.'

Silence followed her request before he said, 'If you mean the body found there, I can't discuss a current investigation with you.'

'Ingrid Donaldson came to see me yesterday. Shona Bain's daughter,' she offered.

A short pause, then he said, 'I know who she is.' The melodious tone had gone, replaced by something much sharper. 'And I've already had a visit from her.'

'She told me about that,' Ava said gently. 'She brought me a copy of our sixth-form photograph. Do you have one?'

She could tell by the silence that he was puzzled by this latest development. 'Not any more. Anyway, what was important about the photo?' he asked.

Ava hesitated before answering. 'She said she'd heard that a modern Viking torc bracelet had been found at the scene.'

Erling swore under his breath. 'That's classified information and hasn't been released to the press or public.'

'So it is true . . .' She halted there and waited.

'What has the bracelet got to do with the photograph?' he demanded.

'In our sixth-form photo, Ben Bradley was wearing a bracelet on his left wrist.'

The depth of silence that followed was filled with her fears and, she suspected, his own.

Eventually he said, 'Can you bring the photograph to the police station and make a statement regarding this.' It wasn't a question but an order.

'Of course,' she said. 'Shall I come now?'

'Yes. Now,' he emphasized, before ending the call.

Ava took the jeep, glad that Dougie had held on to the second vehicle. Before departing the house, she'd written a short note saying she was going to the police station to speak to Erling and that she'd taken the photograph with her.

Now on the main road, she could see Magnus's house, Seaview, and contemplated dropping in to discuss things with him. Not right now, but maybe on her way back from her meeting with Erling.

Magnus had always been the steady one, despite their wild times. She remembered again how he'd been on the beach with Shona Bain that night. They'd believed Shona had had a thing about Magnus in school, although he'd never, to Ava's knowledge, reciprocated that feeling.

Or had he?

She suddenly had an image of Magnus back then. The tallest of the boys, with a shock of blond hair. The only true Viking-like member of the gang. Even as she recalled this, her thoughts went to Ingrid and her long blonde hair. Then to the fact that Shona, Ingrid's mum, had mid-brown hair, as had Ben.

Was there a chance . . .?

Get real, she told herself. Magnus Pirie wasn't a man to renege on his parental responsibilities. But what if he didn't know he had any?

Another reason I need to speak to him, she decided as Kirkwall came into view. *But first I have to face Erling.*

She was shown into his office by a young male officer she vaguely knew from the *Orlova* investigation. He'd obviously been warned of her arrival, because he'd greeted her with a nervous air and, once he'd shown her into the office, he'd immediately closed the door behind her.

Erling was seated behind a desk, looking every inch the Detective Inspector.

He managed a small smile, then directed her to take a seat. She did so, but not before she handed him the envelope.

He held it for a moment, before easing the photograph out and studying it closely.

Ava waited in silence, aware of what he would say before he said it.

Eventually he looked up. 'It's not clear what sort of bracelet it is.' He examined her reaction to that.

'I agree,' she said. 'Magnification might help.'

'Do you remember Ben Bradley ever wearing a torc bracelet?' Erling asked.

She felt bad about her answer, even before she gave it. 'I didn't look at him much. In fact, I tried not to.'

He waited, obviously expecting her to elaborate.

'He didn't want to be seen,' she offered by way of an explanation. 'Because when he was, he was bullied.'

Erling nodded. 'We were cruel as teenagers.' He took another look at the photograph. 'I'll get the Tech folk to examine it more closely. See what they have to say.' He sat back in the chair. 'I'd like you to make a statement regarding your visit from Ingrid and what she said.'

'She didn't do anything wrong,' Ava told him.

'She should have brought this to me first.'

'Maybe she thought you'd brush her off, like you did the first time?' Ava suggested.

'Hearsay in an investigation isn't evidence. There is nothing to suggest the victim is Ben Bradley.' Erling halted there for a moment as though considering what to say next. 'I went to see Shona myself. Explained about her daughter's visit.'

Now this was a surprise. 'Does Ingrid know this?'

'Not unless her mother told her,' he said. 'Anyway, she confirmed that Ben had come back to see her, and promised to keep in touch, but didn't.'

'So why does Ingrid think Ben is her father?'

'I think because Shona spoke fondly of him. Said he was kind and wouldn't desert her and that she was worried something bad had happened to him. And no,' he added, apparently reading her expression, 'I did not ask who Ingrid's father was.'

Silence fell between them, leaving so many things unsaid on both sides. In this room, Erling was a detective inspector and she was an investigative journalist, irritating him with her questions. But there was one final question that did require an answer.

'What if the victim does turn out to be Ben Bradley?' Ava said.

'Then everyone in that photograph will need to be interviewed about their relationship with the victim twenty years ago, including me.' He paused. 'However, we are currently looking into the whereabouts of the Bradleys after they left Orkney and we're fairly certain they headed for Glasgow, because that's what they told the owner of the cottage they rented here on Orkney.'

'And they may still be there?' she asked hopefully.

'That's yet to be established. The family, if you remember, moved around a lot and were a bit . . .' He hesitated.

'Odd?' she tried.

'Maybe more than that.' Erling's expression darkened. 'When I spoke to Shona, she said that Ben's father was a homophobic bastard.'

Now that was a revelation. 'God, so we weren't the only ones persecuting him.'

They were both silent for a little while before Ava said, 'That night on the beach, Shona was with Magnus.'

'Yes, she was.'

'Have you spoken to him about it?'

'A little,' he admitted.

'I think we three have to sit down together and talk through what happened, from each of our perspectives.'

'I think we all remember what happened,' he said. 'All too vividly,' he added.

Ava, noting Erling's expression, drew the swift conclusion that he had no desire to do what she had just suggested. Here in this moment, or anywhere else. His next remark made that clear.

'None of what we've discussed here regarding this photo-graph or anyone in it can be in a podcast,' Erling said, slipping the photograph back in the envelope. 'None of it. Do you understand?'

'I would never use anything without the permission of the participants,' she said quietly.

'That's not how I remember it on the *Orlova* case,' Erling said.

Ava remained silent at the accusation, because she knew it to be true.

16

Glasgow

Sand, she thought, was too simple a name for what she was currently examining under the microscope. The colours and shapes of the grains were beautiful, reflecting both the geological history and the marine life biodiversity of the place in which they had been found. In this case the place being Skaill Bay.

Under the neighbouring microscope was the sample meticulously extracted by Chrissy from the coiled metalwork of the torc bracelet. Equally beautiful, it too reflected the history and biodiversity of its origins.

Chrissy caught her eye as Rhona raised her head from the microscope.

'Well?' she said.

'They're not the same,' Rhona told her.

'So whoever was wearing that bracelet had been on another beach?'

'Yes,' Rhona said firmly.

'I take it you're thinking what I'm thinking?' Chrissy said.

Rhona was contemplating several things, one of them

being the possibility of the other beach perhaps harbouring another buried body.

'I don't think the bracelet was left in the cist by accident,' Rhona said. 'It was either left on Erik's wrist on purpose and came off after decomposition, or it was symbolically placed in there with him.'

'Which suggests either Erik visited this other beach, or his killer did,' Chrissy said, her thoughts echoing Rhona's own.

'We definitely need to find out where that beach is,' Rhona agreed. 'I'll speak to Jen and send her the samples, both for confirmation of your findings, plus hopefully some help on locating the second beach.'

Dr Jen Mackie, a forensic soil scientist, was both a good friend and a definite go-to at times such as this.

Buoyed up by the sand developments, plus the news of the impending arrival of the second batch of forensic evidence from Colin, they decided to end the day on a high.

The torrential rain that had relentlessly pursued them earlier had now departed, giving way to a clear sky and a decided drop in temperature. Chrissy had unearthed another jacket from her cubicle. A supposed snowboarders' clothing item, it was very hairy, and made her look, hood up, like a miniature version of Chewbacca from *Star Wars*. 'It keeps me warm and the rain runs off it,' she told Rhona. 'I should have worn it this morning.'

Rhona, on the other hand, had no back-up jacket, so was glad to find that this morning's one was pretty well dry.

Heading down University Avenue, they found the pavement already glittering with frost and the odd patch of ice. Alongside Rhona, Chrissy's breath was condensing, emerging from the big hood with each determined step nearer the warmth of the jazz club.

There had been no word from either Sean or Connor since they'd last been here. That wasn't unusual between herself and Sean. But she could tell by Chrissy's expression when she flung off her hood on entering the club that she would definitely like to find Connor back in residence.

Chrissy's love life was usually casual and short-lived. The only time it had looked remotely serious had been with her son's father, Sam Haruna, who'd eventually graduated in medicine and returned to Nigeria to practise. He'd wanted Chrissy and wee Michael to join him there, but Chrissy had chosen not to. Things were still friendly between them and Sam had kept in touch with his son. He'd also got married not so long ago, and although Chrissy and wee Michael had both been invited to the wedding, Chrissy had declined to go.

Since Sam, there had been other men in her life, but never for long. Rhona wondered what it was about Connor that had caught Chrissy's imagination, apart from being a handsome Irish musician with the gift of the gab.

All things, she had to be honest, that had appealed to her with respect to Sean – who she'd met in this very club where her mentor and friend DI Bill Wilson had held his fiftieth birthday party. That and the sex. And his cooking. She stopped herself there, because the list was growing too long.

'I'll get the drinks,' Rhona offered, 'if you want to check the back room for occupancy.'

The miniature version of Chewbacca took her at her word and headed off. It was only then that Rhona spotted the tall, auburn-haired figure that was DS Michael McNab nursing a glass at the far end of the bar.

She was about to call to him, then found herself observing him instead. They'd been friends and colleagues for a long time and had fallen out on multiple occasions. At one point she'd been so incensed at his actions that she'd ceased talking to him, unless directly about work.

She made herself also acknowledge the fact that they'd once been lovers, albeit for a short time only, and ended by her.

In fact Michael McNab possibly knew her better than any man could or would again, because of what they'd faced together. *Even unto death*, she found herself muttering.

At that moment, as though sensing her approach, he turned and, seeing her, smiled a welcome.

'I was beginning to think you were avoiding me, Dr MacLeod.'

'Funny, I was thinking the same about you,' she answered, already analysing both his demeanour and his tone.

'You're happy,' she said. 'That's unusual.'

'I am, and it is,' he agreed.

'Things still good between you and Ellie, then?' she asked.

Ellie and McNab had met in a tattoo parlour where she'd been the one to cover the bullet scar on his back with his choice of a skull. He'd taken the said bullet while protecting Chrissy, who'd been heavily pregnant at the time.

The pairing of Harley biker Ellie and McNab had been everything he'd wished for until it wasn't, when Ellie decided being the full-time partner of a detective, who was always on the job, wasn't something she wanted any more.

Happily, in the lead-up to Christmas, it seemed she'd changed her mind.

'She brought my Harley back.' McNab was smiling at the memory.

'That was at Christmas. It's March now,' Rhona reminded him.

'Time travels fast when you're having fun,' he said with a look that spoke volumes.

'And the Artificial Intelligence course?' she said to change the subject from his love life.

'Artificial,' he said, studying the golden contents of his whisky glass. 'Meaning false or fake, mock or reproduction. So not real intelligence at all.' He swallowed the remainder of his whisky as though toasting to that. 'Much like criminal psychology.'

'Which you don't trust either,' Rhona said.

'Your forensic science, on the other hand, is real.'

'So you didn't think the course was worthwhile?' she tried.

'Ollie, our resident super recognizer, wrote an AI program that recognizes faces just like he does, except faster.'

'Which is good,' Rhona said.

'But not intelligent per se. Merely a copycat of the expertise of folk like Dr Styles and Ollie's programming skills.'

'A useful and fast one, though,' she said.

'Could be,' he finally admitted. 'Anything more on the Orkney skeleton?'

'Last I heard, your AI program was working on his face,' Rhona told him. 'However, I have his picture in my mind already.'

'And *you* used *real* human intelligence to do that,' he countered.

'Via scientific knowledge of bone structure. Plus DNA testing to establish his hair and eye colour,' she confirmed.

'What about the PM? Did Sissons work out how he died?' McNab asked.

'The skeleton was in perfect condition in his stone cist. No injuries.'

McNab looked pensive at this. 'A stone cist in the sand dunes. What is it with weird burials and Orkney?' he said.

Rhona knew he was recalling the Sanday murder investigation case and his part in it, which he definitely hadn't enjoyed.

At this point in the proceedings Chrissy reappeared. It seemed McNab at first didn't recognize the hairy-coated Chrissy, because he stepped back as though in surprise.

'If you call me Chewbacca, I'll hit you,' Chrissy told him ominously.

'I heard you got a dog,' McNab said, staring pointedly at the jacket.

Chrissy punched his arm. 'I did. He's called Rocket and this isn't him.' She turned to Rhona. 'Neither Sean nor Connor are here.'

'Connor? Not another Irish musician?' McNab asked.

Ignoring him, Rhona said, 'I'll message Sean. Ask where they are.'

She moved away from the bar, leaving Chrissy to deal with McNab's desire to know more about Connor Maguire. Rather than text, she decided to call Sean, keen to hear the tone of his voice, which often told her more than a text.

It rang six times before he picked up, and she imagined him hesitating before answering it, despite her name being on the screen.

'Rhona,' his voice said. 'What's up?'

She hesitated too because that wasn't his usual way of greeting her.

'Is Connor with you?' she said.

A pause, then, 'He is. Why?'

'Chrissy was wondering where he'd gone,' she said, although now she too was wondering.

There was a short break as he seemed to move into a quieter space.

'Is anyone else asking about Connor?' he asked in a hushed tone.

'No. Why?'

'If they do, say we're away playing some gigs.'

'Are you?' Rhona demanded.

A brief silence was followed by, 'He's in a bit of bother back home. That's why he came over.'

'You said he was one of the good Maguires,' Rhona said.

'He is, but it's not a good Maguire who's looking for him. I'll explain later.'

She wanted to say 'explain now', but didn't get the chance before he rang off.

Chrissy was awaiting her return, and her explanation.

'They're playing a couple of gigs down south,' Rhona heard herself say.

The ever-determined Chrissy wasn't going to take that for an answer. 'When are they back?'

'He didn't say exactly,' Rhona told her, aware of McNab's interest in their conversation.

'You can give Connor a call and ask him yourself,' McNab now suggested.

'We didn't exchange numbers before I had to take off after Rocket,' Chrissy told him testily.

That answer was sufficiently obscure to stop McNab's interrogation.

'Right,' said Chrissy. 'I'm off home.' She gave Rhona a nod. 'Call me later,' she commanded.

'Okay,' Rhona promised, fully aware that the whole conversation with Sean would have to be revealed at that time.

'So,' McNab said as he watched Chrissy leave. 'What's this Connor guy been up to, then?'

For a brief moment Rhona had forgotten just how much of a detective McNab was.

'Sean says he's one of the good Maguires,' she told him honestly.

'With a bad member of the Maguire clan likely chasing him, I'll bet,' McNab said, ordering up another drink. 'And it didn't take AI to work that one out,' he added with an annoying look.

17

Glasgow

The image on the big screen in the meeting room was of the Orkney skull, currently turning on its axis so that the team might view it from all angles.

Most folk believed they knew what a skull really looked like. What they were less likely to know, McNab thought, was what a skull could reveal about its human owner.

At the course, he'd watched as the AI program had built up a series of ancient skulls, some consisting of only partial remains, many with wounds indicating their mode of death. Then he'd viewed what a Neolithic male or female had looked like prior to death, as the hair and eye colour had been added. They'd come alive again at that moment, smiling out at him from beyond the grave.

Now, studying the Orkney skull, McNab found himself identifying the points, according to Rhona, indicating the sex of the Orcadian victim. The pronounced brow ridge, the square chin, the more obvious bump at the back of the skull.

The remainder of the skeleton had told the same story.

And now DNA tests had confirmed this, plus added the hair and eye colour to the description.

At this point his partner, Janice, joined him. 'So we're going to see what your AI course was all about,' she said with a mischievous smile.

'The boss should have sent you on the course,' McNab said. 'You're less of a Neanderthal than me.'

'Which is exactly why he sent you,' she told him as the boss in question, DI Wilson, appeared at the front, followed by Ollie, the super recognizer.

Ollie, looking characteristically uncomfortable when faced with more than one human being at a time, chose to view the screen rather than his waiting audience. McNab, having spent a lot of time in Ollie's company, had come to the conclusion that Ollie felt compelled to commit every face he met to memory, and in detail, which probably accounted for his desire not to study the crowd in front of him now.

After DI Wilson provided a quick introduction, he asked Ollie to take over.

Speaking quietly and continuing to stand sideways to the screen, Ollie set the video in motion.

'This is the skull found in the stone cist buried in sand dunes in Skaill Bay in Orkney. The complete skeleton was also in the cist and looked like this when the capstone was removed.'

An image now appeared alongside the still-rotating skull. The skeleton lay on its right side, knees drawn up, the head also turned to the right.

'This is a common layout of bodies found in Viking graves,' Ollie told them. 'However, from the remains in situ, Dr MacLeod and Professor of Archaeology Colin Nelson deduced that the victim was likely a more recent burial and not Viking in origin, despite the use of what was an ancient cist.

'They also deduced that the victim was probably that of a young male, late teens to early twenties. Incarcerated, they believe, in the region of twenty years ago.' Ollie paused there briefly to let his audience absorb this. 'Both the post-mortem study by an osteologist and subsequent DNA profiling have established this as factually correct.'

He was silent for a moment before continuing.

'The following presentation is generated by an Artificial Intelligence program that draws on the knowledge of experts in facial reconstruction to give you an image of what our victim would have looked like in life.'

McNab had seen this done before, but as Ollie set the program in motion, he found himself entranced yet again by the reconstruction.

First came the placing of the eyes and tissue depth pegs. Then the muscle points began to appear and were put in place. Thereafter followed the careful addition of the main features. The ears, the nose, but not yet the full mouth. Although, side on, they could view the teeth.

'The victim, as you can see, had a full set of healthy teeth with no fillings,' Ollie told them. 'However, if you look at the ear, turned currently towards us, you can see that he also had a condition known as swimmer's ear. Exostosis is abnormal benign growths in the ear canal generally caused by exposure to cold water and wind.'

'Which sounds like a swimmer based in Orkney,' Janice said.

'Now, we put flesh on the bones,' Ollie said, rotating the skull to look straight out at them.

'This is where it gets real,' McNab muttered to an enthralled Janice.

The face began to take on its true and fulsome shape, replacing the gaunt visage of death. Hair appeared, mid-brown in colour and longish as though modelled on styles of twenty years ago. Below the dark eyebrows, a pair of very blue eyes looked out in a slightly surprised fashion, as though Erik, as Rhona had named him, had just spotted that he had an audience attending his rebirth.

There was an audible sound of appreciation as, alongside this reconstructed face, a list of his vital statistics appeared.

DI Wilson allowed the chatter to die down before addressing his officers again.

'The software that produced this has been further developed to hopefully reflect the abilities of a super recognizer. It has been rapidly checking this portrait against all young males reported missing in the last twenty years, both in Scotland and across the UK, which you all know is a considerable number. On average, 171,000 males go missing in any given year and around six out of every thousand are never found.

'Of course, if our victim was never reported missing in the first place, that makes things more difficult.'

He continued. 'The program can also check the national DNA database, to see if our victim has been convicted of a crime. That is ongoing. Then there are other ways we can try to use AI to track our victim's last whereabouts.'

DI Wilson nodded at Ollie to explain.

'The super recognizer software will compare our victim's image to data collected from all available CCTV footage captured in the time zone of his disappearance, as I have done myself in the past. AI, of course, will be able to do this much more rapidly than I ever could. Any possible matches will be passed on to the team to investigate.'

McNab raised his hand and addressed his boss. 'Is the AI version going to be shown to the general public, sir?'

'Yes, if we don't have any luck with our in-house searches,' DI Wilson said. 'I'm wary of putting too much information in the public realm as yet.'

The meeting drew to a close then, and McNab and Janice headed for their desks via the coffee machine.

'Looks like we'll be out of a job soon,' McNab said gloomily as he waited for his double espresso to be delivered.

'Since when have you sat for hours comparing photos with CCTV footage?' Janice said. 'That's been done by either a standard recognition program or Ollie the super recognizer, and even he has to sleep sometimes.'

'Speed isn't everything,' McNab told her. 'There were numerous reports in the US last year about AI-powered facial recognition software failing to accurately identify offenders while producing fabricated cases and falsely accusing the innocent.'

When Janice shot him a look, he continued. 'Last year in Detroit city, Porcha Woodruff, who was pregnant at the time, was wrongly sentenced to eight months in prison for a carjacking based on an AI recognition system. No human involved and guess what?'

'What?' Janice said in an exasperated tone.

'The AI facial recognition system falsely identified her due to her ethnicity. So sure, computers can do the comparisons much faster than Ollie, but Ollie is a human being looking at other human beings. How do you write everything that means into a computer program?'

Now at their desks, Janice took her seat before saying, 'Well, I guess you'll have to ask Ollie that question.'

McNab had tried, more than once, but whatever Ollie told him hadn't made much sense, so he'd eventually given up.

Noting that Janice, now gazing intently at her screen, was no longer listening anyway, he asked what she was looking at.

'There's a message from the boss,' she told him.

'About what?' McNab said.

'He wants us to check out the last known Glasgow address for a family, name of Bradley. They apparently lived in Orkney twenty years ago with their son, Ben, who Orkney police would like to make contact with.'

'They think this Ben might be the Skaill Bay victim?' McNab said.

'The boss didn't say. Although the timing suggests it's an avenue DI Flett wants to check out,' Janice told him.

'Great,' McNab said with a satisfied grin. 'So we're not out of a job yet.'

18

Glasgow

Rhona found herself drawn towards the window as a shaft of light broke through the heavy cloud to pick out the early spring colours of the park below, replacing the dark grey of the morning, which had matched her mood as she'd walked to work.

Despite Sean's promise to contact her the previous night with more information regarding himself and Connor's absence from the club, no such call had occurred. She hadn't been overly worried about that because Sean, like herself, wasn't great at keeping in touch when on the road.

The problem was she knew Chrissy would be eagerly awaiting her arrival with news of Connor's whereabouts and the reason for his swift departure.

Fortunately, it hadn't quite played out like that, due to the early arrival of the new forensic evidence from Orkney.

Chrissy may have been momentarily engaged by the memory of her all too brief evening with the handsome Connor. But her interest in his current whereabouts was now superseded by her excitement at the presence of the new evidence and ancient bones.

Once everything had been checked against the various lists, and the bones all accounted for, Rhona had broken the news of the non-phone call.

'So they're busy.' Chrissy had shrugged. 'As are we,' she'd added, her eyes shining as she viewed the tables laid out with forensic goodies, even more enticing than her other love, food.

Thus the morning and half of the afternoon had passed productively, before the sun came out to light up the park at the same time as the call from Dr Jen Mackie arrived, which hopefully would provide information on the grains of sand Chrissy had extracted from the bracelet.

Answering, Rhona said, 'Jen, hi. How are things?'

'Things in general?' Jen responded, a smile in her voice. 'Or with particular regard to the sand you enquired about?'

'Both,' Rhona said. 'Although I can tell by your voice that you might have some particular news of sand for me.'

'I do,' Jen agreed. 'The grains retrieved from the torc, as you surmised, are not from the Bay of Skaill.' She paused. 'I believe they most likely originated around the coast from there, not far from the Broch of Gurness, on the Sands of Evie at Aikerness.'

Silence followed as Rhona absorbed this news.

'I've sent you over the full analysis,' Jen said. 'And a detailed soil map of the area. Do you know the place at all?'

'No,' Rhona said honestly. 'I've driven along the Evie Road and seen the sign for the beach and car park, but never gone down for a closer look.'

'Well, whoever was wearing that torc *has* been down there at some time. I hope that helps.'

They spoke a little more about work in general before Rhona hung up and immediately pulled up a map of the area they'd discussed on her laptop.

'Fancy a coffee break?' Chrissy said, popping her head round the door ten minutes later.

Rhona nodded. 'Jen's been on the phone. We know where your sand particles originated.'

'Where?' Chrissy said, pleased.

Rhona waved her over to the screen and pointed to Aikerness Bay and the Sands of Evie. 'There,' she told her.

'Any big dunes like at Skaill?' Chrissy asked.

Rhona had switched to a photographic view. 'The bay's more sheltered than the western shore, so doesn't face the might of the Atlantic. It's more like links than dunes.'

'What about a Viking presence?'

Rhona had been checking that too. 'There are a couple of small brochs to the west. One where it seems a Viking jewellery hoard was discovered. Further to the east is the famous Broch of Gurness, with its Iron Age settlement. Now a big tourist attraction.'

Chrissy looked thoughtful. 'If our perpetrator has a modus operandi that involves Viking-type burials . . .'

'I need to tell Erling about the origin of the sand,' Rhona said. 'Let him decide what to do about it.' She paused, thinking. 'I'll also get in touch with Colin Nelson. Ask about excavations in the vicinity over the last twenty years or so.'

Their break for coffee proved short, Chrissy being keen to get back to the new evidence, in particular the cable tie found in the sand at Skaill Bay. When she'd set off to do that, Rhona opened her email to find a video attachment from DI Wilson, which he said showed the AI reconstruction of the Skaill Bay victim.

> You'll be pleased to see that you and Professor Nelson were
> pretty accurate in your description. I hear you've called him
> Erik. Well, here's Erik in the flesh, so to speak. With luck our
> AI program will find a match in our missing persons file.

Rhona launched the video and watched with interest as Erik was reborn to closely match her own image of him. It wasn't the first time she'd seen such a 3D-image being built, but the speed and accuracy of detail with the involvement of AI in the proceedings was impressive. So too was the speed of comparison with other images, which, according to the stats given, were obviously much swifter than even the best of the super recognizers, like Ollie.

She could only hope that the accuracy was as good. Last night, faced with her wait for Sean's call, she'd spent a fair amount of time reading articles on AI's usage in policing, particularly in the United States, and there were some worrying tales, which tended to support McNab's disquiet, even after attending the course.

She'd thought he'd just been his usual querulous self. She well remembered McNab's initial distrust at the involvement of Magnus, a forensic psychologist, in the study of a crime scene. He and Magnus had been at odds a number of times in the past, but gradually, albeit grudgingly, McNab had eventually acknowledged Magnus's contribution to previous investigations.

Developments in forensic science had been viewed in a similar fashion by many involved in upholding the law.

Even now, in court, forensic evidence of all kinds was interrogated with vigour by defence lawyers.

As it should be, Rhona thought.

Now, having satisfied herself on the identification of Erik, Rhona decided that, rather than email Erling, she would call instead to tell him about the origin of the sand they'd recovered from the bracelet.

19

Orkney

Erling studied his ringing mobile and in particular the name on the screen.

If Dr MacLeod was calling him on his direct number, then it must be either urgent or important or both. For a moment he vied with the notion of letting it go to voicemail. That way he could listen to what she had to say, then work out his response in advance.

To prevent himself considering this further, he pressed the answer button.

'Dr MacLeod. I hope the next batch of forensic material has reached you safely?' he said.

'It has,' she confirmed. 'And Chrissy's working on it.'

'Good.' Erling waited with concern to hear the real reason for the call.

'I thought you'd like to know about the result we've received from Dr Jen Mackie, the forensic soil scientist,' she said.

She was obviously waiting for him to respond, but he

120

wasn't sure how. 'Sorry, what was the test about?' he managed.

'Chrissy extracted sand from the coils of the bracelet found in the cist along with the body,' she said as though reminding him of something he already knew.

Despite her explanation, all Erling could think about at that moment was that the bloody torc was becoming the bane of his life.

'Oh, right,' he said. 'And?'

'The sand didn't come from Skaill Bay,' he heard her say. 'It came from the Sands of Evie.'

'Evie?' he muttered. 'That bracelet's been on the beach at Evie?' He tried to make sense of this. Then came the fleeting memory of another of their infamous beach parties. Had Ben been spying on them there too?

Driving this from his mind, he managed to say, 'So the sand definitely didn't come from the burial site at Skaill?'

'No. The grains that were embedded in the coils and extracted by Chrissy did not come from Skaill Bay,' she emphasized. 'Sand is very particular to its location.'

'I'm aware of that,' he said, then instantly regretted his tone, which he couldn't explain the reason for. Not to Dr MacLeod anyway. 'You believe our victim may have been at Evie prior to his death?'

'We don't know for certain that the victim was wearing the bracelet when he was put in the cist. It may have become detached during decomposition or—'

Erling interrupted her there. 'Or it was placed in there symbolically by the killer?'

'Exactly,' she said. 'Either way, the torc has been in contact with sand from Evie. I see that there have been archaeological excavations to both the west and east of Evie.

I believe some evidence of the presence of Vikings was also found in that area, suggesting perhaps that our perpetrator's modus operandi seems to have a Viking link.'

Erling let that sink in while the troubling thought of just how many Viking burials there were across Orkney mainland and all its islands presented itself.

'So what do you advise we do with this knowledge?' he asked cautiously.

Silence followed as though Rhona was preparing to say something she knew he wouldn't like.

'The forensic analysis of sand in the Sanday murder led us to the killer. I think we should follow this forensic clue,' she said.

'And do what exactly?' he said.

'Take a closer look at Evie. There are signs of a burial if you know what to look for,' she said.

'Evie's a different landscape to Skaill. No big sand dunes, only links and machair,' he found himself saying.

'You don't need dunes to bury a body,' Rhona said in return.

'No, indeed.' Erling felt something like despair sweep over him. 'Do you want to speak to Colin? See if he has any info about archaeological digs in the vicinity of Evie Sands in the last two decades. Also, does he know about the sand grains in the torc?'

'Not yet,' Rhona said.

'Then explain about that as well,' he told her.

'Okay,' Rhona responded. 'Oh, and have you seen the video of the AI reconstruction of our victim?' she added.

He took a swift breath. 'Just arrived in my in-box. Haven't had a chance to watch it as yet.'

When the call ended, Erling wondered whether she had

heard the edge in his voice. The underlying tension, and maybe even fear?

Gathering himself, and having made up his mind to proceed as normal, he put a call out to the entire team to come to the upstairs room to view the aforementioned video. Wanting desperately to rule out the possibility that the face on the screen would be that of Ben Bradley, he had considered watching it alone first.

But that would be what a guilty man would do. And he wasn't a guilty man. At least, he wasn't guilty of murder.

Now if it was Ben on that screen, then everyone here would see it at the same time. And . . . if it was recognizable as Ben, he would immediately inform the room that he believed he knew the victim personally twenty years ago.

After which, he would by necessity step down from the investigation and another senior investigating officer, probably from outwith Orkney, would be summoned to take charge.

His team were waiting for him, intrigued and keen to see the face of the entombed victim from Skaill Bay. Attaching his laptop, he kept his back to them, not sure what anyone might read from his expression, especially his second-in-command, DS Green.

Already he was wondering who they might send in to replace him should it be Ben Bradley. DS Green wasn't a local and most of the faces waiting patiently for the show to begin were at least ten years younger than him. So even if born here, they were unlikely to know anything about the Bradley family from twenty years back. Like the many folk who came to try to make their home in Orkney, the Bradleys hadn't lasted very long, never becoming accustomed to either island life or the weather. In particular, the wind.

Even as he thought this, he felt a chill as though a window had been left open. But the sudden cold down his spine, he realized, had nothing to do with a draught, but was a result of dread at what might happen in the next few minutes.

Straightening up, he found the big screen now filled with the image of a slowly rotating skull. Without further ado, he pressed the play button and the intricate rebuilding of the victim's head began.

It was weirdly like a jigsaw puzzle of a face, slowly and carefully being put together, he thought as he watched, the important and self-identifying pieces similarly left until the end.

The ear had a caption explaining the distortion in the bone structure. Saying it was known as swimmer's ear and could be caused by prolonged exposure to cold wind and water.

Both of which were plentiful in Orkney.

He checked his memory again. Had Ben been a swimmer? Since they'd never invited him to their beach parties, he had no idea. Even if he did swim in the cold waters of Orkney, was he here long enough to develop such a condition? The family had apparently moved here from down south some-where. He had no idea where and had never been interested enough to find out.

As the facial features became more apparent, he felt his heart lurch in his chest. Then the hair appeared together with the eye colour, which was blue. He realized he had no idea what colour Ben's eyes were.

And what about his hair? The colour looked like a pos-sible match. But, and it was a big but, the AI program had guessed the length wrongly, perhaps making a judgement on the style of twenty years ago. Ben Bradley would never have let his hair grow long like that. He'd always been a short-back-and-sides guy. In fact he'd been given grief about it.

At that moment, Erling recalled what Shona had said about Ben's father, that he was a homophobic bastard. Maybe that had been the reason for the GI haircut. He hadn't wanted his son 'to look like a pansy'.

With that final thought, he found himself staring at the completed face, the ghost of a smile on its lips, the eyes giving the strong impression that it was reading the room and everyone in it. Especially him.

Erling stared back, mesmerized.

Was that really Ben, though? As his heart began to slow, he knew that he couldn't be sure. He had spent so much time ignoring Ben Bradley that he just couldn't tell for certain. He recalled the school photograph. Was this the same person? He'd recognized Ben immediately from that, but then all the other clues were in there. The blazer that was too small for him, the way Ben always stood a little apart from the others, alone. Always alone.

The AI program didn't know what Ben had been like back then. How he'd kept his head down and never looked you in the eye. He'd been regarded by others, including himself, as a nuisance. An irritant.

The AI program didn't know his character or the way he thought of himself. It couldn't produce his stance. His hidden look. It couldn't show him truly alive.

DS Green, perhaps reading his questioning expression, said, 'D'you think you recognize him, sir?'

'No,' Erling heard himself say. 'No, I do not.'

Even as he said this and meant it, another thought appeared. What if the AI program were to compare its result to the school photograph? Would it match it to the real Ben?

20

Glasgow

The address they'd been given was just off Duke Street, heading eastward.

Janice was quiet in the car, her expression pensive. McNab wondered if he should ask her if everything was okay. They'd been partners for a while now and he liked to think they got on well. Although, if he was honest, when she'd joined the team he hadn't been the gentleman he liked to think or hope he was now.

Yet one thing definitely eluded him. That was his reading of her mood. He'd put his foot in it quite often, although he hoped he was learning from his mistakes. But at this moment he wasn't so sure. Was everything okay on the domestic front between her and her partner, Paula? Should he ask or not?

When in doubt, he reminded himself, stay shtum.

Eventually, he was rewarded for his patience.

'I was just thinking,' she said. 'If the victim was in his late teens in Orkney twenty years ago, isn't it possible DI Flett might have known him back then?'

Now that thought had definitely not crossed McNab's mind. Being a city boy born and bred, the closeness of a small island community was something he hadn't experienced until he'd headed up the murder investigation on the island of Sanday, where the population was fewer than five hundred. All of whom seemed to know their neighbours' business.

Which had, he remembered, helped solve the murder.

'If it turns out that he does know the victim from back then, that could be tricky, especially if they were friends,' Janice was saying.

'It's unlikely he could continue to lead the investigation,' McNab confirmed.

'So they'd send in a replacement officer?' Janice asked. 'Like what happened on Sanday?'

'Sanday didn't even have a local bobby,' McNab told her. 'Turned out they didn't need one, because they basically policed themselves.'

'Which was why you were sent up there?'

'There was a possible link between a killing in Glasgow and the Orkney murder,' McNab said as he drew up in front of the address they'd been given. 'That's why I was sent there.'

Janice, seemingly satisfied with that for the moment, exited the vehicle, McNab following.

The three-storey yellow sandstone building was encased by a high hedge at ground level. Approaching the black-painted doorway, McNab checked for the name Bradley on the buzzer and was mildly surprised to find it there on the first floor.

With a pleased look at Janice, he pressed the button. When it was answered by a female voice, he explained who they were and that they'd like to have a word.

There was some background chat with a male voice, then the lock was released.

'So far, so good,' McNab said to Janice as he pushed open the heavy door and headed upwards.

Reaching the first-floor landing, they found a door partially open with a man, who McNab judged to be in his late fifties or early sixties, awaiting their arrival. The woman, he presumed from the intercom, was hovering behind.

After introducing himself and Janice properly and showing his ID, McNab asked if the man's name was Bradley.

When he agreed that it was, Janice said, 'Did you and your family live for a time at Lochside Cottage, Stenness in Orkney, sir? About twenty years ago?'

The guy looked taken aback by the question, before his expression darkened. 'Why do you want to know?' he demanded.

'Just answer the question, please, sir,' McNab urged.

The woman put her hand tentatively on the man's arm and he glanced down at her in an irritated fashion, before shaking it off. 'We did, but not for long,' he said. 'Why?'

Having decided they definitely had the right Bradley family, McNab said, 'I understand that you have a son called Ben. Is that correct, sir?'

At the mention of Ben's name, it seemed to McNab that the woman's face momentarily lit up, then almost immediately crumpled as though she expected bad news.

The man's expression, however, merely darkened even further. 'I do not have a son called Ben,' he stated firmly.

As the woman looked up pleadingly at him, McNab said, 'We are reliably informed that the Bradley family who were living at that address at that time had a son called Ben, who attended the sixth form at Kirkwall Grammar School.'

'Ben wasn't my son. He was my stepson,' the man conceded, albeit reluctantly.

'Do you know of Ben's whereabouts now, sir?' Janice asked.

He shook his head. 'I do not. I haven't seen him since he walked out of here nearly twenty years ago.'

The woman moved forward at this. 'Has something happened to Ben?' she said anxiously.

'Are you Ben's mother?' When the woman nodded, Janice added, 'Have you been in touch with your son recently?'

The woman seemed to want to answer, then with a guarded glance at the man, shook her head. 'No,' she said. 'Why are you looking for Ben? Is he in some sort of trouble?'

'We've been asked by the Orkney police to check up on his whereabouts. This was the last known address they had for him.'

McNab waited, hoping the mention of Orkney police might persuade her to talk, despite the stepdad being there.

When the woman remained silent, McNab pointedly passed her his card. 'If Ben does get in touch, can you please let us know?'

She glanced at the card and swiftly slipped it in a pocket. 'I will, Detective Sergeant McNab.'

When the door shut, they stood for a moment listening, but all was silence inside.

'Well,' Janice said as they exited the close and made for the car. 'What d'you think?'

'Same as you. She's been in touch with her son behind the bloke's back. Although I don't think it was recently.'

'Will she call, d'you think?'

'If she can get rid of her minder, yes.' McNab had caught the swift glance he'd been given as the door had closed. 'I vote we go find the nearest coffee shop and wait for that call.'

They weren't long seated with their usual order when his mobile rang. McNab picked up immediately. 'Mrs Bradley?' The woman whispered back 'yes', her voice partially drowned out by what sounded like a running tap. 'We're round the corner at the coffee shop. Can you come?'

McNab hoped he'd caught another 'yes' before a toilet was flushed and the call ended.

'We'll wait,' McNab told Janice. 'It sounded as though she made the call from the toilet so he wouldn't hear.'

'Right. I'll go take a look at the cakes, then,' Janice told him. 'What d'you fancy?'

'The biggest one, whatever it is,' McNab told her, thinking she should know that by now.

They were on their second coffee with an added chocolate biscuit when Mrs Bradley walked in. Janice immediately went to meet her and, bringing her to the table, checked what coffee she preferred before heading to the counter, leaving McNab alone with the woman.

'Is Ben in trouble?' she immediately asked.

'Not as far as I know,' McNab told her honestly. 'DI Flett from Kirkwall police station asked us to look into his whereabouts, and the last known address was here.'

The name Flett seemed to perturb her. 'When Ben went to school in Kirkwall there was a boy called Flett in the sixth form with him. They didn't get on, as I remember.'

McNab decided to let that go, and asked instead, 'When did you last hear from your son?'

'When we left Orkney, Ben came with us, but . . .' She halted briefly, before mustering up the courage to continue. 'Ben and Jack, his stepdad, didn't get on. Ben went back to

Orkney to visit a girl there, Shona, I think her name was.' She paused. 'He came back here but only to pick up his stuff. Jack and him fell out again. Ben left. Said he was never coming back.' She shook her head at the memory, then met McNab's eye. 'He never did.'

'But you kept in touch with him?' McNab said.

'For a month or so, yes. He went to London, got himself a job. Sounded okay, happy even. Then the texts got fewer and finally stopped coming. I kept trying but he must have changed his number, because it wasn't available any more.'

Janice, back with the coffee, said, 'That must have been very difficult for you, Mrs Bradley.'

'Annie, you can call me Annie,' she said. 'Yes, it was,' she added, with a catch in her throat. 'I tried to register him as missing, but he was an adult, the police said. And he'd left home of his own free will.'

McNab, reading her expression, decided her son's departure had more likely been caused by force rather than free will.

'I saw something on the news about a body found buried in Orkney,' she said, fear in her voice. 'I was worried that was why you were looking for Ben?'

When Janice glanced at him, he knew she was leaving it up to him to answer that one.

'I don't know,' McNab said. 'But you saw Ben when he came back from his Orkney visit and you kept in touch with him for at least a month, when he moved to London. Right?'

'Yes, that's true.' She considered this for a moment. 'But in the news, it said the remains were those of a young man who'd lain there for maybe twenty years. Can I find out for sure it isn't my son?'

McNab thought about the video they'd just watched, but which wasn't yet authorized to be shown to the public. Maybe once she saw that it would put her mind at ease.

'They plan to release an identikit image of the Orkney victim to the general public soon. It'll be on various news channels and websites. If you think you recognize the victim, please call me right away,' McNab told her.

At this point, Janice asked if she'd considered using social media to try to make contact with her son. 'It's surprising how successful that can be,' she added.

Annie's face immediately clouded over again. 'Jack wouldn't allow that,' she said.

Hell mend Jack, McNab thought, but didn't voice it out loud. 'You have my number. If you think of anything else you'd like to ask or tell us, just give me a ring,' he said instead. 'And thank you for your time, Annie.'

They left her there, staring blindly into her coffee.

'So what do you think?' Janice said once they were back in the car.

'I think Annie has a bully for a husband who made her son's life a misery. So he either decided to leave home or was made to,' McNab said, thinking that his own mum had possibly faced much the same problem, which was why she'd decided to bring him up on her own.

'And that bit about someone called Flett and her son not getting on at school?' Janice said.

McNab shrugged. 'There are a lot of Fletts in Orkney. Also the list of folk I didn't get on with at school is legendary,' he said as he drove away. 'The list of folk I should continually apologize to is even longer. And you're on it.'

Janice laughed out loud at that, which pleased him. Maybe he wasn't doing too bad on the partner front after all.

21

Glasgow

When Erling ended the call, Rhona sat for a moment contemplating their interchange. She didn't know Erling very well and not on a personal level. Yet she felt she knew him enough to sense that something was wrong.

Was that something work related or personal, she wondered.

She'd met his partner, Rory, a couple of times, one of which was at a meal in Magnus's house. It'd been during the investigation into the ghost ship *Orlova*, which had come aground on the cliffs of Yesnaby. Rory, a diver, had been sent down to check whether the hull was intact, but he wasn't an official member of the investigation team.

Rhona recalled Erling's discomfort when Rory had talked openly about the crime scene on board the ship in front of Ava Clouston. Revealing aspects not yet shared with the general public, and definitely not with a journalist.

Separating work from your private life was difficult. She strove to achieve it with Sean and had succeeded, mainly because he never asked questions of her regarding what she was working on. A no-go area she'd established early in their relationship.

Chrissy, she knew, never discussed her work with her mum. Or with the string of casual boyfriends that were permitted briefly to enter her life.

DI Wilson, on the other hand, had at times confided in his late wife, Margaret, and, still mourning her passing from cancer, was, Rhona thought, missing the reassurance she'd often given him.

An image of McNab presented itself at this point. McNab, when obsessing about a case, often forgot that he even had a current partner, which was usually the cause of each and every break-up. Luckily, it sounded as though he and Ellie were still together, despite his best efforts to the contrary.

Which brought her back round to Erling and the phone call and whether his reaction was in fact more to do with the case itself.

DI Erling Flett was a consummate professional, something she knew for certain having worked alongside him on both the *Orlova* case and the Sanday murder, where he'd stood aside at one point, when a family member was briefly identified as a potential suspect.

So the possibility that he may have known the young man buried two decades ago at Skaill Bay would be preying on his mind. She was certain of that. Policing the islands put you much closer to those you policed than could ever be the case in the city. In Orkney, every death became personal.

She now decided to follow up on Erling's suggestion that she call Colin and bring him up to date on current developments.

'And you're sure the sand came from Evie?' he pressed, after she had given him the news.

'Yes,' Rhona told him. 'It's been confirmed by forensic soil science expert Dr Jen Mackie.'

'Then the victim or perhaps the perpetrator had likely been on the Sands of Evie prior to the burial?'

Rhona agreed. 'I believe there have been Viking graves found in that area?' she checked.

'There have. Probably the one you would have read most about was the grave of a female Viking discovered at Gurness. The Vikings often used mounds of earlier settlements as places of burial. There's evidence that other Vikings were buried around there too.' He paused as though considering what their sand discovery might mean. 'You're concerned that there may be another gravesite at the Sands of Evie?' he said worriedly.

'I think we need to be able to rule that out,' Rhona said.

'So what do you want to do?' Colin asked.

'I think we should take a field walk of the area together,' Rhona told him. 'If we register anything suspicious, anything at all, we'll bring in a cadaver dog.'

'Good idea. We've been held up at the Skaill Bay site because of poor weather, but the next couple of days look better. A Dr Gillam from Princeton University is on sabbatical here for a month or so. She can continue with the Skaill Bay site, while I work with you on this. I'll root out the maps I have of earlier digs in the area. In case our killer has a thing about using former Viking graves,' he added.

Rhona didn't need to confirm that this was her fear. 'I'll let you know when to expect me,' she said, already making a plan for her return.

She felt better after the call. One thing she was sure of: any forensic evidence they had must be acted on and swiftly.

Chrissy, acknowledging her return to the lab, asked if anything was wrong.

'I'll tell you about it later,' Rhona promised. 'Any luck here?' she asked hopefully.

Even a single handling of a cable tie could leave DNA traces, and nowadays full profiles might be obtained from just a few cells. The downside of this was, if the tie had been handled by more than one person, then it might have multiple DNA deposits on it.

Chrissy nodded. 'The victim's DNA is on there, as we would expect. But whoever tightened the cable tie left theirs on it too. And that's a match for the trace I lifted from the fragment of tape extracted from the initials on the torc,' she said.

'So it's likely both electrical tape and the cable tie were used to restrain the victim,' Rhona said. 'With the tape as a gag maybe.'

'Plus we still have what feels like a mountain of sand to sift through yet,' Chrissy said. 'Maybe there's more of the tape in there.'

'The devil's in the detail,' Rhona said, glancing at the wall clock. 'Shall we discuss your findings further over a glass of wine?' she suggested. 'I also need to bring you up to date on developments in Orkney.'

Discarding her suit in the changing room, Chrissy, seemingly unable to wait, demanded in her inimitable fashion to know what the developments were.

'Erling agrees that we need to follow up on the sand evidence. So Colin and I will do a field walk together at Evie, paying particular attention to areas of Viking burial sites. If we find anything of interest, we'll bring in a dog to check it out,' Rhona told her.

Chrissy reached for her hairy jacket. 'Orkney's not short on Viking burial sites,' she said.

'I think that might have been Erling's concern,' Rhona admitted.

'Has he had any luck on the origins of the torc? Or the engraved initials?'

That was a question Rhona couldn't answer. 'If he has, he hasn't shared it with me as yet, although making enquiries without actually releasing what he must regard as key evidence will be tricky.'

Their walk down University Avenue was peppered with the sound of passing vehicles swishing through puddles and the whine of a wind that would have cut you in two, according to Chrissy. 'Unless you're lucky enough to own a jacket like mine,' she added, peeking out from beneath the sizeable hairy hood.

'I may have to visit this snowboarding shop you mentioned,' Rhona muttered as they finally left the wide and windy avenue and headed down the back path into Ashton Lane.

A welcome wall of warmth met them on entry to the club, together with the sound of someone playing the piano, accompanied by a saxophone. Rhona wasn't a fan of all the jazz she heard in the club, but what was being played struck her as definitely tuneful.

'It's Connor and Sean. They're back,' Chrissy announced, sounding very pleased.

Just as I'm about to depart again for Orkney, Rhona thought, but didn't say.

A raised saxophone indicated they'd been spotted and Connor paused briefly to give Chrissy a thumbs up.

Rhona wondered if Connor's pursuer had returned to

Ireland, having given up on trying to locate him. The machin-
ations and inter-sibling rivalry of the Maguire family were
a mystery to someone who'd been adopted as a baby by a
loving couple with no children of their own.

Sean, for the most part, seemed to cruise through the
stormy waters, dealing with whatever came his way with
aplomb. Such as recently with the bold Connor.

As Chrissy headed for the bar, Rhona was pleased to
see McNab there, along with Janice. Thinking back to her
earlier ruminations on keeping personal and private lives
separate, she understood why neither Janice nor McNab
ever invited their partners along, because talking shop was
the order of the day here.

She wondered how the demo on the skull had gone
and was keen to tell McNab that she was heading back to
Orkney and why.

He in turn related their story of DI Flett asking the boss
to check out the last known address for the Bradley family,
who'd left Orkney twenty years before.

'Does Erling think he may have known the victim?'
Rhona said, revisiting her earlier call with him.

'No idea,' McNab offered. 'We just checked the given
address as ordered. Luckily, they were still there. Or, rather,
Mr and Mrs Bradley were.'

Janice gave a potted version of what they'd learned from
the visit. 'Bully for a stepdad. Ben left home and went to
London. Kept in touch with his mum for a while, then fell
off the radar. She tried to register him as a missing person,
but he was an adult who left of his own free will.'

It was a common enough tale.

'We have the victim's DNA now and we think also that of
his attacker,' Rhona told them. 'It'll be easy enough to check

whether the victim is Ben Bradley, if his mother agrees to a test.'

Janice came in then. 'Annie Bradley also made a point of telling us that her son and a boy called Flett didn't get on at school in Orkney,' she said, looking to McNab.

'Really?' Chrissy said, all agog.

'As I said, Orkney's full of Fletts, plus I hated most everyone in my class at school. And at the police college,' McNab said firmly. 'But I haven't followed up on it . . . yet,' he added, as Janice punched his arm.

Rhona didn't contribute to the laughter, her thoughts returning to her earlier conversation with Erling, and perhaps the answer to his odd behaviour.

Had Erling's viewing of the reconstruction video prompted his request to Bill to check out the last known address of the Bradley family? Had he thought he'd recognized Erik as the Ben Bradley who may have gone to school with him?

But the timing didn't seem to work for that, she thought. Erling had told her he hadn't viewed the video yet when she'd called him, and it sounded as though McNab and Janice had already been sent out to the Bradley address.

Something else had prompted Erling to seek Ben Bradley's whereabouts, before the video became available. Something else had made him fearful that the victim might be Ben.

There was no need to call Magnus now, she decided, except of course to tell him of her return to Orkney and the reason for that. There would be plenty of opportunity over the next couple of days to ask him whether he had also known this Ben Bradley and why Erling was so eager to establish his whereabouts, or even if he was still alive.

22

Orkney

In the first episode of *The Dead and the Dying* podcast, she'd told the story of the pod of pilot whales coming ashore at Skaill Bay. How local man Will Balfour had come across the beached whales and made his emergency call-out.

In his Orkney voice, he'd told a tale of watching the rollers crash in, moonlight illuminating the scene, only to see a mass of dark bodies being propelled in on those waves, to land one after another and lie thrashing on the silver sand.

She'd followed this with interview material from a few of the traumatized volunteers, who'd fought all night, only managing to refloat two young males. Whether they would survive in the open sea without their pod was deemed uncertain.

Dr Donald Main, director of SMASS at Glasgow University, had then described the procedures taken in the aftermath of such a stranding. He'd also tried to explain why the pod may have beached, and the reason for his decision to bury the newborn calf among the dunes.

The online responses to the first episode and in particular

the death of the mother and her calf had been massive and heartfelt. So much so, Ava wondered if it would drown out what would feature in episode two: the murder and burial of a human being.

Hearing the approach of a vehicle, Ava closed her laptop and went to the window to check who'd arrived. Dougie was out and about on the farm and unlikely to appear again until early afternoon, so it was either the postie or someone else.

She hadn't spoken with Erling since he'd asked her to give a statement on the school photograph and the torc bracelet that Ben Bradley might or might not have been wearing.

Seeing him emerge from the vehicle, she wondered if that was what he'd come to speak to her about. Either that or perhaps her request that they and Magnus should meet and discuss their own stories regarding Ben, in case that became necessary.

Opening the door, she ushered him in and offered him coffee. 'I just made a pot. You like it black as I remember?'

He gave her a swift nod, and took a seat at the big kitchen table, just like old times.

'I've come about the photograph,' he offered. 'I had it examined and the conclusion is that there's not enough evidence, even under magnification, that Ben was wearing a torc bracelet.'

Ava had the momentary thought that he seemed relieved about that, as was she.

He regarded her laptop. 'I listened to the first episode of your Skaill Bay podcast,' he said. 'You captured the scene very powerfully.'

'It was the voices of the people who were there that did that,' she said.

141

'I don't need to remind you that you mustn't reveal anything on the podcast that is part of the current investigation,' he said, meeting her eye.

Ava could feel herself bristle. 'If you're referring to the bracelet, of course I'm aware of that. Although it seems most of Orkney knows about the torc and young folk do use social media,' she reminded him.

Erling didn't respond to this but said instead, 'We now have an AI reconstruction of the face of the victim. It will be released shortly to the general public in the hope that someone will recognize him.'

'You've seen this already?' she said, encouraged by this latest development.

'I have,' he confirmed.

'And?' she demanded.

'I did not recognize it as Ben Bradley,' he said firmly.

Her heart rose a little at this. If that were true, then maybe they could stop worrying about it.

Before she could make mention of this, Erling continued. 'The AI software involved is currently looking for a match in both missing persons and felons, and will also check against CCTV footage collected by Police Scotland. I intend asking that the school photograph be checked too.'

'And if the AI program does flag it up as a possible match for Ben?' she asked.

'Then I step aside from the investigation and someone from outwith Orkney will take my place. The rest of my team are either too young or weren't living here when the victim was killed. Until then, I carry on as normal,' he added.

Ava considered this for a moment. 'Do you plan to tell Ingrid what you've just told me, regarding the identikit image and the bracelet?'

'I do,' he assured her.

'May I tell her first?'

'It's better coming from me. Then she knows it's official.'

It may be official, but that doesn't mean she'll believe it, Ava thought, remembering the determination on the girl's face. Weird as it sounded, it was almost as though Ingrid needed the victim to be her father, to prove that he hadn't left her and her mother on purpose.

'I'd still like we three to meet and talk over what happened back then, in particular at Skaill Bay,' she said.

'Why?' Erling said.

She examined his expression. 'If you're wrong and it is Ben, then everyone in that school photograph will be questioned, and the party at Skaill Bay will be talked about,' she said.

Erling met her eye, and she knew at that point that he remembered the horror and embarrassment of it still.

'If it comes down to that,' he said, 'then we'll each give our honest version as we remember it. Warts and all.'

Ava nodded. 'Okay. Can I ask if Magnus knows about Shona and Ingrid?'

He shook his head. 'I haven't said anything.'

'I think we should,' she said. 'And I'd rather we did it together,' she urged him.

Erling was silent for a moment, before eventually saying, 'You're free to talk to Magnus yourself, of course. And to ask him about Shona. I prefer not to.'

At that point she requested that he send her a copy of the AI image. 'I'd like to take a look at it myself, before it hits social media,' she told him. 'I suspect Magnus would too, if only to put our minds at rest.'

'I can't do that,' he told her firmly. 'You're writing about the case for the *Orcadian*?' he checked.

'I am,' she admitted.

'Then they'll have their copy in good time for publication. You'll have access that way. As for Magnus, he's not officially on the investigation team, so must see it at the same time as everyone else in Orkney.'

And that was the end of their discussion.

What she didn't tell him was that she planned to ignore his wishes regarding Ingrid. Dougie had trusted her to be straight with the girl. If or when Ingrid asked her about the photograph and the torc bracelet, Ava planned to give her an answer.

Returning to her laptop, she now posted up what she'd recorded for episode two. It began with a piece from the local farmer Les Drever, whose machine had been used to dig the grave for the calf. In the interview he'd explained that he'd provided a place on his farm for Dr Main to perform the necropsies, and also transported the carcasses there with the help of locals.

'Dr Main asked me to dig the hole for the newborn calf. He'd decided to bury it in the dunes. It was when I started digging that the shovel hit stone. When we removed the sand, we saw that it was the capstone of a cist, built with flagstones. There have been Viking graves found at the Bay O' Skaill before, so they got in touch with the archaeology professor from the University of the Highlands and Islands and he came down. Professor Colin Nelson's his name and he lives in the Ivy House in Kirkwall. When they took the lid off the cist, that's when they found the skeleton.'

When Ava had prodded him still further, he'd said, 'That's

144

all I know, because I had to go and help Dr Main with the burial of the other carcasses.'

Replaying this, she was struck by how quiet and measured his voice was and also how sad. For those listening, who'd never experienced a beaching and were never likely to, his story would have helped them live it.

Checking back online, she realized things had been moving since Erling's departure. Much of it caused, she thought, by Ingrid and her fellow sixth-formers. Word of the existence of the torc was definitely out there and causing a great deal of chatter. Something Erling wouldn't be happy about. But why? Might it not help with the identification of its maker, and hopefully lead them to whoever had purchased it?

She wondered if there had been anything on the bracelet. An inscription perhaps? A date even?

Erling certainly hadn't mentioned an inscription of any kind. Nor would he, she thought. And judging by the online chatter about the torc, Ingrid didn't know of anything either.

And then it hit her.

The killer, assuming they were still alive, and interested in what was happening in Orkney, would likely also be aware that both his victim and the torc bracelet had been discovered.

What would they do with that knowledge?

23

So they've found him – but only him.

He felt saddened by the discovery but he wasn't worried by it. The boy had been a waif, a stray. Unloved, except by him. For a while at least.

He'd heard about the discovery via her podcast. He'd followed her since the *Orlova* investigation. Marvelled at her investigation skills. Her tenacity. So he'd checked her out, both personally and professionally. He also liked listening to her voice, her Orcadian accent more pronounced at unguarded moments. Hearing it transported him back there, helping him to relive some of his past experiences.

He'd thought she would go back, ostensibly to visit her younger brother, but in reality to find out more about the body they'd found in the dunes at Skaill Bay. She was an investigative journalist, after all.

Funny how they'd found him. He could never have anticipated all those deaths in one place. If they hadn't decided to bury the calf in situ, he would still be there, lying peacefully in his Viking grave.

That was what angered him most.

24

Orkney

Colin met her off the early flight from Glasgow. It had been his idea that she stay at the Ivy House rather than out in Orphir as usual.

'It'll be easier for us travelling to Evie together,' he'd told her. 'Plus the archaeology department of UHI is here in Kirkwall, including my office.'

It had sounded sensible, but she'd still felt a little awkward forewarning Magnus about her imminent trip, while at the same time telling him she was staying with Colin to make it easier to travel to Evie together.

His response, of course, had been 'What's happening at Evie?' to which she'd replied with something vague about sand deposits.

Obviously registering her reticence to divulge anything more, Magnus let it go at that, except to say, 'Well, if you have the time, you and Colin are welcome to come for dinner while you're here.'

Collecting her overnight bag from the carousel, she

headed outside as instructed, to find Colin waiting in a UHI van.

Opening the passenger door for her, he loaded her bag in the back.

'You happy to go straight to Evie?' he said. 'We have a window of decent weather for the next five hours and I have forensic suits and equipment. Can you last that long without eating?' he checked.

'No problem. I had a large breakfast before starting out,' Rhona assured him.

Leaving Kirkwall, they headed towards Finstown, where Colin apologized for the wait at a set of temporary traffic lights, which made Rhona laugh.

'You've obviously forgotten what city driving's like,' she said.

'I have,' Colin admitted, 'although I remember soon enough when I head south.'

Driving through Rendall, they soon met the coastline again. To her left, Rhona could see rust-coloured moorland; to her right, acres of green fields skirting a glittering sea.

A short while later Colin turned onto a single-track road, still tarred, and they headed directly towards what she took to be Aikerness Bay. When the road ended in a small car park with a toilet block, Colin turned onto a muddy and potholed track that headed eastward along the perimeter of the bay.

Drawing to a halt, he said, 'This road's always in a bad condition, so it'll be a bumpy ride. I advise you to make for the beach and I'll meet you at the far end.'

Rhona, taking him at his word, got out and, leaving Colin to negotiate the abundance of potholes and broken edges, jumped down onto the neighbouring expanse of flat white sand.

Standing for a moment, she took in the lay of the land.

The bay was a glorious curve. To her right, in the near distance, the ground rose towards a rocky headland which, she decided, must be the Broch of Gurness. Sheltered by the island of Rousay to the north with the small isle of Eyn-hallow in between, this bay bore no resemblance to Skaill. No crashing waves. No giant boulders tossed ashore. No high dunes behind.

A different land- and seascape and a different sand, she thought, as she bent to collect a sample to take back with her.

Following the van round the curve of the bay, she could make out the area of links ahead. A flat stretch of fertile ground comprising crushed shells and sand, it was similar to the area that bordered the bays around Arisaig on the west coast of Scotland. Known in Gaeldom as the machair.

On the way here, Colin had explained that he'd had a drone cover the links area, and having studied the images, had mapped out the sections he thought they should walk.

Forensic archaeology and her own speciality of buried and hidden bodies had much in common, Rhona acknowledged, as she approached the now-parked van.

'Check the drone footage first,' Colin said, handing her a tablet, 'and where I've marked specific areas of interest on the map. If you spot anywhere else you have questions about, we'll mark and walk them too.'

Rhona sat in the van to watch the aerial survey, looking for the telltale signs of changes in vegetation that might indicate the presence of a grave.

Their reason for being here at all was the sand Chrissy had extracted from the swirls on the Viking bracelet. The torc had definitely been here at some time or other. The question was why and, even more importantly, when and with whom.

She focused now on the area of ground closest to the beach and just inside the fence. You could, she thought, dig a grave here unnoticed if done in the hours of darkness, which Orkney boasted plenty of, especially in midwinter. Just as had been possible in the dunes at Skaill Bay.

But how to entice your victim to either location?

Erik, she believed, had likely known his killer. Perhaps even well. Had he been enticed to Skaill Bay, and if so, what had been the bait? An assignation perhaps among the dunes?

And why not here? More sheltered and secluded than at Skaill, but also rich in Viking heritage. And you didn't bury a body in a Viking grave together with a torc unless both location and object were significant.

This made her think about Magnus and what his considered take might be on the crime, its location and the modus operandi and signature of the killer. As a criminal profiler, he hadn't as yet been asked to advise on the investigation, hence her reluctance to divulge details on the latest forensic evidence and the real reason for her return visit to Orkney.

It would be up to Erling to decide who should be party to such information and when. Although how realistic was it to think that anything regarding this murder could be kept a secret in an island community such as Orkney?

Even now, she thought, her return visit here would likely have been noted, together with the visit of a UHI van to the Sands of Evie. The undulating landscape surrounding them might at first glance look empty, but there were scattered houses tucked in its folds, and the road that encircled the bay before heading to Gurness was in frequent use.

Seeing Colin arrive back from a quick check on the designated search area, she got out of the vehicle.

'So what d'you think?' he said.

'I agree with all your marked locations. There was one more area quite close to the fence – it may be nothing, but I'd like to take a look there too.'

'Right,' Colin said. 'Let's get kitted up and make a start.'

Topography, vegetation, soil type and access were all important when considering the possibility of a buried body in a particular vicinity. This location, Rhona noted, had good access, despite the bumpy track. The soil beyond the fence was a mix of decayed vegetation, crushed shells and sand, which would have provided a relatively easy dig.

Once the body was interred, the killer would need to disguise the spot. Perhaps by replacing the surface divots they'd removed, or using other vegetation or soil taken from nearby. This would create a mound, a significant change in the topography.

As time went by, the body decomposing below would cause the mound to subside, creating a dip. Plus the chemicals released by the decomposition would change the nature of the surface vegetation.

Heads down, eyes constantly focused on the ground for anything questionable, they walked the areas marked, working from west to east. Occasionally they picked up stray items such as bottle tops, remains of packaging from some former beach picnic, sweetie papers that the onshore wind had blown through or over the wire fence.

Colin found a sheep's skull bleached white, partly buried

by vegetation, clumps of its woolly coat still dotting the surrounding ground.

Rhona came across a raven – not long dead, she thought – on its back, stiffened legs pointing upwards, its eyes no longer bright. Crouching beside it, she noted that one wing looked badly broken, perhaps from hitting the fence.

Magnus had once explained to her the raven's place in Norse mythology. How Odin was often pictured with a Hrafn – a raven – on each shoulder. Called Huginn and Muninn, they were dispatched each day, their task being to bring back news of enemy movement. She also remembered him stating, in a serious tone, that even nowadays in Orkney, the appearance of a raven might be considered a pointer to death. 'It was to my late mother, anyway,' he'd added.

It was at this moment she realized that the dead raven lay in the shallow dip she'd made note of from the drone footage. Stepping away from the bird, she now mapped in her mind's eye the surrounding oval shape together with a change in vegetation cover.

The area began a couple of metres inside the fence. Close enough for an easy burial?

Rhona called to Colin, trying to keep her tone measured, even as she felt the rise of excitement mixed with horror at what she may have found.

Holding up her hand to halt him before he stepped into the sunken oval round the dead raven, she watched as he ran his eyes over the ground.

'This is the area you added to the map?' he checked.

'Yes, but I may still have missed it had the dead raven not been lying there.' Rhona didn't expand on her earlier ruminations regarding Magnus, raven mythology and his late mother's beliefs regarding the birds.

'I think we should augur the area,' she said instead. 'We might not be able to detect any odours from that, but a cadaver dog would.'

'What about Magnus?' Colin suggested. 'I understand he has a high sensitivity to smell and we could get him here quicker than a cadaver dog.'

Rhona hesitated. Magnus wasn't officially attached to the case, and there was also the issue of the effect such a task might have on him. Eventually she said, 'I'll give Erling a call and tell him what we may have found and suggest that he might bring Magnus with him.'

Stepping clear of the area so that Colin could begin penetrating the ground with the long sticks they'd brought with them, she selected Erling's number and pressed the call button.

When he answered, she explained what had happened. His answer was a stunned silence swiftly followed by a low curse.

'You actually think you've found a possible grave?' he checked.

'There's an area of subsidence,' she said cautiously. 'Plus a change in vegetation cover. In view of the circumstances, and the Evie sand evidence, I believe we should check what's down there. Colin's rodding at the moment to release any gases. We could request a cadaver dog be brought in, but Colin suggested that Magnus might be able to confirm human remains for us.'

A second silence followed, which Rhona broke by saying, 'If you're happy to involve him, that is?'

'I'll call him now,' Erling said. 'And we'll come straight down.'

*

Ending the call, Erling stared into what felt like oblivion.

Another body – was that possible or even probable? If it did turn out to be the case, then a major investigation team would likely be brought in. And all control of what happened next would move to them.

He felt a mix of fear and relief at this thought, because it would be better than standing down if or when the first victim turned out to be Ben Bradley. Someone he'd tortured, at least mentally, twenty years ago.

Bracing himself, he dialled Magnus's number and listened as it rang out three times, before Magnus answered with a cautious 'Erling?'

He decided to get straight to the point.

'Rhona and Colin may have found a burial at the Sands of Evie,' he said. 'They're rodding it now. Rhona would like a cadaver dog brought in, but Colin suggested you might provide a swifter solution.'

In the silence that followed he could almost hear his friend's thoughts, which, he considered, would be much like his own. For Magnus to revitalize his ability to detect decomposition, especially that of a human being, could and likely would prove traumatic. Especially under the current circumstances.

'If you don't feel able—' Erling began, before Magnus interrupted him.

'I'll head to Evie now,' he said firmly.

Thanking him, Erling said he would meet him there.

Summoning Jo to his office, he explained that Dr MacLeod had returned to Orkney early that morning and was currently surveying an area of land at Evie with Professor Nelson. 'Her forensic analysis of the sand extracted from the coils of the torc suggested it came from there,' he explained.

Erling watched as the meaning of all of this now dawned.

'They think there might be another body buried there?' she said, her eyes wide.

'They've already augured a suspect area to release any gases. You and I will head there now and meet up with Professor Pirie.'

Seeing her consternation at the addition of Magnus to the story, Erling explained about his work with Police Scotland as a criminal profiler, plus his unique scenting ability, adding, 'Believe me, if there is a body buried in the area identified by Dr MacLeod, Magnus will know.'

Their drive to Evie passed mostly in silence. DS Green was a competent officer. Erling both respected and acknowledged her abilities. However, as far as he was aware, unlike him, she'd never been involved in a murder investigation before. And certainly not here in Orkney. Eventually she said, 'If they do find another body, then an outside team will be brought in?'

'We're already prepared for that,' Erling told her. 'We're liaising with Glasgow on the identification of the first victim, with their AI image about to go out to the media. I'm hoping the response will be good.'

What he didn't tell her was his request to Glasgow to check on the last known address of the Bradley family, or why he'd given it.

As they drew alongside the UHI van, he spotted Magnus's car turning onto the dirt track and heading their way.

'Magnus and I will get kitted up. You stay here with the car,' he told Jo. 'Have you ever been at a burial site before?' he asked, noting her expression.

155

'I worked on archaeological sites here as a student,' she reminded him. 'Nothing involving more recent bodies, though,' she added, her expression grim.

'Then stay this side of the fence. If anyone comes along the track, send them back.' He glanced skyward where a threatening cloud formation was approaching from the west. 'Let's hope the weather doesn't intervene before Magnus gets to decide if this is a goer or not.' Even as he said those words, his hopes were for the latter.

Magnus looks like death itself, Erling thought as his friend emerged from his vehicle and came towards him.

The two men now got kitted up and, climbing over the low fence, waited as Rhona and Colin approached from the direction of an area marked out by tape.

Reaching them, Rhona posed the question that Erling had been avoiding.

'Are you sure you're okay to do this?' she said, looking directly at Magnus.

He indicated that he was. 'And I'd prefer to do it alone,' he added quietly, but firmly.

'Of course, We'll wait here,' Erling assured him.

Standing by the fence, they watched as Magnus slowly walked to the marked-out area to first stand among the poles, before dropping to his knees.

Erling swore under his breath at this point, then felt Rhona put her hand on his arm. 'It's okay,' she said. 'He just needs to get closer to the ground.'

Erling, remembering the cruel tricks he'd played on Magnus in the past, which had invariably been followed by the sight of Magnus projectile vomiting, wasn't so sure.

The minutes dragged past before Magnus eventually

stood up and, seemingly composing himself, began to walk slowly back towards them.

Erling, reading the expression on his friend's face, already knew what he was about to hear.

'Something *is* decomposing down there,' Magnus told them.

'Could it be a stock burial?' Erling said, although he was already aware that the only animal to share the same chemical scent cocktail as a human was a pig.

'I believe it's more likely to be human,' Magnus said.

25

Glasgow

Staring at the photograph, McNab was sharply reminded of his own schooldays, although he'd left well before the sixth year. Nor did he recall ever being featured in a school photo. Probably due to his propensity to skive.

He noted that the email together with the image had landed in his inbox in the middle of the night, when even he was in bed, slightly the worse for drinking whisky.

He'd got to know DI Flett when he'd been posted to Sanday. Then they'd connected again via the ghost ship *Orlova*, which had washed up on the west coast of Orkney mainland. Back then, he'd been in Glasgow, investigating the operators of the ship, which may have looked like an abandoned cargo boat, but was being used for something much more interesting and criminal than that.

The email explained that Ben Bradley, who he'd been asked by DI Wilson to try to locate, was in the photograph, along with Erling himself and Magnus Pirie, both in the back row.

On reading this, McNab had looked for Magnus, spotting

his tall blond figure almost immediately. Erling had taken a little longer and even then he wasn't altogether sure, because of the quantity of hair he'd apparently sported back then.

Finally, he moved to the figure who, Erling had indicated, was Ben Bradley. The guy stood a little apart from the rest of the group, as though he didn't belong with them. He also appeared to be deliberately avoiding meeting the camera's lens. McNab, also an outsider at school, immediately felt a connection to the missing Ben.

Then came the request . . .

I want to make sure Ben Bradley is not the Skaill Bay victim. I didn't personally recognize the AI image as Ben, but since the program had nothing to compare it to, I spoke to DI Wilson and he suggested I send through the school photo. It seems to me that the AI program couldn't take account of the way Ben tried to be invisible. Also, his hair was always short back and sides like a marine.

It finished with:

Could you check if the AI program finds the victim is a match for Ben?

McNab's immediate question was what had prompted DI Flett to think that the victim might be his old schoolmate in the first place?

At that moment he recalled Annie Bradley talking about a pupil called Flett not getting on with her son at school, and his own glib reply to Janice's reminder about that. Was that the reason for DI Flett's interest in eliminating Ben as a possible victim?

Then that troubling thought returned. Should the victim indeed turn out to be Erling's old school sparring partner of twenty years ago, then he and everyone in that school photograph would have to be questioned. And Erling would no longer be asking the questions, but answering them.

'Jeez, I should pay more attention to what my partner says,' he chided himself.

But, and it was a big 'but', Ben's mother had said that she'd communicated with her son for at least a month after his supposed last visit to Orkney, and during that time he'd been in London. Or had told her he was.

What if he'd returned to Orkney, unbeknown to her, maybe after they'd stopped communicating?

And the other troubling question: why had he stopped texting his mum?

Because he found himself another life and didn't want to be reminded of the previous one, came the inner reply.

'Or he was killed. And laid in a Viking grave at Skaill Bay,' McNab muttered under his breath.

This largely internal monologue had taken him from his desk to IT in search of Ollie, the super recognizer, who he believed would be able to fulfil DI Flett's request in two ways.

The first, when he ran the AI recognition software against the photograph. The second, where Ollie would give his own, human opinion on a possible match.

McNab knew which he would trust more.

Following his usual pattern when visiting Ollie, he'd gone via the canteen and purchased some goodies, really for himself, but as usual pretending they were a reward for Ollie, who, when he wasn't on a diet, usually received them with relish.

Trouble was, McNab couldn't help but notice when Ollie had stood up in the last strategy meeting to display his latest achievement on the Artificial Intelligence front, he had definitely looked slimmer. And fitter.

With this thought, McNab vowed it was time to get back to the gym himself. A vow he repeated internally, even as he purchased a selection of cakes.

On arrival at the IT suite, he discovered Ollie was no longer at his usual spot, but was now ensconced in the new Cyber Division area, to which he too was permitted entry, having completed the AI course alongside Ollie.

McNab didn't know whether to be pleased or annoyed by this, but decided the more places he could enter the better.

Ollie, usually found surrounded by clutter, was no longer. In fact McNab didn't dare place the bag of goodies down, for fear of messing up the pristine surroundings.

Sensing or scenting his arrival, Ollie turned and pointed to a door leading to what appeared to be a small staffroom.

So that's where we talk and eat now, McNab acknowledged, heading in the direction indicated.

When Ollie followed him through, McNab made yet another note on how much slimmer and fitter Ollie looked, but decided not to mention it lest it go to his head.

'What can I do you for, Sergeant?' Ollie said, accepting the goodie bag and opening it to view what was inside.

For a moment McNab thought he might reject the offering, but no, Ollie carefully selected what was definitely the biggest bun and began eating it.

McNab had bagged that one for himself, but decided not to say. Instead, he explained the reason for his visit.

'Is this an official request?' Ollie said, once he'd demolished the bun and licked his fingers.

'From me, yes,' McNab said. 'A way of testing what I was taught on the course.'

Producing his mobile, he pulled up the school photograph and handed it over.

A swift glance resulted in Ollie immediately pointing out Magnus. 'Professor Pirie,' he declared. 'Looking all of eighteen years old.'

'DI Flett is a couple of places along,' McNab told him. 'The guy Flett and I want to focus on is the one on the second-row end, who looks as though he'd rather not be there at all.'

Back in front of the big screen, McNab watched as Ollie made a copy of Ben for the AI program to use for comparison with the generated image.

'Ready?' Ollie checked.

McNab barely had time to complete his nod before the screen, displaying both images side by side, presented its conclusion.

Stunned by the speed of the comparison, McNab was at a loss for words for a moment, before saying, 'So the program thinks the victim isn't Ben Bradley?'

Ollie, concentrating on the screen, didn't immediately answer. McNab, having seen that look before, said, 'Okay, tell me what you're thinking.'

Ollie turned to face McNab. 'It's not the result I expected,' he said, sounding puzzled.

'What d'you mean?' McNab prodded.

'I don't agree with the program's conclusion. I believe the victim *is* the male in the school photograph,' Ollie told him.

26

Glasgow

Janice listened in silence to his explanation of where he had gone first thing, and why.

'Did you check with the boss first before you headed to IT?' she promptly said. When he didn't answer, she pulled a face. 'Okay, so go check with him now,' she said. 'And maybe apologize that you didn't do that beforehand.'

McNab was already working out how to construct his story in a manner that reflected positively on his actions. 'Right,' he said, rising. 'I take it there's been no progress on trying to locate Ben Bradley in London?' he added hopefully.

'No, there hasn't,' she assured him, with the hint of a smile. 'You can tell the boss that too,' she added.

The interview was going better than he'd hoped. There had been a few awkward moments when he'd explained about immediately acting on the email request from DI Flett without checking with DI Wilson first. He'd apologized, of course, adding that he thought DI Flett, having watched the image reconstruction video, wasn't convinced that the AI program had enough information.

'He sent the school photograph to test the program. I think he was right to want to do that, sir. Plus the AI program declared that the victim was not a match for Ben Bradley, but Ollie, our human super recognizer, says he believes the victim *is* Ben Bradley,' he finished, on what he realized was a triumphant note.

'I am aware of all of this, Detective Sergeant,' DI Wilson said, somewhat drily, before adding, 'Because prior to your arrival here, I received a call from Cyber Division.'

Okay, that had been unexpected, but McNab said a silent thank you to Ollie nonetheless.

By DI Wilson's current expression, he was coming to a decision, which, McNab thought, was likely to involve him in some way or another. Eventually he learned what it was.

'I'd like DS Clark to make contact with Mrs Bradley and request she come in and have a DNA sample taken, so that we might establish whether the Skaill Bay victim is, or is not, her son.'

'Yes, sir,' McNab said, pleased by this.

'Also, you should know that Dr MacLeod flew to Kirkwall yesterday morning, where she and Professor Nelson carried out a forensic examination of an area at the Sands of Evie.' The boss paused there briefly. 'Dr MacLeod confirmed late yesterday that they would start excavating a suspected internment site there this morning.'

McNab, stunned by this latest news, waited in silence for what he feared might follow.

'You will join Dr MacLeod there. Should the first victim in fact prove to be Ben Bradley, then you, as acting Detective Inspector, will take charge of the investigation into his death.'

'Me, sir? But—' he began.

'DI Flett asked for you, since you have experience of working successfully on the Sanday case, when he had to stand aside because of the possible involvement of a relative.'

McNab had a host of reasons as to why he thought this a bad idea, none of which he voiced, predominantly because of the determined expression on his superior officer's face.

'That is all, DS McNab. Tell DS Clark to come in while you make your flight arrangements and inform Dr MacLeod of your imminent arrival.'

'Everything okay?' Janice said on his approach, obviously reading his expression.

'I'm bound for Orkney,' McNab said, still not quite believing it. 'Rhona thinks there may be another body buried somewhere called the Sands of Evie. Also, if the first victim does turn out to be Ben Bradley, then DI Flett will stand down from the case and I'm to take over as acting DI.'

Janice's bemused expression matched his own.

'The boss wants to see you about getting a DNA sample from Annie Bradley,' he added. 'To confirm if the Skaill Bay guy is her son or not.'

As Janice headed for the office, McNab tried to take stock of what had just happened.

'How the hell did I succeed in getting myself sent to Orkney?' he muttered as he contemplated what he had to do to get there today, which included heading for the chopper by way of his flat, in the hope of finding some clean clothes. Something he wasn't confident about.

DI Flett, he realized, had sent him the school photograph to make sure he knew in advance of the possibility of a conflict of interest, should Ben Bradley prove to be the victim.

Which the boss had obviously gone along with, even to boosting his status to a temporary DI.

Bringing up Rhona's number, he pressed the call button.

When it swiftly moved to voicemail, he left a message, explaining that he would be arriving in Kirkwall sometime today.

An hour later he was en route to the helicopter stance with a hastily packed bag containing anything clean he could lay his hands on, while at the same time vowing to keep up with his laundry in future in a timelier fashion.

The call came in from Rhona shortly before he boarded the chopper and he gave her a brief explanation for his imminent arrival in Kirkwall. 'I'll give you the details when I see you,' he added.

'So, for the moment, Erling's still in charge?' Rhona checked.

When he confirmed this, she told him they'd begun the excavation. 'Are you being picked up at Kirkwall?' she asked. When he confirmed this, she said, 'Then tell whoever it is to bring you to the Sands of Evie. We'll still be here.'

The rain came on in a burst as he hurried across the tarmac to the waiting chopper. Safely inside and belted up, he watched as they rose towards a grey blanket of cloud, the sound of the beating rain drowned out by the blades.

As buildings gave way to swathes of open farmland, to be followed by scattered lochs and encircling mountains, he experienced that familiar sinking feeling that always beset him when he departed his city.

Glasgow was full of green spaces and numerous parks. None of which he would be likely to visit by choice. Where he was headed was one big park, comprising seventy or so islands in a variety of sizes. Apart from Hoy, they were all basically flat and green, especially in summer.

No mean streets anywhere, but that didn't mean they didn't require policing. Although Sanday, the island he'd spent time on before, didn't have a permanent police presence.

He found himself recalling his endless attempts to get a mobile signal while there. Plus the fact that Rhona had had to set up a temporary lab to deal with the forensic evidence associated with the case they'd been sent there to investigate.

Nothing had fazed Dr MacLeod, of course. Or Chrissy for that matter. As for himself . . .

His abiding memory was of the night he'd been thrown over the harbour wall behind the Kettletoft Inn by a local, and how lucky he'd been that the tide wasn't out.

Now passing over the Pentland Firth, he couldn't help but acknowledge the heavy swell and crashing waves breaking against the western flank of Hoy, before the pilot turned east towards Kirkwall.

'This may be bumpy,' he was warned.

As they made their rocky descent, McNab decided that, unlike Rhona, he didn't dislike flying. He just didn't like having to fly to locations outwith his city comfort zone.

Released now, he was soon out and walking swiftly towards the terminal building in what proved to be a gusty but dry wind. Entering, he was surprised to find DI Flett himself waiting for him.

Seemingly sensing this, Flett held out his hand and thanked him for coming. 'My apologies if it isn't something you particularly wanted,' he added. 'I'm aware you're not too keen on being out of Glasgow.'

'I go where I'm sent,' McNab said. 'Although I'm puzzled as to why you should ask for me,' he added.

'You've been here before, and have experienced a murder investigation in a small community such as this.'

McNab chose not to respond further as they exited the terminal building to find a police car parked and waiting.

'Dr MacLeod asked me to come straight to the locus,' he said.

'That's where we're heading. I'll fill you in on everything you need to know on the way.'

'You're still in charge, Inspector,' McNab said. He knew there was an edge to his voice but didn't care.

DI Flett waited until they were out of the airport and onto the Kirkwall road before he spoke again.

'I'm aware your super recognizer found a match between the identikit image of the victim and Ben Bradley. And that it contradicted the AI recognition program.'

'Which was odd,' McNab said, 'since Ollie was party to its programming. However, I would put my trust in Ollie's human abilities, rather than the recognition software.' He looked round at DI Flett. 'So what led you to think the victim might be your old school chum?' he asked outright.

'Ben Bradley and I weren't friends. In fact I spent most of my time either ignoring or belittling him.'

'I know,' McNab said. 'Well, I know about you and Ben not being friends.'

'How do you know that?' DI Flett appeared nonplussed by this.

'When I interviewed Ben's mum regarding her son's whereabouts, I mentioned a DI Flett in Orkney. She said Ben had gone to school with a boy called Flett and they hadn't got on,' McNab told him. 'I didn't think much about it at the time, because there are a great many Fletts in Orkney, plus I didn't make many friends in school either,' he added.

Silence fell, albeit briefly, before McNab repeated the question. 'Why *did* you think the victim might be Ben?'

'I gave a talk about becoming a police officer to the sixth form at Kirkwall Grammar School, where all they wanted to discuss was the body of a male of their age unearthed at Skaill Bay. They knew things, even then, which hadn't been released to the public,' he said. 'After which a female sixth-former came to see me, to tell me she thought the victim was her father.'

Now that was something McNab hadn't been expecting.

'Since then,' DI Flett continued, 'and despite our best efforts, information regarding a Viking bracelet, known as a torc, found by Dr MacLeod in the stone cist, has also become common knowledge. Ingrid, the girl I mentioned, maintains that Ben Bradley, who she believes to be her father, is wearing that bracelet in the school photograph.'

McNab immediately pulled out his mobile and brought up the image, enlarging it to see what did look like a metal bracelet.

'I've had it magnified by the Tech team but it's not sufficiently clear to see if her claim is true,' Erling said.

McNab took a moment to consider all of this, before coming to the conclusion that he was here to provide the outsider view on this unravelling scenario. Someone who was unconnected to the location, its history and its inhabitants. While at the same time with an understanding of how things worked here. And some bad memories from Sanday to go with it.

They now turned right onto a single-track tarred road

and headed for the sea. In the distance, he spotted a white van parked at the head of a sea loch. On the other side of a bordering fence, two white suits were at work.

He was back again in Orkney, he thought, and with a vengeance.

27

Orkney

They had come here at first light. She and Colin in one van, his two assistants, both women, in the other. Dr Deborah Gillam, on sabbatical from Princeton University, had been the one to help Colin with the retrieval of the bones and Viking artefacts at Skaill Bay. Dr Francis Semphill was a temporary staffer in Colin's department at UHI in Kirkwall.

Both women had been on numerous archaeological excavations before, but neither had worked on what was likely to be a more recent grave, where smell would be a major issue.

After discussion with Colin, the decision was made that Deborah and Francis would help lay out the grid over the designated area, after which they would be responsible for bagging the extracted soil and transporting it to a lab at the UHI building.

Rhona was already missing Chrissy. As much for her patter as for the fact they'd worked loci such as this one so often together that discussion on method was never required.

Arriving with the promise of dry and breezy conditions, they'd found the cover they'd laid the previous evening still in place. Although there had obviously been rain overnight, as evidenced by the puddled tarpaulin. When removing it, Rhona immediately caught the escaping smell via the rodded surface. As did Colin, just as he'd done at the opening of the cist at Skaill Bay. Even the two women, who she'd asked to stand further away, had caught a waft of it by the expression on their faces.

Once they began removing the layers of soil, the smell of decomposition would become progressively stronger and more difficult to cope with.

That's why she and Colin had taken the decision to perform this task alone, just as she and Chrissy would have done, and put the other women in charge of transferring the soil to the lab, where it might be examined.

It was a painstaking job, as it would have been if they were uncovering a Viking burial. It just wouldn't have been so smelly. Or so Colin had told her, a twinkle in his eye above the mask.

It was Colin who first encountered what turned out to be the top edge of an upright slate. Other slates then began to emerge, seemingly forming the outer rim of the grave. Working their way systematically round, they eventually exposed them all.

The grave, it now appeared, had been constructed in the shape of a small boat, with the bow furthest from the water's edge.

'This isn't a Viking boat grave,' Colin said, 'but it's an attempt at imitating one. Without the actual boat,' he added grimly.

Rhona would never grow used to the scent of death. She had long since accepted that. How she coped with it was to focus entirely on the victim and how much she might learn from their cause of death and burial. That didn't make the smell go away, but it did force it to the back of her mind, for a while at least.

They had not yet reached the actual remains, but they were definitely close, she thought. Glancing over at Colin, she decided that it was time for a brief retreat and a breath of fresher air.

Signalling they should take a break, Rhona, followed by Colin, walked into the onshore breeze and, dropping her mask, took in a deep breath of sea air.

'Just as well our helpers aren't around,' Colin said, after he'd done the same.

It was at that moment Rhona spotted a police car heading down the single track from the main road.

'That'll be DS McNab,' she said. 'Just helicoptered in from Glasgow. Erling called to say he'd pick him up at the airport.'

'Is this DS McNab the cavalry?' Colin said, with a questioning glance.

'Possibly an advance party of what might become a major investigation team. Especially if we uncover a second victim,' Rhona said, unwilling to share the real reason McNab was here.

'So it'll be out of Erling's hands now?' Colin looked concerned by this.

'Not necessarily,' Rhona told him, hoping that was true. 'Just some help in times of trouble.'

Watching the car negotiating the potholes and puddles, Rhona couldn't help but wonder if conditions inside the vehicle were equally difficult.

When she'd spoken to him earlier, McNab had been pretty forthright about his thoughts on being posted back to Orkney. How Erling felt about McNab's arrival here, she didn't know.

She wished she'd been able to speak to Bill Wilson about the latest developments, but hadn't had the opportunity to discuss it with him as yet. However, she was certain that Bill wouldn't have sent McNab north without good reason.

The men were out of the vehicle and walking towards her now. Equal in height and similar in build, McNab's auburn hair was his clearly identifying feature. Even from this distance, she could feel him bristling. Erling, on the other hand, seemed comfortable with the situation he found himself in. Which was also evident in the calm tone he now addressed her with.

'How are things progressing, Dr MacLeod?' he asked.

'We've identified the outline of a grave,' she told him.

'Built with slates arranged in the shape of a boat,' Colin added.

'So a continuation of the Viking theme?' Erling said, his concern showing.

'And the body?' McNab said, sniffing the air.

'Not uncovered as yet,' Rhona confirmed. 'But soon to be.'

'I'll get kitted up and take a look,' McNab announced.

When Rhona checked with Erling on this, he promptly responded. 'Let's both get kitted up and have a closer look.'

The awkwardness of this interchange wasn't lost on Colin, who, catching Rhona's look, raised an eyebrow. In return, Rhona replaced her mask and, nodding to him to follow, headed back to the locus.

'That reminded me of some faculty meetings I'd rather not attend,' Colin said under his breath.

'It might get worse before it gets better,' Rhona warned him. 'McNab definitely doesn't want to be here. On the other hand, I get the impression Erling doesn't mind that he is. Anyway, we have our own job to do.'

By the time the two men arrived at the gravesite fully kitted up, Rhona, having removed the next layer of soil from the bow of the boat, caught her first glimpse of the skull that lay beneath.

Focused as she was on brushing it clean, she didn't immediately register the men's arrival until she heard the smothered sound of someone coughing and looked up.

Her first thought that it might be McNab was proved wrong as Erling took a few steps away from the gravesite and turned his face to the wind.

Moments later, he was back, composed again. 'I was brought up on a farm, so I've smelt plenty of dead animal carcasses. But human remains . . .' He shook his head.

'Are uniquely terrible in their scent,' Rhona confirmed. 'As McNab will testify to, since he avoids entering my forensic tent whenever possible.'

The skull, now fully exposed, was lying on its right side. Rhona thought it likely by its shape to be that of another male. Continuing her soft brushstrokes, she began to clear the area round the neck.

At this moment the sun decided to appear from behind the racing clouds and, shining directly on the grave, found something to reflect off.

'What is that?' McNab said, dropping down beside her.

Rhona had caught the glint too and, suspecting it was likely a piece of jewellery, used careful brushstrokes to expose it further to the light.

Colin, having joined her on the other side, used his brush to help expose the metal torc that encircled the bones of the neck.

'This isn't an actual Viking body?' McNab said.

Rhona pointed to the teeth. 'Not unless they'd invented amalgam fillings back in Viking times.'

'So how long's he or she been here?' he said.

'Let me expose the whole body before I start answering questions about the sex, age or time since death and burial,' Rhona said, before carefully removing the torc from the neck.

'It looks like tarnished silver,' said Colin.

It did, Rhona thought, and was much finer and lighter than the heavy metal torc of the Skaill Bay victim.

'Any engravings?' Erling said.

Rhona took a closer look. 'Those might be initials,' she said, checking with her magnifying glass. 'The torc bracelet had an E M or a B M on it. The second initial here looks again like an M. As for the first letter . . .'

She handed the torc and magnifier to Erling to take a look.

'Second one is definitely an M,' he said. 'The first maybe an L?'

McNab came in then. 'If it's the same perpetrator, the first initial might relate to his victim, and the second to himself.' He halted there for a moment, as though thinking this theory through. 'Ollie matched Ben Bradley from your school photograph to the AI-generated image of the Skaill Bay victim. So maybe it was a B the first time round? Ben or Bradley?'

He continued doggedly. 'If that's how it works, then the second victim's name begins with an L.' He looked to Erling. 'Did anyone whose name starts with an L go missing in Orkney in the last decade or two?'

'As I mentioned in the car coming here, we're still

checking out all young males reported missing over the last twenty years,' Erling said, 'regardless of their initials.'

'What about your fellow sixth-formers at Kirkwall Grammar School? Are they all accounted for now, Inspector?' McNab said sharply.

Rhona came in then. 'Colin and I need to get back to work before the light fails us. DI Flett, could you organize someone to come and guard the grave overnight, please?'

'Of course,' he said, before turning to McNab to say they'd head back to Kirkwall now. 'You're booked in at the Kirkwall Hotel on the front, Detective Sergeant. I'll drop you there and expect you at Kirkwall police station first thing tomorrow,' he said firmly.

McNab accepted this with a nod and then a glance at Rhona, who ignored his semi-apologetic look.

'I had a slight sense of stags at bay?' Colin said as they watched the two men head back to the vehicle. 'And what was all that about the identikit picture and someone called Ben Bradley?' he added. 'Did Erling think he went to school with the victim?'

Rhona didn't see that she had any choice but to explain, so she did.

'Thanks for telling me that,' Colin said. 'I wasn't in Orkney twenty years ago, but I can imagine how difficult that would be for Erling.'

'The image is to be released tomorrow morning, so all of Orkney will be taking a look. Maybe Ollie, the super recognizer, won't be the only one to decide it's Ben Bradley,' she told him. 'Although the only way to be sure is through DNA, and I understand McNab's already been in touch with Annie Bradley, Ben's mother, regarding a sample.'

And the sooner that happens the better, Rhona thought.

28

Orkney

The return journey to Kirkwall was punctuated by calls from various members of DI Flett's team. McNab listened as Flett responded to questions and issued orders, many of which McNab noted were centred on the imminent transmission of the AI-generated image of Erik, as Rhona had named him, both on social media and local and national television.

There was even a call from the *Orcadian*, the local newspaper for the islands, who were planning on running the image on their front page.

Flett, he noted, seemed unfazed by this, or else his preoccupation with perhaps knowing the victim was fading. The call from Janice came as they were entering Kirkwall. His partner's tone, when she spoke, warned him that bad news was on its way.

'It's about the Bradleys,' she said. She paused briefly, and he urged her on.

'I went round to see Annie to ask her to come in and give a DNA sample to eliminate Ben from our enquiries. They weren't there and a neighbour said they'd gone—'

McNab interrupted her before she could finish.

'Gone where?' he demanded.

'On holiday, she said. She thinks Majorca, which is apparently where they normally go,' Janice told him.

McNab swore under his breath. 'Have you tried Annie's phone?'

'I have and it goes to voicemail,' she said.

This time his curse was loud enough for Flett to hear.

'D'you think the husband found out about Annie's meeting with us and removed her before that happened again?' Janice said.

McNab thought back to that large male figure blocking the doorway, the manner in which Annie had been kept in her place. 'Could be, but why exactly?'

'He knows more about Ben's disappearance than he's willing to say?' Janice offered. 'Anyway, I thought you and DI Flett should know right away.'

When she'd rung off, McNab asked how much Flett had heard.

'From your partner's side of it, nothing,' he said, looking concerned.

'Annie Bradley's missing. As is her husband. Gone on holiday, according to their neighbour, and Annie's mobile just goes to voicemail. So we have no way to contact her at present to check Erik's DNA against hers.'

'Erik?' DI Flett said, puzzled.

'Dr MacLeod's name for the victim until we learn his real one. To her, he's not just a body.'

'Nor to me. Nor you, I suspect. And that's nothing to do with the fact Erik might yet prove to be Ben,' he added firmly.

They'd reached the brightly lit harbour and now drew up

outside the imposing three-storey frontage of the Kirkwall Hotel.

'I hear there's a coffee maker in your room, Detective Sergeant, and the food's good. See you at eight tomorrow morning. We're along to the left and up Burgh Road. We'll get you organized with a vehicle then.'

As DI Flett drove away, McNab found himself remembering when he'd been the one under suspicion. How he'd regretted the action that had put him there. How the boss had stood by him, despite his stupidity. As had Rhona. More than once.

It was time he did the same for Flett.

He stood for a moment, breathing in the night air. On the return journey, he'd registered the sky as a multitude of stars. No bright city lights around to mask them.

The boats tied up in the harbour suddenly reminded him of one of the few trips he'd made out of Glasgow with his mum as a boy. They'd taken the train to somewhere on the coast. Wemyss Bay it was. He remembered the station with its beautiful glass ceiling. They'd caught a boat from there to Rothesay and stayed with a pal of his mum's.

He'd liked it, he remembered. The pier with the ferries arriving and departing, where the view of the River Clyde seemed to go on forever, peppered by inlets and sea lochs. But the feeling had soon worn off and he'd longed to be back on the streets he knew, with the noise and lights of the city a cocoon about him.

He turned from the harbour and entered the hotel with thoughts of food and whisky on his mind.

He was installed in his room, with the coffee maker on and the shower running, when another call came in. Not recognizing the number, he hesitated to answer, before the thought occurred that it might be Annie Bradley. She had his number even if she wasn't answering calls to her own.

'DS Michael McNab?' It was a female voice, but it wasn't Annie's.

'Yes. And who is this?'

'Ava,' she said. 'Ava Clouston. We met during the *Orlova* investigation,' she added. 'You tried to help my friend Mark. That's why I have your number.'

He remembered that time, and her, almost too vividly, but still he didn't respond.

She continued regardless. 'I'm currently in Orkney covering the Skaill Bay murder for the *Orcadian* and my investigation podcast,' she said. 'Would you be willing to speak to me regarding that?'

'How did you know I was here?' McNab asked.

'The police helicopter dropped you at Kirkwall airport earlier today, where you were met by DI Flett. News travels fast in Orkney, as you probably remember,' she said.

He did remember, all too well. He left a marked pause before eventually saying, 'Your contact for information about the current investigation would be DI Flett, as I'm sure you're aware.'

He wanted to add that the last time he'd tried to help her had almost cost him his life, but didn't.

Despite his response, she continued. 'A young girl, Ingrid Donaldson, came to me with the school photograph that I think brought you here. She believes that the victim may be her father, Ben Bradley.'

'I know,' he said. 'DI Flett told me.' He waited again.

'I think Erling needs to prove for definite that that isn't the case,' she said.

'Then you should tell him that yourself,' McNab answered.

'It's better coming from you, as an outsider here, and a police officer. He'll listen to you. Erling is too close to all of this.' She paused as though thinking through what she should say next. 'You should know,' she began, 'that there was an incident when we were all in the sixth form together. It involved Ben Bradley. And it happened on the beach at Skaill.'

She had him now.

'Okay,' he conceded. 'Let's talk. I'm staying at—'

'The Kirkwall Hotel,' she swiftly finished for him. 'Can I meet you there in, say, an hour? I'm in the process of finishing my write-up for tomorrow's *Orcadian*. You're aware the front page will be the AI-generated image of the victim?'

He was aware, he told her. 'I'll be in the bar,' he added and promptly rang off.

Heading for the shower, he tipped his head back under the spray and opened his mouth, trying to rid himself of the taste of death, while contemplating what had just occurred.

Instinct told him he should immediately inform Flett of the phone call and yet he knew he wouldn't. Flett was responsible for bringing him here and must suffer the consequences of that. The Detective Inspector was still ostensibly in charge of this case, but might not be after tomorrow.

An hour later, well fed and with a couple of whiskies consumed and another before him, McNab watched as she entered the bar and, catching sight of him, made her way over. Glancing at his chosen drink, she offered to buy him a refill.

'No hurry,' he told her. 'I'm savouring this one. But can I get you one?' he added, rising.

She looked as though she might refuse, then didn't. 'Thanks. I'll have the same as you.'

'Highland Park it is, then.'

Back at the corner table he'd chosen because of its privacy, he set her drink down, took a sip of his own and waited.

Eventually she spoke. 'Have you seen the AI image that's going out tomorrow?'

He gave a brief nod. 'And you?' he said, wondering if Flett had given her access before the release date, which wouldn't have been a good sign.

As though reading his mind, she said, 'Erling didn't show me. In fact he refused when I asked. He said it would arrive at the *Orcadian* for tomorrow's publication,' she explained. 'I've just seen it.'

'And?'

She took a deep breath. 'I think it could be Ben,' she said, obviously distressed by this. 'Although Erling seemed certain it wasn't.'

'Maybe he didn't want it to be Ben, and you did?' McNab said testily.

'Of course I don't want it to be Ben,' she said angrily. 'But it's not what I want, it's what's true that's important.'

This was the Ava Clouston, tenacious investigative journalist, he remembered. The truth meant everything to her and was worth every threatening situation it got her into.

'This girl you spoke about, Ingrid Donaldson. Has she seen it yet?' he asked.

'I assume not, but it wouldn't matter anyway. She just needs to see the proof that the victim is not her father.'

'What's her mother saying about it?' McNab tried.

'She told Erling that Ben was kind to her. That he came back to visit once, but never kept in touch after that, which she'd worried about. We, on the other hand, were mean to him. Mostly by ignoring him, but on one occasion it almost came to blows. Like that night at Skaill Bay twenty years ago.'

It was then the story came tumbling out. Good reporter that she was, McNab could almost feel himself there. The sand and the wild surf, the drink and drugs, the shambolic sex scene between herself and Erling in the dunes, watched by a hidden Ben.

'That's when I screamed. Erling was so angry when he realized why, I thought he would hit Ben, but Magnus held on to him and told Ben to leave.'

'And Ben walked away unharmed?' McNab said.

She nodded. 'Although I remember wondering at the time how Ben got to Skaill Bay in the first place. He didn't have a car and none of our crowd would have taken him there. And how did he get home?' She hesitated for a moment before saying, 'I know you and Magnus are friends . . .'

Friends would be too strong a word, McNab thought, so corrected her. 'Professor Pirie and I have worked professionally together in the past.'

'Magnus was with Shona Bain that night on the beach,' she said. 'She's Ingrid's mother.'

He felt her eyes on him as he digested this piece of information. 'You think there's a chance Magnus may be Ingrid's father?' he said. 'Without knowing it?'

'Maybe,' she said. 'Shona only returned to Orkney a year ago after her husband, Ingrid's stepfather, died. Her married name is Donaldson. Magnus may not know she's back, or that she has a daughter. I didn't, until my brother brought Ingrid to the house and she told me her story.'

'What about asking her mother outright who the father is?'

'If she wouldn't tell Erling, then she won't tell me.' She took a mouthful of whisky as though to boost herself for what she would say next.

And then it came.

'I know you've found another burial site at the Sands of Evie,' she told him. 'A local called me about the white suits and vans down there. Magnus was one of them, so he must have his DNA on the police database for elimination purposes.'

He finished his own whisky before responding.

'You think if we sample Ingrid's DNA as she wants, and compare it to the victim and to Magnus Pirie, we'll get the answer to both questions?'

'Yes,' she said.

'We'd have to ask Magnus's permission first,' he told her.

'I know,' she said. 'And I'm willing to explain why.'

29

Orkney

The drive back to the Ivy House from Evie had a surreal quality about it. With no mountains or even large hills to block the view, the sky in Orkney was king, or queen, of both night and day.

Tonight it was clear, with only an occasional scudding cloud, and plenty of stars on view.

'I can imagine the Vikings looking up at a sky such as this,' Rhona said.

'And the Neolithic peoples before them,' Colin told her.

'Finding and excavating an ancient grave is, I suppose, both exciting and pleasurable,' Rhona said. 'Unlike what we did today.'

'I still feel sad when I excavate an ancient grave,' Colin responded. 'Especially when I realize by the state of the remains that the person buried there was likely murdered or inhumanely executed,' he added. 'We try always to remember that they were people, just like us. The real difference between your job and mine,' he said, 'is that I can never help bring their killers to justice. You can.'

'Not always,' Rhona told him. 'Buried bodies, such as these two, suggest a highly organized killer, who is likely wise to forensics, and has a penchant for young males.'

'Another thing we know about them,' Colin said, 'is that they have a preoccupation with the world of Vikings and they seem to know Orkney pretty well.'

'You think the perpetrator could be local?' Rhona said. 'But killing so close to home in a small community like this would be very difficult. Especially if you were killing other locals.'

'I was thinking more about a regular visitor. Or maybe someone who's been involved in archaeological digs here before.'

'I'd like to discuss the perpetrator with Magnus, now that he seems to have joined the team officially,' Rhona said.

'Well, you can, tonight,' Colin told her. 'He left me a message asking us to come eat with him later. You probably have one too.'

Checking her mobile, Rhona in fact found two messages. One regarding the meal from Magnus. One from Chrissy demanding she call.

'Found it?' Colin checked.

'I have, plus some work stuff,' Rhona told him.

Now upstairs in her room at the Ivy House, Rhona made her first call, which was in fact to PC Ivan Tulloch, currently on duty at the locus at the Sands of Evie.

'Dr MacLeod. Everything okay?' he said.

'It is here,' Rhona assured him. 'What about where you are?'

'All good. A bit windy but your site is well secured. I don't foresee any problems.'

Rhona trusted PC Tulloch's reassurances. A Sanday man himself, he'd helped her a great deal at the excavation she and Chrissy had carried out on his home island.

Now for Chrissy, she decided.

Just as she brought up the number and was about to press the call button, her screen lit up with Chrissy's face on it. Not for the first time did she think her forensic assistant had an uncanny gift for reading her mind, despite the distance between them.

'I was just about to phone you,' Rhona admitted.

'I knew that,' Chrissy assured her. 'So what did you find at the Sands of Evil?'

'The Sands of Evie,' Rhona corrected her, thinking that now Chrissy had planted that version in her brain, it would be difficult to get rid of it.

Mustering herself, Rhona gave a potted version of the day's events.

'So there was another body there,' Chrissy said. 'And the weird Viking burial thing too. I wish I could have gone to Orkney with you,' she added.

'As do I,' Rhona said. 'Although Colin's filling in for you pretty well,' she offered.

This remark was followed by a *harrumph* sound.

Rhona decided to steer the subject elsewhere. 'Anyway, how are things going at your end?'

'I've extracted further fragments of tape from the sand,' Chrissy said in a satisfied tone. 'Plus a small phial that I suspect may have contained a drug of some kind. I'll let you know.'

'Excellent,' Rhona said and meant it.' Then to leave the subject of work, she asked after Connor.

'He's good,' Chrissy said, her tone definitely lighter. 'We're off out tonight, and Mum's looking after wee Michael and Rocket.'

'Just as well you didn't accompany me to the Sands of Evil, then?' Rhona said.

'Made all your calls?' Colin said when she reappeared downstairs.

'Just one left, but I'll do it later,' Rhona said.

'Right. Let's head for Seaview.'

On arrival they discovered a jeep parked alongside Magnus's car.

'He has other guests,' Rhona said, disappointed. 'I was hoping to get Magnus's take on the perpetrator.'

'That's the Clouston farm jeep,' Colin said. 'So it's likely Ava Clouston.'

'So Ava's arrived,' Rhona said.

'You know her?' Colin asked.

'I got to know her during the *Orlova* case,' Rhona told him. 'Is she here on a visit home or has it something to do with Skaill Bay?'

'She hosts an investigative podcast,' Colin said. 'I assume she's covering the Skaill Bay excavation. Probably reporting it for the *Orcadian* too. Looks like you're about to find out.'

Normally, Magnus was alerted to their arrival by their headlights coming down from the main road. In such times he would already be at the door to welcome them. Not in this instance, however. Instead, Rhona found herself reaching for the door knocker, while at the same time aware of an animated discussion going on inside.

Colin, obviously hearing this too, raised a questioning eyebrow. 'So what do we do?' he semi-whispered.

'I suggest you sound the car horn, as though we've just arrived,' Rhona said.

Colin nodded his agreement and did as suggested. Still by the door, Rhona heard silence abruptly descend, then the sound of Magnus's footsteps in the hallway.

There was another silent moment as though he was collecting himself, before the door was swept open.

'Rhona. I didn't spot your lights. Apologies,' he said quietly. 'Ava's here and we were catching up on things.'

He looked her straight in the eye and Rhona took this as a sign he would explain later, perhaps when they were alone.

'Come away through, Ava's looking forward to seeing you again,' he said a little louder this time.

Whatever had gone before, both Ava and Magnus appeared to have put it to rest for the moment, Rhona realized, as the normal conviviality of Seaview rose to the occasion. Drinks were served, one of which Rhona accepted with alacrity, pleased she wasn't tonight's driver.

She and Ava had a brief chat, with Ava explaining that she'd come back to see Dougie but then the *Orcadian* had made contact with her, asking if she would cover the Skaill Bay excavation.

Rhona thought her timeline for this a little skewed, but didn't point that out, because Ava was first and foremost an investigative journalist and so even a scent of the discovery at Skaill Bay would naturally have drawn her home like a moth to a flame.

'I'm also featuring the story on my podcast,' Ava was saying. 'I have a big listening community, particularly after the *Orlova* case. I'll feed out the AI image on social media when it goes live tomorrow. Plus it'll be on the front page of the *Orcadian*.' Ava paused, her keen eyes trying to read

Rhona's expression. 'I've discussed all of this with Erling, of course,' she added.

'Good,' Rhona said. 'It's a worrying time for him.'

'I know.' Ava looked as though she might say something more, then stopped herself.

So there is more to all of this, Rhona thought, determined to get Magnus on his own to ask him.

The moment arrived when he indicated he was about to serve up the meal. 'You know your way around my kitchen, Dr MacLeod. Would you like to help?'

Rhona nodded and swiftly followed him through, where he shut the door behind her.

'I heard you two talking earlier, what's going on?' Rhona immediately asked.

'Ava, Erling and I all went to sixth form with a boy called Ben Bradley. We were less than pleasant to him when he arrived at the school. He might be your Erik,' he said, before briefly describing a drunken party at Skaill Bay twenty years before where Erling and Ben had almost got into a fight. Something that was obviously worrying all three of them.

'Erling says the image is definitely not Ben,' Magnus told her. 'Ava has seen it via the *Orcadian* and thinks it could be. I won't see it until tomorrow,' he finished.

'That was the argument I overheard?' Rhona said, still unsure she'd got the whole story.

Magnus seemed to consider his answer for a moment before he admitted that it wasn't.

'That part was about Ingrid Donaldson, a friend of Dougie Clouston, Ava's brother. Ingrid is apparently convinced that Ben Bradley is her birth father and wants Erling to have a DNA test run to prove if that's the case.'

Magnus halted there, his face clouding over – with what? Anger, disappointment, fear?

'What is it, Magnus?' Rhona demanded.

'Ava wants me to agree to a paternity test too.'

'You, but why?' Rhona said, perturbed.

'That night twenty years ago on the beach at Skaill Bay, when the fight happened, I was there with Ingrid's mother, Shona Bain.'

'You had sex with her that night?' Rhona said.

'I did, but we weren't an item and I didn't see her again. We all left the island after that summer, including Shona. It was only when Ingrid turned up at the police station to tell Erling the body might be her father that I even knew Shona was back and with a daughter.'

'What do you plan to do?' Rhona asked gently.

'I want to speak to Shona myself, because of this.' He pulled out his mobile and, selecting an image, handed it over.

'This is Ingrid, taken recently by Ava.'

The girl stood next to Dougie. Tall, her long blonde hair framing an open and striking face, she wore a determined smile.

'You think that's your daughter?' Rhona said quietly.

'I don't know, but I'd like to find out,' Magnus said.

30

Orkney

Morning had dawned windy and wet, which wasn't unusual for McNab, coming from Glasgow. Although Glasgow was more often wet than windy.

Rising, he'd showered and drunk a double espresso before going downstairs to sample breakfast. Having helped himself to a portion of everything available, he headed for a window seat and proceeded to demolish the eggs, bacon, tattie scones, haggis, black pudding and sausage piled on his plate.

A young woman brought him coffee and they exchanged a few pleasantries, before she asked if he was the detective from Glasgow and whether he'd seen today's *Orcadian*.

'I am the detective from Glasgow,' he confirmed, and told her he hadn't seen the *Orcadian* as yet. At which she promptly fetched him a copy, and there was the AI-generated image filling most of the front page.

A quick glance at the words alongside proved them to be by investigative journalist and Orcadian Ava Clouston, whose true crime podcast *The Dead and the Dying* was covering the story online.

McNab cursed himself inwardly at this. Although Ava had clearly mentioned the podcast yesterday evening, he hadn't checked it out before going to sleep. And he should definitely do so before reporting for duty this morning.

'Have you listened to the podcast?' he checked with the young waitress called Katrin, who, she'd informed him, was considering joining the police herself.

'I have,' she said. 'It's really good. Episode one sets it all up with the attempted rescue of the whales at Skaill Bay, then episode two is about the discovery of the actual body in its stone cist,' she told him. 'Oh, and there was a taster put up last night, about recent police activity spotted at Evie Sands.'

McNab inwardly groaned at this, before saying, 'Then I'd better have a listen.'

When Katrin departed to go and serve another guest, McNab went in search of *The Dead and Dying* podcast, puts his headphones in and settled down to listen.

The title for the investigation, Ava explained at the onset, had been inspired by the images from that fateful night, and the testimonies of the volunteers who had tried so hard to keep the whales alive.

Listening to the voices of some of those present that night painted a visual horror of the proceedings, and despite McNab's annoyance and concern about the dissemination of information to the general public, he couldn't help but admire how truthful it strove to be. This wasn't sensationalist clickbait, but honest reporting.

The second episode featured the discovery of the body in its stone cist buried in the sand dunes and its subsequent removal. Both Rhona and Colin were revealed in their professional capacity, but, he noted, no mention was made of the existence of the torc bracelet. So Ava was definitely following police protocol on that.

As for the taster for episode three, it mentioned that locals had reported seeing police activity at the Sands of Evie. That was all she knew at present, but would update listeners as she learned more.

McNab now turned back to the article in this morning's *Orcadian* with Erik's face staring out at him. For some reason he looked even more real than the image on the video screen in the strategy room.

'Who are you, Erik?' he muttered under his breath. 'And who put you in the ground?'

He wondered how many Orkney folk were asking themselves that very same question this morning, and which of them would pick up the phone to call Kirkwall police station to tell them who they thought it might be.

How many, if any at all, would mention the name Ben Bradley?

Swallowing the remainder of his coffee, McNab rose and, waving goodbye to Katrin, set off for the police station.

Instead of taking the route Flett had suggested the previous night, McNab turned right, intent on walking through the old town. The rain had ceased and, in the narrow flagstoned thoroughfare, he was sheltered from the wind.

Too early for most shops to be open, there were nevertheless a few folk about, and whether it was his imagination or not, he felt his own presence being noted.

Thinking about the torc bracelet found in the stone coffin of the first victim, he paused before each of the shop windows advertising locally made jewellery. Although there were Viking-styled bracelets, none looked like the heavy handcrafted one they'd found in the stone cist. According to Flett, they'd had no luck as yet in tracing its maker.

Walking the length of the narrow flagstone street, he found Erik's face staring out at him from every newspaper stand. Surely such exposure locally, plus on social media, would provoke some response about his possible identity? Ava too had urged her listeners to contact the police with any information they might have.

As St Magnus Cathedral appeared, he made a right turn, aware he would have to double back to the police station. He was passing the impressive Library and Archive building, and pondering why their forecourt was scattered with an array of large stone balls, when his mobile rang.

Checking the screen, he registered it was in fact Erling's number, and wondered if in his wanderings he'd made himself late.

'Where are you, Sergeant?'

'Minutes from the front door of the station,' McNab said, upping his pace.

'I'll meet you outside.'

This response from DI Flett led him to believe they might be going somewhere other than a strategy meeting.

He was right. Entering the car park, he found Flett waiting next to a police vehicle.

'Get in, Sergeant. We're heading for Evie.'

'Can I ask why?' McNab said as he buckled up in the passenger seat.

'When Dr MacLeod and Professor Nelson arrived to begin work on the grave this morning, they found PC Ivan Tulloch, who was guarding the locus last night, lying unconscious. He's currently in hospital.'

'He was attacked?' McNab said. 'Who would do that and why?'

'According to Dr MacLeod, they also attempted to wreck the locus,' Flett said worriedly.

'I didn't think Orkney had a problem with vandalism,' McNab said.

'We have our fair share of hooligans on Orkney like every-where else,' Flett told him. 'But what appears to be an attack on a police officer so as to carry out the carnage is not the norm,' he said grimly. 'And why choose to wreck an actual crime scene?'

'They didn't want it excavated in the first place?' McNab said, then after a moment of thought added, 'Maybe because they feared what might be discovered there?'

While Flett considered this explanation, McNab's brain went into overdrive.

'Assuming the perpetrator is still alive, they will no doubt have been following with interest any reports on what's been happening at Skaill Bay. Maybe even listening in to Ava Clouston's podcast.' He halted there in order to marshal his thoughts before continuing.

'Maybe they believed that nothing uncovered at Skaill Bay could possibly lead us to them. Then got freaked out when we somehow identified a second locus at the Sands of Evie,' he finished as Flett drew up next to the UHI van.

Their arrival had obviously been spotted because the suited figures of Rhona and Colin were coming towards them.

As they got closer, McNab could immediately tell by Rhona's expression how concerned and upset she was by what had happened.

'Any word on PC Tulloch?' she immediately asked.

197

'He's conscious, but not yet able to give a proper statement as to what he remembers,' Flett said. 'What about the site?'

'Whoever attacked PC Tulloch removed the tarpaulin, exposing the area to the weather,' Rhona told him. 'It appears they made an attempt to unearth the skeleton and some of the bones have been scattered. Colin and I have been collecting and identifying them,' she said. 'Since we've not been able to locate the skull, we have to assume they took that with them.' She looked even more distressed by this. 'I wanted to exhume the skeleton in its entirety, so as not to miss anything. I wish now we'd taken away what little we'd already exposed last night.'

'You had no reason to suspect that this would happen,' Flett said firmly. 'Plus I'd placed an officer on duty overnight – though I likely should have had two . . .'

'I called Ivan last night as soon as we got to the Ivy House,' Rhona said. 'He said all was well and not to worry.'

'When we get to talk to PC Tulloch, we'll hopefully get a better idea of what actually happened,' Erling offered.

'Maybe whoever did this was after the skull,' McNab said. 'Possibly because they didn't want the same job done on its AI reconstruction as happened with the Skaill Bay victim.' Then a thought occurred. 'The image went online at midnight and is in the print press this morning. So there's a good chance whoever did this saw it,' he added.

'Well, they've failed on that score,' Rhona said. 'I took photographs and 3D video footage of the skull from all angles. Plus there were amalgam fillings this time, which I noted and also photographed,' she added.

'Male or female, would you say?' McNab asked.

'By the forehead size and eye sockets I'd hazard a guess at

male,' Rhona told him. 'When we've retrieved all the bones, we'll rebuild him, and DNA testing will prove me right or wrong on that,' she added.

'Is this burial more recent than the one at Skaill Bay?' McNab asked.

Colin glanced at Rhona before saying, 'We believe so.'

'How long has he been in the ground?' McNab said.

'In these soil conditions, perhaps a decade, but we'll confirm that once we get him back together.'

'What about age? Any clues about that from what you've seen so far?' Flett said.

'Again, this would need to be verified by the forensic pathologist, but from my initial study of the skull, I noted that the third molars were coming through, which normally happens somewhere between the ages of seventeen and twenty-one.'

'Which, if true, suggests we may have a perp who's targeting young males,' McNab said. 'And he's still out there, and likely still plying his trade.'

31

Orkney

They worked steadily through the occasional showers both heavy and light. In between these, when the sky cleared, the sun seemed to seek out the burial site and its surroundings as though trying to help them locate the scattered remains.

Colin and Rhona walked in tandem, heads down, eyes scouring the ground, foraging among the dead grasses, hoping every slight change in colour or texture might reveal another bone.

When success did occur, and a bone was identified, the bone chart was updated.

The desecration of the grave continued to hang heavily on Rhona, as she suspected it also did with Colin. No matter what Erling had said, Rhona knew that the responsibility for the grave, and more specifically its victim, lay with her.

And she had failed in protecting both.

The fact that she'd called Ivan last night showed that it had been playing on her mind.

In circumstances where the scene could be protected by a forensic tent and work might be done by arc lights, she would have remained with the body until they'd retrieved all of the remains.

But this was windy Orkney, where forensic tents simply blew away.

Rising with a groan, she registered yet another squall currently playing out over Rousay and likely heading their way.

'Time for coffee in the van,' Colin shouted, 'until that' – he gestured at the blackening sky – 'passes.'

Reaching the van just in time, they watched the rain peppering Eynhallow Sound on its swift way towards them. Colin, seemingly unfazed, poured her a hot coffee from a tartan flask and handed her a bannock.

'Cheese and home-made pickle okay?'

'More than okay,' she said with a grateful smile. 'It's usually Chrissy, my forensic assistant, that supplies the food.'

'I'm delighted to fill in for her,' Colin said. 'But I bet she wishes she was here?'

'More than you can imagine,' Rhona told him. 'But she's still processing the forensic material from the first burial. In fact it was the tiny grains of sand that Chrissy extracted from the torc that brought us here.'

The squall having passed, a low sun broke through again.

'How much daylight do you estimate we have left?' Rhona said.

'Another hour of half-decent light, then we're done,' Colin told her. 'Anyway, we're nearly there with the bone chart and we've bagged most of the disturbed soil. We'll be able to examine all of this and piece the skeleton together again at the UHI lab. What shall we call this one? I'd rather we gave him a name,' he added. 'I like to do that with the Vikings I unearth.'

'Then you choose the name this time,' Rhona said.

Colin nodded thoughtfully. 'I'll have to think about it,' he said.

A police car appeared on the track as they were beginning to pack their findings in the back of the UHI van. This time, Rhona noted, the vehicle held DS Green and a constable.

'Well timed,' Colin said, as they both climbed out. 'We believe we've retrieved what we can from the gravesite.'

'The tarpaulin's on again?' DS Green said.

'It is and Colin's helpers will be back tomorrow to make sure we haven't missed anything,' Rhona told her.

'DI Flett wants a guard on it tonight again,' DS Green said. 'That'll be PC Gowan and myself,' she added. 'Until two a.m., after which someone else will take over.'

'Hope you've plenty of hot coffee and food?' Colin checked.

'We're well supplied,' DS Green assured him.

The sun was already dipping as the UHI vehicle climbed the long, low hill towards the main road.

'We'll unload, then back to the Ivy House for a shower and food . . . and drink,' Colin told her. Glancing round at Rhona, he added, 'What happened last night wasn't your fault.'

Rhona accepted this without comment, well aware that it didn't and wouldn't alter her thoughts on the matter.

'The desecration of a grave is as much a crime as the taking of a life,' Colin said. 'Whether in Viking times or now. All the more reason we will do everything in our forensic power to point the police towards the culprit.'

Acknowledging this, Rhona said, 'That we will,' with a determined smile.

On entering Kirkwall, she asked if she might be dropped at the hospital. 'I'd like to check on Ivan Tulloch.'

'Okay,' Colin said. 'I'll take the material to the lab and return for you later.'

'I think I'd like to walk back,' Rhona told him. 'It's not far.'

Noting her resolve, he readily accepted this. 'Then I'll see you at the Ivy House.'

Minutes later, she was entering the hospital and asking at the desk about PC Tulloch.

'Are you a relative, miss?' the receptionist asked.

'No. My name's Dr Rhona MacLeod and Ivan knows me. We've worked here and on Sanday together.'

A light dawned in the woman's eyes. 'DI Flett said you might call in. You're the forensic scientist from Glasgow?'

'I am,' Rhona confirmed.

'Very good. Well, PC Tulloch's on the mend, I'm glad to say. That picture of the poor lad you found at Skaill Bay is on the front of the *Orcadian* today. What a terrible thing to have happened here on Orkney. And now Ivan attacked out at Evie.' She shook her head in disbelief, before giving Rhona instructions on how to find PC Tulloch.

Ivan was sitting up in bed, a large bandage round his head. He had the news playing on the nearby television and was listening with interest.

As she drew closer, Rhona noted that there was an image of Erik on the screen and the announcer was asking for anyone recognizing the man in the image to contact the police immediately.

Realizing who was standing at the foot of his bed, Ivan turned the TV off.

'Dr MacLeod, what are you doing here?' he said in a shamefaced manner.

'I came to see you, of course, before I have Chrissie McInsh on the phone demanding to know why I let this happen to you.'

Ivan reddened a little at this. 'Chrissy's okay?' he said.

'Yes, and asking after you. She's got a rescue dog now, name of Rocket, who is in the habit of taking off like a rocket and having everyone out looking for him.' Rhona halted there to give him an appraising look. 'How about you, Constable?'

His hand went automatically to his bandaged head. 'Fine, Dr MacLeod. How I let someone creep up on me, I don't know. There was a wind and rain, of course. I'd just stepped out of the vehicle to—' He halted there, obviously embarrassed.

'To relieve yourself,' Rhona finished for him.

'Yes. And the next thing I remember was coming to in the ambulance.'

'So you didn't get sight of your attacker?' Rhona said.

He indicated not. 'How the hell he got so close, I don't know. Last thing I remember is being pushed and going down hard. That's when I hit my head on a stone, I think.'

'So you never saw headlights on the road?'

'No. He must have walked in.'

'What about by water?' Rhona said, wondering if that was also the way the second victim had arrived.

'I suppose that's possible,' Ivan said. 'Anyway, I feel a fool, Dr MacLeod. And your crime scene. I'm really sorry about that.' He looked rueful. 'I heard they took the skull.'

'They did, but not before I'd captured it on video,' she told him.

That brightened him up.

'So you can give it a face like the first one?' he asked.

'Not me, but an AI program, which doesn't appear to have a name as yet,' Rhona said. 'Or not one that I've been told.'

They chatted on for a little while, before Rhona said her goodbyes.

'I'll be out of here tomorrow,' Ivan told her in a determined fashion. 'You can tell Chrissy that if she asks.'

Rhona promised him she would.

Arriving in the centre of Kirkwall, Rhona decided the next conversation she wanted to have was with McNab, and hopefully alone, which wouldn't be possible at tomorrow's strategy meeting, so she should try now.

Her call to his mobile was quickly answered and his response to her question regarding his whereabouts was equally fast.

'I'm in the bar at the Kirkwall Hotel, where I've ordered a drink and plan to have dinner. Why not join me, Dr MacLeod?'

Rhona decided she would, but first she would call Colin and let him know that she was eating out.

32

Orkney

McNab looks well on the Orkney air, Rhona mused as she took a seat opposite him. She didn't tell him this, of course, because he wouldn't like it. Instead, she asked him to give her the full story behind his deployment to Orkney.

'I'll order another drink before I do that,' he said with a half-smile. 'And what would you like, Dr MacLeod?'

'A dry white wine,' she told him.

'Small, medium or large?'

'How long is your story?' she asked.

'Medium to large,' he offered.

'Okay, make it a large. Provided we're ordering some food soon.'

'I plan on fish and chips, same as last night, and excellent,' McNab said.

'Then I'll have that too,' Rhona told him.

Watching him head for the bar, she decided that despite the fact he obviously didn't want to be here, things had definitely improved since his first visit to the Evie locus with Erling. So what had happened between then and now?

Back from ordering, he settled down opposite her and lifted his glass in a toast.

'Here's to you, Dr MacLeod, who, together with your excellent assistant, Chrissy McInsh, will forensically solve this case.'

Rhona savoured her wine, but didn't respond to the toast.

'So,' she said instead, 'let's hear the whole story of your defection from Glasgow to Kirkwall.'

He took a moment before answering, then said, 'DI Flett asked for my presence here on Orkney with regard to the Skaill Bay case.'

Now that was a surprise. 'Do you know why?' Rhona asked.

'Well, it began with his request to the boss that we try to locate the Bradley family who were resident in Orkney twenty years ago,' he said. 'Remember we spoke about it that night at the jazz club? Janice wondered back then why Flett wanted to make contact with their son Ben Bradley, who, it turned out, he'd gone to school with.'

'I do remember,' Rhona said.

'As you know, Janice and I had no idea initially why we were looking for Ben. Then Flett sent me a school photograph, with the boss's approval. He wanted the AI program – which Ollie now calls Orak, because of some old TV programme he discovered online – to compare the identikit image to a real photo of this Ben guy. Anyway, he said he thought the AI image wasn't Ben, but wanted Orak to confirm.'

'And did Orak do that?' Rhona asked.

'Oh, Orak did agree with Flett on that. Said there was no match. Trouble is, Ollie disagreed. He said your Skaill Bay guy *is* Ben Bradley. And I'm inclined to believe Ollie.'

He continued. 'So there's a good chance if, as you say, the body's been in Skaill Bay for close to a couple of decades, and it is this Ben Bradley, that Flett will need to step back from the investigation, and he wants me to head it up as acting DI,' he finished, the surprise on his face obvious.

Rhona was thinking about the previous evening at Seaview and Magnus's explanation about his argument with Ava.

'What?' McNab demanded.

'You know Ava Clouston's here, don't you?' she asked.

'I do. I met with her last night at her request.'

'Really, why?' Rhona said.

'She sought me out to tell me how mean they'd all been to Ben Bradley when he arrived in the sixth form at Kirkwall Grammar School. All about some wild party they had at Skaill Bay, where Flett and Bradley had an altercation of sorts.'

'So you know all about that?' Rhona said.

'As, it seems, do you.' McNab raised an eyebrow.

Rhona explained about her arrival the previous evening at Seaview and the heated discussion that was going on in the house.

'Let me guess,' McNab said. 'Ava asked Magnus to check he wasn't the father of this Ingrid girl.' He observed her reaction. 'I take it this is where our two stories collide?'

'Looks like it,' Rhona said. 'Are there any other updates we should share?'

'One, I think,' McNab told her. 'Ben Bradley's parents have apparently gone on holiday. To Majorca, the neighbour thinks. And Annie Bradley's not answering her phone.'

'So no hope of a DNA sample from her for comparison with the victim?' Rhona said.

'Nope.' McNab glanced up with a smile as a young woman arrived with their meals.

'Katrin,' McNab said. 'Meet the famous forensic scientist Dr Rhona MacLeod. Rhona, meet Katrin, who keeps me up to date with what folk around here know, about you, me and, more importantly, the current investigation.'

The girl looked a mixture of embarrassed and flattered by his introduction.

'So what's the news on the street, then?' McNab said.

'That the grave at Evie was defiled and the skull's missing,' she said.

McNab looked to Rhona. 'News travels fast around here.'

'And Ivan Tulloch's in hospital, but he's okay now,' Katrin said, sounding relieved.

'You know Ivan?' said Rhona.

The girl nodded.

'Any ideas on who attacked PC Tulloch?' McNab asked.

'No, but folk think that whoever it was likely came to Evie by boat,' she said.

'Why do they think that?' Rhona asked.

'There were no lights seen on the road to the Sands of Evie,' she said firmly.

'What about lights on the water?' Rhona tried.

'A boat can come in there without lights, if they know the place well enough,' Katrin told her.

'So you think someone local attacked PC Tulloch and took the skull?' McNab said.

'Or someone who knows Orkney well.'

McNab smiled his thanks. 'Anything else you want to tell me' – he handed her his card – 'just give me a call.'

'Will do,' she promised with a satisfied smile.

When she'd left, McNab set about his meal. 'Eat up,' he

told Rhona. 'We'll discuss my local informant and other things after.'

The plates now taken away by someone other than Katrin, and two more drinks served, Rhona asked what had been the response to the published photograph.

'Big,' he said. 'The local calls are being dealt with here, and the lines have been busy all day. Folk are taking this task seriously. Outwith Orkney, the calls are being dealt with in Glasgow, where they have the manpower.'

'Anyone suggesting the Skaill Bay victim is Ben Bradley?'

'We'll hear the details tomorrow morning at the strategy meeting. I'm assuming you'll be there?' McNab said.

Rhona nodded. 'Colin will begin reassembling the second victim at the UHI lab, and two of his people will go out to the Evie site to tidy up.'

'Any idea how victim number two was killed?' McNab said.

'The skull and neck area were intact. No blunt force trauma. I suspect we'll not find any injury on the skeletal remains we've just retrieved.'

'Which suggests the two deaths are similar?' McNab said.

'They look that way. Plus Chrissy found a tiny phial when she sieved the sand from Skaill Bay,' Rhona told him.

'A drug of some sort?'

'She's running tests on it. She's also retrieved DNA samples from a fragment of plastic caught in the initials on the torc and bits of a cable tie.'

'So we have DNA to run through the database?'

'We do.'

'And what's your scenario of what went down at both Evie and Skaill, Dr MacLeod?'

It had been the question she'd been asking herself from

the moment she and Colin had slid open the capstone at Skaill Bay and met the escaping scent of decomposition.

She now put her thoughts into words.

'I think a young male was brought to each locus, hands bound and mouth taped. There they were injected with a substance that rendered them unconscious. The fastenings were cut off and they were stripped naked. At Skaill the victim was laid in the cist, previously emptied of the Viking remains Colin found in the surrounding sand. The tape and cable tie were thrown away too and the lid shut and covered with sand.'

The effect of her re-enactment was obvious on McNab's face. 'And the drug used?'

Rhona had also thought about this in advance of Chrissy's testing of the phial.

'Probably ketamine, available two decades ago, used widely by farmers for anaesthesia. And available over the counter too. It came in small phials like the one Chrissy found.'

'And even easier to get since,' McNab said.

33

Orkney

Both mother and daughter were sitting in reception even at the early hour of his own arrival at the station.

Erling, caught off-guard at seeing them there, was momentarily at a loss for words.

Thankfully the desk sergeant helped him out by explaining that Mrs Donaldson and her daughter, Ingrid, had asked to speak to him personally.

'It's regarding the identikit picture on the front page of the *Orcadian*, sir,' he finished with.

Erling managed to rally himself and, thanking the sergeant, asked the two women to please follow him into his office, which they duly did.

Setting out a couple of chairs, he took his own place behind his desk, feeling like a barrier between them and him might be a good thing.

Ingrid, even seated, was obviously taller than her mother. Dressed like before, this time her blonde hair was tied loosely back. Nothing about her reminded him of Ben

Bradley, and surely if the girl had studied the school photograph she would see that.

'You wanted to speak to me about the identikit picture?' he said.

Ingrid gave her mother a look, which obviously demanded that she should be the one to speak.

So she did.

'Ingrid would like to be allowed to give a DNA sample to be sure that the man in the photo is not her father,' Shona said, obvious pain in her voice. 'I'd like to give my permission for that to happen,' she added.

'Okay,' Erling found himself saying. 'If you're sure?'

It was Ingrid who spoke this time. 'I'm sure,' she said firmly. 'And I want to know about the torc bracelet in the school photo I brought you.'

Erling nodded. 'Yes, you should be told about that. I requested the photograph be examined by experts and the result was that the bracelet you saw is unlikely to be the one found in the grave.'

Ingrid didn't look convinced by that, but thankfully didn't argue.

At this point, Erling used the intercom to ask that DS Green come to his office immediately.

'My detective sergeant will organize the DNA sample,' he explained.

Minutes later, the pregnant silence was ended by Jo's welcome arrival.

Without explaining the whys and wherefores, Erling asked her to please take Ingrid to the medical room and obtain a DNA sample.

When the door closed behind them, Shona said a heartfelt thanks. 'No matter what I've said about her parentage, and believe me I have stressed that Ben wasn't her father, she wouldn't let it rest until this was done,' she explained.

Erling waited, certain by her expression that there was more to come.

Eventually it arrived. 'I also wanted to speak to you about the photo in the *Orcadian*,' Shona said.

'And?' Erling hoped his expression didn't convey his own thoughts on this.

'I believe it is Ben,' she finally said. 'Don't you?'

'No,' he told her honestly. 'I don't, but I had it run through the new AI recognition program in Glasgow using our school photograph as a comparator.'

'And?' she said, waiting.

'The program said it wasn't a match for Ben.' As he watched her absorb this with some relief, he quickly followed with, 'However, an expert human super recognizer did the same comparison and he said he thought they were a match.'

'So what's the decision?' she demanded. 'Is it Ben or not?'

'We made contact with Ben's mother and stepfather earlier in Glasgow. However, they have since gone to Majorca and we haven't managed to make contact there as yet to ask Ben's mother for a DNA sample for comparison,' Erling told her.

Shona's face twisted with anger. 'I told you Ben's stepfather was a homophobic bastard. God, what if he had something to do with Ben's disappearance?'

'Annie Bradley said Ben went to London to live after he visited you in Orkney,' Erling explained. 'He kept in touch for a while and seemed happy in his new life, then went off the radar. She tried to report him missing, but . . .' He tailed off.

'The police didn't fancy looking for him?' she said angrily.

'D'you know how many young men walk out on their lives by choice?' Erling said. 'If they don't want to be found—' He halted there.

Shona shook her head in a determined fashion. 'Ben loved his mum. He said she understood him. He wasn't afraid of her. I think he would have stayed in touch with her whatever it took,' she said. 'No, some bastard got him. In London, I'll bet.'

'But if that's true, why bring him to Orkney to kill him?' Erling said.

'You're the detective,' she was saying as the door opened and Jo and Ingrid walked in.

'Well?' Ingrid looked to her mum. 'Did you tell him that you thought the picture on the front of the *Orcadian* was Ben Bradley?'

Shona nodded. 'I did. And you got what you wanted. A DNA test.' She rose. 'Now I want to go home.'

At a glance from Erling, Jo offered to show them the way out.

Minutes later, she was back again. 'Want to tell me what that was all about?' she said.

'I'll explain at the strategy meeting, which is' – he checked his watch – 'starting shortly. Has Dr MacLeod arrived yet?'

'She's just got here,' Jo confirmed.

'Then can you ask DS McNab to come through. I'd like a word with him before we start the meeting.'

Erling watched as Jo exited and closed the door behind her. His detective sergeant was wise enough to understand the situation he now found himself in. As did McNab. The question was, what was he going to do about it?

He'd spent the previous evening ruminating on it. After,

that is, he'd tried unsuccessfully to make contact with Rory again. What he would have given to talk things over with his partner.

But were they still partners? he wondered. It wasn't that unusual for Rory to be off-grid during a job, but something felt wrong about it this time. Or maybe it was merely tainted by his memory of the torc bracelet he thought he'd once seen Rory wearing.

His thoughts on that got no further before the door opened and McNab walked in.

'Detective Sergeant,' Erling said. 'There's something we need to discuss before the meeting.'

McNab nodded. 'Yes, sir.'

Erling, studying the man who he'd chosen to replace him, found himself pleased with his decision. The rapport between DS McNab and Dr MacLeod was obvious. It seemed to him they fed off one another. Though he knew their relationship had been spiky in the past, there was no doubt that as a pair they were impressive in an investigation.

'I've spoken again to Detective Inspector Wilson and, as agreed earlier with him, you will assume the role of acting DI on this case while in Orkney.'

McNab's expression didn't change at this announcement.

'Until we know for certain that the Skaill Bay victim is Ben Bradley, you and I will work together on this case. I'm about to announce this at the meeting, Inspector.'

'Right, sir.'

'So no more "sirs" are required, Inspector McNab.' Erling walked to the door and opened it. 'Let's go meet our team.'

34

Orkney

The teenager she'd just seen exiting the police station had been easily recognizable as the girl in the photograph Magnus had shown her, Rhona thought, as she made her own way upstairs to the meeting room.

Rhona wondered then if Magnus had already approached Shona regarding her possible parentage. She wondered too why both mother and daughter had been at the police station and at so early an hour.

It was at this point McNab entered the room alongside Erling and came to stand next to her.

'What's going on in that head of yours, Dr MacLeod?' he said.

'I just saw Ingrid Donaldson leaving the station with her mother,' she told him. 'I wondered why they were here.'

'That's easy,' McNab said. 'She came in for a DNA test. Plus her mother wanted to register the fact that she recognized the identikit image as Ben Bradley.'

A double whammy for Erling, Rhona thought, before adding, 'And you saw the girl?'

'I did and you're right, she could well be Magnus's daughter. Or the daughter of any one of the other Viking-type men on these islands,' he added. 'Or maybe a visiting Swedish student or holidaymaker. There's no way of knowing for definite unless through DNA. But, then again, I don't need to tell you that, Dr MacLeod.'

His tone being decidedly cheerful, Rhona wondered why.

'Right,' he said, before she could ask. 'I'm off to the front with DI Flett.'

Spotting Magnus, Rhona wove her way through the crowd towards him. There was no time to greet him, however, except with a smile, before Erling began to address the assembled company.

By his demeanour, Rhona wondered if Erling might have made the decision he'd long been wrestling with.

In the following minutes, she realized she was right, as Erling revealed to his team that acting Detective Inspector McNab would be working alongside him on the current investigation, before explaining the reason for this.

'There have been a number of rumours circulating suggesting the Skaill Bay victim may be a Ben Bradley,' he began, 'who came to live in Orkney just short of two decades ago and became a sixth former at Kirkwall Grammar School at the same time as myself.

'I can therefore confirm there was a Ben Bradley, who joined our sixth-year group from down south.'

He continued. 'At this time and place, despite our best efforts, we have not yet proven or disproven whether the victim is in fact Ben Bradley. I therefore sent DI McNab a school photograph for comparison purposes, using the AI program that produced our identikit image.

'The result of this was that the program declared them not to be a match.'

As a ripple of sound filled the room, he went on. 'Whereas,' he stressed, 'the current resident human super recognizer in Glasgow, with years of experience and success, pronounced that he believed they *were* the same person.'

The waves of murmurs at this grew, and understandably, Rhona thought.

Erling waited for the noise to die down before he revealed his request to DI McNab to locate Ben's family in Glasgow, his success in doing so, and the discovery that Ben had left home shortly after the family's departure from Orkney and had, according to his mother, gone to live in London.

'Although they lost touch soon after,' he continued. 'We've tried to contact his mother, Annie, to ask her to give a DNA sample, to eliminate Ben from our enquiries. However, both she and Ben's stepfather are reported as having gone on holiday, possibly to Majorca, and Annie Bradley is not answering her phone.

'Subsequently, in view of my history with our probable victim, I spoke with DI McNab's commanding officer and requested that DI McNab, who I've worked with previously, join us here as Senior Investigating Officer on this investigation.'

Rhona caught Jo's eye at this moment and was pleased to see her approval at the announcement.

Erling continued. 'As you are aware, DI McNab's arrival also coincided with the discovery of a second victim at the Sands of Evie. The investigation there by Dr MacLeod and Professor Nelson was prompted by forensic work done on the torc bracelet, which uncovered grains of sand in the ornamental swirls in the metal, identified as coming from this area.

'At this point I'm going to ask Dr MacLeod to give us an update on her forensic findings and perhaps an indication of her thoughts on how the first victim died.'

Magnus threw her an encouraging look as Rhona made her way to the front.

Looking out at the sea of faces, she registered the intensity of their expressions. Not one murder victim but two, found in a small community such as this, had had a profound effect on everyone, but especially on those with the task of identifying and apprehending the perpetrator.

She began with a description of the first locus and the subsequent discovery of victim one, using photographs and video clips they might not have seen as yet.

Then followed the forensic examination of the fragments of tape, together with the cable tie.

And, finally, she brought up the image of the phial sifted by Chrissy from what must have felt like a mountain of sand removed from the locus.

'My forensic assistant,' Rhona said, 'is currently testing the phial, which we believe held a drug used to render the victim unconscious, before they were stripped naked and laid in the stone cist.'

'Ketamine,' someone called out. 'That's a ketamine phial.'

Although this was yet to be established, Rhona acknowledged the likelihood of that: ketamine injections would have been readily available at that time, particularly in the farming community in Orkney.

She continued. 'I believe on the evidence so far that the victim was abducted and taken to Skaill Bay, or perhaps went willingly with someone they knew and trusted. The

220

existence of the fragments of insulation tape and cable tie suggest they were bound at some point in the proceedings, which may have been sexual and consensual. After which a dose of a tranquillizing drug was injected.

'The victim was placed in the cist as you can see from the photographs, in a form similar to those found in Viking burials in the area. The victim was likely wearing the torc at this time, which eventually fell from his wrist as the body decomposed. The capstone was used to seal the grave, which was then covered with sand.'

Rhona now referenced Chrissy's work on the torc, with a slide showing the tiny sand granules multiplied in size to emphasize their shape and colour.

'These are what led us to the Sands of Evie, where a second grave was identified, with the help of Professor Nelson and Professor Pirie.'

Her video and stills of the second grave now appeared on-screen, together with those of the missing skull and the silver torc necklace.

'The perpetrator prepared this grave by peeling back the surface vegetation like a blanket, so that it could be easily re-laid afterwards. Flat stones were then inserted to produce the shape of a ship's bow. After the body was laid inside, the curtain of vegetation was drawn over it once again. Any decomposing body will change the nature of the overlying growth. It will also sink a little.

'As I understand it, livestock burial can produce similar patterns, but when the area identified was rodded, Professor Pirie, who has a highly developed sense of smell, believed we should investigate the area for human remains.

'I've already sent the skull video recordings to Glasgow for the AI reconstruction of the second victim's head. So we should have a portrait soon. I also expect our second victim will prove to be a young male,' she finished.

A hand went up. 'Any idea how long the second body's been there?' an officer asked.

'Not as yet,' Rhona said.

McNab now followed, with an update on the results of the front-page appeal in the *Orcadian*, confirming that a number of former pupils at Kirkwall Grammar had got in touch regarding the image, with at least a third of them suggesting that it might be Ben Bradley.

'As you're aware,' he said, 'gossip about such a possibility is circulating widely, mostly fuelled by a current pupil at the school. We are dealing with this in an appropriate manner. All suggestions as to who it might be are being recorded, both here and in Glasgow, where they are dealing with the social media responses. Police Scotland has had a great deal of success in locating more recent cases of missing people via online appeals. This one, however, is a couple of decades old. Nevertheless, we remain hopeful.'

Erling took back over then and spoke of the attack on PC Tulloch at Evie and the subsequent desecration of the grave and removal of the skull.

'Reports from residents indicate that no vehicle lights were seen in the vicinity,' he said. 'I'm inclined to believe this. Since the exhumation began, locals have watched the proceedings from afar via binoculars and telescopes, and on one occasion a drone, the owner of which has been located and questioned.

'That leaves us with the possibility that whoever attacked PC Tulloch may have arrived by water. However, the modus operandi of our perpetrator does not appear to square with what took place at Evie. At this point I'd like to ask Magnus Pirie, Professor of Criminal Psychology, to come up and talk us through the mind and actions of our killer.'

Magnus arrived at the front, his tall figure easily visible. Rhona knew what he was about to say, but still found his voice in its summation on the mind of their killer mesmerizing.

'Firstly, I would stress that the perpetrator, as DI Flett suggests, is an organized killer,' Magnus said. 'Nothing they do is random. Hence, neither the death at Skaill Bay nor Evie were spur-of-the-moment decisions, unlike the attack on the Evie grave.'

He continued. 'Now, to remind you of the terminology that strives to understand a killer's motivations and actions, we must first consider their modus operandi.

'The modus operandi, or the operating mode of a killer, typically includes any actions that are necessary for the completion of the crime. In both our cases, the killer needed to capture his prey either mentally, or physically, or both. He needed then to transfer them to the burial site, either before or after their death. For this to work he would have chosen the site already, and also prepared it for the burial as Dr MacLeod has outlined.

'At Skaill Bay, I believe it likely they discovered the original Viking grave, possibly by chance, and decided to make use of it to fit their fantasy. I think they knew there were other Viking burials in that area, which you can of course find details of online. It was an ideal place for all this to play out.

'Now let's take a look at the signature,' he said. 'The signature describes any actions that are unnecessary, and are there only to serve the emotional and psychological gratification of our killer.

'That, I suggest, would be the Viking nature of the burial, the nakedness of the victim and how they were laid out in the grave. It would also include the Viking jewellery left in the cist.'

Rhona raised her hand at this point. 'Both items of jewellery had initials engraved on them, which may also be a part of the killer's signature,' she said.

'I agree,' Magnus said, bringing up an image of both items of jewellery on the screen, enlarged so that the initials were now obvious.

'As you can see, the bracelet has either an E M or a B M engraved on it. As for the necklace, it is quite clearly an L M,' he said.

McNab came in then. 'I believe the second initial may refer to our perp. The first initial to his victim. If Ben Bradley turns out to be the first victim, then it's definitely a B M on the bracelet.'

'Any luck identifying the source of these items of jewellery?' Rhona asked.

'That's an ongoing task,' Erling told her. 'In fact we've recently received information on a possible local craftsman for the bracelet, who has been off island for a time, which will be followed up later this morning.' He gestured at DS Green, who acknowledged this.

When no more questions were forthcoming, Erling wound up the meeting after encouraging his team back to work.

Exiting alongside Rhona, he asked how long they could hope to keep her here.

'Until Colin and I have recovered all the evidence from Evie and rebuilt our second victim,' Rhona assured him.

Erling nodded, his relief at this obvious on his face.

'I'm glad McNab's here now,' she told him. 'He can be a pain at times, but his instincts are sound and he never *ever* gives up.'

Erling smiled. 'I know. That's why I asked for him.'

35

Orkney

Turning down Erling's offer of a lift in a police car to the Archaeology building, she'd explained how she found walking through Kirkwall a pleasure. Plus it gave her time alone to think.

However, she'd barely begun her fifteen-minute walk to UHI when her mobile rang. Glancing at the screen, she found Ava's name. She briefly contemplated letting it go to voicemail, so that she might listen to the message at leisure. Then somehow the insistence of the ring changed her mind and she answered.

'Rhona, are you free for a chat?' Ava asked, her tone cautious.

'Can I ask what it's about?' Rhona said.

'It's about the podcast, but I don't want to ask you any questions,' Ava added hastily. 'I want you to take a look at something and tell me what you think.'

'What is this something?' Rhona asked, a little intrigued now.

'It would be better if you read it for yourself. Could we meet?' Ava said.

Rhona had reached the main street now, so she said, 'I'm near the Ivy House. What about we meet there?'

A small silence followed, then, 'That would be great. I'm at the *Orcadian* office, but I'd rather we discussed this in private. Is Colin about?'

'No, he's already at the Archaeology department,' Rhona told her.

'Okay, I'll see you at the Ivy House,' Ava said.

Rhona had barely had time to put on the coffee machine before she heard a knock at the door.

'It's open,' she called, then watched as a wide-eyed Ava entered the flagstoned kitchen in much the same way as she'd done herself, barely over a week ago.

'Does it live up to your expectations?' Rhona said with a smile.

'Definitely. At least the kitchen does,' Ava added.

'Well, the rest is equally impressive,' Rhona told her. 'You could ask Colin to show you around sometime. He loves showing it off – the restoration is pretty amazing.'

'I think I will.' Ava fell silent then, before taking out her laptop. 'Can I log on here?'

Rhona passed her the card with the password. 'The walls are thick, like Seaview and probably your place, but the signal's still good.'

She watched as Ava logged on, then brought up what looked like a true crime website.

'I'm not doing an interview,' Rhona reminded her firmly when she registered the banner headline to be that of Ava's podcast.

'I'm not asking you to,' Ava said. 'Have you listened to the podcast at all?'

'I have,' Rhona admitted. 'As has McNab. He told me about it over dinner last night. He also told me about your conversation with him regarding Magnus and Shona.'

Ava nodded in a perfunctory manner, as though that wasn't why she was here. 'Good. Magnus needs to sort that out,' she said.

'You should also know that Shona and Ingrid were at the police station this morning,' Rhona told her. 'Ingrid to have a DNA test. Shona to tell Erling that she thinks the AI image is Ben Bradley.'

Ava raised an eyebrow at this. 'I guess my chat with DS McNab proved successful, then.'

'So why come to me and not McNab with whatever this is about?' Rhona asked.

'You have a forensic eye,' Ava said. 'If you think it worth pursuing, you can take it to Erling or McNab and they'll listen. Though I'm not certain they share their own thoughts fully with one another,' she added.

'McNab's acting SIO on the case now,' Rhona told her.

'Because of the Ben Bradley thing?' When Rhona nodded, she said, 'I'm glad Erling's seen sense there. For the sake of his career here on Orkney.'

Ava pushed the laptop towards Rhona, then began her explanation.

'There's a chat aspect to the podcast, where those who follow the story discuss it afterwards and what the latest information might mean for the actual investigation,' she explained. 'For listeners, it's like solving a puzzle.'

'But they don't have all the evidence. Especially the forensic evidence,' Rhona said.

'I know, but I've often found they throw up ideas that may seem off target, but are worth considering.' Noting Rhona's expression, she continued, 'For instance, one listener, revealing she'd heard a rumour that the second skull had been taken and the grave messed with, immediately said that the real killer would never desecrate their own victim's grave, because that would be sacrilege.'

'That's already under consideration,' Rhona said, 'especially after Magnus's talk this morning regarding the MO and signature of the perpetrator.'

'Good,' Ava said, 'because I suspect our perp may be closer than we think.'

'What d'you mean?' Rhona said.

Ava brought up the chat page on her screen.

'You believe there's someone in your chat group who may be the perpetrator?' Rhona said.

'Some perps like to be part of the investigation. It stokes their ego. Some feed inaccuracies to muddy the waters,' Ava said. 'As an investigative reporter, I've seen it all, and often from the most unlikely people. The guilty often turn out to be the ones you believe to be entirely innocent.'

Rhona acknowledged the truth of this. Even forensic evidence, factual as you believed it to be, could be fabricated.

'Anyway, there's something about one contributor's postings that raises a red flag with me,' Ava told her. 'I may be entirely wrong, or I might be right. I'll let you be the judge of that. Read everything on there and see what you think. I have a couple of things to do at the *Orcadian*. I'll leave you to it and be back in, say, half an hour?'

Rhona readily agreed, having no desire to have Ava watching while she digested the contents of the chat stream.

As she began trawling her way through the conversations,

she was reminded of Erling's concerns about amateur investigators turning up in Orkney and causing problems. Luckily, the folk who appeared to be logging in from across the UK and beyond weren't discussing any trips to Orkney to pursue their enquiries.

There was, however, much discussion on the apparent Viking nature of the two graves found so far, plus quite a few folk reminding everyone that a perpetrator became a serial killer once a third body was found.

Something she, and no doubt Erling and his team, were already worried about.

Then an entry around this topic caught her attention. It read:

A decade between kills seems long. Then again, the decade length may in itself be significant for the killer. If so, then we are two decades past the original kill and should perhaps expect another kill to happen soon. M

Rhona reread it, before coming to rest on the initial that followed the statement.

Was this the message Ava was alluding to?

Rhona swiftly scanned through the entries again, looking this time for the same contributor.

There were two more comments, evenly spaced out among the chat entries, and this time she paid them more attention, despite their seemingly innocuous contents.

Those buried in sand take a long time to decompose. M

The Vikings included favoured items of jewellery such as torc bracelets and necklaces in the grave to wear in the afterlife. M

She registered that all three entries appeared to be from the same person, calling themselves M. One displayed knowledge regarding the length of time it took a body to decompose in sand. The second showed familiarity with Viking burials.

However, it was the post in which the timing of the murders was mentioned that worried her the most.

M was quite right when he said that the first death had been two decades ago. That had been widely publicized in their search for the identity of the victim. But the police had not released any information regarding how long the second grave may have been there. Even today at the strategy meeting she'd skirted just such a question from those present.

In fact only Colin, Erling and McNab were aware that this was her current estimate.

So how did this M presume to know this information?

At that moment, the kitchen door opened and Ava came in, a questioning look on her face.

'You've read them?'

Rhona indicated she had.

'And?' Ava tried.

Rhona contemplated how much she might say about what had raised her suspicions and why.

As though reading her thoughts, Ava said, 'I'm worried about the comments by the one calling themselves M. And I can tell you why,' she offered.

'Okay,' Rhona said.

'Because they, or he – because I think it is a male – mentioned the second body having been in the ground for a decade,' she said. 'When at no time has that been revealed by the police or I suspect as yet forensically proven by you.'

Rhona waited in silence for what was yet to come.

'Plus I didn't like the mention of a possible third grave since a decade has passed from the second one,' Ava said. 'It's almost as if he already knows there is one, or there's about to be.'

36

Orkney

Exiting the meeting room ahead of Erling and Rhona, McNab made his way out to the car park, intent on accompanying DS Green on her trip to the torc craftsman mentioned earlier.

Since he'd arrived here in Kirkwall, there had been little opportunity to engage with Erling's second-in-command. Now was that time, he decided, as he called out her name.

Just about to get into the police vehicle, she paused and awaited his approach.

'You're heading for the lead on the bracelet?' he checked.

She confirmed this with a nod, her expression blank. McNab wondered what she made of his presence here and how willing she would be to work with him, now that he appeared to have usurped DI Flett's position.

'I'd like to come with you, if that's okay, 'McNab said.

She gave another nod. 'Would you like to drive, sir?'

'No thank you, Sergeant,' he told her. 'I suspect you know your way around the island much better than I do.'

'Round the mainland, sir,' she corrected him. 'In Orkney, this is the mainland.'

'So what's the real mainland called, then?' he said.

'Scotland,' she told him.

He contemplated this as they headed out of Kirkwall along the coastal road past Hatston Pier, where a large cruise liner was docked.

'I understand you haven't been in Orkney very long?' he said.

'Six months, sir,' came the clipped reply.

'And where were you stationed before?' he asked, registering now the difference in her accent from that of the other serving officers here.

'Caithness and Sutherland, sir,' she said.

McNab rummaged around in his brain for where Caithness and Sutherland were exactly on the map of Scotland.

Seemingly sensing this, she said, 'On the other side of the Pentland Firth, s—'

He interrupted her before she could get the 'sir' out again.

'I'm only acting DI while I'm here, Sergeant. Back in Glasgow I'm a DS just like you, and my partner there, DS Janice Clark, calls me McNab. I'd be happy for you to do the same.'

When she looked surprised by this, he added, 'Also, DI Flett asked my boss to send me here because we worked together once before. I'll admit I didn't want to come, but I'm here now. And just like you, I'm determined to work out who the hell killed two young men and buried them here in Orkney. So no more sirs, please,' he said. 'And may I call you Jo?'

'Jo's fine,' she said, with the hint of a smile.

'Good,' he said. 'So where are we bound, Jo?'

'Birsay,' she told him.

'Is that anywhere near Skaill Bay?' he asked, registering that they were heading west.

'We could go via Skaill Bay. I take it you'd like to see where we found the first body?' she said.

'I would, and in real life, not in a video,' he added.

McNab also wanted to get a sense of the size and layout of the island the locals called mainland, his only real experience of policing in Orkney up to now having been centred on the small northern island of Sanday.

He decided it might be useful to reveal that story to Jo now, and so he did.

'I wondered where it was when the boss mentioned at the meeting that you'd worked together before,' she said.

'So how did *you* end up here?' he asked.

'I worked here before as a student on archaeological digs in the summer holidays. So I knew what I was coming to.'

Now that is interesting, McNab thought. 'Any chance our killer did the same?' he ventured.

'I wondered that myself, so I've been trying to get info on volunteers who've worked here over the past two decades,' she told him.

'Good thinking,' he said appreciatively. 'So where are we now?' he asked as she did a right turn off the main road.

'We're heading for the Ring of Brodgar, between the two lochs of Harray and Stenness,' she told him. 'Just ahead, on your side, is the house where the Bradleys lived.'

Shuttered, with a red corrugated roof and an air of abandonment, its presence was an immediate reminder of why he was here, and of course of Annie Bradley, who'd now disappeared, just like her son.

'I take it there's still no word on Annie Bradley?' Jo said.

McNab shook his head. 'But I'm holding out hope that she'll see the identikit image somewhere and get in touch to tell us whether it's her boy or not,' he said.

He fell silent then, waiting for that moment when the sea would come into view, remembering the footage he'd viewed of the bay with its beach a graveyard of whales.

'Are you a volunteer with the whale watchers?' he checked.

Jo shook her head. 'DI Flett is, though. He was there that night. I don't think I could bear to be at a beaching. It's the stuff of nightmares,' she told him.

'Much like our job, at times,' McNab said.

Turning into a parking space, the car pointing towards the Atlantic ocean, they now drew to a halt.

McNab didn't need to step out of the vehicle to appreciate the vastness of the bay, the giant boulders rounded by the force of the sea, and above them, the waving grasses of the sand dunes.

'Just to your left is where they unearthed the stone cist with the body inside,' Jo told him.

When McNab stepped out of the car, the wind immediately caught him, snatching the car door from his hands to slam it shut. Head dipped, he walked towards the fluttering yellow crime scene tape that still outlined the locus.

He thought about the party held here twenty years ago and tried to picture Magnus and Shona Bain on the shore by the bonfire. Ava and Erling lying together among the dunes, Ben Bradley watching them.

Back then, it had been a calm, mild summer night, according to Erling. Although the drink and drugs they'd consumed would have countered anything the weather might have thrown at them, McNab thought.

How, he wondered, had Ben got himself here from the red-roofed house by the two lochs? How had he got home again? He thought about Ben's stepfather. The obvious dislike he'd had for his gay stepson.

McNab replayed the cafe scene again in his head, reminding himself that despite Annie's obvious fear of her husband, she'd been determined and brave enough to come and speak to them. If she hadn't given up then, he thought, why would she do so now?

Back in the car and heading for Birsay, McNab called Janice to ask for an update.

'On what exactly?' she checked.

'Everything,' McNab told her.

'We've been inundated with folk getting in touch about the identikit picture. Most of them way off the mark, claiming the image was that of a young male who'd disappeared within the last few years. Or even the last few months.'

'Anything on Annie Bradley?' he asked.

'Yes. We checked on flights and they are in Majorca. We've not confirmed exactly where yet, but hopefully soon.'

His heart rose at that. 'When you do, can you get the local police to check with Annie there? Show her the photograph. Find out what she thinks?'

'That's the plan,' Janice assured him. 'Don't worry, I'm on top of my side of the investigation,' she said firmly. 'Also, the AI-generated image of your second victim will be with you shortly, Detective Inspector. Anyway, how are you coping with all that fresh Orkney air?'

'I've just left the first locus at Skaill Bay where it almost blew me away,' he told her. 'We're now on our way to Birsay to talk to the person who may have made the torc bracelet.'

'We?' Janice said.

'DS Jo Green, who knows her way round Orkney better than me.'

'Good. Give her my commiserations on having to work with you and tell her I'm glad of the break,' Janice finished with.

When she'd rung off, McNab relayed the last message to Jo, and was rewarded with a smile.

The workshop of Viking Island Crafts was a long, low, stone building next to a more modern L-shaped bungalow.

Approaching the large open doors, McNab could hear the grinding sound of metal being worked.

'You lead on this,' he suggested. 'I'll definitely sound like a Glasgow cop as soon as I open my mouth.'

'Okay,' Jo agreed.

The man, having spotted their presence in the doorway, stopped whatever he was working on and came towards them. McNab registered a male probably in his fifties with a shaven head complemented by a substantial black-and-grey beard.

Jo introduced herself and McNab, and reminded Mr Forrester why they were there.

When he spoke, McNab decided the voice hadn't been forged in Orkney, but more like Newcastle.

'I'm sorry it took me a while to get in touch,' the man told them. 'We were away south at a family funeral, otherwise I would have contacted you as soon as the call went out about Viking bracelets made here in Orkney.' He directed their gaze to a board where at least a dozen similar torcs were on display. 'Most of the ones I make are sent off island,' he said.

Jo handed him a high-resolution photograph of the one they were interested in. 'There are initials on the end swirls,' she said. 'Is this one of yours?'

He studied the image closely. 'I think it could be. You said twenty years ago?' When Jo nodded, he added, 'I was just starting out. Had come up from Newcastle with my wife, Janey, and a new baby. Bought this place and set up shop.' He pointed at the swirls. 'I'm better at that now. Smoother. The initials weren't done by me, though. They've been marked on afterwards, I'd say.'

'How did folk order back then?' Jo asked.

'I advertised locally in the *Orcadian* and in a few UK magazines. Vikings weren't so popular at the time, but being an early computer geek, I created a basic website. Orders came via the website, followed by a cheque in the post. Or folk just turned up here. Especially visitors to Orkney who were interested in the Viking history of the place. More recently, it's folk from the cruise liners who arrive in a group, visiting the official craft trail.'

'I assume you keep a record of all your sales?' Jo said.

He nodded, pleased. 'I do and did even back then, when I was selling next to nothing. Wanted to grow to be a proper business. Got myself an Apple computer and kept everything on a spreadsheet, and banked the few cheques I got in Stromness,' he said. 'When I knew you were coming, I took a look at the orders from the time you asked about, and found three possibilities.'

He went over to a desk in the corner and returned with a sheet of printer paper. 'Here they are.' He handed it to Jo. 'One order was sent to the States, Philadelphia in fact. One to a London address, and one was bought locally, so

I assume they turned up here in person to collect it,' he finished.

Jo viewed the list then handed it on to McNab, her expression suggesting a win of sorts.

There were three entries, consisting of one female and two males. The female was the American buyer, living in Philadelphia. The first of the men, a Thomas Montgomery, had given a London address; the second, George Whitelaw, an Orkney one.

'Whoever George Whitelaw was,' she said, 'it looks like he was staying at the Bradley house when he bought the torc.'

Turning back to Forrester, she pointed to the name. 'The guy who bought the torc in person. Do you recall anything about him? Anything at all?'

Forrester wanted to help, that was obvious from his expression, but eventually he shook his head.

'I don't even recall the sale, except it must have happened, because it's here on record.'

Accepting this, Jo changed tack, asking if Forrester also made silver torc necklaces.

Forrester, obviously taken by surprise by the question, said, 'There was nothing mentioned about silver when the police called.'

'I'm asking you now,' Jo said firmly.

'Well, the answer's no. I don't work in silver, but there are plenty silversmiths here in Orkney.'

'If you saw a photograph of a Viking silver necklace, would you know if it was the work of a local artist?'

'I might do,' he offered. The existence of the necklace in the second grave had not become public knowledge as yet. They could warn Forrester not to discuss their interest in it

239

with anyone else. But, if he did recognize the work and told them the name of a possible silversmith, the word would get out there anyway.

McNab watched as Jo took out her mobile and brought up two images. One of the front of the torc necklace, the other of the back.

The man studied each in turn. 'It's good work, but it's quite tarnished,' he finally offered.

Jo didn't elaborate on the reason for that. 'Any ideas?' she probed.

'My near neighbours in Birsay, Viking Silver,' Forrester said. 'They would be the ones to ask.'

'That will do nicely,' Jo said and thanked him.

Back in the car and heading for the Viking Silver premises, McNab congratulated her.

'That was impressive, DS Green,' he said, with an appreciative nod.

Jo accepted his praise without comment, then said, 'Don't you think it weird that someone ostensibly staying with the Bradleys bought a torc bracelet around that time?'

'Yes, I do, and I'd like to ask Annie about that,' McNab said. 'Also, the London order was for a Thomas Montgomery, with an M.'

'I spotted that too,' Jo said. 'We need to check out the London address.'

'We do, but does anyone still live in the same place they did twenty years ago?' he said.

'My parents do,' Jo told him. 'And most Orkney folk do too. If they have spare land, then their kids build their homes alongside. Same happens in Shetland.'

'But London?' McNab queried.

'The Bradleys moved to Glasgow twenty years ago and were still at their forwarding address,' she reminded him.

'We'll definitely have the London address checked out,' McNab confirmed. 'And see if Annie Bradley can tell us who George Whitelaw is, or was.'

'We'll need to find her first,' Jo reminded him.

'We've established she's in Majorca. DS Clark will find out where,' McNab assured her.

Viking Silver had a small shop attached to a long stone-built house with a slate roof and plenty of parking space outside.

'So how do you want to play it this time?' Jo said as they drew up outside.

'I assume a police car doesn't often come calling, and Viking Silver weren't forewarned about our visit like Forrester was,' McNab said.

'I'm not a total stranger,' Jo admitted. 'I've had a couple of dates with a nearby farmer,' she explained with a semi-embarrassed look.

'A date with a local farmer no less?' McNab responded. 'Then you will take the lead again, Sergeant.'

The shop bell signalled their arrival and seconds later a young woman emerged from somewhere in the back with a welcoming smile. Catching sight of Jo, she immediately said, 'Jo, how are you doing? I haven't seen you since—'

'The young farmers' dance,' Jo finished for her.

'That's right.' She moved her interest to McNab, before saying, 'And this is?' with a raised eyebrow.

'Shirley, this is Detective Inspector McNab, from Glasgow,' Jo said.

The young woman's welcome smile faded.

'You'll be here in Orkney because of that business at Skaill?' she said pointedly.

McNab didn't respond, but instead left Jo to explain that they wanted to check if a piece of silverwork had been made here at Viking Silver.

'Okay,' Shirley said. 'Should we go into the back room, in case someone comes in?'

'That would be good,' McNab told her.

Shirley ushered them into a room that seemed to serve as part store, part small kitchen.

'Right,' she said, dread obvious in her voice, 'show me.'

When Jo brought out her phone, she looked mildly perplexed.

'I might not be able to tell from a photograph,' she said apologetically as she accepted the mobile.

'There are two images. One a front view, one a back. You can swipe between the two and resize if needed,' Jo told her.

McNab knew instinctively that she did recognize either the work or the distinctive design, and waited to hear if it was because it was one of theirs, or perhaps fashioned by another Orkney silversmith.

'I think this is one of our earlier designs,' she eventually said. 'I can't be sure because of the staining, but I think you can just make out our mark here.' She pointed to a small symbol on the rear image, at the centre bottom of the curve. 'If or when it's cleaned up, that would be a V with an S overlaid.'

She looked directly at Jo, before saying, 'As to who might have purchased it and when, that's a lot harder to say. Our jewellery goes all over the UK and the world, especially since Vikings have become such a thing. However, most of our work is bought by distributors, so we have little contact with the end buyers.'

'Was the shop here a decade ago?' McNab checked.

'Yes, it was.'

'And this design?'

'Yes, I think so. But even had someone bought it from the shop, there would be no record of who it was, which is what you really want to know.'

The conversation obviously at an end, McNab thanked the woman and, leaving Jo to say her own goodbyes, took himself outside.

The day was drawing to a close, the western sky clear of cloud and now turning red in the rays of the setting sun.

McNab felt himself lost in the vast emptiness of land, sea and sky, a mere dot on this northern landscape. He didn't know how things worked here. How people worked. It was just like being back on Sanday, apart from the fact he had a phone signal.

He also wondered whether he might turn out to be more of a hindrance than a help in all of this. Locals definitely preferred being questioned by a local officer, rather than someone flown in from Glasgow. Seeing Jo in action had made that plain.

Should he speak to DI Wilson and explain why he should come back to Glasgow and leave it to Erling and his team? Would the boss even listen? The ringing of his mobile took a moment to register. Checking the screen, he didn't recognize the number, but answered anyway.

'Detective Sergeant McNab?' a foreign-sounding male voice said.

McNab was about to correct his rank, then didn't. 'Yes, this is he.'

'Comisaría de policía, Puerto Pollensa,' the voice said. 'I have a Señora Bradley wishing to speak with you.'

'Annie?' McNab said, his heart rising. 'Annie it's me, DS McNab.'

'Jack has my mobile,' Annie said. 'But I wanted to check in with you about Ben. So I came to the police station. I've now seen the identikit picture, and—' She halted there a moment, her voice choked. 'And I think it is Ben. I've explained who I am and given them a DNA sample, so you can find out for certain. Also, Ben fractured his left wrist when he was six years old. I didn't know about it at first, and it healed badly. At the time he told me he fell off his bike, but I learned later that Jack had twisted his arm.'

'Annie, I can arrange for you to be brought home,' McNab said.

'It's better if I stay here for now,' she said, her voice suddenly breaking. 'When you're certain it's Ben and I can bury my son, then I'll come home.'

'Annie—' he began, intent on asking her about George Whitelaw, but now prevented from doing so by her sudden ending of the call.

37

Orkney

Although Ava had initially suggested that Rhona be the one to show Erling or McNab the chat around her podcast, Rhona had persuaded Ava that she needed to be there too.

'They'll have questions only you can answer,' Rhona had told her.

So they'd walked back to the police station together, and asked to speak to DI Flett or DI McNab, whoever was available.

'DI McNab has left the building,' they were told by the desk sergeant. 'I'll let DI Flett know you're here.'

Minutes later, they were back in Erling's office, Ava's laptop open on the desk. Ava delivered the same introduction to Erling that she'd given to Rhona, then the two women remained silent as Erling studied the contributions.

Erling, she observed, was struggling with the idea of Ava being party to the investigation, yet unsure how he could ignore her contribution. It was, Rhona thought, his earlier fears made manifest.

After his first reading, he immediately scrolled back and

read through again. At the end of his third reading, he sat back in his chair.

'So tell me what you think about all of this,' he said, looking directly at Rhona.

With a quick glance at Ava, Rhona set about her explanation. 'As I understand it,' she said, 'at no time have we made public that the second body had been in the grave for a decade. That has yet to be established.'

Erling nodded. 'I agree, although I believe that information may already be in circulation locally.'

'In what form?' Rhona said.

'Gossip, innuendo, loose talk by police officers. It makes a good story.' He looked to Ava. 'Didn't you set up this podcast to do that?' he asked. 'Tell a good story and get folk talking about it?'

Ava didn't like the veiled accusation. Taking an obvious breath, she said, 'I'm an investigative journalist. That's what I do, investigate. The true crime podcast is a part of that. And I am considerably more careful and accurate in what I publish than any newspaper or social media platform,' she added firmly.

'But, judging by the responses on here, you've managed to whip up a frenzy anyway,' Erling countered.

Rhona, growing uncomfortable at the increasingly personal nature of Erling's remarks, decided to intervene at this point.

'In my opinion, digital forensics needs to take a good long look at this, in particular the contributions by the one signing themselves as M.'

She continued. 'Ava obviously wasn't at the meeting this morning so wasn't party to our discussions about the initials engraved on the bracelet. Yet she still picked up on the three

246

contributions signed by M. One of which definitely raised a red flag with me.'

She thought she'd gone too far, until she saw Erling's expression begin to change, before he said, 'I'll get DI McNab to take a look when he comes back from Birsay. As SIO, he'll be the one to contact Glasgow and ask that this be investigated by digital forensics.'

'So do I keep the podcast up and running?' Ava said.

'Again, that will be DI McNab's decision. Although I suspect his answer will be yes. He'll want to see what else is discussed on the chat forum, and in particular from the one signing themselves as M,' Erling said. 'I also think it likely he'll want Magnus to take a look at the chat and see what he thinks about the postings.'

'Right,' Rhona said, relieved. 'If you'll excuse me, I'm required at UHI to reassemble a skeleton. I take it there's no word on the missing skull as yet?'

'Nothing but false sightings, which I believe are the work of a prankster, who's going to be very sorry indeed when I catch them,' Erling told her.

The light was already fading as Rhona walked towards the UHI building, the short day consumed by the strategy meeting and the extended discussions regarding Ava's podcast.

She suddenly found herself longing to be back in her own lab with Chrissy, after which she would head back to her flat, her cat and perhaps Sean. Once she and Colin finished their forensic examination of the skeleton, she would go home, she told herself.

Yet, after reading the messages from M, a troubling thought had reoccurred. Even though she hadn't yet confirmed the length of time the second body had been in the ground, she knew a decade was a likely estimate, which – if the ten-year interval was a significant part of the killer's signature – meant they were currently in the danger zone, or worse still, something bad had already happened. They just hadn't discovered that something yet.

That thought stayed with her en route to the archaeology department. Forensic analysis took time, she reminded herself, which meant it never seemed quick enough, especially when you were working to prevent the next crime from happening.

The first grave had led them to the second, not by luck, but because of the careful forensic examination of what had been found in the stone cist.

Magnus had said in the strategy meeting that he believed the killer to be an organized planner, who would have chosen the gravesites in advance and duly prepared them.

If she was right in her thoughts regarding the second victim being buried a decade ago, then wouldn't it be likely that the next location had at least been chosen? And if so, where might it be? Another beach with a Viking history, of which there were many in Orkney?

As Colin and her own online searches had told her, the Orkney archipelago had the largest concentration of pagan Norse graves in Scotland. Which included several cemeteries of varying sizes. One of which, she remembered, was just across Eynhallow Sound from Evie, on the island of Rousay.

But what was the significance of Viking graves? Because the perp had read about them? Or lived in proximity to one or more of them? Or watched a Viking drama on TV or one of the streaming services? People did become obsessed with stories and films and the characters involved, thinking of them as real.

Erling hadn't as yet ruled out a local perpetrator, although in a community this size, he would have expected a line of enquiry around that possibility to have emerged by now. Especially when some of Ben's former schoolmates had already called in to say they thought the identikit image was Ben.

So maybe the perpetrator was familiar with Viking graves in Orkney because they'd been involved in their excavation. And since Orkney had the largest concentration of Norse graves in Scotland, this was where they may have come twenty years ago.

She thought of the chat posts from M. The discussion of decades. Did the perpetrator only visit Orkney every ten years or so? Or did they come on digs in between, familiarizing themselves with an area and preparing the groundwork for when they would return to make it their own?

Did they choose their victim while on the dig and on a return visit together orchestrate their death? Or select them elsewhere and bring them here?

There were plenty of stories of grooming nowadays through online apps, but twenty years ago, it had been done differently.

She remembered herself as a young teenager, on her first visit to London with a pal. They'd split up, each going off to see something of interest alone, having arranged to meet again at an agreed spot in the railway station. She'd been back first and had been standing watching the crowds for her friend, when a well-dressed man had approached and suggested she might like to come and have something to eat with him.

She'd turned him down, of course, explaining she was

waiting for her friend, but he'd been persistent up until she told him she would scream if he didn't go away.

Her thoughts moved to the teenage Ben Bradley, leaving home for London, desperate to escape his bully of a step-father. Wanting to go where he might be permitted to be himself.

His mother had believed him to be happy in his new life until he stopped contacting her. Something she didn't think he would do by choice.

Rhona's own son, Liam, had kept in contact with her. Messages continued to arrive from various parts of the world – wherever his work with an aid agency took him. How would she feel if his messages and intermittent phone calls, however brief and awkward they were at times, were to suddenly stop?

She'd never had the relationship with Liam that Annie Bradley had had with Ben. Annie had raised her son herself. Not given him up for adoption, as she had done with Liam.

Nothing much had changed since Ben had disappeared. The young and vulnerable were still drawn to London, although now the grooming didn't have to start in a London railway station or even a nightclub. It most likely began via your mobile and the numerous dating apps now available.

Arriving at the UHI building, she found Colin at work on the skeleton. Suited up, she joined him. In the neighbouring lab she could see the two figures of his assistants working their way through the sand removed from the site. Rhona hoped they might be as successful as Chrissy had been with the sand from Skaill Bay.

Smiling at her arrival, Colin asked how the strategy meeting had gone. After she'd given him a quick résumé, she brought up the subject of Ava's podcast, describing the posts by the character signing themselves M.

'Well, well, well,' he said. 'So this poster knew about the whole decade thing. Or acted as if they knew the killer's timeline?'

'That's what spooked me and Ava the most,' Rhona said. 'That and the "those buried in sand" bit, as well as the fact he mentioned torc bracelets and necklaces in particular.'

'Viking graves do sometimes contain jewellery if the dead person was wealthy, but it's usually tools and items thought to be useful in the afterlife,' Colin said.

'I was also thinking on my way here,' Rhona began. 'About the possibility that the perpetrator might be someone who has been actively involved in Viking excavations in Orkney. That would allow them to choose a suitable site and use it when it was no longer under investigation.'

Colin nodded. 'That could explain the time lapse between the graves,' he said. 'And the obvious knowledge of the area. Plus the fact that the Skaill Bay victim was buried in a former Viking burial cist. Which the killer could have identified during a dig trip.'

'Do you keep contact details on the people who volunteer on your digs here in Orkney?' she asked.

'I have done since I arrived here twelve years ago.'

'What about your forthcoming dig on Rousay this summer? Will the same volunteers as last year return, do you think?'

'More than likely, although there's always a small turnover.' He paused for a moment. 'Once we finish our work with Sigurd here, we'll definitely check out all the volunteers who've spent time here on Orkney.'

Now focusing on the fully assembled – apart from the

missing skull – skeleton, Rhona asked why Colin had chosen the name Sigurd for him.

'Because Westness, the estate on Rousay where we're working, is mentioned in the *Orkneyinga Saga* as the home of Sigurd, a powerful chieftain. So until we discover this young man's real identity and give him back his own name, I decided to call him Sigurd.'

38

Orkney

Rhona missed going to the jazz club after work with Chrissy and, despite the wonders of the Ivy House, she longed to return to her own flat and her view of Kelvingrove Park.

Tonight Colin was out, so she'd arranged to meet McNab in the Kirkwall Hotel bar, prior to which she was scheduled to chat to Chrissy, this time on a video call.

Chrissy was to be the one to call her, so Rhona was sitting at the kitchen table, laptop open and ready. She was looking forward to seeing Chrissy's face as well as hearing her news, regarding the case and in general.

So when the *bebop* sound of the incoming call arrived, she immediately answered.

'Hey there, boss,' Chrissy said with a grin. 'How's it going in the Northern Isles?'

'You first,' Rhona responded.

'Okay,' Chrissy conceded. 'On the work or home front?' she checked.

'Home front first,' Rhona said.

'Well, wee Michael's really enjoying nursery, as is Mum.

She takes Rocket for a walk while Michael's there, and she made a friend in the park who was also there with his dog. He's a widower called Harry, and she likes him.'

'That's good news,' Rhona said. 'And what about Connor?'

'He's fine,' Chrissy said. 'But we're keeping it casual,' she added.

'Is that your decision or his, or both?' Rhona said.

'A bit of all three. What about you?'

'Keen to get home,' Rhona admitted.

'When will that be exactly?'

'Once Colin and I have dealt with Sigurd,' she said. 'We've managed to rebuild him after the attack on his grave, but there's still no sign of his skull.'

'A careful killer would never desecrate one of their graves, which is, let's face it, a place of significance to them,' Chrissy said, her voice serious.

'That's the opinion up here too,' Rhona told her. 'Plus Erling's been getting prank phone calls about where the skull can be found. He's pretty mad about that.'

'So now the update on where I am on the work front,' Chrissy began. 'We have two DNA profiles from the tape used to gag the victim. The same with the cable tie. One of each being a match for the victim and the other, we assume, being that of the perpetrator.'

'Have you run the perp's DNA through the database?' Rhona asked.

'We have and without a match,' Chrissy confirmed what Rhona had already feared.

'And the phial?' she said.

'It held ketamine, as no doubt you suspected,' came the reply. 'So we now have a picture of how Erik was killed. What about Sigurd?' she asked.

'No obvious evidence of blunt-force injury. I took a video and photos of the skull in situ,' Rhona told her.

'And the neck?' Chrissy checked.

'Hyoid bone is intact. As is the remainder of the skeleton, which on a full examination looks to be male and around the age of the first victim. When I bring him down, Dr Sissons will have his say, of course.'

'Anything in the grave soil?' Chrissy said.

'Not so far,' Rhona confirmed. 'Although I plan to join the team on that tomorrow.'

'I could always come up and help?' Chrissy offered.

'I'll be down soon, I hope, together with Sigurd and the soil.' Rhona didn't add, *Provided another body doesn't turn up*.

'What about McNab?' Chrissy said.

'Acting SIO, so he's here for the duration. Unless the body at Skaill turns out not to be Ben Bradley,' Rhona told her.

'I can feel his wrath from here,' Chrissy confirmed. 'Tell him I miss him. Oh, something else I wanted to mention. This decade thing. Shouldn't we be worrying about an impending third victim?'

'We are worrying,' Rhona confirmed. 'And we still have no idea why a decade should be significant,' she added.

'The number ten in the Bible represents completeness, perfection and God's divine order,' Chrissy told her. 'You know, the ten commandments and all that.'

With Rhona momentarily at a loss for words, Chrissy added, 'I'm trying to look at it from the killer's point of view. Isn't that how we catch them?'

The walk to the pub was wet and windy. Seeing Chrissy on screen had both cheered Rhona up and plunged her into despondency. She hoped food and a large glass of white wine would help. She was also interested to hear McNab's thoughts on Ava's podcast and the chat forum.

The wind met her full-on as she exited Bridge Street at the harbour, where ship lights shone from the darkness.

Entering the bar, she was pleased to discover McNab already there, whisky glass in front of him.

'Dr MacLeod, you still on the white wine? If so, I suggest a repeat of last night's meal.'

Rhona was happy with fish and chips again and told him so.

Something's happened, she thought, watching McNab's tall figure approach the bar. But was it something she already knew about or not?

She found out on his return.

'Annie Bradley called me from a police station in Majorca,' he told her. 'She confirmed that the identikit picture was her son and she's given a DNA sample to the police there to be sent through to us.'

'Wow. So Ollie was right after all?'

'Looks like it,' McNab said. 'Although I never doubted him, especially against an AI program.'

'Is Annie okay?' Rhona said.

'I offered to bring her back, but she said she would only return when she could bury her son.'

'But she's a witness to what happened back then,' Rhona said.

'And will need to be interviewed, I know,' McNab responded. 'And definitely away from her husband. But I couldn't emphasize that. Not at the moment.'

They both fell silent at this, and Rhona knew McNab well enough to appreciate how much the thought of Annie was worrying and distressing him. So she gave it a few moments before relating her recent conversation with Chrissy.

'She says to say she's missing you,' she added.

McNab's grin at this was infectious. 'And I her,' he said.

'So,' he continued, 'we have the perp's DNA, and we know his MO, but he's not on our database. Which means he's not been in trouble with the law, despite his murderous intentions.' He thought for a moment, before saying, 'From what you've seen of Sigurd so far, I assume you believe he likely died in a similar fashion to the Skaill Bay victim?'

'I don't think there's a question regarding it being the same perpetrator,' Rhona confirmed. 'Or the fact that it happened around a decade ago. Has Erling talked to you about the chat forum on Ava's podcast?'

'He has, and normally I'd be with Flett on this. Online sleuthing can be seriously disruptive to an investigation. It can bring hordes of folk down on the location involved. Luckily, getting to Orkney is neither cheap nor easy, so we seem to have avoided that so far.'

'But?' Rhona prompted.

'I've got digital forensics on it, headed by Ollie. It's not the first time a perpetrator has tried to insert themselves into the investigation of their own crime. It happens more than the general public are aware.'

'What about the timing?' Rhona said. 'Twenty years ago, ten years ago . . .' She tailed off.

'I have a gut feeling that that particular timing only relates to their crimes here in Orkney,' McNab said. 'I suspect such an organized killer won't have waited ten years to kill again. MO. Means, motive and opportunity. You know the drill, Dr MacLeod. A killer will rarely stop killing once they have a taste for it. Hence Janice is checking out any discovered remains and missing persons in Scotland and south of the border that might show similarities to what we have here.'

'Around archaeological digs?' Rhona said, before describing her recent discussion with Colin regarding volunteers.

'Great minds think alike,' McNab said. 'Jo – DS Green – suggested exactly that today when we were visiting Birsay. So Colin has lists of his former volunteers?'

'Over the twelve years of his tenure here, he says, but he seems to think he can locate some from further back too,' Rhona said, before enquiring why they'd been visiting Birsay.

McNab smiled. 'I keep forgetting we don't have Chrissy on the case,' he said, 'spreading knowledge among the interested parties without the need for a strategy meeting. Anyway, the torc bracelet was crafted by a John Forrester out in Birsay. He gave us three names from orders back then, when his business was in its infancy. Two were men. One order was sent to a Thomas Montgomery at a London address. The other, a George Whitelaw, bought it in person, while claiming to be staying at the old Bradley place, which is not far from the Ring of Brodgar.'

Rhona, keen to hear more, waited in silence for what was to come.

'Jo did the interview and she showed him the images of the silver torc necklace,' McNab continued. 'He then directed us to nearby Viking Silver, who claimed it as one of theirs. However, their work is sold throughout the UK and beyond, so they have no idea who purchased it.'

'And the initials?' Rhona checked.

'In both cases, they confirmed they'd likely been added later by the owner, and definitely not by them,' he finished.

'So the killer chose Orkney-crafted jewellery and put the initials on themselves?' Rhona said.

'Which leads me to think that there was a relationship of sorts between the killer and his victims prior to their murder, which may have been more than fleeting.'

Rhona thought about her earlier musings regarding grooming.

'What?' McNab said, reading her expression.

'I think you may be right about the idea of a relationship between the killer and his victims,' she said. 'If there was, it would have been easy to lure them to Orkney and the place he'd chosen for their graves.'

McNab agreed before suddenly cursing. 'Annie was really upset when I last spoke to her and rang off before I got the chance to ask her about the guy, George Whitelaw, who claimed to have been staying at their house when he bought the torc. I should have asked her about it straight away,' he chided himself.

'You'll get a chance to do that when you speak to her next,' Rhona sympathized.

McNab gave a nod to her empty wine glass. 'You for another? I'm having one.'

Rhona thanked him but declined. 'I need my bed,' she said.

'I could walk you round to the Ivy House?' McNab offered.

'I'm safe enough on Bridge Street,' Rhona said with a smile.

'Funny that,' McNab countered. 'I feel I have eyes on me wherever I go in Orkney.'

'You have,' Rhona told him. 'Everyone knows that the tall guy with auburn hair is the ace detective sent up from Glasgow to solve the case.'

'That's why I need another drink,' McNab said, rising and heading for the bar.

39

Orkney

McNab carried his drink upstairs, aware he had a bottle of Highland Park, which he'd earlier purchased, waiting in his room. He wondered briefly if his visit to the nearby supermarket had been noted and discussed, and couldn't imagine that it hadn't been.

Chrissy's retinue of spies throughout Police Scotland was legendary. He wondered if her reach might even stretch as far north as Kirkwall. That thought lightened his mood, which the whisky had notably failed to do.

Stripped and headed for the shower, he made note that he was almost out of clean underwear. So sometime tomorrow he would need to locate a launderette or else purchase more.

His thoughts drifted to Magnus and he dawdled with the idea of asking if he might do his laundry at Seaview. Magnus, he knew, wouldn't balk at such a request, nor cast it up to him later. Magnus wasn't that kind of a guy, which was good, of course, yet it irritated him nonetheless.

No, it would be new underwear plus a launderette visit,

he decided, emerging to towel himself dry. And he would ask Jo Green to recommend where he should go for both.

It had been a good idea to accompany DS Green on her trip to Birsay. He'd liked her professionalism, and her way with folk. Back in Glasgow, questioning the general public was different, because you were unlikely ever to meet them again. Here, however, they were often your neighbours, or someone you met at the young farmers' dance.

He smiled at that thought, recalling Jo's embarrassment at the mention of her dating a local farmer. As for him, he would settle for a date with anyone, or at least some female company that had nothing to do with work.

That thought immediately led to Ellie, which was, he'd finally accepted, a definite dead end. They were over for sure. Her choice, of course, and he couldn't blame her. Christmas had been ace after she'd returned his motorbike, but all it had been was festive sex, which didn't last beyond Twelfth Night. Something he hadn't chosen to broadcast, and definitely not to Rhona.

Donning his last clean boxers and T-shirt, he ceremoniously opened the bottle of Highland Park, poured himself a large one, then settled on the bed with his laptop, his intention being to check in on Ava's podcast and associated chatroom.

Despite his reservations, he found her voice to be captivating as she spoke about the Orkney residents' reactions to the release of the identikit image of Erik, and explained the reasoning behind the nomenclature until his real name might be restored.

There followed a piece she'd written for the *Orcadian*, with some interviews with locals sounding determined to do all they could to help the police in their enquiries.

He noted that she had little new to say regarding the discovery of the second body. No mention of the torc necklace, which he was pleased about. Although that story would no doubt appear soon, as a result of his visit today to Viking Silver. The defiling of the grave and the removal of the skull she did speak about, demanding its immediate return.

McNab now turned to the chat forum, noting the increase in the number of comments since he'd last looked earlier in the day. However, a swift scan through found nothing further from M, which immediately concerned him.

Had M become aware that the website was now being monitored by Police Scotland?

The possibility of a play-off between the hunter and the hunted made his brain hurt, so he rose to top up his drink. As he was doing this, his mobile rang. Reaching for it from the side table, he answered.

'DS McNab?' a female voice said.

'Katrin?' McNab tried.

'Yes. I need to see you, *right now*,' she emphasized.

'Okay, I'll come downstairs,' he said, eyeing his trousers at the bottom of the bed.

'No.' She sounded decisive and worried at the same time. 'I'll come up if you give me your room number. Please,' she added, 'it's important.'

He did as requested, then, scrambling into his trousers, he waited for her knock at the door.

When it came, the knock was firm and demanding. As he opened the door, she immediately swept in, then asked that he lock it. 'It locks automatically,' he reminded her. He'd only ever encountered Katrin when she was waiting tables. Standing in front of him now, a small backpack slung over her shoulder, her hair wild from the wind and a silver ring piercing her nose, he found it difficult to reconcile this version of Katrin with the one who served him his morning coffee.

Seeing his surprised expression, her hand rose to her nose. 'I can take it out, if you like,' she said, in an effort to lighten the moment.

'Not on my account,' he told her. 'So what's so urgent and secretive that it won't wait until the morning,' he said, becoming increasingly conscious that he had a young woman of maybe seventeen in his hotel bedroom with the door locked.

Perhaps sensing this, she gave him a look that suggested she wasn't here to molest him or be molested. Removing the bag from her shoulder, she set it on the bed and unzipped it.

Out came a towel wrapped around something. Moments later, he discovered that something was a skull. *The* skull, he presumed.

'Where the hell did you get this?' he demanded.

She shook her head. 'No need for you to know that,' she said. 'You've got it back now. That's what's important.' Her look defied him to argue. Heading to the window, she beckoned him to join her there. Puzzled by this, he did as bid.

'Now, kiss me,' she ordered. 'And look passionate about it.'

McNab shook his head. 'No way,' he stressed, 'is that going to happen.'

She looked set for an argument, then seemed to change her mind. 'Okay, so I need to stay longer.' Deserting the window, she headed into the bathroom, brought out a plastic glass and poured herself a whisky.

'What the fuck is going on?' McNab said, exasperated.

'I made it plain to my mates that I was visiting you in your room, and it wasn't to deliver a skull,' she said. 'The kiss at the window would have backed that up.'

'Who's out there?' McNab headed for the window again, spurring her into action to join him there.

'Just look like you're pleased to see me,' she ordered.

The only alternative being to manhandle her away from the window, McNab tried his best to look happy.

'Why all the subterfuge?' he asked.

'I told my pals I fancied you and planned to confront you about it in your room,' she told him, swallowing some whisky. 'I could hardly tell them I was returning the skull.'

'They were the ones who took it?'

'No, but I have no intention of telling you who did. It's back now anyway.' She drained the remainder of her whisky.

'Hey,' McNab said. 'Are you even eighteen?'

She laughed. 'A bit late to ask that now.' Seeing his horrified expression, she added, 'Yes, I am, and I'm still planning on joining the police . . . in Aberdeen or maybe Glasgow, definitely not here.' She gave him a cheeky grin. 'So you're safe from any accusations of a sexual nature,' she added. 'Provided you don't tell DI Flett that I gave you the skull.'

'So what's my story?' McNab said, already thinking that Katrin would make a pretty good undercover agent.

'You opened your room door tomorrow morning and found it there.'

'That would be lying,' McNab reminded her.

'In a good cause,' she said, opening the door a little to check the corridor. 'Right, I'm off,' she told him. 'See you at breakfast without the nose ring.'

And she was gone.

40

Orkney

Bridge Street and the connecting Albert Street were, as predicted, completely empty except for herself and the echo of her footsteps on the flagstones.

Walking here alone so late at night had so far caused Rhona no concerns at all. Unlike when she was in her home city.

Yet her city wasn't a stranger. She knew it well enough to choose the paths she thought safe, and take precautions when she felt they were required, such as avoiding the city centre, especially late at night, and swiftly passing the many back lanes that criss-crossed the inner-city grid.

Now, on the winding sheltered tunnel that was Albert Street, she began to register just how many narrow and often dark passages led off on either side.

Aware she was spooking herself for no real reason, she nevertheless quickened her step, keen to reach the stone certainty of the Ivy House, to pass through its gates and into its welcoming kitchen again. When she did, she found Colin sitting at the big table, his laptop open in front of him.

'How did it go with our SIO?' he said. 'Has he okayed the check on Ava's podcast?'

'He has,' Rhona confirmed. 'Is that what you're looking at?'

'No. I'm going back through my volunteer lists and the timings and locations of the various digs.'

'Is there a George Whitelaw or a Thomas Montgomery anywhere on your lists?' Rhona said as she discarded her coat.

'You think there's a possibility there might be?' he asked.

Rhona took her time, giving Colin a full explanation of McNab and DS Green's visit to Birsay, first to the maker of the torc bracelet and secondly their visit to Viking Silver after John Forrester had recognized the necklace design as perhaps coming from there.

'So both items of jewellery we found in the graves were fashioned here in Orkney?' Colin considered this for a moment, then looked to his laptop. 'These are the volunteers on digs here for the past twelve years. Let's see if there's a Whitelaw or Montgomery on the list.'

Rhona moved to sit alongside Colin at the table as the list ordered itself alphabetically by surname.

'Bingo,' Colin said softly, and pointed. 'There was a Thomas Montgomery as part of the volunteer team working near the Broch of Gurness.'

'That's near Evie Sands?' she checked. When he indicated it was, Rhona asked when exactly that had been.

'In the summer after I arrived.' Colin glanced her way. 'But he could have been a volunteer earlier than that too.'

'The initials on both items of jewellery include an M,' Rhona said. 'Plus it's the signature initial of the seemingly knowledgeable contributor to the chat forum.'

Colin pointed to the screen. 'There are four more volunteers with surnames starting with an M,' he said. 'Who would be just as knowledgeable about Viking burials,' he offered.

'But they haven't bought Viking jewellery in the past, as far as we're aware,' Rhona said, frustration taking over.

'You need to go to bed,' Colin suggested. 'As do I. That was just a list of names. I'll have their contact details somewhere. I'll root them out tomorrow, plus hopefully anything I can find on the people who volunteered before I took over here. As for George Whitelaw, if he did stay at the Bradley house as he claimed, Annie Bradley would be the one to talk to about him.'

'McNab's onto that already,' Rhona told him.

'Right, we rest now and rise to fight another day,' he said encouragingly. 'We've made a good start.'

Reaching her room, Rhona looked out of the window on to Albert Street to see three young women walking along the road together, talking and laughing. Standing in the darkness of her room, she realized she recognized one of them as Katrin, who McNab had introduced her to in the pub the previous evening. She wondered where they'd been and what had made them so cheerful.

Then she remembered that when you were young, you had much to be cheerful about. Except if you were someone like Ben, pictured in that school photograph, when the world and your peers seemed set against you.

She'd turned her mobile to silent during her talks with McNab and later with Colin, so now in bed and ready to turn off the light, she checked whether she'd missed anything important.

She noted that Sean had tried to call her when she'd been

with Colin, and that shortly after she'd missed a call from McNab.

Why would McNab call so soon after they'd seen each other, she wondered, and contemplated calling him back. Then reminded herself that when she'd left him, he'd been topping up his whisky at the bar. So surely whatever he wanted to talk about could wait until the morning, she decided.

Then there was the missed call from Sean. She wasn't concerned about the late timing of it, because it fitted in with his playing schedule.

Pressing the return call button, it rang out only once before Sean answered.

'Rhona,' he said. 'I thought it might be too late for you to call back.'

'Where are you?' she said, pleased to hear his voice with its Irish lilt.

'At your place. I thought Tom might be in need of some company. A bit like myself,' he added. 'When are you back, d'you think?'

'Soon,' she said, hoping that was true. 'Unless . . .' she found herself saying.

'Another body turns up,' he said gently. When she didn't respond, he added, 'I know the drill.'

He did, because they'd been together long enough for him to know what was worrying her.

'I plan to come back the day after tomorrow,' she said and meant it. 'Has Chrissy been by the club?'

'She has,' Sean said, 'because of Connor, I suspect. He has a light in his eye,' he added.

'She told me they were good, but casual,' Rhona said with a laugh.

'Not the way I've seen it.'

'So he's staying for a while?' Rhona checked.

'He is,' Sean confirmed. 'Not sure Chrissy believes it, though.'

They fell silent for a moment until Sean asked if he might cook for her on her return, or whether she'd prefer to eat out.

'I'm missing my flat . . . and other things,' she added. 'Let's eat there.'

Perhaps it was the longing in her voice that prompted him to ask if she was really okay.

'I am now,' she told him honestly.

As she rang off, a text arrived from McNab. It read:

We have the skull. You can collect after the strategy meeting tomorrow.

So that was what the earlier contact had likely been about. She was sorry that she hadn't returned his call. Too late now, she decided, as briefly contented, she got under the duvet and switched off the light.

If the skull was back, she registered as she drifted off, then Sigurd was complete and could now be taken to Glasgow for a forensic pathologist to study in more detail. Although she doubted whether Dr Sissons would disagree with her and Colin's findings up to now.

41

Orkney

He'd unwrapped the skull with gloved hands and placed it upright on the towel it had arrived in. McNab had little doubt that it was the strangest item ever to have been put on Flett's desk.

'It's definitely the one from the grave at Evie?' Erling said.

'I've compared it to Dr MacLeod's video. It's definitely Sigurd,' McNab told him.

'And you found it outside your hotel room door this morning?'

'That's what I'll write up in my report.'

'But it's not what really happened?' Erling said.

'I have to protect my sources,' McNab said. 'They took a chance bringing it to me.' When Erling looked as though he might question him further, McNab said, 'As SIO on this, it's my decision and it's on me if this issue comes back to bite. The important thing at this moment is that we have the skull back.'

Flett, he should have realized by now, was a straight-up kind of a guy, as evidenced by him owning up to a possible connection with the first victim, and then asking for a replacement, i.e. him, to be sent here as SIO.

But now that Annie had identified the victim as her son, unless the DNA sample she'd provided to prove her parentage somehow disproved this, then he was definitely in the driving seat for the duration. Flett could ask for the identity of the person who'd returned the skull, but he couldn't command that he be told it.

Taking note of Flett's expression, McNab decided he could offer a little more.

'It was a teenage girl who brought it to me,' he told him. 'I don't believe for a moment that she was involved in taking it. I think she knew how important it was that we get it back, plus she was trying to protect whoever did it, because they were too scared to return it themselves,' he explained.

Flett nodded, his expression changing for the better. 'Thanks for telling me that.'

'This is your patch,' McNab said. 'You'll have to live with the fallout from this investigation even after we bring it to a conclusion. You and DS Green, of course, who I've discovered is an excellent partner. Much as my DS Clark is in Glasgow.'

Flett's Orcadian feathers now smoothed over, McNab glanced at the wall clock.

'Okay, we're up in ten minutes and I want to call DS Clark before the meeting. Find out where we are with Annie Bradley's DNA test.'

Taking the hint, Flett made to exit his own office, before McNab stopped him.

'I'm happy talking to her from my room. I'll see you upstairs in ten,' he said.

They'd given him what amounted to a cubbyhole, which

he didn't mind, because he could go in there, shut the door and be free to think. He knew the rest of the team would have been happier had the victim not turned out to be Bradley, as this would likely have meant his departure.

That was unlikely to happen now. Sad for them, and even more sad for him, he thought.

Shutting the door firmly behind him, he made his call to Janice, who answered almost immediately.

'Before you ask, we have Annie's DNA sample and it's being run against Ben's as we speak,' she told him.

'Good. We have the skull back,' he countered with his own success.

A small silence fell as she digested this. 'How?' she checked.

'A local girl brought it to my room last night. She wasn't involved in taking it in the first place,' he added, to clear that up in advance.

'So how did such a good deed come to involve you?' Janice said in her usual dry manner.

'She works in the dining room of my hotel. She's my eyes and ears on the ground.'

'As long as that's all she is,' Janice said.

McNab remained silent at this, well aware of what Janice was referring to and having no wish to revisit his past mistakes.

To end the stand-off, he brought her up to date on the torc and necklace makers. Then asked about Sigurd's AI identikit picture.

'It's ready and winging its way towards you as we speak,' she told him.

'You know I don't want it up on social media?'

'I know, but I'm not sure why exactly?' she said.

'I want both Orak and his human counterpart to run a check on all available missing person databases, CCTV footage and crime files first,' McNab said.

'I take it Orak's your name for—'

McNab cut her off. 'It's Ollie's name, not mine,' he told her. 'I want to know who the second victim is before the general public gets involved. I also don't want the killer to know we've identified him. Let him think we haven't, maybe because of the skull going missing.'

'But what if we don't ID him?'

McNab didn't have an answer for that, so didn't offer one. 'Also, we need Annie and her husband brought back from Majorca. The bold Jack has questions to answer in all of this.'

'Okay, boss. I'll see to that as well.'

'Right, now I'm off to tell the team here what the plan is,' he said.

'Well, if you're as bossy with them as you are with me . . .' Janice said, an obvious hint of laughter in her voice.

'If you're acting SIO, you've got to act like it, Sergeant,' he said before ending the call.

Standing for a moment, he took stock of how he was going to outline his wishes to those waiting upstairs. Would they go for his plan to keep the identikit image of victim two under wraps both locally and further afield?

Added to that, should he actually show the team the AI image at all? His instinct was to keep it to the inner circle of Flett, DS Green, Rhona and Professor Nelson initially, mainly because of how fast news travelled around here. Show or tell one person something and the entire population of the Orkney mainland appeared to learn it too.

He knew this because he'd been here before. Well, he'd

been to Sanday before with a population of less than five hundred and, at the time, little chance of a mobile connection anywhere. And yet, despite all of that, folk would know when and why he'd gone somewhere on the island before he even got there.

Bracing himself, McNab departed his cubbyhole and headed upstairs.

The meeting room was nothing like the one in Glasgow. One wall here consisted of big windows looking out towards the sky and sea. Today, the view was peppered by rain beating against the glass.

At this moment, he also registered another sea, this time of faces turned towards him, with Flett at its centre. Everything he'd been thinking about downstairs came back into play and he made his mind up there and then to get them on side, by explaining what he wanted and why, with perhaps a little humour thrown in.

Walking to the front, he thanked them for all they'd done up to now, and for what they had yet to do. Then he told them about the return of the skull and was immediately pleased that he had done so. Judging from Flett's expression, he was too.

'I've shared this information with all of you because it's important that you know the skull is safely back in our hands. However, it's equally important that you share this with no one. And I do mean no one. If anyone says there's a rumour that this has happened, you shrug and say we're still looking for it. Even to your nearest and dearest. So tell no one. Not even the dog, because it will immediately run off and tell all the other Orkney dogs, who will, of course, tell their owners.'

There was a ripple of laughter at that.

'The reason for this is because we do not want the perpetrator, wherever they are, to know that we have the skull back.' He paused to hopefully let that sink in. 'We also now have an AI-generated image of victim two, currently christened Sigurd, which was created using the stills and video footage Dr MacLeod took of the skull prior to its disappearance.

'However, although you will have access to it, the image will *not* be posted anywhere, including on social media, but will be run against missing persons' data files across the UK.

'In order to do this, I require two officers to work in tandem with Glasgow.'

When a couple of hands were immediately raised, one being DS Green, McNab found himself smiling, before finishing with, 'DI Flett is your immediate go-to on all of this, as per usual.'

42

Orkney

When Rhona entered the police station, she found Ava already waiting in the entrance hall.

'I didn't know you'd been called in,' Rhona said.

'It's all your doing,' Ava responded with a wry smile. 'If you hadn't made Erling take the comments in the chatroom seriously . . .'

Rhona shrugged. 'It was definitely forensic evidence,' she said. 'Just digital instead of biological. I take it the strategy meeting is still on the go?'

'I assume so. They're all upstairs anyway.'

Rhona wondered if Ava was aware of the return of the skull and suspected not. McNab may well have chosen to keep that information out of the public domain, and thereby out of sight of the perpetrator. If so, any identikit image produced via her video of the skull would also stay under wraps.

At that moment Erling appeared and, seeing them both waiting, asked that Rhona come with him to the evidence room.

'DI McNab will take you into my office,' he told Ava. 'We'll join you there shortly.'

Pretty sure she was off to see the skull, and that her thoughts on who was likely to be party to its return were correct, Rhona followed Erling to the evidence room.

Ushering her inside, he shut the door, then drew her attention to what she assumed was the said item, covered by a brightly coloured towel.

Unwrapping it, Erling stood aside to allow her to take a look.

Drawing close, Rhona checked for the telltale signs that told her this was indeed the skull she had studied in situ and photographed extensively, down to the noted fillings on the lower and upper jaw.

'It's definitely Sigurd,' she said, pleased. 'McNab texted me to say you had it last night, but he didn't mention how that came about?'

Erling looked nonplussed by the question, before saying, 'It was delivered to DI McNab's hotel room, by person or persons unknown.'

Rhona almost smiled, immediately aware there was a bigger story here, which she would definitely extract from McNab when they were next alone.

'Excellent,' she said. 'We can have it bagged properly now, together with the towel, and I'll take both to the lab after the meeting. Colin will be very pleased to see it.'

Noting Erling's relief that she hadn't questioned his somewhat flimsy explanation regarding the skull's return, Rhona followed him into his office, where she found McNab and Ava as expected, now with the addition of Magnus.

'We have more room upstairs,' McNab said, 'but it seemed appropriate to meet here in DI Flett's domain, especially when not everything we say is for outside consumption. Firstly,' he said, 'I've now received word from Glasgow that the DNA sample given by Annie Bradley confirms her as the mother of the Skaill Bay victim.' He stopped there, obviously aware that this was both the news they'd been expecting, but didn't necessarily welcome.

He continued. 'We can also tell Ingrid Donaldson that the victim is not her father.' He nodded to Ava at this point.

Rhona's glance towards Magnus was met by a small shake of his head, which she read to mean that he, too, wasn't Ingrid's father.

'Right,' McNab said. 'Now let's talk about the podcast and the role it appears to be playing in this investigation. A role that I, like DI Flett here, was initially unhappy about.' He indicated that Erling should take over at this point.

Erling switched on the wall monitor linked to his laptop. On it was the chat forum, which looked busy.

'Ava,' Erling began, 'together with Dr MacLeod, brought our attention to some questionable entries on the chat forum. Further to this, DI McNab and I decided to have the site digitally monitored from Glasgow where they are currently seeking to identify the contributor who signs themselves as M.

'I've asked Magnus, in his role as criminal psychologist, to update us on his thoughts on the podcast and the resulting online chatter and, of course, the contributions of the said M.'

'I believe,' Magnus began, 'that a highly organized killer such as we have would seek out Ava's investigative podcast because, firstly, she's Orcadian and is currently reporting from here during the live investigation. Secondly, Ava has an international reputation for exposing the truth, which will, I assume, have caused our perpetrator some concern, or at least sparked his interest.'

He went on. 'As to our killer's status and MO, I believe he has strong links with Orkney, either as a visitor or perhaps a former resident in some capacity. He is captivated by its Viking history, which is demonstrated by his actions and his signature.

'His choice of victim could imply he has a propensity for young males, late teens to early twenties. Also, the modus operandi would lead us to believe they're not killed at random, but perhaps groomed, leading eventually to a visit to Orkney, or in the case of Ben Bradley, a return visit to Orkney.

'The two murders identified so far appear to be a decade apart. I would suggest that such an organized killer would not wait ten years for each kill. So our perpetrator, if he began twenty years ago, has killed more than once since then, and not necessarily only in Orkney.

'The self-belief of such an organized killer can, of course, lead to their downfall. They effectively cannot stand back from any investigation of their crime, but instead feel compelled to take part in it. These comments lead me to believe that this is possibly happening in the chatroom.

'After reading through the increasing number of comments, I noticed others whose use of words are not dissimilar. Perhaps also posted by M in an effort to muddy the waters. Some of these I noted were signed with a W. Which is in effect an upside-down M,' he added.

'Finally, as you are aware, not all serial killers will try to engage with an investigation. These, though, tend to be spur-of-the-moment killers, who, when presented with a possible victim, enact their fantasy. They do not plan. I don't believe the man we're looking for is in that category. I believe he thinks we're not clever enough to catch him, and therefore enjoys watching us fail. Let's be honest here. Had a pod of pilot whales not beached at Skaill Bay, his crimes would have gone undetected.'

After that sobering thought, McNab came back to say that the entries that had raised a flag for Magnus had been passed on to digital forensics, and some headway had been made in trying to identify and locate the contributor involved.

'We're talking a language here in terms of internet searches, IP addresses and VPNs that I'm not able to either explain or describe,' he said. 'However, I'm confident we will track down the person or persons involved.'

He continued. 'There is also a suggestion that the killer may have identified our two burial sites while working as a volunteer on Viking digs in Orkney. I understand that Professor Nelson has been looking back over his volunteer lists?' He looked to Rhona at this point.

'He has,' she confirmed. 'And late last night we discovered a Thomas Montgomery was part of the volunteer team working at the Broch of Gurness, near Evie Sands, twelve years ago. That same name, I understand, was given by a buyer of a torc bracelet at Viking Island Crafts, such as the one found in the Skaill Bay grave,' she finished.

'Any sign of the other torc buyer, George Whitelaw, in the prof's lists?' McNab immediately asked.

Rhona indicated not. 'But the names we looked at only covered the time since Colin first arrived in Orkney to take over the expanded archaeology department. He did indicate that volunteers tend to come back on a regular basis. He plans to look for contact details for that list, including those of Thomas Montgomery, today, which he'll then pass on to you. He's also trying to find any records of dig person-nel before his time here,' she added.

After Rhona's contribution, McNab confirmed that he wanted Ava to continue with her podcast, and okayed her to release the news that Ben Bradley had been officially identified as the first victim. He also asked her to encourage anyone who may have been in touch with Ben after he left Orkney, or who may have met him in Glasgow or London, to contact Police Scotland.

The meeting over, McNab suggested he would run Rhona up to UHI, if she could wait ten minutes. Realizing there were things he probably wanted to tell her in private, she agreed.

Rhona suspected Ava had realized something was up when Erling suggested she meet him in the evidence room. Wise enough not to ask why, Ava confirmed instead that Magnus wasn't Ingrid's father.

'I think he may be just a little disappointed by that,' she said. 'Ingrid's a great kid, after all.'

'And Ingrid?' Rhona asked.

'She deserves to learn who her real father is. If it had turned out to be Magnus, I think she would have been pleased,' Ava told her.

They'd parted company then, and Rhona, along with Erling, had collected the now-bagged skull.

'That was a pretty good double act,' Rhona offered as he walked her to the front door.

Erling nodded. 'DI McNab and I have come to an agree-ment,' he told her with a wry smile.

'I can see that,' Rhona said. 'And I'm glad.'

43

Orkney

Erling had asked Magnus to wait in his office as McNab and the others had left.

McNab hadn't questioned him as to why, aware, Erling was certain, that the two men needed to discuss the announcement that Ben Bradley, their classmate of twenty years ago, had been officially confirmed as the Skaill Bay victim.

Something they'd been dreading since the beginning of the investigation.

Urging Magnus to take a seat, Erling said, 'First of all, tell me about Shona and Ingrid.' Magnus, he noted, seemed happy to do so.

'I spoke to Shona and she told me that I wasn't Ingrid's father. She was quite adamant about that and I believed her,' Magnus told him. 'She said, though, that she was happy for me to check for myself via a paternity test and provided me with the means to do that. Which I did, and it turns out she was speaking the truth.'

'Did she tell you who Ingrid's father is?' Erling tried.

'No, and I didn't ask. That's between mother and daughter, but I do remember she went off on holiday that summer after the party on the beach. So I assume . . .' Magnus halted there. 'But that's not really why you wanted to speak to me, is it?'

'No, it isn't,' Erling confirmed. 'I wanted to explain that DI McNab will be the one to interview you and myself about Ben, and the questioning will, of course, cover the Skaill Bay night. He will also interview Ava. The rest of our sixth-form class, those still here in Orkney, will be interviewed by DS Green as she has no link to the victim.'

Magnus acknowledged this with a nod.

'I don't believe we have to confer about anything,' Erling said. 'We should all tell our own story as we remember it.'

'From my experience, people's memories about what happened twenty years ago can be limited and muddled,' Magnus said. 'Especially if they'd been drinking or taking drugs at the time.'

'And yet traumatic events can still stay with us, despite the drugs and the time interval,' Erling said. 'I, for one, since the discovery of the first body, have experienced constant flashbacks from that night. The problem is they're not coherent or complete, which makes me want them to continue until I get the full picture.' He paused there briefly. 'For instance, when did Ben arrive at Skaill Bay and how did he get there? It's almost six miles from the Ring of Brodgar and his house. I suppose he could have walked there and back, but wouldn't we have spotted him on the road?'

'Maybe he got a lift from someone,' Magnus said. 'People usually stop to give folk a lift here, especially twenty years ago.'

'Did you know there was someone staying with the Brad-leys back then?' Erling said.

'No,' Magnus confirmed. 'But if this George Whitelaw was staying with the Bradleys, he may well have given Ben a lift. I certainly can't imagine his stepfather doing it. Not after hearing about that man from Shona.'

They both fell silent for a moment, before Erling said, 'They're bringing Annie Bradley and her husband back from Majorca as we speak. McNab plans to interview them with his sidekick in Glasgow.'

'Remotely?' Magnus said. 'Or is he planning to fly back down?'

'He hasn't confirmed that as yet, but it appears Annie Bradley trusts him, so it might be better for him to be physic-ally in the room with her,' Erling said. 'This other name that came up, Thomas Montgomery, who gave a London address to Forrester. He also bought a bracelet just like the one found in the cist around the same time as George Whitelaw.'

'You're thinking of the M and W inversion I mentioned?' Magnus said.

'Both the bracelet and the necklace had initials marked on them. The torc was either E M or B M. I suppose now that it's been confirmed as Ben Bradley . . .' Erling tailed off.

'Which, if true, supports the idea that Ben and his killer were in some sort of relationship,' Magnus said. 'Not exactly an engraved wedding ring, but a Viking bracelet with their initials side by side is not dissimilar. If so, then that might explain why Ben came back, one assumes willingly, here to Orkney,' Magnus said.

'But why Orkney, when his memories of this place, and us, couldn't have been good?' Erling said.

LIN ANDERSON

'He'd already come back once to see Shona,' Magnus reminded him. 'So we know the memories weren't all bad.'

Erling strove to bring his thoughts back to the matter at hand.

'Well, if we manage to identify the second victim and either his first name or surname starts with an L . . .' Erling shrugged. 'We may prove our theory true.'

Magnus nodded his agreement, before glancing at his watch. 'I have an online lecture shortly. So, if that's all for the moment, may I leave?'

'Of course,' Erling said. 'I'll be in touch about the interview with DI McNab. And thanks,' he added, 'for all your help on this.'

'I'm glad we know the truth now about Ben,' Magnus said. 'Although I would much rather have heard he was alive and well and living as his true self down in London, or anywhere else he chose.'

'Me too,' Erling said.

Magnus gone, Erling located Jo to tell her that he was heading out for a while, and only to call him if he was needed back. Nodding, she gave him a sympathetic look, and not for the first time did Erling think he had struck it lucky with his new second-in-command.

His plan was to simply drive round his patch, or at least the mainland part of it.

He needed, he knew, to settle some things in his mind. He had dreaded this moment for so long, and now that it had arrived, he had to find a way to deal with it.

His behaviour towards the teenage Ben, he now acknow-ledged, had been fuelled by his anger towards himself. He hadn't wanted to be different, and had chosen to subdue any impulse to admit that he was. Ben, he'd sensed, had

286

already accepted the fact he was gay, despite having to deal with a homophobic stepfather.

Ben had been the brave one, while he had been the coward.

That night in the dunes, he'd turned on Ben, because Ben had been there to see his moment of truth. As had Ava, but his anger was all directed at Ben. He'd called him all the names he'd imagined might be used against himself.

He decided to head west, not certain which route to take, although he thought the likelihood would be that he would make his way to both the Bay O' Skaill and Evie.

He knew every road that criss-crossed the island, plus he knew most folk who lived here. Not all personally, of course, and there were new people coming and going now, more often than back when he was a teenager. Not to mention holidaymakers and folk from the regularly docking cruise ships.

And yet he always felt visible and noted, and would be now, more than ever. Once the news was out that the victim was confirmed as Ben Bradley, a former pupil at Kirkwall Grammar School and a classmate of Detective Inspector Flett, it made the murder personal to both himself and every-one else on the island, especially those like Shona who'd known Ben back then.

Erling had the sudden feeling that he should ask for a transfer and move to the anonymity of a city like Glasgow, or Edinburgh, or Aberdeen.

McNab, he thought, could investigate a murder without being concerned that the victim might be known to him. Or if they were, he could choose to stand back from the inves-tigation, because there would be plenty of other officers to replace him.

He had tried to do that here, even before the identity of the body buried in the dunes at Skaill had been proven to be Ben. But, and it was a big but, here in Orkney the link between him and the murdered Ben could never be broken or forgotten. It would become part of his and the island's story.

Seeing the sign for the Ring of Brodgar ahead, he signalled to turn right. Even now, he thought, the police car and its travels would have been noted and questioned, especially given the heightened awareness of the investigation.

He realized as he made his way past the standing stones of Stenness that he wanted to see the old Bradley house. He'd known where Ben lived, mainly because of the tales of the pigs they'd kept and the smell they'd caused. God, how cruel they had been about that, mocking incomers who didn't know what they were doing, or how to live or farm here.

The joke was, as a teenager himself he'd hated the idea of running a smallholding, and his greatest wish had been to get off the island as soon as possible and move to a city. And while he'd managed to do that, he'd been as much of a failure as a townie as Ben had been here as an islander.

Reaching the red-roofed building, he drew alongside the open gate and stepped out of the car to take a walk around the property. The farmer who now owned the place, who had given them the Bradleys' forwarding address, had eventually stopped renting out the three-bedroomed cottage, rather than having to renovate it.

In truth, it couldn't have been a great place to live twenty years ago, Erling thought. The pervading smell of the pigs. The mud that went with them. The surrounding field, where the pigs had nosed about, was neatly grassed over now, and the quaintness of its situation so near to Brodgar and the two lochs would no doubt feature in tourist photographs.

In fact he remembered sometime in the past when Rory had got him to stop the car so he might take one himself. After which, Erling had told Rory about the boy from the south who'd come to live there and smelt badly of pig manure. The memory of Rory's laughter at his much-embellished tale made him cringe now.

Back in the car, he continued on the route taken that night in the dark with Magnus and Rhona. Back then, they'd seen nothing but what the headlights had picked out of the road and its verges, and of course the stars above.

Now, approaching midday, he could see the way clearly.

He tried to imagine the lone figure of Ben trudging the single-track road that ran alongside the Loch of Skaill and in that moment he had a flashback to his own wild driving on this very road. His near miss with an oncoming car, and the imminent possibility of ending up in the reedy water, which had caused hilarity all round.

God, when you're young, you cannot imagine being courted by death, much less facing it, he thought.

Yet it couldn't have been long after that very night that death found Ben.

When he reached Skaill Bay, he parked the vehicle to face the sea and, checking his mobile, was relieved to find no messages from DS Green, nor DI McNab.

He'd spoken the truth when Dr MacLeod had commented on the easier relationship he and McNab now had. It was ironic, he thought, that the identification of Ben as the first victim had made that possible, because it meant his team could accept McNab's intrusion into what they saw as their investigation. It also meant that McNab himself felt better about being here.

It was at this point in his thoughts that his mobile did ring, with DS Green's name on the screen.

'Apologies for calling, boss, but I thought you'd like this news right away,' she said, her tone excited.

'Go ahead, Sergeant,' he told her.

'The Met's been in touch. They checked out the London address for Thomas Montgomery as requested and he still lives there, although he's away from home at the moment.'

As his hopes had risen, he now found them falling again, before Jo came back in.

'A neighbour says he may have gone north to his holiday cottage,' she began.

'Where?' Erling demanded.

'That's just it, sir. That's why I'm calling. It's in Stromness.'

'Stromness?' Erling found himself repeating.

'Yes, sir.' She quoted him an address. 'I've sent you a link to it on Google Maps. It's at the water's edge, just off Alfred Street.'

Erling almost laughed. He knew Stromness and Alfred Street well enough, if not the name of every little wynd and lane leading to the water's edge.

'Thanks, Jo. I'll head there now.'

His drive of shame brought abruptly to an end, Erling turned the vehicle and headed south to Stromness.

44

Orkney

She'd extracted the full story of the return of the skull from McNab on the short journey to the archaeology department. Although she was pretty sure she hadn't heard all the details of what had gone down in his room before Katrin had left him holding the baby.

As he drew into the car park, she resolved to have McNab repeat it in fuller detail the next time they met over a drink in the Kirkwall Hotel bar. She didn't think anything untoward had happened between McNab and Katrin, but she did think that Katrin had got the better of him in some form, which he had yet to convert into an amusing anecdote.

What she was sure of, however, was that he'd given Katrin his word that he would keep her role in this a secret. A secret he'd now revealed to her, on the understanding that she would keep it too.

And she fully intended on doing so.

As they drew to a halt, Rhona asked if he planned to come in with her, and he told her he did.

'I'd like a word with Colin about his list of volunteers. I'm also keen to see his reaction when we deliver the skull. Did you tell him we had it?' he said.

She indicated not. 'I didn't mention it this morning. I wanted to make sure it was Sigurd first.'

What she didn't say was, once Sigurd was complete, she would accompany him to Glasgow for his official forensic post-mortem. She had the feeling that her presence here had suited McNab, making him feel less of an intruder in the Orkney investigation.

Once she left, he would be on his own.

Dismissing that thought, she led the way to the archaeology department and its lab. Colin, spotting their arrival through the glass partition, waved and indicated he would come to speak to them, at the same time gesturing that they should help themselves to coffee in his office.

Minutes later he appeared and, seeing the evidence bag, raised a questioning eyebrow.

'It's Sigurd,' Rhona told him. 'Delivered to McNab's room late last night,' she added.

Colin had a quick look inside and a wide smile enveloped his face. 'He's not damaged?' he checked.

'No. He's fine. Whoever took him looked after him well,' Rhona said.

Colin turned to McNab. 'Any idea who took him, or brought him back?'

'Not the same person,' McNab said. 'I *am* sure of that.'

Perhaps taking note of McNab's closed expression, Colin didn't pursue that line of questioning any further. Instead, he gave a deep and satisfied sigh. 'So we can put Sigurd back together again. And maybe have him identified?'

Rhona looked to McNab, wondering what he planned to say, since Colin was part of the team, despite the fact he hadn't been at the police station that morning.

McNab responded. 'The AI software built an identikit picture via the photos and video that Dr MacLeod supplied, so we already have a likeness available. However, we're not making that image public, nor are we announcing the skull's return,' he added. 'Not even to your colleagues here. News travels too fast in Orkney,' he finished.

'Understood,' Colin said with a firm nod. 'I take it you don't want Sigurd's killer to be aware that we have him back together again?'

'Exactly,' McNab said. 'We intend on running his likeness through every database we have. I'm hopeful we might find a match somewhere in missing persons. We also have his DNA, which we'll use in the same manner.'

'Right,' Colin said. 'Now, has Rhona explained about the volunteer registers?'

'She has,' McNab said. 'I'm hoping to hear more from you on that.'

'Good, because there is more. I managed to find the address files of the volunteers over my period of tenure, with just a few exceptions. Although only some gave their home addresses, the others where they were staying here in Orkney during the summer excavations.'

'And the ones who volunteered prior to your arrival?' Rhona asked.

'I haven't located their files yet,' he said apologetically. 'But I've made attempts to contact previous personnel who might point me to their location.'

Colin had moved to his desk and, opening up his laptop, said, 'Firstly, a Thomas Montgomery, the name you were particularly interested in, was staying in Stromness as a volunteer, although he didn't say where exactly. What's even more interesting is that he also worked on an earlier Viking exploratory dig at Skaill Bay.'

'At Skaill Bay?' McNab repeated in surprise.

Colin explained. 'In the 1990s, a cist was excavated at the south end of the bay. It was found to contain the remains of a young male who'd been buried in the mid-sixth to late seventh century AD. The cist was close to the site of another Viking burial, located in 1888, which was also found to contain a male skeleton and grave goods. We had another look at the area in 2000,' he added.

'And Thomas Montgomery was part of that team?' McNab checked.

'Looks like it,' Colin said.

Rhona met McNab's eye. This was good news, if true.

'Anything on our other torc suspect, George Whitelaw?' McNab said.

Colin shook his head. 'Maybe he was just on holiday when he stayed with the Bradleys?'

One possible lead was good. Two would have been even better.

'Annie Bradley will be able to tell you about him,' Rhona reminded McNab.

McNab didn't respond, just said he needed to get back to the office. After checking if Rhona planned to join him to eat later, he headed off.

'I need to find those earlier records,' Colin said. 'If you want to complete Sigurd, I could try to do it now?'

Rhona was happy with that arrangement and said so. 'How's the soil-sifting progressing?'

'I meant to speak to you about that,' Colin said. 'Deborah and Francis have departed as of today. They told me to tell you they found a few small items you might be interested in. I assume when you and Sigurd go south, the soil will go with you?'

They hadn't discussed her departure, although Colin was aware she would likely go soon – unless, of course, another victim was discovered.

'I'll take a look,' she said. 'After Sigurd.'

Kitted up now, Rhona removed the skull from its protective covering and, placing it on the table, began her close study. She hadn't viewed the AI-generated image made available this morning, and wanted to reformulate her own thoughts on what Sigurd looked like, now that she had his head once more in front of her.

She contemplated this as she carefully brushed and swabbed him, wondering where he had been since his removal from the ground, even as she imagined him fleshed out as a young adult male, with small ears, a square chin and slim nose. The DNA would have confirmed his hair and eye colour, which would then be reflected in the iden-tikit image. Rhona imagined his eyes to be blue, his hair fair, and she looked forward to finding out if she was right about that.

Eventually, placing his head back in its rightful place, she took a seat beside him and wrote up her findings beneath her headline Gladstone quote:

Show me the manner in which a nation cares for its dead
and I will measure with mathematical exactness, the

tender mercy of its people, their respect for the law of the land and their loyalty to high ideals.

'We have you back, Sigurd,' she said. 'And I promise we will do everything in our power to find out who took your life before you had a chance to live it.'

Her work with Sigurd over, Rhona moved to the area in the lab where the grave soil had been examined, to find a note from Deborah and Francis.

It's been both a pleasure and honour to help on the excavation. We have individually bagged the items we found of interest, for you to take a closer look. Thanks again, Deb and Francis

The three individual bags were laid out side by side. Rhona picked up the first one and examined its contents through the clear covering. It was, she thought, an earring. Emptying it into her gloved hand, she moved to a microscope and slipped it under the lens.

It was indeed the loop of a black metal earring, marked by what looked like Viking runes. In the accompanying note, Deborah had described it as being found in the soil on the left side of the skull, so it had likely fallen from the victim's left ear as the body had decomposed.

The second item was also made of metal and had been found in the soil between the thighs. Extracting it from its clear pouch, she slipped it under the microscope, although she was pretty sure already what she was looking at, having seen one before in previous remains.

Under magnification it was, as she'd suspected, a type

of genital piercing, although she would have to look up its exact name.

The third and final plastic bag contained something that didn't require study under the microscope. It was a small, empty phial, which was undoubtedly the hallmark of their perpetrator.

45

Orkney

There was nowhere quite like Stromness, Erling thought, and not for the first time. Stretching along the shore of Hamnavoe, an inlet of Scapa Flow, its main street, at the core of the town, twisted and turned for over a mile.

Erling had followed the instructions given by Jo, but the problem was, this entire stretch of Alfred Street looked the same.

Comprising a row of fishermen's cottages, which stood side on to the main thoroughfare, each had its own set of steps leading to its own small jetty. Each also had a harbour wall.

He'd already walked down the trio of flagstone passageways to knock on the front doors, and found no one home. He suspected all three were Airbnb rentals, because they each had the look of a house not lived in full-time.

It was when he decided to head back to the police car that he heard a shout from a building on the opposite side of the street and, turning, saw an elderly man emerge from the front door of a two-storey house.

'Who are you looking for, officer?' he asked.

Mindful of not giving too much away regarding his reasons for being there, Erling said he was looking for a man called Thomas Montgomery, who he believed might be staying in one of the trio of cottages he'd just visited.

When the man looked thoughtful, Erling added that the house was Mr Montgomery's holiday home and that he understood he was visiting it from London.

The old man's puzzled expression strengthened, as though he was trying to either figure something out or remember something.

'There is a man comes here on occasion,' he said. 'Tall, maybe in his fifties. Dark hair. If that's your guy, he stays in the middle cottage when he's here.'

'And is he here at present, Mr . . .?' Erling said.

'Jim Rendall,' the man told him. 'And you're Detective Inspector Flett from Orphir,' he added with a knowledgeable look.

Erling nodded. 'That's right,' he said.

'I knew your parents from way back,' the man told him, a nostalgic look in his eye. 'They were sad when you left Orkney,' he added.

'Well, happily I'm back now,' Erling said with a smile. 'Have you seen this man recently?'

'I noticed the light was on last night and there was a big black pickup truck parked outside, so someone was there. But,' he emphasized, 'I think he rents it out. Makes money from the Airbnb.'

'You didn't happen to take note of the number plate of the vehicle, Mr Rendall?' Erling tried.

His question was rewarded with a shake of the head. 'I'm not that nosy, Inspector,' he said with a laugh.

Erling thought for a moment, before deciding to recruit Mr Rendall to the cause.

'A relative from London is trying to contact him, and asked us to check here in case he was back visiting Orkney. So if he does appear, could you give me a call?' he said, handing him a card. 'Don't worry him, though. Just call me and an officer will come and speak to him. Can you do that?' He smiled.

'I can do that, Inspector, and with pleasure,' the man said.

Deciding he'd done all he could here for the moment, Erling thanked him.

This was met by a broad smile. 'Me and your dad used to go to the dances in the Orphir Hall together, before my family moved to Stromness. He met your mum at one of those dances.'

Not sure how to deal with this information, Erling thanked him again for his help and headed for his vehicle.

It was just as he'd been contemplating during his trip of shame, he thought to himself as he drove away. Folk here knew everything about you. And what they didn't know, they made up.

It had always been this way, and always would be, he told himself, before he remembered that you could die in a city and your absence remain unnoticed, your body only discovered months, even years later.

At least that would never happen here.

Not unless your killer buried you in a stone cist among the dunes at nearby Skaill Bay.

He called Jo before he drove away.

'Any luck?' she immediately asked.

'Some,' he told her. 'We're looking for a black pickup

truck seen outside the cottage belonging to Mr Montgomery. Sadly, no licence plate number known.'

'Black pickup trucks are not uncommon here,' she reminded him.

'This one could have come off a ferry recently. From Scrabster or Aberdeen. Or maybe hired here and picked up at Kirkwall airport.'

'Okay, boss, I'm on it,' she told him.

'Also, can you warn the airport not to let anyone with the name Thomas Montgomery get on any outgoing flight? The same goes for the ferry terminal.'

'Will do,' Jo said with enthusiasm.

'And,' Erling came to a quick decision, 'I know we're short-staffed on this, but we need an officer through here, watching the cottage, in case Thomas Montgomery comes back.'

'PC Tulloch's back at work as of today,' she said. 'Shall I send him?'

'Yes. Do that,' he said, thinking Ivan would be safe enough on Alfred Street, especially with Jim Rendall on guard opposite. 'And last thing, Sergeant, I'd like a search warrant for the address you sent me, just in case he escapes us.'

As he headed back to Kirkwall via Orphir, he questioned the idea of the killer choosing to return to Orkney in the midst of an investigation. Of course, Thomas Montgomery might well turn out to be an innocent bystander in all of this, his only crime being his interest in Viking archaeology, like all the other volunteers who visited Orkney in the summer months to help on the current digs.

Suddenly realizing he'd turned onto his home road from habit, his thoughts went to Rory. There had still been no word from him, wherever he was in the North Sea.

His initial concerns had eventually led him to think that he was being blown off, and he'd increasingly thought he would get home late one of these nights and find Rory had come to Langwell and cleared out his things whilst he was at work.

That hadn't happened yet, but . . . He was stopped in these thoughts because, with Langwell now in view, he'd spotted a vehicle parked there that was definitely Rory's.

Drawing in behind it, he jumped out and, hurrying down the steps to the door, threw it open, shouting Rory's name.

His call being met with silence, he set off through the kitchen and neighbouring sitting room as far as the bathroom, where he could hear music playing alongside the sound of running water.

Grasping the handle, he threw open the door to find Rory standing under the shower.

His relief at this welcome image made him realize just how freaked he'd been by Rory's absence and even more by the non-communication that had accompanied it.

At this moment Rory turned and, spotting him, immediately stepped out of the shower to wrap his arms about him. Erling's laughing attempts to remind Rory how wet he was were then silenced by a long and forceful kiss.

Eventually pulling himself free, Erling demanded to know where the hell Rory had been and why he'd never answered his texts or calls.

Grabbing a bathrobe, Rory said firmly, 'I told you before I left that communication would be difficult.'

'But why?' Erling said. 'You've always managed before?'

'This job was different,' Rory told him. 'It was under the radar.'

'Whose radar? Not the police anyway or I should have been told,' Erling protested.

'Not the police.' Rory shook his head. 'And just as you don't tell me about your work, at times I won't tell you about mine. That was what we agreed.'

The stand-off lasted just long enough for Erling to remember the rules he'd laid down at the beginning of their relationship.

Perhaps sensing this, Rory came back in with, 'Despite the radio silence from me, I do know what's been going on here, mostly via your pal Ava's podcast.'

When Erling looked surprised at this, Rory added, 'That torc bracelet found in the cist with the first victim? I have – or had – a bracelet just like that one, back when I first met you.'

In that instant, Erling had to decide whether to come clean.

'I know,' he said. 'You were wearing it that night in the pub.'

Rory gave him a surprised smile. 'You remember that?'

'I thought maybe a former admirer had given it to you,' Erling said.

'One did,' Rory said. 'It was before I moved here. I came diving with some mates and I met this guy in the same pub as I met you. It was years ago,' he added.

'How many years ago exactly?' Erling said.

'Maybe eleven. I was in my early twenties anyway, my marriage pretty much over. Why?' Rory added.

'What was the guy's name?' Erling said, trying to keep his voice steady.

'We weren't a thing,' Rory said with a questioning look.

'What was his name?' Erling demanded again.

'I don't remember, except it sounded Viking. So I thought he was having me on about it.'

'And you didn't go with him?' Erling checked.

'No. Even when he gifted me the bracelet,' Rory said firmly. 'And it shouldn't matter if I did. It was long before we met.'

Erling fought to temper his manner. 'Can you describe this man?' he said.

Rory threw him a pained look. 'I didn't go with him,' he repeated.

Erling realized he would have to give more context to his questions. 'We're currently looking for a guy who came regularly to Orkney, we think, to help on archaeological digs. He had or has a cottage on Alfred Street in Stromness, and he bought a bracelet like yours in Orkney back when the first victim died.'

Rory was staring at him like a man who'd just woken up to the idea that he may have met a killer.

'Was he offering you sex?' Erling asked.

'Undoubtedly. He'd obviously clocked me as gay, although I wasn't really out back then.'

'Can you describe him?' Erling said firmly.

'God,' Rory said. 'Can I get dried and dressed and I'll try?'

Erling told him to be quick and went to wait in the sitting room, his thoughts turning somersaults. When a fully dressed Rory appeared minutes later, he forced himself not to ask anything more and to let Rory take the lead.

'Okay, before I tell you the little I remember, you have to know that we'd been diving in Scapa Flow and were high on the experience. We'd also drunk copious amounts of beer. I needed to pee and went to the gents. That's where I first saw this guy. I knew he was looking at me. I realize now that gay men can spot one another, even if one of them is acting straight.'

Erling couldn't stop himself. 'What did he look like?' he asked again.

Rory took a breath. 'Heights with me. I remember that. Maybe ten or a dozen years older than me, so he would probably have been in his early to mid-thirties. He had dark hair. Well built. Good-looking. I was really broad Scouse back then. When he spoke, the voice was a more cultured London accent. I remembered being flattered that he'd sought me out to be his toy boy.'

'His toy boy?' Erling repeated.

'That's what it felt like. And for a working-class gay Scouser who didn't have the nerve to admit to something about himself that this guy could obviously see, it was a pretty powerful draw.'

'So what stopped you?'

'One of my mates came in and the moment passed. But before I left he came and gave me the bracelet. Slipped it on my wrist as a *memory of what might have been*, he said.'

'You'll need to give a statement about this to DI McNab.'

Erling watched as Rory's expression darkened. 'McNab's here? The Glasgow officer who worked on the Sanday murder?'

Erling nodded. 'He's SIO on the case, because—' He halted there.

'Because what?' Rory demanded.

'I asked that he be sent here, because I suspected the first victim might be someone I knew in school.' He hesitated, aware he would have to say more than that and looking for the right words. 'I was pretty mean to Ben Bradley at senior school. There was a time I could have hurt him at a party at Skaill Bay, if Ava and Magnus hadn't stopped me.'

Meeting Rory's intense look, he added, 'Is there a reason you don't want to meet DI McNab again?'

Rory was struggling with his answer, almost as much as Erling had.

Eventually he said, 'Yes, because he recognized me in Sanday. That night at the end of the investigation when the locals held the bonfire party at Cata Sand? I saw him studying me. Checking me out. He knew me from somewhere. He just couldn't place where or why. But if he's as good a cop as you say he is, he'll have found out all about me by now.'

46

Orkney

McNab headed for the police station, keen to catch up online with both Ollie and Janice before the interview with Annie Bradley.

 He was still unsure whether he'd made the right decision not to head for Glasgow and conduct Annie's interview in person, but his rational self had pointed out that Janice would be there, and Annie would know he was in Orkney because he was doing everything he could to find her son's killer.

On arrival, he was immediately met by DS Green, who swiftly related the tale of the Met's information on Thomas Montgomery, which had led DI Flett to a fisherman's cottage in Stromness.

'This guy's here on the island?' McNab immediately demanded.

'Possibly, although we don't know that for sure.'

As she outlined DI Flett's orders around this possibility, McNab found himself impressed at Flett's quick decisions, even while he acknowledged that preventing a suspect from departing an island was a mite easier than on the UK mainland.

'DI Flett's on his way back now, sir,' she finished.

'Thanks, Sergeant. Is my room set up for the Glasgow interview?'

'It should be,' she told him.

'Good work,' he said. 'DI Flett is lucky that you came his way from the other mainland,' he found himself adding, which brought a surprised smile.

Fetching himself a double espresso from the machine, he headed for his room where, as promised, the large screen was currently showing a Glasgow interview room. Settling himself at his desk, he made his planned video call to Ollie, who was prompt to answer.

Never one to waste words, Ollie told him that they believed they'd found a match for the second victim.

'Vouched for by you and not Orak?' McNab checked.

Ollie confirmed this. 'Full details are on their way to you,' he said. 'Also, we're on track to locate M from his contributions to the podcast you've alerted us to. There is also some suspicion regarding someone signing themselves as W.'

'Professor Pirie mentioned that earlier at our meeting, pointing us to W being an inverted M.'

Ollie almost smiled at this, something that didn't happen very often. Magnus, it seemed, was a kindred spirit.

'Good stuff,' McNab said. 'Subsequent to our request to the Met to check out a London address for a Thomas Montgomery, it appears he has a holiday home here in Stromness and may be currently staying there.'

Ollie absorbed this, before saying, 'Is he our only suspect?'

'There is also a question mark over a certain George Whitelaw, who was apparently staying with the Bradley family prior to them leaving Orkney. He too purchased a torc bracelet similar to the one found with the first body.'

'There's likely to be more victims than the two you've found in Orkney,' Ollie offered.

'Exactly, but these two are the only ones we have to work with as it now stands,' McNab said.

'We've been looking for a match to the perp's DNA profile on the National Database,' Ollie told him. 'No luck as yet, so we'll now search for a familial match.'

The truth, McNab suspected, was that their perp had been killing over the last twenty years and maybe even before. They just hadn't found the bodies . . . yet. Hence they hadn't collected their killer's DNA.

McNab ended the call then, conscious of time passing and the upcoming interview with Annie.

Marshalling himself, he now positioned his chair so that he might be in full view of Annie when they went live. Just as he did so, DS Clark entered the interview room and waved up at him. 'This feels a bit weird, but I think it'll work,' she said.

'You take the lead when she's brought in,' McNab told her. 'Annie trusts you as much as she does me.'

Minutes later, the door opened and another officer ushered Annie inside.

She looks pale, McNab thought, despite the tan she'd obviously picked up during her sojourn in Majorca.

When Janice explained the situation and the whereabouts of acting DI McNab, Annie raised her eyes to look towards his screen image.

'Hello, Annie,' he said quietly. 'It's good to see you again and to be able to offer my condolences about your son, Ben.'

She gave a small nod. 'I always knew if Ben was still

alive I would have heard from him,' she said. 'So it wasn't a surprise to hear you'd found his body. But in Orkney?' She looked puzzled by that part.

'We think Ben may have come back here for a visit with a man he possibly met when he moved to London,' Janice explained. 'We also think that the man may well have been Ben's killer.'

Annie appeared to take time to absorb this before looking directly at McNab and saying, 'How did my boy die, Inspector?'

McNab didn't hesitate. 'We think he was probably drugged, then suffocated,' he said quietly. 'There were no wounds or evidence of violence. He was likely unconscious when it happened.'

'So no pain?' she checked.

'No pain,' McNab repeated. 'We also suspect Ben was in an intimate relationship with his killer, so was unlikely to be fearful in his company.'

Annie was silent for a moment before saying, 'I think that's the cruellest relationship of all. When you believe yourself to be loved, yet the truth is you're merely being controlled.'

Indicating with a look to Janice that they should give Annie a few moments before they continued, McNab wondered if she was in fact talking about her own relationship with her husband, Jack.

They soon found out when Annie began speaking again.

'I knew my boy was gay,' she said. 'Even before he knew it himself. Jack knew it too, and Ben was only ten when I met Jack. Jack never mentioned it at first. Not until it began to be more obvious. Then he would torment the boy, tell him to man up, when he was being bullied.

'That's why we ended up in Orkney. We thought it would be easier there, but it wasn't. Bullies exist everywhere, don't they?' She looked to McNab.

He didn't answer except with a small nod.

'He had a tough time in Kirkwall at the school, but not everyone was mean to him. There was a girl – Shona, I think she was called. They weren't going together, of course, but Jack laid off Ben after he mentioned her. For a while at least.'

McNab, thinking this might be the time to mention the presence of George Whitelaw in their house, gave Janice the nod.

'Annie,' she said. 'Did you have someone staying with you in Orkney back around that time?'

Annie looked momentarily surprised by the question, before saying, 'Yes, we did, but not for long. He was helping out at one of the archaeological digs. Gosh, I'd forgotten about that. Why are you asking?'

'Do you remember his name?' Janice tried.

Annie thought for a moment, 'I think I do,' she said. 'It was Gary something. Ben brought him home with him one night, because he was looking for digs for a few weeks and we needed the money. They'd met in a pub in Stromness. Ben wasn't far short of eighteen at the time and I didn't mind him going to the pub. In fact going there was better than staying at home with Jack nipping at him every time he came out of his room.'

'And the man's surname?' Janice said.

'It began with a W, I think,' Annie said. 'Maybe White?'

'Whitelaw?' Janice suggested.

'That's it, George Whitelaw, though he used the name

311

Gary.' Annie looked to McNab. 'What's Gary got to do with anything?' she asked.

'So he and Ben were pally?' McNab said.

'Well, they went out for a run in Gary's car now and again,' she told him. 'He was a fair bit older than my Ben. Maybe ten years. But he never made fun of him. Treated him well.'

'Have you any idea where Gary was from originally?' McNab asked.

'North of England, I think. His accent sounded as though he came from there at least,' she said.

'And what did he look like?' Janice tried.

'Quite handsome, I suppose. Taller than Ben, slim-built but not thin. Muscled, maybe from working on the digs. His hair was mid-brown. That's all I can remember.'

She fell silent then, an obvious thought crossing her mind. 'You don't think Gary had anything to do with what happened to my Ben?' she said worriedly.

'We're exploring everything about Ben's time in Orkney, including who he knew back then,' McNab told her honestly. 'And the girl Shona you mentioned. She spoke highly of Ben and he did come back to see her once, before he went to London,' he said.

'Maybe if he'd been a different kind of boy, they might have been together,' Annie said wistfully.

'Shona said Ben was the kindest boy she'd ever met,' McNab said.

'Kind and trusting,' Annie said. 'Which is probably why he died.'

After Annie had been shown out, McNab and Janice sat in mutual silence. Dealing with the mother of a murdered child was one of the hardest parts of the job, and in this case, where twenty years had passed, Ben was still the teen-age son Annie had last seen alive and well, and heading for London.

Eventually Janice said, 'Can you face Jack Bradley now, or should I ask another member of the team to sit in with me?'

'I'll stay, and be thankful I'm here and not across the desk from him,' he told her.

'My thoughts exactly,' Janice said. 'Shall I do the talking?'

'Yes, to begin with anyway,' McNab said.

He'd only seen Jack that one time, his big face staring out through the half-opened door of the Bradleys' flat, but McNab recalled it very well. He also remembered the man's hand grabbing at Annie when she wanted to speak to them.

He's a controlling bastard, he thought, as Jack took his seat in a nonchalant manner at the table opposite Janice. *He's also happy that it's a woman he has to deal with*, he decided, before Janice launched into a little speech about Detective Inspector McNab, 'who is the Senior Investigating Officer in the case of your stepson's murder'.

When she indicated McNab's God-like presence just above the bastard's line of sight, Jack's expression shifted a little, before it moved back into self-satisfied innocence.

Janice gave the usual spiel about the DNA identification of Ben's body, then asked Jack to describe his relationship with his stepson.

The question definitely caught him off-guard and he looked nonplussed for a moment, before saying, 'I thought you were going to tell me how he died.'

'Answer my question please, Mr Bradley,' Janice insisted.

'He was Annie's son, not mine. She was too soft on him.

I tried to be firmer. If he'd listened to me he wouldn't have ended up dead,' he finished.

'How do you work that one out?' McNab said.

Jack studied McNab's long-distance face for a moment. 'He would have married a nice girl, instead of heading for London to find a man to have sex with. Men who would play him like . . .' He halted there as though looking for the right ending to that sentence.

'Like *you* play *your* wife?' McNab found himself saying.

Janice came back in then to prevent him from being even more stupid.

'Your stepson returned to Orkney to see a Shona Bain,' she said, 'who he was friendly with at school. Then, as I understand it, he returned to his mum in Glasgow, where there was an altercation with you?'

Jack's face coloured at this recital of events. 'He should have stayed in Orkney with the lassie. She cared about him. He would have been happy there. But naw. He had to go where he could be himself, so I told him to get out and he went to London, where he could do what he liked with whoever he liked. And look what that got him.'

He slumped a bit in the seat then, and for the first time McNab thought Jack Bradley was sorry for what had happened to Ben, and not just sorry for himself.

Janice gave him a minute before bringing up the subject of George Whitelaw.

'He stayed with you for a time while working on an archaeological dig?' she said.

Jack shot her a look that McNab couldn't interpret.

'What's Gary got to do with this?' he said sharply.

'What was Gary like?' Janice persisted.

'He was okay,' Jack said. 'Him and Ben got on well. Ben started acting like a man when he was about.'

'They liked one other?' Janice said.

'Not the way you're saying it. Gary wasn't queer. He was a straight guy, who Ben liked and listened to. He used to take Ben round some of the sites he'd worked on. Got him interested in archaeology . . .' He tailed off.

'Can you describe Gary for us?' Janice said.

'God, it's twenty years ago and I didn't pay much attention to what he looked like back then. Annie would be able to describe him for you,' he said, his voice softening a little on her name.

McNab came back in at that point. 'Do you want to know how Ben died, Mr Bradley?'

The fear that flew across Jack's face suggested that was something he wasn't keen to know, but McNab now related the information exactly as he'd told Annie.

His explanation was followed by silence before a pale-faced Jack said, 'For Ben to go to Orkney with this guy means he wasn't afraid of him. And I bet the bastard told Ben he loved him,' he added, his expression a mixture of anger and pain.

Jack did care for the boy, McNab thought. He was just so afraid of Ben's sexuality, he couldn't show it. McNab thought about Annie, and realized she probably knew that too.

'Why did you take your wife to Majorca, and remove her phone so she was out of touch with us?' he said.

Jack looked straight at him. 'Annie had come to terms with not hearing from Ben. She'd convinced herself that he was happy in his new life. That thought made her happy. Then you two turned up. After that, she was beside herself thinking Ben had been murdered. Spent all her time on social media trying to find out if he was alive. While waiting for you to call.' He shook his head. 'So I took her away for a while to try to stop all that. I thought I was helping her.' He paused there, looking up at McNab on the screen. 'I was wrong.'

They finished the interview at that point and McNab's last image of Jack was of a beaten man, who knew that he'd screwed up and was even more aware of how he could never make that right.

'D'you think Annie'll leave him?' Janice said, when Jack Bradley had departed the room.

'I suspect he thinks she might,' McNab said.

After a moment's silence, he said, 'We need a true image of both George aka Gary Whitelaw and Thomas Montgomery. Surely in the world of social media and Orak, we can find a picture of each of these two men?'

'What if those names aren't their real ones?' Janice said. 'Most serial killers adopt multiple aliases and addresses,' she reminded him.

McNab had already done his own worrying along those lines. 'Magnus says he's an organized killer, who hasn't been caught for twenty years, and never would have been, if a pregnant whale hadn't got into trouble off Skaill Bay. Plus there is no record of his DNA on the database, which means he's never been caught for anything before. He knows that, and he's an arrogant bastard. My bet is he's living as he always has done.'

'And is watching our non-progress with relish, via Ava's podcast?' Janice suggested.

'That just about sums it up,' McNab said.

47

Orkney

McNab emerged from his office to find a solemn-looking Flett waiting for him.

'Were you back in time to view the interviews with Annie and Jack Bradley?' McNab asked.

'I was,' Flett said, his expression unchanged.

'And?' McNab said.

'It definitely puts George Whitelaw in the picture,' Flett said. 'And I agree with you on the need to get images of both him and Thomas Montgomery, although maybe not broadcast them as yet. If one of them is our perp, it'll give him time to go to ground. Something I think he'll do.'

Flett, he knew, was only echoing his own thoughts and would be aware of that, so why the long face, McNab wondered. Rather than ask him, he moved on to the report regarding the possibility of Thomas Montgomery being currently in Orkney and what Flett had done to make sure he couldn't leave undetected.

'That was good work in Stromness,' he offered.

Still Flett's expression didn't alter.

'Are you going to tell me what the bad news is?' McNab finally demanded in frustration.

'Dean Watters,' Flett said. 'He's here to be interviewed by you.'

'Dean Watters,' McNab repeated, questioningly at first, then as the name and its significance came back to him, he said, 'I take it you're referring to your current partner, Rory?'

'So you did check him out?' Flett said.

'I wouldn't be a good detective if I hadn't,' McNab told him, finding himself thankful that this particular subject was finally out in the open.

'Can I ask you when you did that?' Flett asked.

'Immediately I got back to Glasgow, I used the photograph I took of you two together on Sanday,' he said.

'At the community bonfire on Cata Sand?' Flett said.

'Exactly. I sent it to Ollie and he came up with the goods,' McNab said.

'And you didn't report it?'

'No,' McNab confirmed. 'I parked it. Did you know back then about Rory's past?'

'I knew he'd been married before he came out as gay and that his ex-wife had remarried and they were on good terms. I knew nothing about his real name and former convictions. Until today,' he added.

'So he told you about that,' McNab said, surprised. 'Why now?'

'He's been away for work and we haven't been in direct contact, but he had been following Ava's podcast. He saw the image of the torc bracelet and admitted to me that he'd been given one just like it in a Stromness pub maybe eleven years ago, by a man who'd chatted him up.'

McNab felt the hairs on the back of his neck rise up. 'Name of?'

'They didn't exchange names,' Flett said. 'Or anything else,' he added, obviously reading McNab's expression. 'Their meeting was brief, but Rory was certain he was being solicited. As the guy left, he slipped the torc on Rory's wrist, in memory, he said, of what might have been.'

'Have you seen this bracelet he's referring to?' McNab demanded.

'When we were first shown the torc recovered from the cist, I had a vague memory of seeing Rory wear one like it when I first met him. I couldn't ask because he's been off-grid since this began. So I searched through his stuff, without asking.' Flett looked uncomfortable about that. 'When he told me his story of where he got the torc, I said he needed to come in and speak to you about it. He asked me why you were back in Orkney and I explained about Ben and my connection to him. That's when he told me who he really was and that he suspected you knew that already.'

'So confession time all round,' McNab said. 'Right, I suggest DS Green takes his statement regarding the bracelet. And anything and everything Rory can recall regarding this guy. And I mean everything,' he added.

'You don't want to interview him yourself?' Flett said, looking surprised.

'I do not,' McNab said firmly, before changing tack. 'I also think you should speak to Shona Bain. Ask if she'd like to contact Annie Bradley. You probably heard in the interview that I told Annie what Shona had said about Ben. I'm sure Annie would love to hear it from Shona herself.'

Flett nodded. 'If Ben had turned out to be Ingrid's dad, Annie would have had a grandchild.'

'Well, if she and Shona make friends, Annie could have a proxy grandchild. After all, Ingrid tried very hard to adopt Ben as her dad.'

Even as he said all of this, McNab imagined Chrissy McInsh's surprised but pleased expression. Maybe even Rhona's too.

'Now, I'm due to meet with Dr MacLeod and find out what's been happening with Sigurd, who I've subsequently learned is a missing eighteen-year-old from London, as agreed by both our AI program and our human super recognizer.'

He continued. 'So you're back in charge here, DI Flett. Contact me if any other news comes in, of course. Other that that, I'll see you back here in the morning. Oh and,' he added, 'tell Rory to give his interview as his current self, not using his former persona. That's between you and me,' he said firmly.

McNab felt strangely elated as he began his walk down the now-familiar Albert Street, heading for the Kirkwall Hotel.

He should have clocked that DI Erling Flett had no idea that Rory had more than a failed marriage and a hidden sexuality in his past. Especially after Flett had brought him up here on the faint chance he'd known the Skaill Bay victim in senior school. Flett was a straight-up guy, he'd already decided that. Today's revelation merely confirmed this.

McNab took a swift run through his own past endeavours, going way back to school, where he'd done his own fair share of bad things. Then, on to how many times he'd screwed up on the job, and in his personal life too. If his boss, DI Wilson, hadn't believed there was a good detective in there, as well as an arse, he wouldn't have kept his job. A job he loved, despite the toll it took on his personal life.

And there he was again, blaming the job, when the truth was, it was him to blame for messing up every relationship he'd ever had.

Including, he acknowledged, the brief one he'd had with Rhona MacLeod. All of three months' duration. She'd told him from the onset it was casual. He hadn't accepted that, thinking he might persuade her differently. Of course, you couldn't persuade Rhona to do anything she didn't want to do.

So more fool him. If he'd played his cards right, like Sean Maguire, by not putting any pressure on Rhona, he might have been where the Irishman was now.

With that forlorn thought, he entered the Kirkwall Hotel and headed for the bar.

48

Orkney

Colin reappeared as she was completing her notes on the three objects found in the grave soil, which, together with the necklace, offered an image of victim two, along with the modus operandi and signature of the killer.

Looking up as he entered, she read by his expression that he too may have had some success.

'How'd it go with Sigurd?' he said.

'Good,' she told him. 'Plus your helpers did a fine job with the soil.' She indicated the evidence bags. 'Did they tell you what they'd found?'

'Something about more jewellery,' he said. 'And that they'd left notes for you.'

'In fact they found a black earring with Viking runes, which was located close to the left ear,' Rhona told him. 'A genital piercing, and perhaps most importantly, a glass phial.'

'So the pattern of death was likely the same?' Colin said.

Rhona gave an affirmative nod. 'What did you find?'

'A name on last year's Rousay dig. A guy holidaying

here in Orkney volunteered for a week. In truth, I don't recall him. Anyway, he signed himself Gary Whitelaw, with Stromness as his address.'

'You're thinking Gary as a pseudonym for George?' Rhona said.

He nodded.

'Any contact details?'

'Sadly no. He turned up after I let it be known that we were looking for volunteers to take part as diggers. Sometimes we need experienced volunteers, other times we'll take first-timers and give them on-site training. I was happy to do that at the Viking dig on Rousay.'

'Well, if it was the George Whitelaw who bought the torc bracelet and claimed to be staying with the Bradleys twenty years ago, he's one more lead that needs to be followed,' Rhona said.

'I think he came to us via the Orkney Archaeological Society, so I'll check with them tomorrow,' Colin said, glancing at the clock.

'God, is it that time already?' Rhona said. 'I have a Zoom catch-up with Chrissy in five minutes.'

'What are you doing about food tonight?' Colin checked.

'Meeting McNab again,' she said. 'Although I may have something other than fish and chips,' she added.

'Try their beef and Guinness pie,' he suggested. 'I'm out tonight too, so I'll see you back at the Ivy House later.'

As quiet descended on the lab, Rhona poured herself a coffee and settled at her laptop for the approaching Zoom call from Chrissy. Sitting in the waiting silence, she tried to come to a decision regarding when she should head back to Glasgow. A question Chrissy was very likely to ask. Maybe even before she gave her own news.

It turned out she was wrong, because when a very animated Chrissy appeared on her screen, her first and only interest was to tell Rhona that she'd heard on the grapevine that the second victim had been identified.

Chrissy was rarely wrong with such announcements and Rhona immediately wondered if the news had reached McNab yet. She learned the answer to that at the onset of the tale.

'McNab will know by now,' Chrissy told her. 'I got an inkling an hour ago. It seems the AI recognition software picked out three images it thought matched the identikit reconstruction of your second victim. However,' she paused dramatically, 'Ollie agreed on only two of them.' She hurried on. 'One was the photo supplied eleven years ago by the family of a missing person. The other was from CCTV footage of the same person leaving a gay bar in Vauxhall, London.'

'Do we have a name yet?' Rhona said.

'We do,' Chrissy told her. 'If Orak and Ollie are correct, and I definitely trust Ollie on this, then your second victim is eighteen-year-old Lucas Mason.'

Rhona's first thought following Chrissy's pronouncement was that they needn't use the name Sigurd any longer, because they now knew the real name of the teenager they'd found buried near the Sands of Evie.

'Have you viewed Orak's image of him?' Chrissy said.

'Not yet,' Rhona told her, 'although I'm keen to know if how I imagined him, together with what we learned from the DNA, will be a match.'

'Here you go,' Chrissy said, sharing her screen. 'Our boy Lucas. Taken not long before he disappeared.'

And there he was in two versions. One constructed by

Orak from the skull photos she'd taken. And the one from the photograph used in the police search for him.

How young he looks, Rhona thought, as she noted that she'd imagined the correct eye colour and was close on the hair colour. DNA had signalled it as light, but in the photograph he'd dyed it a glossy golden blond.

Interestingly, in the real photo he was wearing an earring like the one they'd found in the grave soil.

'Well, did you get it right?' Chrissy said.

'Orak and I agree on the eyes and hair colour, before he dyed it blond,' Rhona told her. 'Also, we found three items in the soil. One was an earring that looks like the one in the photo.'

'It had Viking runes on it?' Chrissy asked.

'Yes. We also found a genital piercing, and' – Rhona paused – 'an empty phial.'

'I guess we were right, then,' Chrissy said, her tone reflecting her sadness. 'The guy in Evie Sands is Lucas Mason and he was killed by the same person as Ben Bradley.'

They didn't talk much after that, their mood coloured by the images and what they meant. Rhona didn't ask after Connor, the moment seeming wrong. She also didn't mention that she'd been in touch with Sean either, and for once Chrissy didn't ask.

Any elation created by discovering the identity of the second victim had been washed away by seeing a picture of him when alive. That had always caused in Rhona a mixture of sorrow and anger, which would last at least as long as it took to identify his killer. And even longer if they didn't.

Slipping her laptop in her bag, she fetched her coat, deciding to head for the Kirkwall Hotel regardless of whether McNab would be there yet.

Outside was crisp and dry, the air fresh as always. Overhead, the sky glittered with stars, and when she reached the harbour, the scent of the sea washed her lungs clean. But she realized that she missed walking home through Kelvingrove Park, among the cyclists and joggers, the folk heading home from work, or perhaps already on their way for a night out.

If she felt like that, what on earth must McNab feel like by now? The thought made her smile. She would find out soon enough, she supposed.

Pushing open the door, she made for the table where McNab normally placed himself. He wasn't there yet. Neither was he chatting at the bar, something he was wont to do when alone.

Despite his dislike of the countryside and practically anywhere that wasn't inside the Glasgow city boundary, he was good at ingratiating himself with locals. Which was obvious by the way he'd managed to recruit Katrin to his cause, thereby retrieving Lucas's skull.

Ordering a glass of wine, she checked out the menu, looking for Colin's suggested choice for tonight. Once she found it, she decided to text McNab to see if he was headed here within the next half-hour. If not, she'd order her own meal.

That was another thing she missed, she realized. Chrissy's filled-roll breakfasts, picked up on her way to work, kept her going much longer than Colin's healthy breakfast of overnight oats and fruit, with tea and toast.

Twenty minutes later, and prompted by a delivery of what looked like the beef and Guinness pie at a nearby table, the smell of which she could longer ignore, Rhona rose and headed for the bar to place her order.

It was at that moment McNab strode in and came to join

her. Listening to her order, he upped it to two, then asked for a whisky and another white wine, 'for Dr MacLeod', before leading the way back to their table.

Having listened to his tone when ordering and viewed his expression, Rhona found herself unable to gauge his mood, which was unusual, because she'd been reading McNab for a very long time.

Seated now, she wondered if she should go first with her news of what had been discovered in the grave soil, or wait for McNab to lead, no doubt with the story of Sigurd's official identification as Lucas Mason.

What she didn't expect was to hear another story. One she hadn't anticipated.

49

Orkney

McNab, having told Rhona his tale of today's proceedings, including both Annie's and Erling's stories, now awaited an update from her.

'So a George Whitelaw did lodge with the Bradleys that summer before they left. And Annie liked him and thought him a good influence on Ben?' Rhona now checked.

'Even Jack Bradley thought that. He also stated quite firmly that this Gary bloke was straight,' he added.

'*A* Gary Whitelaw was back here in Orkney last summer,' Rhona said. 'Colin discovered his name as a late volunteer on their project on Rousay.'

McNab groaned. 'Where the hell is Rousay?'

'It's the big island just off Evie over Eynhallow Sound,' Rhona told him.

McNab, who had no difficulty with brain maps of Glasgow, even with all its street intricacies, had still failed to establish a mental picture of mainland Orkney, let alone the other islands.

'There's a dig on this island too?' he said in frustration.

'At a place called Skaill Farm, where they've discovered the foundations of a Viking hall,' Rhona explained.

'And our Gary was on that dig?'

'It seems so, according to Colin's records. Except he doesn't remember him.' She paused, obviously taking note of his expression. 'The weather here means volunteers are well wrapped up, whatever the time of year,' she added.

'Did he get paid for it?' McNab said, nursing a forlorn hope that there might be a paper trail.

'They're volunteers. That means they dig for free,' Rhona said with a sympathetic look.

McNab mumbled a few curses under his breath before saying, 'You think he was scouting for a new grave?'

'Maybe,' she offered.

'Maybe,' McNab repeated. 'Maybe the perp is called Thomas Montgomery. Maybe he's called George or maybe even Gary. One thing's for sure, he's making a right dick out of us.'

Rhona gave him a rueful smile. 'I think Colin and I should take a look at the site on Rousay.'

McNab, inwardly praying they would find nothing of significance, said, 'Of course you should. I take it there's a ferry to this Rousay place? Or do you need the police launch?'

Rhona considered this. 'I'll check with Colin and get back to you on that.'

'So you'll go to Rousay tomorrow?'

'Yes,' she confirmed. 'If there's nothing there of interest, I should head back to Glasgow with Lucas and the evidence retrieved from the soil from the second grave.'

He felt his face fall, despite all his efforts to prevent it. Rallying himself, he said, 'Of course, or else I'll have Chrissy

329

McInsh arriving by police helicopter to whisk you back herself.'

The look she gave him then showed she was well aware of how he felt at her imminent departure.

'Right,' he said, getting to his feet. 'Time to call it a day, and in the hope of a decent sleep before we're back to the fray tomorrow.'

His small speech over, he wished Rhona goodnight, adding, 'There's a strategy meeting at nine tomorrow morning. If you want to head straight to Rousay, I can present your findings on Lucas and the soil evidence.'

Rhona gave a nod to that and rose herself.

This time he didn't offer to walk her back to the Ivy House.

Once she'd left, he headed to the bar and, ordering a double whisky, took it back to his table. Despite his reference to bed, he had no intention of heading there yet. Today had presented him with much to mull over, including this latest news regarding the elusive Gary.

The Gary who they now knew had met and befriended Ben all those years ago. And was around the night Ben had arrived at the beach. Maybe Gary had been the one to run him there and take him home afterwards. Maybe Gary had even viewed the shenanigans that had taken place there. Or maybe Ben had confided in him about them afterwards.

Gary Whitelaw was no longer a ghost name, not since Annie and Jack Bradley had given their picture of him in today's interview.

As for Thomas Montgomery, he had a London address and appeared to be a real person, who also owned a holiday home in Stromness. Although, if he had been staying in the harbour cottage, he hadn't apparently returned there today, or they would have heard about it by now.

Flett's decision to pursue a search warrant for the cottage had been a good one, he acknowledged. That way they could hopefully obtain some DNA evidence, so that they might yet eliminate Thomas from their enquiry. Although, if the cottage was let out as an Airbnb, his wouldn't be the only DNA in there.

Plus they only had the neighbour's word that it was the owner staying there recently. Eye witnesses were notoriously unreliable. Except this was Orkney, he reminded himself, where everybody knew your name and your business.

As for Flett's alert to the ferry service and the airport, they'd been informed that no one with that name was booked in or out of Orkney.

Anyway, does a serial killer ever use their own name when out on a planned job? He thought not. Even a seasoned and successful one, such as they undoubtedly had here.

It was at that point a text buzzed in. Bracing himself, he took a look at the name, then checked what they had to say.

Meet me upstairs. There's someone you need to speak to.

So Katrin was back on the job, he thought. She hadn't been serving the coffee at breakfast for the last couple of mornings and he'd thought she'd moved shifts. Or was done with him.

Tossing back the remainder of his whisky, McNab headed for the stairs. Anything Katrin had to say was worth a listen, and anyone she thought he should meet was worth his time.

331

Approaching his door, he noted that she wasn't waiting outside and neither was anyone else. Assuming if he went inside, he would hear her knock soon enough, he tried his key, only to discover that the door was unlocked.

Cautious now, he entered and flicked on the light switch to find no one inside. Or no longer inside, at least. Glancing round, he tried to check if anything was missing. At this point the bathroom door opened and Katrin appeared.

'Jesus,' McNab said. 'How the hell did you get in here?'

Without answering him, Katrin beckoned to whoever was still in the bathroom.

A teenage boy now emerged, looking suitably worried about being there. Almost as tall as McNab, he was slim and lightweight, with long, dark hair knotted in a bun and an earring hanging from his right ear.

'This is Calum,' Katrin told him. 'He needs to speak to you.'

'About what?' McNab demanded.

'About the skull,' Katrin said. 'And other things. And you have to listen and not shout at him,' she added.

Christ, McNab thought. *She's beginning to sound like Chrissy.*

'Go ahead, Calum,' he said.

Obviously keen to get this over with, the boy's Orkney voice rose and fell softly and fast, and the tale he told was an interesting one.

It seems he'd been one of the two guys who'd travelled to Evie by boat and had taken the skull. Why they'd done this wasn't clear and, McNab thought, probably had come about through drink, drugs and teenage stupidity. Something he'd been familiar with when a teenager himself.

Waking up the next day, they'd apparently rued the antics of the night before, but Calum's erstwhile companion already had a police record, so they didn't come forward to return the skull. Calum had thrown a heartfelt look towards Katrin at this point, which made McNab think they might be an item.

'Anyway,' Calum said, 'Kat here brought it back to you.'

'So this is just a confession?' McNab said sharply.

'Wait,' Katrin said. 'There's more.'

Calum took a breath. 'There was someone else there that night. Apart from PC Tulloch.'

'Who landed in hospital,' McNab reminded him.

'That wasn't us did that,' Calum said. 'But that's why we left. We already had the skull and were heading to the boat when we heard Ivan's shout.'

'And you didn't go back to help him?'

Calum shook his head. 'No, we ran along the beach and back to the boat.'

'Did you see the other guy at all?' McNab tried.

'No, and there was no car apart from the police car.'

'So how did he get there, then?' McNab said.

'He must have walked in or he came by water,' Katrin told him.

'So did you see another boat?' McNab demanded.

'No, but I thought afterwards that something I did see may have been a beached kayak,' Calum said.

'A kayak,' McNab repeated. 'You think the guy who attacked PC Tulloch got there by kayak?'

Calum nodded.

And there it was. They'd talked about how the assailant might have come by water. It now seemed both sets of visitors to Lucas's grave may have done exactly that.

'Who do you think that was?' McNab tried, in case it had been someone in an opposing gang.

Katrin came in with the answer. 'We think it was the killer you're looking for, keen to take anything from the grave that might incriminate them,' she said.

McNab considered what Rhona had just revealed about the three items sifted from the grave soil, including the jewellery and the phial, and decided they might be right.

If they were, then the perpetrator had been here on Orkney mainland and recently. Plus they'd rattled him enough to have him try to remove items from the grave. Most likely he'd wanted the skull in particular, because of the image they might generate from it.

'You were both right to come and tell me this. Thank you.' He paused before addressing Katrin directly. 'I assume you would let me know if you and your team got wind of who this possible kayaker is, and where he might be staying? If he's still around.'

Katrin glanced at Calum before saying, 'We will.'

When they left shortly after that, McNab sat down on the bed with the remains of the whisky bottle to think through everything that had happened, both earlier in the day and just now.

50

Orkney

Ava rose before dawn and headed for the shower, hoping that the pounding water would waken her properly, after what had been a very few hours of sleep.

This was the way she'd always worked, she reminded herself, once she had her teeth into an investigation. Surely she should be used to it by now?

The problem, she registered, was that Orkney was more than 700 miles north of London, and the further north you went in winter, the shorter the days became. Which messed with your internal clock.

Also, what little sleep she'd had last night had been troubled because of Ingrid's reaction to the news that Ben wasn't her father. For some reason, the girl had fastened on this as something she wanted. Perhaps because Shona had spoken fondly of him. Or maybe because, if Ben had been her father, it had only been death that had stopped him from being a part of her life.

Later, after Dougie had driven Ingrid home, he'd returned to question Ava more closely regarding her involvement in the investigation. Even to the point of asking why Magnus had been to see Shona, and what was it that they – meaning herself, Erling and Magnus – knew about the dead Ben Bradley.

Now they were certain the victim was Ben, Ava had felt free enough to explain about their troubled relationship with the teenager.

'You were all mean to him?' Dougie had said. 'Even Magnus?'

'Magnus not so much, although even if we weren't openly abusive, we made it up by ignoring him.'

'Because he was gay?' he'd said in astonishment.

'I don't think we actually knew Ben was gay. We didn't talk openly about such things back then,' she'd told him.

'But Erling's gay,' he'd countered.

'He didn't come out until much later,' she'd explained.

Eventually he asked the question she'd been expecting and was now, she thought, prepared for. What had really happened at Skaill Bay the night of the party?

So she'd told him everything she could remember about that terrible night. Of Magnus and Shona on the beach, of herself and Erling in the dunes, and Ben spying on them. And, of course, the resulting fight when Erling had spotted him.

Watching the wealth of emotions crossing Dougie's face, she knew he'd begun now to understand their reaction to the discovery of the body and the worrying possibility that it might be Ben.

'So that's the reason Erling brought in DI McNab from Glasgow?' he'd said quietly.

'Yes,' Ava had said. 'Erling's a good person and a good police officer.'

'And Magnus?' he'd said.

'We all three regret we weren't kinder to Ben. Maybe he would have stayed here, even after his mother and step-father left for Glasgow, if we had been.'

'*You* left Orkney and no one had been mean to you,' Dougie had countered.

'That's true,' she'd conceded. 'So did Erling for a while, and Magnus doesn't live here full-time.'

'I think Ingrid will leave too,' he'd said, sadness in his voice. 'She's planning on going to college in Glasgow.'

'But she'll come back to see her mum, and you,' Ava had said, hoping that would be true.

'She's not happy about her mum not telling her who her father is. I wish it was Magnus. I think Ingrid would have liked that.'

'Despite what I said about Shona and Magnus on the beach together that night, Magnus is definitely not Ingrid's father. Shona told him he wasn't and encouraged him to take a paternity test to prove it. Which he did.'

Later that evening, after the kye had been dealt with, and they'd eaten, Dougie took himself up to his room and Ava stayed on in the kitchen with Finn for company, settling down to the task she'd been surveying this morning before deciding what to do with it.

She'd continued to follow what was happening on the chat forum, although now that it was being closely moni-tored by Glasgow, she was happy enough to leave it to their digital team to try to identify M and W.

So she'd returned to a different, but related task.

She hadn't mentioned this aspect of what she was inves-tigating to anyone here as yet, although it had been going on for some time, and had expanded considerably since the discovery of the two bodies in Orkney.

When she'd begun her true crime podcast, her intention had been to focus on unsolved murders in the UK, in particular those associated with buried or hidden bodies.

From there, she'd initially selected a half-dozen which, she believed, would be interesting to study in more detail. These involved the discovery of hidden remains, sometimes found in undergrowth, some of which had been discovered in the walls or under the floors of buildings. Others that had been unearthed when an area of land had been newly ploughed over or during an archaeological excavation.

It was the three belonging to that last group that she returned to now, because of their links with former Viking settlements in England.

The first was in North Yorkshire, where an excavation of what was believed to be a Viking graveyard had unearthed newer bones mixed in with the old. When these were re-assembled, the skeleton was found to be incomplete. However, what they did retrieve marked the remains as being those of a young male, late teens to early twenties. There was no clothing, or any items with the body, apart from a ring on the fourth finger of the left hand. The ring was described as silver, with Viking markings.

The second one of interest involved a possible Viking burial north of York, uncovered when a field was being ploughed. When the remains were fully exposed, they turned out to belong to yet another young male, estimated to have been in his early twenties. Identity unknown. Manner of death undecided.

And the third unsolved case came from a church graveyard

in Cumbria. Initially it was believed to be the remains of a male Viking, due to the age of the items found buried with him. However, the forensic examination proved the victim to be a modern adult male, buried there little more than a decade ago. Who he was and how he'd died also remained unresolved.

Hearing Dougie moving about upstairs, she rose and put the kettle on to boil, then fetched eggs and bacon from the fridge.

She was well aware that Dougie, resourceful and self-sufficient as he was, was more than capable of feeding himself. Something that was obvious from the broadening of his shoulders and his healthy countenance.

However, that didn't stop her from playing big sister while she was here.

When Finn led the way into the kitchen minutes later, followed by a smiling Dougie, she was glad she had.

'I usually wait to eat until after the kye get theirs,' he said as she laid the filled plate on the table.

'I know, but I'm up early so . . .' she said.

Glancing towards her side of the table at her laptop and notebooks, he gave her a studied look.

'What are you up to now, big sister? I thought the police had taken over the monitoring of your chatroom responses?'

'They have. This is something else,' she told him.

'Do I want to know what?' he asked, in between mouthfuls.

'I'd been working on an idea for the podcast, before everything at Skaill Bay happened, which would involve buried or hidden bodies of as yet unidentified young males.' She turned her laptop to face him. 'These three were unearthed by chance and in places associated with Viking burials,' she said.

Dougie gave a whistle as he scanned the short descriptions, setting Finn, sheepdog that he was, on high alert. Giving the dog a reassuring pat on the head, Dougie said, 'So what do you plan to do with this?'

'I think I'll run it past Dr MacLeod in the first instance. As far as I'm aware, there was no DNA recorded of a possible perpetrator in any of these three cases. That may be because such evidence wasn't collectable at the time. Or its existence wasn't put in the public domain. I think Rhona's better placed to find that out than I am.'

Dougie's expression suggested he agreed with her decision, especially when he added a nod and a 'Sounds good', before rising. With a whistle to the waiting Finn, he said, 'I'm off to do the kye plus multiple other jobs. I'll see you later?'

She told him yes. 'And there'll be food then too,' she promised.

Once he'd left, she selected Rhona's number and pressed the call button. When it wasn't immediately picked up, she thought about cancelling. But just before she did, Rhona answered.

'Ava. You're up early.'

As Ava began to apologize, Rhona came back in. 'Great, because I am too. How are things with you?'

'Better since I made a full confession to Dougie regarding our treatment of Ben Bradley and what went down at the Skaill Bay party.'

'Good. But I don't think that's what you called about,' Rhona said, obviously reading her tone.

'No,' Ava admitted. 'But it is in connection with the case – and your forensic expertise,' she added.

'D'you want to tell me or show me in person?' Rhona immediately asked.

'In person would be better,' Ava agreed.

'Okay. Come by the Ivy House and we'll talk.'

51

Orkney

Rhona had given up on sleep when her brain had insisted on replaying everything that she'd learned the previous evening. Over and over again.

Now up, showered and dressed, she headed downstairs to the kitchen, which was gloriously warm even at this early hour, and put the kettle on.

Shortly after this, Ava had called, sounding surprised but pleased to find she too was awake.

Rhona had known that the early call meant something was afoot. And hearing Ava's voice only strengthened that belief. Hence her suggestion that they meet in person.

The pot of coffee made, she settled down with her own laptop and awaited Ava's arrival, while checking her emails on the chance there was anything new through from Chrissy.

The drive from Orphir, she knew, took just over ten minutes, so she was ready for the knock when it came at the door.

'No traffic?' she said as she let Ava in.

'An empty road,' Ava confirmed. 'It's still too early and dark for most folk. Just not if you live on a farm,' she added with a smile.

Pouring her a coffee, Rhona beckoned Ava to take a seat at the table. Waiting until she was settled, she then said, 'So what's this about? You said it's something to do with the case?'

Ava nodded and, taking out her own laptop, set it up to face Rhona. 'Take a look at these,' she ordered, her voice shaky with either excitement, Rhona thought, or fear.

'What are they exactly?' Rhona said, pulling the laptop towards her.

'Details of three finds at Viking sites in northern England,' Ava told her.

Rhona read the three paragraphs regarding bodies of young males unearthed by accident close to or on existing Viking burial sites. As she did so, she felt her own pulse quicken.

'How did you find these?' she asked.

Ava then explained how she'd been searching for material for future true crime podcasts involving buried and hidden bodies.

'These three appeared as part of my original research. This was before the body was discovered at Skaill Bay,' she added.

'No wonder you came home when you heard about that,' Rhona said.

'The thing was, I didn't initially link it to my original research, because the Viking aspect wasn't so obvious at the onset. Not until the presence of the torc bracelet was made public. By then I was so absorbed with my podcast on Skaill Bay, and Erling's fear that it was the body of Ben Bradley that had been exhumed, that I forgot about this research for the next true crime investigation,' she said.

She continued. 'Then the chat forum became the focus, until the responsibility of that was taken over by the Glasgow digital team. Although, I must confess, I still read all the comments.'

'Me too,' Rhona said, before asking, 'What do you want to do about this' – she indicated the screen – 'and how can I help?'

'I think I've exhausted all the avenues I have to learn anything more on these three cases. I don't know, for example, if DNA was collected, which might be compared to that collected by you at the current crime scenes. None of that information is available in the public domain. We know our perpetrator has been operating for some time, and chooses, it appears, similar victims. Young, male and likely gay. The fact that I can't unearth any information about these three young males points to their vulnerability. As for the location of their burial . . .'

Rhona waited for what she suspected would be the request.

'I know this is a Police Scotland investigation,' Ava said. 'But I'm assuming you're in touch with police forces in northern England, as well as the Met?' When Rhona nodded, she went on. 'Then you might be able to ask for the full details about these three similar cases, especially regarding the forensic evidence collected?'

Rhona agreed. 'That seems not only sensible, but also imperative,' she said. 'I wasn't going to this morning's strategy meeting, but I think I should now, to present your material, if you're in agreement? However,' she added, 'should we gain access to the said forensic evidence, I couldn't reveal that to you. It would be restricted information.'

'I know,' Ava told her. 'But if it helps catch the bastard, I'm happy with that,' she added vehemently.

When Ava departed, after transferring the necessary files to Rhona's laptop, Rhona sent a message to McNab to inform him that she would be at the nine o'clock meeting, after which she and Colin would take the local ferry to Rousay.

Hearing Colin heading down the stairs, she set about making fresh coffee, keen to tell him what Ava had just told her and to show him her notes. At the same time hoping that Colin might be aware of the archaeological sites involved.

'Do you know any of the places mentioned?' she asked, once he'd finished reading.

'The north of England is rich in Viking sites, but I don't recall these three in particular,' he admitted. 'I certainly wasn't aware of unidentified remains found in the areas mentioned. Of course, her research goes way back, more than two decades.' He looked impressed. 'She never gives up, does she?'

'No, she doesn't,' Rhona agreed. 'Which is why I intend to inform the team about her research this morning at the strategy meeting.'

'You should be able to gain access to the police files on these three cases?' Colin checked.

'I would hope so. Especially if it's decided they may be linked to our current investigation. However, the wheels of the justice system grind exceedingly slowly at times,' she added.

'Yes, but they also grind exceedingly fine,' he quoted back at her. 'So we catch the ferry a little later?'

'I'll call when I leave the meeting,' she promised.

'And I'll come round and pick you up,' he told her. 'The

forecast is for wind and rain. Plus there's no shelter where we're headed. And it'll be muddy underfoot.'

'I'll dress like a volunteer,' Rhona told him.

McNab's call came as she stepped out into the weather.

'Why the change of plan, Dr MacLeod?' he demanded.

'I had a visit from Ava first thing, and I believe you and your team need to hear what she's discovered.'

There was a pregnant silence before he said, 'Can I ask what it's in reference to?'

'Similarities between our victims and discoveries at three archaeological sites in northern England,' she told him.

'You think they might be the missing pieces of the time jigsaw?' he said.

'Possibly,' Rhona told him.

'Right, I'm assuming you're still heading for Rousay later, despite the weather?'

'We are,' she said.

'Then you definitely need to hear what I have to say.'

He rang off then, before Rhona could ask what that was. She thought she'd already been brought up to date last night in the bar.

Free now of the sheltered centre of the town, the squall met her head on, causing Rhona to up her speed until she reached the police station.

She registered the palpable buzz in the air as she headed upstairs to the meeting room. Something obviously had happened that she didn't know about as yet. Either that or the team had heard rumours of a breakthrough and were anticipating being told about it.

Seeing her enter, McNab beckoned her to the front beside Erling, then opened the proceedings with a story about the night the skull had been removed from the second grave.

Listening to the tale of two male teenagers who, high on something, decided to take a boat to the site at Evie and steal the skull, sent waves of astonishment through the assembled group. Everyone currently present in the room had something in their teenage past they would rather not be reminded of, including both Erling and McNab, which McNab made plain.

'One of the culprits, who will both remain unnamed, came to me with a full confession,' he said. 'He also told me something equally important to our investigation. They managed to creep in and remove the skull unnoticed, and were already leaving when they heard PC Tulloch's shout. Thinking he'd spotted them, they ran along the beach to their boat. At that point, they realized someone else had been there and possibly hit or knocked Ivan over. However, they did not return to check.'

There were murmurs of disquiet at this. The 'But' that followed silenced them.

'But they did see what they thought was a kayak on the beach.' He paused here briefly to let this sink in. 'Which all goes to prove,' he continued, 'that our earlier theory regarding the thieves arriving by boat was correct. Also, I suggest, did our perpetrator, keen to remove anything of significance he thought was in that grave, including the skull.

'If the skull was his prime concern, that means he was worried about the AI image it would produce and suspected it might lead to sightings of the victim, perhaps in his company?' McNab finished.

The significance of this lead wasn't lost on the team as Erling now stepped up to the front.

'As you know, we have two possible suspects. Thomas Montgomery, who had one of the original torc bracelets sent to his London address, and who owns property in Stromness, and has allegedly been seen there recently. In view of the possibility of him still being on Orkney mainland, we have now received a warrant to search his cottage.

'Secondly, we have confirmed that a George or Gary Whitelaw, who purchased the second torc, did in fact lodge with the Bradleys twenty years ago and was friendly with Ben. We don't have an address for him, although Annie Bradley recalls him having a north of England accent. However—'

Rhona chose this moment to raise her hand. Having been given the go-ahead, she explained about Whitelaw volunteering last summer at a dig involving the excavation of a Viking hall at Skaill Farm on Rousay, as recorded by Professor Nelson.

'You think, assuming he's our man, he may have been scouting for another burial site?' Erling said.

'It would fit with our perp's MO,' she said. 'The prof and I plan to check out the Rousay site after this. And, as you're all aware, Rousay is just over Eynhallow Sound from Evie.'

McNab then checked if this was everything she'd planned to tell the team. Confirming there was more, Rhona came forward and, connecting her laptop to the screen, brought up the three entries from Ava's research.

'Prior to the current investigation,' she began, 'Ava had been collecting information regarding unsolved murders involving hidden and buried bodies, which is, as you know, my area of expertise. Her research on this spanned the whole of the UK. The three on the screen appeared as part of that research, all of which were found prior to the discovery of the cist at Skaill Bay.

'The significance of the Viking element to both murders

here on Orkney mainland, plus our belief that a serial killer is unlikely to repeat the pattern only once every ten years, sent her back to her previous research. The result of which is here on the screen.

'What she couldn't find was a mention in the public domain of DNA samples taken from any of these three crime scenes. Which is why she approached me. I would like to pursue this lead, as I believe the circumstances of these three deaths and burials form a pattern similar to what we're dealing with here.'

Silence followed as the team grasped that it was increasingly likely that what they were dealing with here was only a small part of what had been happening in the decades leading up to now.

McNab came in then, to confirm that he would be in touch with his counterparts in the north of England regarding any DNA evidence they had on the three similar cases on their patch.

At this point, Erling and Jo left to accompany the search team to Stromness, and Rhona indicated she would head for Rousay.

52

Orkney

McNab had been here before and now took a moment to glory in the belief that a possible breakthrough was imminent. 'Possible' being the appropriate word, because he knew that it was as yet only a gut feeling.

And a gut feeling, although promising, didn't automatically guarantee success.

After all, the killer they sought had operated under the radar for twenty years or more and hadn't made a slip-up during all that time. And might never have done, if the pod of whales beaching at Skaill Bay hadn't provided them with the evidence of what he'd been up to.

Glancing at his watch, he realized he would only just have time to fetch a coffee before Ollie's promised video call, which he hoped might provide yet another piece of the jigsaw. Or maybe a proper image of the man they sought.

The scarcity of images available for both Montgomery and Whitelaw could, of course, be explained in terms of a simple dislike of social media. Something he himself could relate to.

McNab groaned inwardly, remembering the occasions

he'd fallen foul of having photos taken of him and then posted on social media, causing problems almost too big to be solved. Since then, he'd taken even more care never to have his photograph taken in any circumstances. A wise move for a serving police officer, especially when on the job.

So the two men keeping their heads down might well be innocent, if it weren't for the threads that seemed to weave them into the story of a murdered young man in the first instance.

As the laptop announced Ollie's arrival online, McNab downed the remainder of his coffee with an internal wish that IT might yet be able to present him with the likenesses he sought.

'Ollie. What's happening?' he addressed the familiar face on the screen.

'Between Orak and myself, we have created a likeness of the male leaving the gay club alongside Lucas Mason. This is him,' Ollie said as his own face on the screen was replaced by another.

'Do we know who he is exactly?' McNab said, his heart skipping a beat.

'We know he frequents gay bars and clubs in London, because we've matched him to other CCTV footage. We don't yet have a name, just an AI-generated photograph.'

McNab brought up the photo Annie had sent him and stared from it to the one on the screen and back again, before saying, 'Annie Bradley found a snapshot she'd taken of Gary Whitelaw with her son. It's twenty years old. I'll send a copy through. I can't see the resemblance to your guy, but you would be able to tell if it's him or not.'

'Send it over and I'll get back to you,' Ollie told him.

'Soon?' McNab checked.

'Orak's quicker than me, but we're not always in agreement,' Ollie reminded him.

'It's you I'll believe,' McNab said. 'Always.'

As Ollie departed, Erling's call came in. 'You ready for this?' he said, when McNab answered.

'Ready for what exactly?' McNab said.

'We're inside the fisherman's cottage. It is as expected operating as an Airbnb, so there's nothing personal in it and it's also very clean. There's a set of instructions on how everything works, plus a number to contact in case of an emergency,' Flett told him. 'I rang it and a Mrs Pyper answered. She's the cleaner. She also told us that a company called Walker-Montgomery Holdings owns the cottage, and that a man calling himself Montgomery visits on occasion. He's been here recently, she said, with another man. Considerably younger than himself. She sounded disapproving.'

'He's left now, I take it?'

'He informed her he was leaving and asked her to clean. Before we forewarned the airport and ferry service,' Flett added.

'Any chance of a DNA sample?' McNab said.

There now came what sounded like a laugh from Flett's end.

'What?' McNab demanded.

'Mrs Pyper had already cleaned the cottage thoroughly by the time we arrived. However, she hadn't washed the bedding as yet, so the answer to that is a resounding yes. One last thing,' he added. 'There's a two-person kayak on the jetty, which I don't remember being here on my previous visit.'

53

Orkney

The weather had worsened by the time they reached the jetty at Tingwall, where Colin joined the queue of cars waiting to reverse down the slipway and onto the MV *Eynhallow*.

Their vehicle now secured in the hold, they headed for the passenger lounge, where they sought a window seat to watch Orkney mainland fade from view.

'D'you think we should have waited for an improvement in the weather?' Rhona said.

'It's March in Orkney,' Colin told her. 'This *is* the weather. Anyway, look,' he said, pointing at the now-scurrying clouds and brightening sky. 'It's clearing up for us.'

He rose. 'I'm going for a chat with the crew. They know me from the summer dig. There aren't many visitors to Rousay at this time of year. So any non-locals using the ferry will have been noted.'

Twenty minutes later, as they drove off on the other side, Colin told her that he'd learned that a couple of walkers with a black pickup had been ferried across in the past couple of days, and as far as they knew they hadn't yet left the island. Plus a guy who'd come prepared to camp, which the crew had told him was unwise.

'Any descriptions?' Rhona tried.

'All male. All wearing wet-weather gear. Ages unknown, although one, they thought, was younger than the others,' Colin told her.

It wasn't the first time Rhona bemoaned the fact that they had, as yet, no current likenesses of their two suspects. All she did have was a photograph McNab had sent her, which she'd shared with Colin, of a snapshot from twenty years ago, taken by Annie Bradley of her son, Ben, and Whitelaw together.

As for the London-based Montgomery, there was only a loose description of a man who might be the owner of the fisherman's cottage in Stromness, plus a flat in London.

Turning her mind from what they didn't have, Rhona focused on their plan for today. They'd already mapped out the area they believed they could cover in the daylight left to them, including the Skaill Farm dig, plus the land between there and the ruins of St Mary's church.

This stretch of ground seemed even more pertinent now, after the earlier revelation regarding Ava's findings.

At Skaill Bay, the choice of burial site would have been made simple by the discovery of a stone cist. As for Evie, the area chosen had been close to a Viking burial ground and was both accessible and easily dug up.

Once a site was selected and prepared, the perpetrator, she believed, would have marked its location in some manner, ready for when the time came to dispense with his next victim. All of which she and Colin had discussed, with respect to the areas they were about to search.

Colin, they'd decided, would check the area he knew well in the surrounds of the Viking hall. Whereas Rhona would focus on the stretch of ground between there and St Mary's churchyard.

'We're not necessarily looking for evidence of a burial,' Rhona reminded him. 'It may just be a marker of some description, indicating the possible location of a future grave. If your volunteer Gary Whitelaw is our perpetrator, then his visit here last summer is unlikely to have been an innocent one.'

They parted then, with Rhona heading westward, following the shoreline, looking for any sign of a marked area, a change in surface vegetation or evidence of clearing or digging.

It was a walk she'd done in other locations, usually prompted by a single bone picked up by a walker or their dog. Or a farmer ploughing a field, only to churn up more than they'd bargained for.

On a couple of occasions her eyes deceived her, and an area of interest turned out to have nothing notable about it at all, once she grew close enough to examine it properly.

She was halfway between St Mary's and the remains of Skaill Farm when she finally found what she was looking for.

The rectangle had been fashioned using small flat stones, facing longways to the nearby shore.

Approaching, she lifted a couple of these, taking note that the grass below had been cut through, likely by a spade.

Further investigation revealed that this had been done on three sides of the rectangle, allowing the grass cover to be drawn back like a curtain, as had been the case at the burial site at Evie. Crouched alongside, she pulled back a corner to discover that the mix of earth, shells and sand had been worked loose, and some of it already distributed on the nearby shore.

This was it, she acknowledged. This was the prepared grave. Ready and waiting for the next victim.

Her heart thumping, she rose and shouted for Colin. Hearing her call, he came swiftly towards her. His expression when he looked down at the stone-marked perimeter reflected her own. Without speaking, he crouched and, like her, lifted a corner of the turf to check what lay beneath.

Rhona waited as Colin rose to his feet and gathered his thoughts.

'I'd say this is what we've been looking for,' he said grimly. 'A likely grave, prepared, but not made use of . . . as yet.' He looked out over the frothing waters of the Sound. 'Easily accessible from the water,' he added. 'Just like at Evie.'

'I don't think this was dug during the summer,' Rhona said. 'The vegetation cover wouldn't look like this. Plus the material that's already dug out is still in piles on the edge of the beach, but the autumn and winter swells would have distributed it.'

'So it's pretty recent?' Colin said.

'I would say so.'

While Rhona set about photographing and videoing the prepared grave, Colin fetched a tarpaulin from the car to protect it from the incoming squall.

The break in the weather over, both the sky and the sea had grown equally grey and troubled.

'We'd better head for the ferry,' Colin told her as they secured the tarpaulin. 'We can return tomorrow for a better examination in daylight.'

'Will the ferry still be running?' Rhona said as they drove back to the landing point.

'If there is a problem, I have friends here who will put us up for the night,' Colin told her.

As it was, the ferry was ready and waiting for its last run back to Tingwall, before finishing early due to the deteriorating weather.

Once their vehicle had been loaded, Colin told her he wanted to talk to the crew again, keen to know which, if any, of the visitors they'd mentioned had left the island during the intervening time.

Arriving minutes later in the passenger lounge, he slid into the seat beside Rhona.

'Any luck?' she said.

He nodded. 'It turns out that camping guy has departed due to the weather, as they suspected he would. They haven't seen the other two men again.'

'So they must still be on Rousay,' Rhona said.

'What are you thinking?' Colin said, reading her worried expression.

'That we should have shown the crew the photo Annie took of Ben and Gary Whitelaw together. Just to be sure it wasn't Gary they saw,' she added.

'You're right. Let's do that, once we dock,' Colin said. 'They'll have their hands full until then.'

The usually twenty-minute crossing took almost double the time on the way back, and Rhona was relieved when their car was finally on the slipway and her own feet were on solid ground again.

While Colin went to show the crew the photograph, she called McNab to give him news of their discovery.

He listened in silence before saying, 'Good work. Can you come directly to the station? Things are moving at a pace.'

As he rang off, Colin appeared, indicating with a shake of

his head that the crew hadn't recognized the older guy in the photo.

'They did recognize Ben, though,' he said. 'They'd seen his picture in the *Orcadian* and knew the whole story about him and Skaill Bay. I shared a copy of the photo with them and they confirmed that they'll get in contact if they're suspicious that anyone using the Rousay ferry might be the man we're looking for,' he added.

They both sat in silence on the way back to Kirkwall, Rhona deep in thought regarding what McNab had meant in their brief phone call when he'd said, 'things are moving at a pace'.

Arriving in the still-driving rain and gusting wind at the police station, Colin dropped her off and indicated he was heading back to UHI.

'Let me know what's happening later. I'll be at home tonight and there will be food prepared, in case you and DI McNab fancy a change from the bar menu at the hotel.'

The police station seemed eerily quiet on entry, in complete contrast to her earlier visit. Rhona assumed Erling and Jo and their SOCO team weren't back yet from Stromness and their examination of the fisherman's cottage.

Making her own way first to Erling's office to find it empty, she then sought McNab out in his cupboard.

On her entry, he looked up, and the ghost of a smile crossed his tired face. 'Welcome back, Dr MacLeod. Take a seat and tell me exactly what you found on Rousay.'

Rhona took her time, explaining how they'd gone about their search and what exactly they had found.

'So it was worked on recently?' When Rhona nodded, he added, 'How recently exactly?'

'Very,' she confirmed.

She told him about Colin's conversations with the crew and what they could recall about their most recent passengers.

'The single man planned to camp, which they advised against,' she said. 'The other two men, one of whom was younger, didn't say why they were going, but were dressed for walking and the weather.'

She then explained about showing the crew the old photo of Gary Whitelaw with Ben. 'They knew Ben from the *Orcadian*, but they didn't recognize the man with him.'

At this point, they heard Erling and Jo return.

'Let's take the meeting up to DI Flett's room,' McNab said, rising.

As he moved towards the door, his mobile rang. Glancing at the screen, he said, 'I have to take this. You go ahead and I'll be up shortly.'

54

Orkney

McNab shut the door behind Rhona, then sat back down at his desk.

'Okay. Tell me what you have.'

Janice's voice was clear and full of emotion. And he could understand why.

What she was saying blew everything wide open. As he attempted to work out what had happened and what might still happen, he was grateful for the professional manner in which she delivered the information.

'Right,' he eventually said. 'I'll go tell the team. And keep me up to date on any further developments.'

The trio of DI Flett, DS Green and Dr MacLeod fell silent as he entered. Perhaps it was his expression, McNab thought, looking even darker than usual.

'What is it?' Rhona immediately said.

McNab took a breath before beginning his revelation.

'The guy with Ben in Annie's photograph is not a match for the man seen leaving the gay bar with Lucas Mason.

That's been confirmed by Ollie via DS Clark.' He paused there to let that part of his news sink in.

'In fact,' he continued, 'the man Annie and Ben knew as Gary Whitelaw is dead. He died eleven years ago from a heart attack and is mourned by a wife and a teenage son.'

'Then who volunteered last year on Rousay?' Rhona asked.

'We believe it was his son, who shares both his father's name and apparently his interest in archaeology,' McNab told her.

'So we've been chasing ghosts?' Erling said in astonishment.

'Only one ghost,' McNab said. 'Both Ollie and Orak initially thought that the man caught on CCTV with Lucas Mason was our other suspect, Thomas Montgomery, of the London-based financial firm Walker-Montgomery.'

He watched their expressions as that sank in.

'M and W, the two signatures on the chatroom posts,' Rhona said.

'Exactly,' McNab said. 'However, that name, they now believe, is only one of many aliases used by this man.' He paused there briefly to allow them to digest what had been said up to now, before continuing.

'When the Met contacted the company enquiring about a Thomas Montgomery, they confirmed that he is not one of their employees. He is also not the man currently living at the address we have for him in London. Although it's likely he did stay there at one time.'

'So this man, under one of his aliases, is our killer?' Jo said.

McNab nodded. 'It was his posts on the chat forum of Ava's podcast that eventually led us to him. He thought he was clever enough to cover his tracks, but Cyber Division eventually tracked him down.'

He watched as the enormity of this result became apparent on their faces.

'Magnus was right,' he said, 'our perpetrator is an organized killer, and confident that he won't be caught, but he still couldn't stop himself from contributing to the conversation surrounding the investigation.'

Jo came in then. 'I take it this is the male who bought the torc bracelet twenty years ago and who has volunteered on archaeological digs here?'

'We believe so,' McNab said.

'And who we think has now left Orkney?' Jo added.

'Perhaps not,' McNab said, nodding to Rhona to explain, which she duly did.

He watched Erling as Rhona described her visit with Colin to Rousay, and their discovery of what she believed to be a recently prepared grave.

As she drew to a close, McNab heard Erling swear for the first time. Long and loud. 'So the bastard could still be here in Orkney?' he said, before another thought obviously occurred. 'This young guy he's with. Is he in danger?'

This had been McNab's primary concern as he'd climbed the stairs to the meeting room. Why bring a young sexual partner up here, if not to treat him in the same way he'd treated the other two they already knew about?

'I'm assuming that was his intention. In Dr MacLeod's opinion, the likely burial place on Rousay has been prepared very recently. Possibly within the time we think he's been here.' McNab paused for a moment then continued. 'Added to that, since we chose not to release Lucas Mason's identikit image either online or to the newspapers, he may believe we still don't have the skull and have been unable to identify the second body.'

'Which,' Rhona said, 'convinces him that we're not much closer to identifying him.'

'But that's where he's wrong,' McNab said. 'We have his image with the last known sighting of Lucas Mason. We're also soon to have his DNA, courtesy of Mrs Pyper and the unwashed sheets at the fisherman's cottage.' He threw a half-smile in Erling's direction. 'We just need to apprehend him before he claims another victim.'

Erling came back in then. 'The ferry crew, did they mention if the two men travelling together took a vehicle across to Rousay?' he asked.

'They were in a black pickup truck,' Rhona told him.

'It was a black pickup truck parked outside the fisherman's cottage,' Erling said, his expression fearful. 'Right,' he said firmly. 'There are limited places to stay on Rousay, especially over the winter months. If they haven't caught the ferry back as yet, then they must have accommodation on the island,' Erling said.

'And you know all the places they could stay?' McNab checked. When Erling nodded, he said, 'Right, as SIO I'm now handing over the search for these two men to DI Flett. He knows his patch and his people, and I for one will be doing whatever he asks of me.'

Erling's look of surprise was swiftly replaced by resolve.

'Thank you, Inspector McNab. First things first. Jo, I'd like you to call all the numbers on the list I'll send you. Don't alarm folk, just say we're looking for two walkers currently stranded on Rousay. I'll give the ferry crew a call. Check on when they're likely to resume crossings. Also, we'll ready the police launch and take it up to Tingwall. It can cross in weather the ferry can't cope with.'

McNab signalled to Rhona to follow him out.

'You okay?' she said as he halted outside the room.

'Out of my depth where islands and wild water are concerned,' McNab told her. 'This is definitely DI Flett's domain. Plus I promised to be on call for Glasgow. There's information updates coming in regularly from DS Clark and, of course, Ollie. I'm of more use here,' he said. 'What about you?'

'I'll ask to go with the police launch. If something untoward has happened, I'll be there on the scene to do my job,' Rhona told him.

When she went back in to discuss this with Flett, McNab headed to his office. Resting back in his chair, he waited for the phone calls that were yet to come.

55

Orkney

The rain had passed, and the evening sky was now clear, with the waning moon lighting their passage across Eynhallow Sound.

Back when the whales had come ashore, she remembered, the moon had been full, shining its light on the carnage on the beach below.

Please let there be no death this time, she found herself repeating.

Erling's takeover of proceedings had been swiftly followed by the ordering of the launch and the call round to everyone offering accommodation on Rousay. It had taken only a half-dozen calls for the cottage they had rented to be identified.

Whether they were still in residence wasn't known.

'Well, they won't be leaving without us knowing about it,' had been Erling's response to this, while Rhona kept thinking that it had never been the killer's intention for them both to leave. Or perhaps even for the vehicle to leave.

A man who could assume aliases at will could no doubt

change his appearance to match. And once he dispensed with his victim and the vehicle, he wouldn't be recognizable maybe even to the ferry boat crew.

Chrissy had said that you had to think like a killer to catch a killer, something Rhona had had to do at every crime scene she'd ever been called to, including the two on mainland Orkney. And, she thought with horror, the scene she'd already identified on the fast-approaching shoreline of Rousay.

'You okay?' Erling checked.

'Just thinking about the prepared grave,' she said.

'You want us to go there first?' he said.

'*I'd* like to go there first,' she told him.

'Okay, Jo will go with you, while the rest of us head for the rental cottage. I've arranged for transport to meet us at the ferry terminal.'

There were three vehicles ready and waiting in the landing area, and more available if required, Erling was told by the group of men.

Erling split his team up, allotting an off-roader, driven by a big farmer called Sam, to Rhona and DS Green.

As they climbed up and in, Rhona explained that they needed to be taken as close to the shoreline at Skaill Farm as possible. Without questioning why this should be the case, Sam took off westwards, his big beams lighting up the road, the fields stretching down to the wild sea on their left and the dark shadow of the central hill rising on their right.

56

Orkney

Erling had encircled the cottage, then with a loudhailer had announced their presence and asked that those inside come out.

When no one responded, he'd repeated his request.

The lights were on and smoke curled up from the chimney with the sweet scent of peat burning, but yet he sensed there was no one home.

He felt his heart beat hard and fast in his chest, all the while thinking that they were too late. Whoever had been here was already gone. But where and how?

He thought about the launch, lights full on, skimming across the Sound of Eynhallow, warning whoever was looking out that the police were on their way.

Or maybe the two men had left earlier in the day on the ferry that went by way of Wyre and Egilsay. If they'd travelled separately, they may not have been noted.

And all the time those thoughts flicked through his head, he knew that if this was the man they sought with his impending victim, then only one of them would likely have left alive.

Calling his men to follow him, he tried the door and, finding it unlocked, moved inside.

The small two-bedroom house was easily and swiftly searched to find nothing. The two men had gone from the cottage and probably from the island itself, leaving no sign of them ever having been there at all.

At least that was what he'd thought, until the call came from DS Green, who provided him with an alternative story of what had happened.

A story with an equally bad ending.

57

Orkney

'These guys we're looking for,' Sam said as he made a swift turn onto a rough track leading towards the sea. 'They're something to do with young Ben Bradley, the guy found buried at Skaill Bay?'

'One of them is,' Jo answered.

A short silence followed before Sam said, 'And the other one?'

'A possible victim,' Rhona told him.

A grunt followed her reply, before he swerved to the left, entering through an open gate, and suddenly they were bumping across a field. As light from the half-moon now merged with their headlights, Rhona saw that they were heading directly towards the still-frothing waters of the Sound.

Once they reached the shoreline, she asked Sam to go slowly west towards the ruined church and its graveyard.

He did as requested, until she asked him to stop, but to keep his beams on, so that she could check if they'd reached the right place.

The glint from the tarpaulin suggested they had.

Even before she was out of the vehicle, she knew something was wrong. Very wrong. The tarpaulin was no longer as Colin had left it, anchored with stones, in case it blew away.

'Quick,' she shouted to Jo, 'help me pull it back.'

Sam, seeing what they were trying to do, arrived to grab the heavy tarpaulin and, lifting it, dropped it free of the grave.

Rhona was already on her knees, hauling at the corner of the grass mat that covered the grave. Jo took hold with her, dragging it back to expose the mix of soil, sand and shells Rhona and Colin had found earlier.

All three set about scooping out the soil. Sam in the middle, Rhona and Jo on either end. Rhona had made the assumption that the victim would have been laid down facing the water and she was right. Less than six inches below the surface, she felt the outline of his face beneath her fingers.

While she attempted to fully expose his head, she shouted to Sam to fetch her forensic bag from the vehicle and call 999 for an air ambulance. 'You can guide them in when they come.'

Unblocking his nostrils and clearing his mouth, she bent her face to his, praying that she might find him still breathing. And there it was, a faint touch of air against her cheek.

'He's alive. Just,' she said to Jo.

If his killer used the same routine they suspected he had with the others – administering ketamine to subdue them, before burying them to suffocate – then there would be no sign of trauma. But they had to check.

'Help me clear his body of soil,' Rhona told Jo. 'Look for blood and obvious wounds.'

In the brightness of the headlights, his body was smooth, hairless and unmarked apart from a tattoo on his upper right chest that looked like a Viking warrior. And, round his neck, the telltale sign of a Viking cross.

'What if it's an opioid overdose,' Jo said worriedly, 'and not ketamine like the others?'

Rhona had already considered this. The naloxone syringe in her bag would counteract an opioid overdose, but . . .

'If there's a possibility he's been given ketamine, we cannot administer naloxone,' Rhona told her. 'It could kill him.'

Remember, to catch a killer, you have to think like one.

'An organized killer sticks with his MO, especially if it's worked up till now,' Rhona said, hoping that was true. 'We need to put him in the back of the vehicle,' she told Sam. 'And turn the heater on full blast.'

Sam did as she asked and, arranging the body in the recovery position, Rhona got in alongside him and wrapped them together in a foil blanket, all the while repeating the words, 'Live. Please live,' softly in his ear.

58

Orkney

Rhona had climbed into bed just as the sun had begun to rear its head.

Although she hadn't for a moment imagined she would sleep, she in fact did, long and soundly, waking up close to midday to the sound of Colin moving about in the kitchen below and the scent of something frying.

Rising, she jumped in the shower and replayed last night's events as she washed.

She'd been allowed to accompany the victim in the air ambulance to Balfour Hospital, where she'd sat in the waiting room until they'd come to tell her that he was alive and likely to remain that way.

When they'd asked her who the patient was, she had no answer to give, either on his name or a next of kin. So she put her own name down along with DI Erling Flett's.

It was obvious from the reaction to her arrival with the naked, half-dead young male that his discovery had something to do with the Ben Bradley case, although no one had asked her outright, just muttered their anger and sorrow at what had happened to this unidentified young man.

Eventually Erling himself had appeared to tell her they hadn't as yet found the elusive Thomas Montgomery, but now they had an image of him, it was being circulated widely in Orkney. They believed he was still here some-where, and that his notoriety would have every inhabitant on every one of the islands in the archipelago looking out for him.

That thought was comforting, but not as good as if she'd learned that he was already in custody.

Heading downstairs, Rhona found eggs and bacon awaiting her, with bere bannocks and coffee. Lots of it.

'I heard you up and about, and knew how hungry you'd be,' Colin said. 'Eat first and we can talk after.'

While she did as ordered, he brought her up to date on this morning's news.

'I checked with the hospital and the boy's stable. It seems he's been talking to DI McNab.'

'And the suspect?' Rhona said.

'There's been lots of phone calls to the police hotline. He won't get off the islands unless he swims. I bet he wishes he hadn't left that kayak behind at Stromness.' Colin's tone was light, but Rhona still heard the concern behind his words.

When her mobile rang, she was glad to see McNab's name on the screen.

'I'm on Albert Street,' he told her. 'Are you fit for a visit?'

'I am,' she said. 'And the coffee's on.'

'Make it strong. I'll be there in a moment. And well done last night. You were right. The killer stuck to his MO. The victim had taken ketamine and consumed a large quantity of alcohol.'

'You've spoken to him?' she asked.

'I'll tell you all about it when I arrive . . . which is now,' he announced.

At that moment, the kitchen door opened and McNab's auburn head ducked to enter.

Had Colin not been present, Rhona realized she might have risen to hug him. As it was, she poured him coffee instead.

Settled at the table, he told her what he'd learned at the hospital.

'The victim's name is Danny King and he's from Sunderland originally. He doesn't remember being buried alive, just what went before. He said it was a Viking ritual. His current partner, whose name he gave as Philip Whitby, was into that stuff. When I showed him the image of our suspect, he confirmed it as his partner.'

'So he had no idea what was about to happen?' Rhona said.

'None. He apparently met our man at King's Cross railway station a couple of months ago. Phil, as he calls him, had offered to buy him a Big Mac. He'd accepted because he had no money and nowhere to stay.'

'So they were in a relationship?'

'He thought so. They came up here on a break so that Phil could show him some of the Viking burial sites he'd worked on. In his words, they stayed a couple of days at a cottage in Stromness, then headed for Rousay, where Phil had booked another Airbnb. Their aim being to have some fun down at the Viking hall.' He hesitated there. 'The thing is, he still hopes this Phil will come and get him. That the burial must have been part of the game.'

'It's just as we thought,' Rhona said. 'He builds a relation-ship with them before he kills them.'

'And they believe it's true,' McNab said.

Rhona found herself imagining Ben heading to London from Glasgow and meeting a man he grew fond of. A man who suggested they go back to Orkney, perhaps to lay the ghost of Ben's past to rest there.

'You're thinking about Ben Bradley,' McNab said, catch-ing her eye.

How well McNab knew her. Too well at times, she thought.

Colin's voice broke the silence that followed. 'Any word on this Phil's whereabouts?' he asked.

'DI Flett believes he's still on Rousay. They're searching for him along a place he called Faraclett Head Walk. Flett describes the area as having caves among the overhanging cliffs. He might be in one of them.' He gave a half-smile. 'Not exactly my territory,' he added. 'The police launch is up there, plus the helicopter. I'm awaiting updates as we speak via DS Green. Who, I understand it, has proved herself pretty good in a tight spot.' He looked to Rhona.

'Definitely,' Rhona said.

'Right.' McNab rose. 'Back to the office. Assuming they pick our man up soon, I'll accompany him down to Glasgow in the police helicopter. I'll let you know when, in case you and Sigurd need a ride,' he told Rhona.

'His name's Lucas Mason,' she reminded him. 'And I believe Lucas and I would prefer to make our own way back.'

Once McNab had left, Colin indicated he would head up to the UHI building.

'I'll follow you on foot,' Rhona told him. 'I need to chat to my assistant, Chrissy, first.'

When Colin left, Rhona refilled her coffee cup, then fetching her laptop, set up a video call to Chrissy at the lab.

'Hello, stranger,' were the first words spoken. 'And before you give me the story,' Chrissy said, 'I know a lot of it already. The mad dash on the police launch, the body buried alive on the beach—'

'Near the beach,' Rhona corrected her.

'Okay. I'm not on the ground there and have to rely on PC Tulloch for any updates when you're unavailable.' Her voice grew serious. 'They haven't picked up the perp yet, I understand. But the victim's okay, thanks to you.'

'Physically okay. I'm not sure about mentally. According to McNab, Danny thinks they were playing some sort of fantasy game about Vikings. And he still expects the man he thought of as his boyfriend to come and collect him.'

Even Chrissy was at a loss for words to reply to that. 'When are you headed home?' she said instead.

'Soon. Very soon,' Rhona promised.

At that moment she heard the sound of a message arriving on Chrissy's phone, followed by a small squeal of delight, before Chrissy reappeared on the screen.

'PC Tulloch says they have him. He'd fallen from a cave into the sea. He's being winched aboard the police helicopter as we speak,' she said. 'Right, now you can definitely come home,' she added firmly.

59

Orkney

Erling had been more than happy when DI McNab had indicated that, as SIO on the case, he would be the one to immediately transport the suspect to police headquarters in Glasgow, where he would be questioned with respect to the earlier murders of Ben Bradley and Lucas Mason on mainland Orkney, plus the recently attempted murder of eighteen-year-old Danny King on the Orkney island of Rousay.

They'd stood face to face in Erling's office, as they had done back when McNab had arrived, at Erling's request, to take over as SIO.

'I knew I was doing the right thing asking for your help,' Erling said.

The wry look McNab directed at him suggested he had thought differently, and maybe still did.

'It was an experience. One that I have no desire to repeat,' McNab offered with a raised brow. 'Of course, we'll keep you informed about next moves, and you'll be free to join in with our interviews with the accused. Maybe even find out his real name.'

'What about Ava's leads to the other cases in northern England?' Erling said.

'I'm assured that the relevant police authorities are looking into our suspect's possible connections to those,' McNab told him. 'Sadly, they may not be the only ones. He's had twenty years or more at this. Right,' he finished. 'I'll take him off your hands now, and hopefully Orkney can get back to normal.'

The parting over, and McNab having departed, Erling went to find DS Green to ask that she take over, so that he might head home to shower and change.

'I suggest you catch some sleep as well, sir. I can handle things here,' Jo told him with a smile.

'That you can, Detective Sergeant. That you can,' he said gratefully.

The drive home was quiet. Both in terms of traffic and the weather. Scapa Flow no longer seethed and there were no gusts of wind to buffet the car.

As he drove, Erling found himself overwhelmed by a feeling of relief.

Relief that they'd caught the killer. That his latest victim had been saved and, on a more personal note, that they'd found the man who'd pretended to be Ben's friend and lover, only to bring him back to Orkney and take his life.

Approaching Langwell, he saw by the parked car that Rory was back from Flotta. Drawing in alongside, he sat for a moment, collecting his emotions before going in to face his lover and, he hoped, long-term companion.

Rory had been honest with him about his past, and he

378

had duly been honest with McNab, never expecting the response he'd got.

Things were, he hoped, back to where they had been between them. Or maybe even better, because they each knew of one another's past mistakes. And definitely the important and far-reaching ones.

Rory must have heard him arrive, because he was waiting at the open door.

'You got the bastard,' he said, hugging him. 'You got him. I heard it before I left Flotta.'

They moved inside and Erling found himself apologizing for having been up all night and being badly in need of a shower.

'I don't give a fuck about that,' Rory said. 'We celebrate first, then we shower together.'

He released Erling to go and pour two large drams.

'D'you want to see his picture?' Erling said. 'In case he was the guy who gave you the bracelet in Stromness all those years ago?'

'Go on, then,' Rory said, taking a mouthful of whisky.

Erling brought the image up on his mobile. 'Here he is, shortly after we brought him into the station.'

Rory stared at the screen, his face a mix of emotions.

He knows he's looking at a killer, Erling thought. *But is he also thinking that he might have been one of his victims, if he hadn't said no that night?*

Rory looked at him, and gave a shrug. 'I don't know. To be honest, if I heard his voice, maybe. But I don't want to hear his voice,' he said. 'Just yours.' He threw back his whisky. 'You ready for that shower, Detective Inspector?'

60

Glasgow

Her journey home was in darkness, allowing Rhona to pretend she wasn't up in the air, with only a whirring set of blades keeping her from plunging to earth or sea.

Closing her eyes, she imagined instead that she was on the Glasgow subway, rumbling below ground towards her destination, where she would step out onto the platform, her feet once again on solid ground.

Her thoughts during the journey were a patchwork of images from that first night in Kirkwall, sitting round the dining table in the Ivy House, the faces of her fellow diners talking and laughing, the rain running down those famous yellow-framed windows, all in the glow of the fire.

That scene led swiftly to the vast beach at Skaill, the crashing surf and the row of headlights picking out the whales that lay strewn across it, the figures of humans moving among them, desperately trying to keep some of those stranded alive.

Reliving the moment when the digger met stone and they'd discovered the cist, she recalled Colin at first excited and intrigued by the find, then as realization dawned, so did the horror.

She stopped herself there, aware such memories would play out in her dreams for at least a while, before being supplanted by others.

This was her job. And she was grateful for it.

She must have slept, because when she opened her eyes, the chopper had landed, the whirring ceased.

'You're home, Dr MacLeod,' the pilot told her. 'And I should warn you, it's raining.'

Rhona laughed. 'Now there's a surprise,' she said.

Stepping onto the glistening tarmac, she spotted the forensic van waiting, and wondered if Chrissy might be there to pick her up, despite the late hour. But the tall figure that stepped out wasn't Chrissy, she registered; it was McNab.

'Welcome home, Dr MacLeod. I'll take charge of your cargo now,' he told her, 'and see it safely to the lab. You are to head straight home. And there's a car waiting to take you there.'

When she looked doubtful, he added, 'That's an order, Dr MacLeod, from the SIO on the case.'

The rain had stopped by the time she reached her flat, and when the police car left, she stood for a moment looking out at the lighted pathways of the park below and the brightly lit gothic splendour of the university atop its hill.

With a smile, she registered how good it was to be home.

At that point, her mobile rang, Sean's name on the screen.

'Are you coming up?' he said. 'Or are you planning to stand out there admiring the view all night?'

'I'm on my way,' Rhona said, anticipation in her voice.

EPILOGUE

Two months later

Erling had been the one to meet Annie Bradley from the plane.

He'd been unsure when he'd contacted her whether she would agree to come, but the surprise and joy in her voice when she'd accepted had brought a catch to his throat.

The sun had chosen to shine that day, although the scudding clouds moving swiftly through the blue sky reminded Annie she was back in Orkney.

She'd told him then that she'd liked living in the red-roofed house close to the Ring of Brodgar, and hadn't really wanted to leave.

'I should have let Jack go, and maybe Ben and I might have made a go of it here, after all,' she told him.

When the two of them reached St Magnus Cathedral, they were all there and waiting.

As he pushed open the glass door and urged Annie to step inside, she'd made a little sound of surprise.

'I didn't realize,' she said, 'that there would be so many.'

Aware now of their entry, the assembly rose to greet them, with Jo standing centre aisle.

There was no sombre music to accompany their walk to the front, just the quiet reverence of the ancient edifice and the flooding Orkney light streaming through the stained-glass windows.

Their walk led them past rows of locals, many of whom hadn't known Ben, but had been moved to attend having followed Ben's story written by Ava in the *Orcadian*.

On one side of the front row were Erling's team, including PC Ivan Tulloch, Professor Nelson, Magnus and Rhona.

On the other were those who had become closest to Annie. Ava and her brother, Dougie, with Ingrid and, most important of all, Shona, who welcomed Annie with open arms.

As the organ began to play, Erling saw that she was smiling.

Acknowledgements

With thanks to:

Forensic scientist Dr Jennifer Miller. Inspiring and supportive, she is my main go-to for all things Rhona. In the case of *The Dead and the Dying*, her expertise on buried and hidden bodies was invaluable.

Dr James H. K. Grieve, emeritus professor of forensic pathology at Aberdeen University, who is more than generous in answering all my queries regarding modes of death.

Professor Lorna Dawson of the James Hutton Institute for her advice on the sands of Orkney and for inspiring the creation of forensic soil scientist Dr Jen Mackie.

Professor Colin Richards of the Archaeology Institute UHI Orkney, who inspired the creation of archaeologist Professor Colin Nelson.

And, finally, a big thanks to my wonderful editor Raphaella Demetris and all the team at Pan Macmillan for their help and support with this long-running series.

Introducing Rhona MacLeod . . .

Lin Anderson's series of crime novels featuring forensic scientist Rhona MacLeod are set in and around Scotland. From the beautiful remoteness of the Orkney islands to the dark underbelly of urban Glasgow, the locations she chooses to write about play as much a role in her novels as the characters that she populates them with.

Go back to where it all began with the thrilling first novel in the Rhona MacLeod series.
Read on for an extract now . . .

I

THE BOY DIDN'T expect to die.

When the guy put the tasselled cord round his neck, grinning at him, he thought it was just part of the usual game. The guy was excited, a dribble of saliva slithering down his chin and falling onto the boy's bare shoulder. He nodded his agreement. He was past feeling sick at their antics. He lay back down, turning his head sideways to the greyish pillow that smelt of other games, closed his eyes and shifted his thoughts to something else. There was a goal he liked to play out in his head.

On the right, the Frenchman, arrogant, the ball licking his feet, thrusting forward. The opposition starts to group and there's a scuffle. Bastards. But no worry 'cos the Frenchman's through and running, the ball anchored to him, like a child to its mother. The crowd breathes in. Time stretches like an elastic band. Then the ball's away, curving through the air.

Wham! It's in the net.

The boy can usually go home now. Not this time. This time, before the ball reaches the net, his head is pulled back, then up. The intense pressure bulges his eyes, bursting a myriad of tiny blood vessels to pattern the white. His body spasms as the cord bites deeper, slicing through skin, cutting the blood supply to his brain. At the moment of death his penis erupts, scattering silver strands of semen over the multicoloured cover.

2

SEAN WAS ALREADY asleep beside her. Rhona liked that about him. His baby sleep. His face lying smooth and untroubled against the pillow, his lips opened just enough to let the breath escape in soft noiseless puffs. No one, she thinks, should look that good after a bottle of red wine and three malt whiskies.

Rhona has given up watching Sean drink. It is too irritating, knowing the next morning he won't have a hangover. Instead he'll throw back the duvet (letting a draught enter the warm tent that had enclosed their bodies), slip out of bed and head for the kitchen. From the bed she will watch (a little guiltily), as he moves about; a glimpse of thigh, an arm reaching up, his penis swinging soft and vulnerable. He'll whistle while he makes the coffee and forever in her mind Rhona will match the bitter sweet smell of fresh coffee with the high clear notes of an Irish tune.

They have been together for seven months. The first night Rhona brought Sean home they never reached the bedroom. He held her against the front door, just looking at her. Then he began to unwrap her, piece by piece, peeling her like ripe fruit, his lips not meeting hers but close, so close that her mouth stretched up of its own accord, and her body with it. Then, with a flick of his tongue, he entered her life.

When the phone rang, Sean barely moved. Rhona knew once it rang four times the ansaphone would cut in. The caller would listen to Sean's amiable Irish voice and change their view of answering machines, thinking they might be human after all. Rhona lifted the receiver on the third ring. It would be an emergency or they wouldn't phone so late. When she suggested to the voice on the other end that she would need a taxi, the Sergeant told her that a police car was already on its way. Rhona grabbed last night's clothes from the end of the bed.

Constable William McGonigle had never been at a murder scene before. He had stretched the yellow tape across the tenement entrance like the Sergeant told him and chased away two drunks who thought that police activity constituted a better bit of entertainment than staggering home to hump the wife. Constable McGonigle didn't agree.

'Go home,' he told them. 'There's nothing to see here.'

He was peering up the stairwell, wondering how much longer he would have to stand there freezing his balls off when he heard the sound of high heels clipping the tarmac. A woman leaned over the tape and stared into the dimly lit stair.

'Sorry, Miss. You can't come in here.'

'Where's Detective Inspector Wilson?'

Constable McGonigle was surprised.

'Upstairs, Miss.'

'Good,' she said.

Her fair hair shone white in the darkness and Constable McGonigle could smell her perfume. She lifted a silken leg and straddled his yellow tape.

'I'd better go on up then,' she said.

The click of Rhona's heels echoed round the grimy stairwell, but if she was disturbing any of the residents, they didn't show it by opening their doors. No one here wanted to be seen. If there was a fire they might come out, she thought, in the unlikely event they weren't completely comatose.

A door on the second landing stood ajar. She could hear DI Wilson's voice inside. If Bill was here at least she wouldn't have to explain who she was. She could just get on with the job, go home and crawl back into bed.

The narrow hall was a fetid mix of damp and heat. The sound of her heels died in a dark mottled carpet, curled at the edge like some withered vegetable. She paused. Three doors, all half open. On her right a kitchen, on her left a bathroom. She caught a glimpse of a white suit and heard the whirr of a camera. The Scene of Crime Officers were already at work.

The end door opened fully and Detective Inspector Bill Wilson looked out.

'Bill.'

'Dr MacLeod.'

He nodded. 'It's in here.'

He allowed himself a tight smile. The two other men in the room turned and stared out at her. Dr MacLeod was not what either of them had expected.

Rhona looked down at her black dress and high-heeled sandals. 'I came out in a bit of a hurry.'

'McSween will get you some kit.'

Bill nodded to one of the men, who went out and came back minutes later with a plastic bag.

Rhona pulled out the scene suit and mask, put her coat into the bag and handed it to the officer. She took one shoe off at a time and, hitching up her skirt, slipped her feet into the suit. Only then did she step inside.

Rhona took in the small room at a glance. The hideous nicotine-stained curtains stretched tightly across the window. A wooden chair with a pair of jeans and a tee-shirt thrown over it. Two glasses on a formica table. A pair of trainers on the floor beside the bed. A divan, three-quarters width, no headboard but covered with heavy silken brocade in an expensive burst of swirling colours.

The boy's naked body lay face down across it, his head turned stiffly towards her, eyes bulging, tongue protruding slightly between blue lips. The dark silk cord knotted round the neck looked like a bow tie the wrong way round. The body showed signs of hypostasis, and the combination of dark purple patches and pale translucence reminded Rhona of marble. Below the hips blood soaked into the bedclothes.

'I turned the gas fire off when I arrived,' Bill said. 'The smell nearly finished off our young Constable, so I put him on duty outside for some fresh air.'

'Did anyone take the room temperature?'

'McSween has it.'

Rhona took a deep breath before she put on the mask. The smell of a crime scene was important. It might mean she would look for traces of a substance she would otherwise have missed. Here the nauseating odour of violent death mixed with stale sex and sweat masked something else, something fainter. She got it. An expensive men's cologne.

'McSween and Johnstone have covered the rest of the room. The photographer is working on the kitchen and bathroom.'

'What about a pathologist?'

'Dr Sissons came and certified death. Then suggested I get a decent forensic to take samples and bag the body because he needed to get back to his dinner party.'

'Important guests?'

'He did mention a "Sir" somewhere in the list.'

Rhona smiled. Dr Sissons preferred analysing death in the comfort of his mortuary. Taking samples of bodily fluids in the middle of the night he regarded as her territory.

'That's some bedcover!'

'We think it might be a curtain, but we'll get a better look once we take the body away.'

'Did the doctor turn him over?'

'Just enough to tell if he's been moved. He said the left side of the face, the upper chest and hips had been compressed since death occurred. He's lying where he was killed.'

Rhona opened her case and took out her gloves. She knelt down beside the bed.

'There's a lot of blood under the body.'

Bill nodded grimly. 'You'd better take a look underneath.'

Rhona lifted the right arm and rolled the body a little. The genitals had been gnawed, the penis severed by a jagged gash that ran from the left hand tip to halfway up the right side. One testicle was mashed and hanging by a thin strip of skin.

'This must have been done after he died or the blood would be all over the place.'

'That's what Sissons said.'

Rhona let the body roll back down. The boy's head nestled back into the dirty pillow.

'Any sign of a weapon?'

Bill shook his head. 'Maybe it wasn't a weapon.'

'A biter? Did Dr Sissons check for other bite marks?'

'He muttered something about bruising on the nipples and the shoulder.'

'I'll take some swabs.'

'How long do you think he's been dead?' Bill said.

Rhona pressed one of the deepening purple patches, and watched it slowly blanch under her finger. 'Maybe six, seven hours. Depends on the temperature of the room.'

Bill risked a satisfied smile.

'Matches the Doc.'

Rhona raised her eyebrows a little. She and Dr Sissons didn't usually agree. He had a habit of disagreeing with her on points like the exact time of death.

It was almost a matter of principle. Rhona had done three years' medicine before she switched to forensic science. She liked to practise now and again.

'How did you find him?'

'An anonymous phone call.'

'The murderer?'

'A young male voice. Very frightened. Maybe another rent boy came here to meet a client?'

'Alive, this one would have been pretty,' Rhona said.

Bill nodded. 'Not the usual type for this area,' he said. 'A bit more class, but rented all the same. I'll leave you to it? Just shout if you need anything.'

She was nearly an hour taking samples of everything that might prove useful later on. After she'd finished with the surrounds, she concentrated on the body, under the fingernails, the hair, the mouth. Dr Sissons would take the anal and penile swabs.

The skin felt cold through her gloves, but with the blond hair flopped over the empty eyes, he might have been any teenager fast asleep. Rhona lifted the hair and studied the face, trying to imagine what the boy would have looked like in life. There were none of the tell-tale signs of poor diet and drug abuse. This one had been healthy. So how did he end up here?

'Finished?' Bill's timing was immaculate. 'Mortuary boys are here.' He looked at her face. 'Go home and have a hot toddy,' he said.

A hot toddy was Bill's answer to almost any ailment.

Rhona got up from the bed and unwrapped her hands. 'Any idea who he is?' she said.

'Not yet. But I don't think he was Scottish.' He pointed to the hall. Behind the door hung a leather jacket and a football scarf. 'Manchester United,' he said in mock disgust.

'There are people up here who support Man U,' Rhona suggested cheekily, knowing Bill was a Celtic man.

'Yes, but they wouldn't flaunt it. Not in Glasgow anyway.'

Rhona laughed.

'All right then?'

'Yes.' She began to pack her samples in the case.

'The Sergeant will run you home.'

He walked with her to the front door.

'How's that Irishman of yours these days? Still playing at the club?'

'Yes, he is.'

'Must get down and hear him again soon. Good jazz player. You'll ring me as soon as you've got anything?'

'Of course.'

Sean was still asleep when Rhona got back. With the heavy curtains drawn the room was dark, although outside dawn was already touching the university rooftops. She had stopped at the lab on her way home and checked the swabs for saliva. It was there all right.

She left a note on the bench for Chrissy in case she got there first, giving her a brief history of the night's events, then she headed home for a few hours' sleep.

Rhona pulled her dress over her head, kicked off her shoes and slid under the duvet. She wrapped her chilled body round Sean's. He grunted and moved his arm over to take her hand.

'Okay?' he mumbled.

'Okay,' she said, but he was already back asleep.

Rhona closed her eyes and tried to relax into his warmth. She had been at many murder scenes, some more horrible than the one tonight. Death didn't scare her, not when it was reduced to tests and samples. But tonight was different. There was something about that particular boy. Something she hadn't been able to put her finger on. Not until the Sergeant had put it into words for her, coming back in the car.

The boy who had been abused and strangled in that hideous little room looked so like her, he could have been her brother.